BECOMIN

Book 1, Exilon 5 Series

About the Author

Eliza Green tried her hand at fashion designing, massage, painting, and even ghost hunting, before finding her love of writing. She often wonders if her desire to change the ending of a particular glittery vampire story steered her in that direction (it did). After earning her degree in marketing, Eliza went on to work in everything but marketing, but swears she uses it in everyday life, or so she tells her bank manager.

Born and raised in Dublin, Ireland, she lives there with her sci-fi loving, evil genius best friend. When not working on her next amazing science fiction adventure, you can find her reading, indulging in new food at an amazing restaurant or simply singing along to something with a half decent beat.

Becoming Human, *Altered Reality* and *Crimson Dawn* make up the Exilon 5 series so far. *Derailed Conscience* is her interesting foray into psychological thrillers with a sci-fi twist.

Feeder, brand new young adult sci-fi, coming soon November 2016. Preorder the e-book at www.elizagreenbooks.com

www.elizagreenbooks.com

Becoming Human

Eliza Green

Eliza Green

Third edition. Updated 2013, rewritten from 2012 original.

ISBN-13: 978-1481082938
ISBN-10: 1481082930

Cover Designed by Andrew Brown
www.designforwriters.com

Editor and Proofreader: Averill Buchanan

Becoming Human

To Nigel, for your advice and support

This book demonstrates why I read Indie books and have enjoyed doing so immensely. Yes, some self-published books don't deserve to see the light of day, but this isn't one of those. Far from it. It was exciting and it had mystery.

The Masquerade Crew

Eliza Green had me from page one. Her creative world-building constructed a panoramic view of the consequences of two worlds colliding where both sides want to win, neither trusting the other. Will good conquer evil?

Top 500 Amazon Reviewer

At the back of this book, I have included a list of organisations, characters and locations.

Prologue

They watched the multiple independent re-entry vehicles approach in the night's sky, illuminated by a string of bright lights along their exteriors. The A.I. system guided the vehicles along a predetermined trajectory towards the planet. The next succession, fired from the nearest planet's surface, was already on its way to Exilon 5. The race wouldn't live long enough to witness their arrival.

The multi-launch command came from the Zodiac 117B ship that hovered in the great expanse above Exilon 5. The super heavy-lift vehicles, tightly packed with as many cluster bombs as possible, contained terraforming chemicals. Solid fuel engine rockets drove the expendable vehicles towards the atmosphere where their outer shrouds would separate away and burn up. With just one chance to get the rockets there safely, force fields protected the shrouds to prevent the payload from early destruction. The bombs would alter the atmosphere. A successful strike would result in many unavoidable deaths.

The MIRVs, specifically designed to make light work of the atmospheric layer, tore through space towards the planet. When the terraforming process was over, others could begin the next phase of the operation.

The race huddled together protectively, unsure what the lights were or where they originated from.

7

Some of their young played chasing games, oblivious to the danger that faced all of them. Those with more empathy noticed the adults' mood and clung tightly to their legs for protection.

Distant rumbling filled the skies above them as thousands of MIRVs burned bright upon entry. They resembled stars, except these were growing in size. There was no immediate sanctuary, no place for them to hide in the desolate open. Motionless and deathly quiet, they watched and waited. Some had already sought refuge in the tunnels beneath the surface. For those that remained, only the sound of heavy breathing and bare feet scuffling across the earth could be heard as their young continued to chase each other.

The A.I. system deactivated the force fields around each launch vehicle and the outer shrouds fell away piece by piece. A flimsy wire mesh remained to protect the payload. Shiny chemical-filled spheres jostled about inside their last housing, eager to break loose with every twist of hot metal. As the mesh cage disintegrated, several spheres broke free, clashing together and cracking open on impact. Hot liquids and inert gases leached out from their containers and quickly merged. The liquid toxins dropped to the earth like torrential rain. The gases, slightly heavier than the atmosphere, sank more slowly. As more bombs broke free, the payload leached out of tiny fissures that had appeared in their design. A thick gas cloud lingered just below the skyline, waiting.

Few moved as the lights neared them and they sensed an immediate change in the air. The young lost their enthusiasm for the chasing game. Looking towards the adults, they searched their faces for a reason not to continue. The young interpreted their silence as an affirmation to keep playing.

The first drops of acid rain hit their faces and burned their skin. They struggled to protect themselves in the vast open. The air transformed into static as the terraforming chemicals affected the electrons around them. The statically charged air nipped at their skin. Dropping to their knees, they picked up handfuls of soggy earth and smeared it over their faces, their chests, their arms and legs, to try to lessen the effects. The acid rain-sodden ground they used only aggravated their condition. The adults' screams pierced the contaminated air. Hot, salty tears fell from their inflamed eyes. Equally afflicted now, the young struggled to stay on their feet. Shiny spheres dropped to the earth in bundles, splitting apart and unleashing the gases within just before impact. The chemicals worked silently on their breathing, forcing several of them to grasp at their necks.

Broken pieces from the cluster bombs rained down steadily as the last of the mesh cages melted away. Unbroken bombs transformed into mini projectiles, destroying anything they touched. The liquid chemicals sprayed upwards and out, falling like a gentle mist.

With heavy legs and weak bodies, they staggered towards the tunnels for protection. Some crawled with young on their backs, exhausted from the effort of breathing.

New lights appeared in the skies—brighter and bigger than the ones before. These were not MIRVs designed to break apart. These did not carry explosives. Their sole purpose was to ignite the gases and permanently alter the atmosphere. Their impact was controlled, their explosions timed. Little remained in the aftermath, and whatever had survived would not last for long.

The controllers aboard the Zodiac 117B monitored the MIRVs' trajectory closely. They reported to unseen people about the even dispersion of gases across the sky. The liquid that had seeped into the soil would correct the pH balance so the terrain would accept plants and trees at a faster rate.

Everything had happened exactly as planned. It would be a while before they could inhabit the planet, but for now, stage one was complete. They would make time to celebrate properly when they arrived back on Earth.

1

April 2163, Exilon 5

In the heart of New London, Bill Taggart sat alone in Cantaloupe restaurant at a table by the window. Feeling exhausted after a long day, he hungrily tucked into his steak and chips. Cantaloupe was his favourite restaurant and the best New London had to offer. It was not one of the more affordable establishments on Exilon 5, which used real, not replicated, ingredients to make its old-fashioned fare. Since the World Government—his bosses and the biggest powerhouse on Earth—was picking up the tab, he made sure to indulge as often as possible. The World Government, an organisation made up of the world's twelve leaders, had been set up after the collapse of the United Nations in 2078.

Bill picked up his coffee mug—his fourth refill in the restaurant—noticing the way his hands trembled as the rim neared his lips. The warm liquid soothed his throat but the caffeine only made his tremors worse. His hands continued to shake as he returned the black mug to the table and he quickly interlocked his fingers. He couldn't blame the caffeine this time; there was something else on his mind.

He played with his food while he watched the crowds on the streets outside rudely pushing past each other; never once did they stop to look around and actually appreciate how lucky they were. Exilon 5—or New Earth, as the residents had christened it—was their future now. The new residents should be viewing Exilon 5 as a fresh start, not a reason to continue with the bad habits of the old world. Conditions were so dilapidated on Earth that the government was working on ways to transfer the entire population.

At present, there were not enough cities on Exilon 5 to accommodate everyone, the numbers standing at just six: New Delhi, London, New York, Taiyuan, Vienna and Copenhagen. The World Government had strived to keep the most familiar parts of Earth's urban centres so that people would adapt quickly to their new lives. The first batch of transfers had included doctors, engineers and teachers to help set up industries before the rest of the population transferred. The government's extremely ambitious plan, to move all twenty billion inhabitants of Earth to Exilon 5 over the next twenty years, was questionable. Currently, there was just a fraction of the population living on the exoplanet; that was well below expected targets. If the World Government was serious about transferring all inhabitants of Earth, then Exilon 5 needed more cities, more housing—more of everything.

Bill had an ulterior motive for choosing Cantaloupe that day. He touched his skin that still prickled with the residual energy in the air; the change in the air was attributable to the static charge the alien race emitted. The children referred to them as 'Shadow People'. He knew them by another name—Indigenes. He'd been waiting a long time to come face-to-face with one of them—two years to be exact. His role as Investigator for the World Government's International Task Force division was a neat cover. He was using the mission to uncover a personal matter and he wouldn't stop until he found out the truth.

He took another sip of coffee. The caffeine jolted his heart into more feverish action, but its effects weren't as strong or his heartbeat as fast as before. He held his hands out in front of him; the tremors were still very much there. The other patrons watched him warily as if he was on something, but he was not a city junkie. There were far more dangerous men than him out there. An old adversary sprung to mind—Larry Hunt—and he instinctively touched a spot on his shoulder where an old injury had once been. He would probably agree that the new cities needed to be policed better, but to his mind, there were other reasons that made it dangerous to live on Exilon 5. The residents were being fed half-truths about their new home.

His wife Isla came to mind; the personal matter he wished to uncover. He fondly recalled her: rosy cheeks, waist-long brown hair, a dimpled smile. A sudden pain gripped him so tightly and sharply he thought he was having a heart attack. But it subsided and he kneaded the pain away as he always did when memories of his happier life became too much. Isla's easy-going nature had always been a good fit for Bill's more cynical side. With her, life had seemed less complicated, even if it was not. Without her, he was a shadow of his former self. He owed it to her to continue in his search.

Isla, I promise you, I won't give up.

Remembering their life together was difficult for him. He couldn't recall the last time he had smiled since she'd disappeared, even though smiling was a rare enough action for him. Isla, an optimist, had always hated his pessimistic streak.

'Turn that frown upside down,' she had said to him one evening when he was in one of his moods. Sitting on one end of the sofa with her legs curled underneath her, she had shot him a look and, fascinated by stories about life in the twentieth century, turned her attention back to the tome she was reading on the history of Earth. Strands of her hair fell on the page she was reading and she dramatically flicked them behind her. She unfurled her legs and placed her feet on the floor. Then she crossed her legs in a way that always made them seem longer and more appealing.

On the other end of the sofa, Bill sat in silence. He didn't react to the first of the clichés.

'We're here for a long time, not a good time.' Cliché number two usually snapped him out of it, although not always. 'The grass is usually greener on the other side.'

The last one caught his attention. He slowly turned, a smile tugging at the corners of his mouth. 'Isn't it "the grass is *always* greener"?'

She briefly stuck her tongue out at him. 'I was just checking to see if you were listening.'

He laughed, noticing her legs for the first time that evening. 'It's hard not to. Any more anecdotes up your sleeve?'

She uncrossed her legs and slid over to sit directly beside him. She gathered up the ends of her waist-long hair and tickled his face, giggling lightly when he squeezed his eyes shut. 'Not today, but it's working. I can already feel the seismic shift.'

Bill failed in his attempt to look angry. Instead,

he gazed at her soft face, and at her fine hair that seemed to tangle at the hint of movement or a breeze. It had taken her many years to grow it out, and many times he'd wondered if it was worth the daily maintenance. 'Have you ever thought about cutting your hair?' he said.

'No. It makes me feel feminine. It's also where my strength lies, like Samson,' she joked, gathering up a bunch of it and studying the split-ends closely. 'It's taken me so long to grow it. I guess it would feel like I had lost a part of me.' Isla let go of her hair and swept it behind her. She settled into the soft sofa back and pulled her feet underneath her, staring at the imitation fire that never needed stoking.

'Do they allow you to wear it down for work?'

'No. That's why I wear it like this.' In a moment, she had swept her hair up into a ponytail and created a swirl on top of her head. She removed a few pins from her pocket—her 'emergency supply'—and secured the swirl into place.

'That better?'

His face softened into a smile. 'I thought you didn't like to wear it up like that?'

'I know it bothers you because I leave so many hairs everywhere, so just think of it as me doing you a favour.' She winked at him.

He shook his head. 'I was trying to be subtle.'

'Not your strong point, love.'

Bill's good mood shifted to a different plane. 'Knowing what you do, would you really want to live out your entire life here, on this planet? Wouldn't you prefer to take the easier way out?'

'Termination?' Her expression had changed and she stared at him, her green eyes filled with pity—or disappointment; he hadn't been entirely sure.

15

'Never! Life is for living. I'm not here to exist and neither are you. Why would you even consider that?'

Bill shook his head again. 'Hypothetical, love. Not for me but for others. Things in general aren't good here.'

He stood up and walked to the window, his eyes struggling to see anything of significance in the murky day. It was 3 p.m. and the world outside was void of life other than human. The forecast was for worse to come. 'This is no life for any of us, Isla. Look at where we live now—the planet. Study the people's faces. Why exist for this kind of life?'

She joined him and rubbed his back gently, staring out at the congested landscape that was crammed with tall buildings and a thick grey fog that never lifted. 'There's a better life on Exilon 5, I've told you. It's magical—what Earth used to look and feel like. Why do you think I read so many history books? It won't be long before I travel there on assignment and I can't wait.'

He had turned towards her and cupped her face in his hands. 'I wish I could join you.' The lines on his forehead deepened with every word spoken.

She held his wrists. 'Me too, but we're working to make it safer. It won't be long before everyone can live there without a fear of death hanging over them.'

Bill leaned in and kissed her gently, savouring every moment he had with her. If he had known that their life together would be cut short, he'd have kidnapped her and hidden her somewhere safe. The 'somewhere safe' had been a wild concoction in his head, an afterthought after Isla's disappearance, or death—he still wasn't sure. He was still looking for the truth. He would have given anything to spend the rest of his life on Exilon 5 with Isla. In his mind's eye, he could see her standing in the middle of New London, ignoring the rude people around her, grinning at him as her hair danced in the breeze and tickled the faces of those that got too close. He would give anything to feel her arms around him again, to see that smile that was only meant for him.

The smell of fresh bread wafting from Cantaloupe's kitchen filled his nose and interrupted Bill's thoughts. He turned his head to the side and discreetly thumbed a tear from his face. He shook his head, sat up straight and tried to remember why he was there. With so many others around him, he struggled to focus on what mattered.

Cantaloupe restaurant, with its trademark red-and-white chequered cloth-covered tables, was filled to capacity for the dinnertime rush. He watched as overly friendly servers took new orders and well-off patrons settled their bills at the counter with a brief scan of their identity chips. Several children protested loudly at their parents' suggestion that they try real vegetables but calmed down after the promise of ice cream. It chilled him to think that one or more of the Indigenes had been here in this very restaurant, so close to children and right under his nose. Normally nocturnal creatures, the Indigenes' appearance during daytime hours marked a change in behaviour for them. They were becoming bolder and riskier in their choices.

Bill knew Cantaloupe intimately, having been there several times, but this time he studied its layout in minute detail. While it killed him to be so close to where Indigenes had been, he had to put himself in their shoes to try to understand their motives. *Why choose this place? Are they hunting for their next victim?*

He rubbed the lingering static from his arm; it was stronger outside, a sign that one of them had recently been in the area. World Government intel given to the ITF had reported that an Indigene was on the verge of making contact with a human. At just forty-five, Bill was younger than most to lead such an important mission—with humans living a century and a half, anyone under sixty was considered young— but his persistence and ability to do the job had won him the role. In addition, he needed to be part of the mission, for his own sake as well as Isla's.

He polished off the last of his steak and ordered a light beer. The alcohol soothed the fiery edges of his nerves, which was something the coffee only seemed to aggravate. He glanced at the time projection on the wall: it read 6.30 p.m. At the counter, he charged the meal to his World Government account by scanning his identity chip.

On the walk home to his ITF-issued apartment, Bill tilted his head upwards until his face found the sun. He allowed it to scorch his naturally aged skin. Around him, people chatted noisily, drawing in the sweet, clean air, never needing the gel breathing masks that were mandatory on Earth. Earth's air was poisonous and carried with it a risk of organ failure due to long-term exposure. Most people couldn't afford lung replacements, so the population did as they were told. It would be easy to forget the planet located thirty light years away had it not been for the life he shared with Isla there. Earth would always be a part of him as long as Isla was.

He arrived at his apartment block located in the New Westminster area and watched a man drop a broken chair from a window above to the side alley below. The smell in the side alley was overpowering, the alley filled with more than just unwanted furniture. Remembering that the cleaning autobots weren't scheduled for a few days, he picked up a couple of rubbish bags that littered the pavement outside the entrance to the block and tossed them out of his way. A sudden waft of rotting food and disinfectant forced him to pinch the end of his nose tightly. He hurried inside the block as quickly as he could. It wasn't illegal to dump rubbish in an area where cleaning was scheduled and was one of the World Government's ill-thought-out plans to help smooth the transition to the new planet. While there were many positives about the new planet, the six cities were far too overcrowded and had already become derelict in parts. Humans had only been occupying the planet for a short twenty-five years.

His ITF-owned apartment overlooked Belgrave Square Gardens, a close replica of the same gardens once seen in London on Earth; green open spaces on Exilon 5 had been one of the main requests on the transferees' 'wish list'. Bill unlocked the front door and tread as lightly and stealthily as possible across the floor while his eyes scanned the layout of his apartment for signs of disturbance. His job was to draw out enemies into the open, but on occasion, they would try to seek him out.

His apartment was sparsely decorated and any personal items were locked away safely in a suitcase in his bedroom. Every surface was deliberately thick with dust; an informant had advised him once it would be easier to spot when things had been moved. His eyes examined the surfaces in microscopic detail. Old circular imprints left by the legs of chairs remained hidden as they had done that morning. He drifted into his bedroom and pulled open the wardrobe doors to check on his suitcase. He quietly closed the doors and moved silently into the bathroom.

He thought about getting a second apartment on Exilon 5, a place that the World Government or ITF knew nothing about—like the one on Earth that he and Isla owned—but the stress of keeping one apartment hidden from them was enough.

When he wandered into the living room again, a brief flash of light caught his attention. The Light Box—a virtual information system that contained programmable artificial intelligence—shimmered in a ghostly way on the wall above his cherry-coloured three-seater sofa. He hadn't activated the virtual avatar that came as standard, and had only ever used the security and secretarial facilities, and the twenty-four hour news feed. So the flash of light meant that the ITF were watching him again. But they didn't know that he'd already located some of their bugging devices: two in the base of the table lamps, one inside a disused cupboard in the kitchen and one underneath his bed. And those were only the ones he could find. He had no idea of the levels of surveillance they were carrying out on him—their best investigator. At the beginning of his career, he'd made the rookie mistake of failing to read the small print on his employment contract. While he was used to their intrusion, there were moments when he craved privacy. He stopped short of saluting the air at them. Many times, he had fantasised about settling in one place, but as life became more complicated it seemed like less of an option. Born in Edinburgh, he hadn't set foot in Scotland for several years, and he didn't see that changing anytime soon.

Bill sat down on the sofa and pulled his digital pad, or DPad, out of his bag. He placed it on the glass table in front of him, suddenly reminded of the strings he had had to pull with Daphne Gilchrist, the Earth Security Centre's CEO, so that he could be put on the current mission. The World Government was in charge, and the ESC handled international security matters for them. While initially Gilchrist had been against his involvement because of what she reasoned to be his inexperience, something—or someone—had changed her mind. The ITF handled the grunt work for the ESC—investigations, arrests, policing—and nothing ever happened without Gilchrist's say-so.

Bill stood up and studied his face in the Light Box's virtual façade. He pulled at the skin around his eyes, noting how tired and old his genetically unmodified face was looking. He ruffled his dark brown hair and examined the extra spattering of grey flecks dotted throughout. He faked a smile and counted the lines around his eyes. Everything seemed more exaggerated in the Light Box's façade. Isla had once told him that no matter what advances were made in age alteration, it was important that he was always able to recognise himself in the mirror. He hadn't given too much thought to it over the years, but the advice seemed more pertinent now that she was gone. Memories of her tore at his chest and he looked away from the screen, refusing to allow whoever was watching him to share in his private moment.

In the kitchen, Bill grabbed the black handle of his coffee pot and waited for the H2O unit to fill it with water. He added the water, then fresh coffee granules to a machine and brewed some coffee the old-fashioned way. A delicious aroma filled the room as the black liquid streamed steadily into the pot. He licked his lips. He knew his addiction was becoming a problem, and for some reason the coffee didn't taste as good when he was taking Actigen, pills that allowed him to skip sleep. It had been a long time since he'd enjoyed a decent night's sleep—two years since Isla's disappearance he reckoned—and tonight would be no exception. The Indigene's meeting was anticipated for the following morning and, if World Government intel was correct, it would occur in the hour after dawn. The Indigenes, unable to survive in the temperatures on the surface, had figured out a way to surface safely.

The problem of the indigenous race was not an easy one to solve. With the conditions that prevailed on Earth there were only two options for humans: move to the new planet or die on the old one. The Indigenes were preventing full human integration into society and he suspected they knew exactly what had happened to Isla.

The coffee pot finally sizzled and Bill filled his favourite 'I heart Boston' mug to the brim; Isla had bought the mug for him in an antique shop a few years back. He ran a finger over the cracked rim and examined the heart design, the red colour largely faded where he rested his fingers most. He believed the mug helped to focus his mind—or maybe it was just the coffee. Whatever the reason, it was an important link to his past and he vowed never to part with it. Adding cream substitute and artificial sugar to his steaming coffee, he settled on the sofa again. He placed his DPad on one knee while he precariously balanced the mug on the other. He resumed his review of the government's files on the alien race, blowing on the coffee before taking a cautious sip of the hot liquid. While the caffeine stimulated his senses, he expected the crash would come later on—it usually did.

2

With a dry mouth and feeling colder than normal, Stephen finally realised the danger he was about to face; exposing his fragile skin to the Exilon 5's sun could come at a price. It would be the first time the Indigenes had tried anything like this. He could almost feel his translucent skin blister at the very thought of it. He imagined how it might feel, like an uncomfortable build up of heat beginning in the pit of his stomach, then spreading to the rest of his body. *Is that what it will be like when Indigenes burn?* He had never stayed in the sun long enough to find out.

Stephen paced the length of District Three's laboratory, taking long, even strides. All previous attempts to make contact with Surface Creatures— what they called the race that lived above ground— had always been at night and protected by the cover of darkness. If he was to be successful, this mission could change how the Indigenes lived. Everything had to go according to plan. Time might be short to get the information he needed before a Surface Creature noticed him.

He was aware of what the Surface Creatures' children called the Indigenes: Shadow People. The name was right, he felt, because some of his kind hunted more than just animals in retaliation for what the surface dwellers had done to their race. He understood the reasons that fuelled the predatory motives of those who could not forget the past. In weaker moments, he sympathised enough with them to consider joining them on their nightly hunts. After the explosions had occurred and with so few of the Indigenes surviving the blasts, he cared little for their children. Stephen had known his friend Anton since they were young Evolvers, but Anton was not scarred by events of the past like Stephen was; Stephen had seen the land explosions and the early changes to their society—changes that had later killed his parents. Born after the worst was over, Anton was not consumed by thoughts of revenge as some of the others were.

At least the tunnels of District Three and other districts that ran underneath Exilon 5's surface had preserved what was left of their species, giving them a chance to start again. The tunnels had been a lot simpler back then. Changes had been necessary when the surface was no longer habitable.

Stephen tried on the artificial skin that Anton had designed, but it felt strange to him—an additional weight that weighed almost nothing. Changing his appearance bothered him but he had to try, for the sake of the mission. He brushed his face with the tips of his fingers and the delicate silicone yielded to his gentle touch. How could something so fragile feel so heavy? He was proud of his appearance and of the fact that he was a unique member of a great society. It was necessary that he change. What happened the next day could shift the power back into their hands long enough for them to figure out what to do next.

The differences in his appearance did not allow him to blend in naturally with the Surface Creatures. When they passed him on the street, he could feel the heat from their warm-blooded bodies. Their

25

proximity only served to fuel a deep hatred that made his blood run hot, but not as hot as theirs did naturally. The static electricity from his body irritated theirs. The Surface Creatures didn't struggle with the sun like the Indigenes did. Their skin was less transparent and capable of withstanding fluctuations in temperature, something Stephen's body would not allow. The silicone skin was designed as much to protect his skin as to allow him to disguise those differences.

The Indigenes carried different skills. Anton's skill was manipulating technology, in particular, the technology that belonged to the Surface Creatures. He had discovered an alternative use for their silicone skin. Surface Creature literature declared its main use, in its original state, was to make deep-sea diving suits light, while other materials protected the wearer from the effects of abnormal pressures. Anton found a way to alter the molecular structure of the silicone to make the artificial skin that was both lightweight and wafer thin and with the ability to cool the skin upon touch. He then added some pigmentation until it resembled the Surface Creatures' opaque appearance. While the skin worked well, there were still obvious flaws; the uneven density didn't allow natural light to penetrate it. It would give a degree of anonymity, but how much Anton couldn't say.

Stephen and Anton had talked several times about the day the Surface Creatures arrived twenty-five years ago. A pair of curious Evolvers, they had kept their distance while large cranes removed pallets of materials from smaller spacecrafts. A piercing screech had filled the air as their equipment drilled downwards. Fires released noxious gases as they burned what they didn't need. The sound of fighting and yelling had filled the void the drills left vacant when they weren't running. To the relief of all in the districts, the Surface Creatures had not drilled down far enough to discover the beating heart of the planet. They remained as artificial as the structures they forced upon the land—it was the reason for their name. Central Council had not been able to guess how many Surface Creatures arrived that day or now lived on Exilon 5, only that the numbers were far greater than that of their own population. For the Indigene race, which had existed for ten thousand years, this was the first species to arrive on Exilon 5 and attempt to take over the planet.

Stephen focused his mind on the current task and grabbed an air filtration device from the table before relocating to another tunnel not far from the laboratory. Inside the tunnel, he touched the rock face made of insignia, with its ability to trap cocoons of surface air in its wall. It gently vibrated in response to him. He smiled and quickly set up a device powered by the amplifying strength of gamma rock, in front of the wall. The device drew a single cocoon of air from the wall and stretched it until it was large enough for Stephen to stand inside.

He drew in a deep breath from District Three's strictly controlled atmosphere and opened his hand. The air filtration device came in three pieces, clear in colour. He fitted the two smaller pieces into his nasal cavities and the third, larger piece at the back of his throat. He rested his hand on the outside of the cocoon and gently pushed through until he was inside. The first breath of contaminated air burned his lungs and he waited for the single-charge micro filter to restrict the flow of oxygen to his lungs. When the device caught up to his air requirements—to the point when he could breathe normally—he exited the cocoon and carefully removed it. He remembered Anton's warning about the one-hour time limit. He could swap a depleted device for a new one, but not without risking contamination to his lungs. Anton's team was working on a better, rechargeable version using the body's kinetic energy, but it would be months before it was ready for production.

Stephen leaned against the wall and tried to think of what advantages he had over the Surface Creatures, things that would guarantee his safety the following day: speed, strength—intellect? As far as intellect went, the Indigenes fared better. But the Surface Creatures had a better understanding of cunning and deception that put him at a disadvantage. He pushed away from the wall and paced the length of the tunnel. What else could he use—his vision?

An Indigene's vision worked best in low levels of light; it allowed them to make sense of the dark. It was why they preferred to surface at night, the tactic they had used early on in their need to find out more about the race that lived above ground. Stephen recalled the night several of them had surfaced, dressed in cheap costumes and without the silicone skin to protect their identity, on the back of Central Council orders.

An irrational fear had caught hold of him that night when three of them surfaced from the tunnel entrance and his feet had rooted to the spot. Had he not been physically pushed by one of the Indigenes, he wasn't sure how long he might have stayed there. They had approached the city border for New London and wandered through the streets looking for willing individuals to question. They spotted seven of them—all children—standing outside a replication terminal building. Stephen had caught the smell of alcohol long before they were close enough to smell it on their breath. They stopped a short distance from the children.

The atmosphere changed as whispers replaced the loud chatter. Up went the invisible barriers that only a self-assured approach would break down. The boys had been curious about the three oddly dressed strangers that approached them, so that was a good start. But Stephen struggled to speak. What did he want to say exactly? *Your parents are murderers and you will grow up to be one too.* Not exactly the best way to get them talking, he felt.

To his relief one of the other Indigenes had spoken first. The innocent enquiries and retorts were bandied back and forth until the other two Indigenes changed tack, asking questions that were more personal. The boys whispered to each other, but the Indigenes' sharp hearing meant they had been able to hear every word.

'Who the fuck are these losers?'

'I know. I'm losing me buzz.'

'I'm bored.'

'C'mon, let's show these clowns what dirt tastes like.'

'Yeah!'

'I wanna go home.'

'Stay where you are, Jason. Everybody's stayin' put.'

'D'ya think they're some kind o' military?'

'Dunno. They're not wearing uniforms.'

'Don't wanna to get into no trouble.'

'Don't be an idiot, Jason. Do as I say.'

'Seven against three.'

The children surrounded them and,

instinctively, Stephen took a step back. It was an irrational thing to do; he was stronger and faster than they were, but the way they circled him put him on edge.

'Seven against three,' they had said, slurring their words.

They suddenly threw themselves at Stephen and the others, arms flailing and legs kicking, fuelled by a mixture of alcohol and stupidity. Before the boys' punches could reach them, Stephen ran away. The other Indigenes had the good sense to follow him. They listened from a safe distance.

'Where … where'd they go?'

'What the fuck?'

'It's like them Shadow People I keep hearing 'bout.'

'Don't be an idiot, that's just legend—a story to scare the little kiddies so they don't fall 'sleep.'

'No, I heard them people's real. They hunt late at night and they eat kids and adults if they sleep. Sometimes they catch them out here.'

'That doesn't even make sense, Jason. We're out here ev'ry night, and I ain't seen no Shadow People.'

'Well what'dya call them people just here then?'

'Fucking losers.'

It was the first time Stephen had heard the term 'Shadow People' and Central Council had no idea who among their race was hunting Surface Creatures in this way. No matter what rumours existed about the Indigenes and their way of life, they had to be more careful. They needed a better plan.

It was at the next council meeting that Stephen had presented his own plan to District Three's

Council elders, Pierre and Elise. His anger had got the better of him as he put forward a bolder, more daring strategy that would mean surfacing during the day. Pierre had seen the logic in his plan while Elise, Pierre's wife, had not.

But Stephen had a target in mind: a boy whom he'd been watching for a while who was not aggressive like the earlier targets were and was always alone. He explained to the elders how he planned to use the boy's natural curiosity to gain his trust. Pierre's faith in him had swung the votes of the representatives.

Stephen had worked hard to look like and move the way the Surface Creatures did, even though the very thought of being close to them made his skin crawl. He had no choice: he had to immerse himself in their lives. The target must not become suspicious.

He took out a box and rummaged through the items that had been 'acquired' from the Surface Creatures over the past few months. He fished out a thumb-sized digital recorder that Anton had retrieved from a female's bag. The tiny recorder was barely the size of his thumbnail.

He moved to an adjoining room off the tunnel where he'd tested the air filtration device—a rough square room with a metal table in the centre flanked by two chairs. A soft hue illuminated the white walls, the light feeding through a shaft linked to tiny solar-powered discs embedded into the wasteland above. He placed the tiny recorder on the floor, near one of the table legs. He waved his hand over the device and the first of the recordings began.

A high-resolution 3D image of the restaurant burst out of the recording device, instantly filling the otherwise plain room with a low-light colour. The wall's surface bounced the images back into the room. Stephen watched through pale Indigene eyes as Cantaloupe restaurant came into focus. It felt forced and unnatural to him to sit in a place where people served you, and even more bizarre to pay for the experience. Stephen had never eaten anything he hadn't killed himself, but the decline of the Primoris—a native animal on Exilon 5—had forced their race to seek alternatives to a raw meat diet that was rich in iron. Animal hunting merely satisfied a primal urge but was no longer necessary to survive; a synthesised protein substitute kept them alive. The animals the Surface Creatures had brought with them tasted strange—the composition of their blood different. In the end, the taste of warm blood and fresh meat from the new animals was enough to suppress their desires, even if the product didn't adequately satisfy their hunger.

Stephen took a seat at the table and aligned his body to mirror one half of a Surface Creature couple, immersing himself into their timeline as they ate. It was unnatural for him to sit; he preferred to stand. He gripped the steel edges of the chair and carefully watched the recording, observing the way they used their hands to gesture. He listened intently to their conversation. When he watched the Surface Creatures through recordings like this, he could be clinical in his observations—no hate, or panic or fear to get in his way. His lips moved in perfect synchronicity with theirs. Their hands danced, almost as if they were conducting a musical score. He picked up the pattern of their hands easily enough. He had replayed the scenario so often he could recite every movement by heart. But he planned to watch it right up to the break of dawn, when he would finally leave for the surface.

Anton had recorded the scene a month ago while pretending to wait in the restaurant for someone. Even in his disguise, he said the Surface Creatures had noticed him, but nobody approached other than the female attendant who'd asked if he was ready to order. A lone male sitting by the window had watched him for a while before returning to his private solitude.

While the couple ate their meal, a different couple argued behind him.

'But I want us to sleep at my place tonight,' the young female said.

'My place is nicer. Yours is too small, and I think your cat hates me.'

The silence that followed said more than words ever could.

'Can't we just give it a go?' the male pleaded. 'I'll even walk you to the train station in the morning.'

The young female folded her arms and sighed.

Sweat glistened on the male's forehead. 'Okay, your place it is.'

Only one of them was smiling by the end of the conversation and Stephen idly wondered if they were still a couple. The recording looped, and this time he looked beyond the arguing couple. A much older male sat to his right.

How long can they live? If the Surface Creatures were to die out suddenly, would the Indigenes survive them? The oldest living Indigene on record was one hundred and ninety-eight. He knew their species' bodies were the same—one heart, one liver, two kidneys and one brain—but there were still fundamental differences between them. The Indigenes' bodies and minds didn't suffer deterioration because all their cells could regenerate. An injury that could take weeks to heal in a Surface Creature would only take minutes in an Indigene's body. Having studied their physical composition, he discovered that the cells in their brains and spinal column possessed no regenerative ability. Instead, the Surface Creatures relied on the production of synthetic cells to combat brain injuries, old age and paralysis. Disease was uncommon among the Indigenes, because it was impossible for an infected cell to manipulate a healthy one when the body was already expelling it.

The male sitting by the window looked familiar to him, even though he was sure he'd never seen him before. A sudden feeling of contempt for the male surprised him, so he turned around and concentrated on his doppelganger's meal to regain a little control. The recording looped for the third time and, right on cue, a female came to the table and filled their glasses with water. He'd read somewhere that Surface Creature's bodies contained ninety per cent of the stuff, although they didn't always drink it in its purest form. The same female handed a beer to the male by the window. The alcohol reminded him of the children they'd encountered not that long ago. While the Indigenes could drink water, it didn't 'quench' their thirst as the Surface Creatures claimed it would in their advertising. Not having discovered where the planet's water supply existed, the Surface Creatures had brought their own when they relocated to the planet. By adding a chemical compound, they were able to multiply what little quantities they did find.

The longer Stephen sat at the table the more he struggled with the idea of how a less intelligent race such as the Surface Creatures could successfully destroy so many Indigenes. It was almost as if they had prior knowledge of the Indigenes' existence. He continued to watch the recording, allowing the scene to loop a fourth time until the images were ingrained in his long-term memory. He watched their movements and their familiar ease with one another, but refused to acknowledge the similarities that existed between each race. There were plenty of differences too, one being the speed with which both species moved. The Indigenes regularly conversed in thought alone—words weren't always necessary to convey a message. Stephen was not used to speaking aloud and he would have to learn how to slow down his speech if he was going to converse successfully with a child. He turned off the recording, feeling his body relax as soon as he did. He needed one last thing: a set of lenses that would protect his retinas from the harmful daytime sun. Anton had a few left over from his time on the surface.

Stephen stood up, scraping the chair's metal legs on the stone floor, and rummaged through the box once more. He fished out a mirror and pushed the table towards the wall. He placed the mirror on the table and used the wall to prop it up. With a clarity of vision he was not used to, he examined his strange image, distorted by the silicone skin. He practised his eye movements, his speech and his hand gestures, finding it difficult to contort his face into unusual expressions. He kept rehearsing until the movements felt a little less obvious and more natural. He reminded himself he would only have to act the part for a short while.

This will be easy.

So why did he feel unsettled about the trip the next day? Maybe it was the idea of coming face-to-face with one of 'them' and having to hide his true feelings. In his mind, his family had died unnecessarily so the Surface Creatures could live. Every fibre of his body screamed at him to stay.

But he had to go. Not only was Central Council relying on him to find out details about the Surface Creatures but he also needed to understand them. Maybe he could sleep better at night. And if the mission failed, would he be allowed to try again?

He dismissed the idea of failure and left the room in search of Anton.

3

That evening, Bill received a call from Daphne Gilchrist, the CEO of the Earth Security Centre. Never really sure who was listening, he always made sure to treat each call with the same seriousness as if he was talking directly to Charles Deighton, CEO of the World Government. While he had only spoken to the man a couple of times before, it was twice too many. He didn't need to 'profile' Deighton to know there was something seriously wrong with him.

'Are you all set Bill? I don't want anything to go wrong tomorrow,' Gilchrist said. There was an edge to her voice.

'I'm ready, and so is my team.'

'What are your plans?'

'To observe the Indigene and see what it does.' He could hear her tapping her nail on something hard.

'That means no interference from you or your team.'

'I understand that.' He knew she meant him.

There was a brief silence before she spoke again. 'Are you sure you're up to this? I am aware of your … situation.'

Bill spoke forcefully, but respectfully. 'I wouldn't have pushed for the role if I wasn't up to it. What happened—well, it was a long time ago now.'

'Yes, but these things have a habit of rearing their heads at the wrong time. I know the … problem you have with the Indigenes.'

'Not all of them,' he said a little too quickly, before being forced to add, 'I mean—I don't know them. I'm interested in them in the same way the World Government is.' As soon as he'd said the words, he knew how meaningless they were.

'Look, Bill. I'm not going to sugar-coat it for you. This could be a turning point in the investigation or an all-out disaster. Whatever happens, I need to know I can count on you to keep it together.'

Bill's heart picked up speed as he answered, 'Yes, you can.'

'Good. And remember why we picked you. It was because of your success with Hunt. Deighton's expectations are high.'

Larry Hunt—hearing his name made him touch his shoulder again. Even while he was incarcerated, the man just wouldn't go away. To say the World Government was regretting their involvement with the most successful man in the food replication business was an understatement. The government had a lot to lose, but equally plenty to gain from their majority stake in Hunt Technologies, a company that controlled seventy per cent of the food replication market.

'Understood,' he managed to say, just before Gilchrist clicked off.

Bill picked up his DPad and pulled up Larry Hunt's photo. Staring back at him was the criminal he'd helped to put behind bars. An ordinary looking man, nothing special, but then most of the serious criminals looked like family men with nothing to hide. Bill had expected Hunt to seek retaliation for his involvement in bringing him to justice, but he hadn't been ready for how he felt afterwards; the catch was too easy, almost like he'd been set up to succeed. When Hunt Technologies had released their latest food replication model, the Replica 2500, the government had become jumpy and the ESC ordered Bill to intervene. The hundreds of businesses that bought the model were touting it as a fake.

Daphne Gilchrist had ordered him to a meeting. When he arrived, she handed him a list of numbers.

'What do you see?' Her expression was cold, her mouth set in a tight line.

Bill scanned the information. He recognised the format of prices against amounts. 'Shares.'

'Exactly. We think Mr Hunt has been pulling a stroke, overvaluing his stocks to gain a better share of the replication market. Naturally, the World Government board members are upset at this revelation. If the Replica 2500 isn't genuine, the company's value will drop into negative equity. That's a loss nobody wants.'

Bill looked at her. 'You want me to profile him?'

Gilchrist placed her hands on the table and leaned forward. She locked her cold eyes on him. 'I want you to take the son of a bitch down.'

Bill had spent months trying to get inside the head of the man who had dominated the food replication world for an aeon. Slowly, he established patterns in Hunt's carefully orchestrated, yet sometimes erratic, behaviour. More importantly, he'd identified who Hunt relied on and who would have access to personal information—his secretary.

He called Hunt Technologies to arrange a business meeting with her. When they met, he tried to be smooth, maybe flirt a little. Hunt's secretary was attractive enough, but not his type and far too young at only twenty-five. In fact, she was too young for the job of gatekeeper to the most powerful business person on Earth. He wondered what her relationship was with Hunt; it had to be more than sexual. While he spoke to her, he caught her glancing discreetly at the time projection on the wall numerous times. The vacant look in her eyes told him everything he needed to know. Hunt's people had been coached.

Bill concentrated his efforts on others who Hunt's secretary may have been connected with. He began tailing lower level workers out on their lunch breaks. At one of the food replication terminals, he had chatted with an employee and feigned interest in working for Hunt Technologies. He casually steered the topic around to the person of interest to him, asking whether he would better his chances if he spoke to her directly.

'Nobody gets to see Theresa without an appointment. Even her boyfriend has to take a number,' the male employee replied. He thumbed over at a skinny twenty-something man who was sitting at another table, hunched awkwardly over his lunch.

'What section does her boyfriend work in?'

'Storage.'

Bill had to stop himself from getting up. *You're too eager. Play it cool.* He had found his way in— why he hadn't thought of the secretary's boyfriend, he didn't know. Maybe it was because she didn't come across as the sociable type. He couldn't picture the moderately attractive girl with the grim smile making time for anyone other than Hunt.

In the end, the boyfriend had been of little help, perhaps even a little scared of her. But a colleague of the skinny boy had no loyalty to anyone in particular.

A little bribe helped loosen his lips.

Bill recalled his only encounter with a couple of Hunt's henchmen shortly after his indictment. He'd tried to shake his pursuers as they chased him through London's dark streets, but as his lungs burned and his breath shortened, they quickly cornered him. A nearby street lamp flickered overhead and then went black, as if it didn't want to see what happened next. One of the men had grabbed his arms so roughly he almost dislocated Bill's shoulder. The other produced an antique knife from his pocket. The blade gleamed as the light from the streetlamp above them reflected off the metal. There had been an excitement from the men that was palpable and raw. Bill drew in a sharp breath as the knife-wielding man stepped forward and plunged the blade into the soft area of his left shoulder, the blinding hot pain disarming him instantly.

A fucking antique knife, he thought. There had to have been easier ways to kill him. The attack came with a verbal warning attached.

'Hunt wants you to remember this.'

Bill idly touched the area where the knife had penetrated his skin that night. Although it was fully repaired with no sign of a scar, he remembered exactly how it had felt when the blade tore through his muscle and poked out the other side. Thinking about that night sent a shiver through his body. With shaky hands, he picked up the DPad; the tremors were worse. He inhaled deeply and released a slow breath. His stomach felt sick, but his body was buzzing with caffeine-induced adrenaline. He wished for it all to be over so he could get his answers.

In his apartment, Bill combed through the dozens of files the World Government held on the

Indigenes. So far the information was limited. Irritation suddenly caught hold of him and he clasped his hands together to steady their shaking. An earthy scent hit his nose and his craving for coffee kicked in. He prayed that the following day would give him a lead—any information at all—on what had happened to his wife.

There were so many files to choose from, but the one about the government's capture of a young Indigene always caught his attention. The young alien had not survived long after the capture because of its inability to survive in the same conditions as humans. Bill found interesting details about an atmosphere-controlled containment unit existing in facilities on the outskirts of New London. The unit had yet to receive its first prisoner.

Gilchrist's face popped into his head. She wasn't the worst person, certainly not as bad as Deighton, but what concerned him was the close working relationship she had with the CEO of the World Government.

'Apprehend the subject, but make sure it's alive,' Gilchrist had said at the last briefing. She tapped her nail on the polished table in the boardroom next to her office. 'And make sure those idiots we assigned you don't go off half-cocked.'

What Bill had requested from the World Government was Special Forces. What they stuck him with was Armoured Division, minus the heavy artillery. 'Divide and Conquer' was their motto. Yes, he would make sure to keep the alien alive. When he had finished with it, then the World Government, the ESC—or whoever wanted it—could do what they liked with it.

Memories of his wife were clearer, more vivid

than usual. Maybe it was because he was cradling the mug she gave him, or because he was inching closer to the truth about her disappearance. When his mind wasn't occupied with work, he gave every spare thought he had to her. He trawled through his past memories, looking for clues about why she'd disappeared. The government had been helpful enough in the beginning, but it didn't surprise him when they eventually stopped looking.

The World Government, the powerhouse in Washington D.C., was in charge of all Earth's business. The charcoal grey borders that surrounded the slick black windows gave their offices a foreboding yet unique look. Majestic height and angular lines towered effortlessly above the other buildings that surrounded it, leaving smaller constructions to cower in its icy shade. The building stretched for miles into the low-lying steely skies around Washington D.C., punching neat holes into layers of atmosphere as it searched for a way out of the restrictive cityscape. In the face of all that magnificence, the building was a ruse, a decoy for something greater. The real World Government offices lay deep below the surface, protected by force fields that formed graduating rings, each more impenetrable than the one above it. The building represented what the World Government stood for on Earth—hope and order, power and impenetrability.

What twenty-year-old could resist the government's representation of hope and order, disguised by miles of steel and glass but emphasised by unimaginable luxury inside? Mottled blue granite floors and walls created the interior, with precious jewels dripping from the lighting fixtures. He realised later on that the place was designed to be aesthetically appealing to impress the potential recruits that sought out work there. Large advertising screens dressed the walls and promoted too-good-to-be-true career opportunities. The decision for Bill to join their organisation had been a no-brainer—there wasn't any other place like it on Earth.

But his need for excitement had pulled him in a different direction early on, something his job in the public documents section had not provided. He sought out another path, one that would take him places and satisfy his wanderlust. The ESC's military training programme ticked all the boxes, in particular the job of Special Operations agent.

It was where he'd first met his wife. Isla had looked so cute standing at the top of the class while she taught self-defence skills to men stronger than her. Bill desperately wanted to ask her out, but she was an instructor.

'It's less about brute force and more about negotiation,' she had said.

The all-male class laughed at her suggestion, but she earned their respect when she broke up a fight between two men the following day using only words.

Bill struggled to concentrate on the lessons, especially when the sound of Isla's gentle Scottish accent gave him butterflies. He recalled very little about the class work, but remembered having to rely on notes to catch up on his studies at home. Isla's hair had been shorter back then, hanging just below her shoulders. Her warm blue eyes had sparkled and her face was as soft as her smile. She was the complete opposite of him, and he'd wanted her.

Bill's natural flair for reading people had earned him a place as a Special Operations agent. The

ESC had tried to send him to India to complete his training—something he vehemently resisted. He enlisted Isla's help in getting them to change their minds.

'What can I do to help?' she said, looking sceptical.

'I need to stay in the UK. My parents are here and I'm all they have.' He hated lying to her but he couldn't bear the thought of leaving her behind. Both his parents had died in a bullet train accident years earlier.

'I'll see what I can do.' She had smiled at him in a way that almost made him break the instructor–pupil rule.

When he was assigned to the International Task Force in London, he was sure of two things: that she had helped, and that he loved her. A month after he graduated, they began dating. Soon after, she asked to meet his parents. She angrily punched him on the arm when he'd handed her an urn with their ashes still inside.

An ache built up inside his chest when he remembered the happier times with Isla. He distracted himself at the window and looked to the street below. Resting his face and hands on the cold glass, he stared at Belgrave Square Gardens through a fog his breath had created. An automated vehicle pulled up outside and several children and a woman—presumably their teacher—alighted from the vehicle's left side. The children screamed excitedly as they bolted for the swings in the park. The teacher yelled after them to come back but they were running free and wild, and without parental supervision.

He thought about Isla's love of children, and

the window fogged up more as his breathing became laboured. She had always been open with him about her desire to have children, but he hadn't been as keen as her. He didn't think Earth was the right environment to bring up children and had promised to think about it again when they transferred to Exilon 5. Now Isla was gone and suddenly he wanted a child— her child, a little version of her to make him laugh the way she always could. But Exilon 5 was no safer than Earth as long as the Indigenes existed. They had taken from him the one person he cared about the most.

Isla was in his head: 'Forgive them, Bill.'

'Forgiveness is earned,' he said coldly. If it came down to it, would he really grant it to the Indigenes?

He buried his nose in the transcripts from the previous week's surveillance operation, his heart hardening as his eyes stopped at the detail about the male Indigene's attempts to talk to a boy in the square opposite his apartment. The mother had reacted quickly and the boy was led away. His team reported how the same Indigene had watched a different boy for a while, a skinny lad with black hair.

Their attempts to surface are always at the same hour, just after sunrise, Bill noted. Now he waited for the following day to arrive and the expectation that the Indigene would try to make contact again.

4

While eight-year-old Ben Watson waited for the next automated bus to arrive, he watched with interest as the stranger made his way towards the bench, eventually choosing a seat right beside him. He sneaked a glance at his unusual appearance, trying to guess where he was from. He ran through the list of countries he knew from his school lessons. There were the six cities on Exilon 5 and other than the obvious ones on far-away Earth, he struggled to think of more. It was too difficult to concentrate in his geography class when all he really wanted to do was send digital notes to his best friend, Peter.

Syria and Nepal popped into his head and he wondered if the man was from there. He remembered them from his classic Earth adventure series on the Light Box. In one episode, the criminals had escaped from prison and were running from the law. Somehow, they'd ended up in both locations. But the criminals from his stories were meaner looking and had plenty of facial scars. He wondered whether the stranger was a spy. He couldn't see any visible scarring, so maybe he was a spy for the allies.

His level of excitement rose so much that he almost squeaked with joy. What if he's a real life spy, he wondered, right here in the middle of New London. A grin transformed his face, and his mood.

As he ran through the idea in his young mind,

he noticed the man briefly glance in his direction. Maybe he's lost, Ben thought. Bravely meeting the stranger's eyes, he quickly lost his nerve and looked away. He remembered from his adventure stories that you should never look directly at a spy because they might have to kill you. He didn't care that he'd broken the number one rule; he was pleased that he'd been brave enough to try, braver than his best friend, Peter, he imagined.

He sneaked another glance, this time at the man's clothes. It was a strange outfit: a long brown coat with matching hat, like the ones the old detectives used to wear in the antique comic books he collected. The clothes were old. A musty smell lingered in the air between them. He didn't know why he'd expected a spy to wear a black ninja outfit. But maybe that was what made a good spy—when he didn't look like everybody else.

While the man was busy looking elsewhere, Ben noticed his skin for the first time. He fidgeted uncontrollably with his hands, eventually having to sit on them to keep them still. The movement attracted the man's attention. That unnerved him. Eye contact is too risky, he decided. The stranger could be anyone, working for the government—or his mum. He wasn't supposed to be out alone, and out of habit he glanced nervously over his shoulder.

Nervousness quickly changed into annoyance as he silently wished that his mother would mind her own business. He'd heard her complain to friends that he was just like his father, always somewhere else, never where she wanted him to be. She called his actions 'getting into trouble'. He preferred to call it 'going on an adventure'. Ben dreamed of becoming an actor so he could live the life of his adventure-story heroes—dodging bullets, getting into trouble, travelling to places like Syria and Nepal. The closest he came to that was his Saturday trips around New London, while his mother slept in late. Anywhere was better than home, waiting for her to get up after another late night session on the Light Box.

Ben slipped his blue backpack off his shoulders and perched it on his lap. He pulled open the flap and peered inside. Last night he'd packed enough supplies to keep him going for a couple of hours, enough to cover his entire trip. He pulled out his DPad—his avatar had loaded it with a map covering a five-mile radius of the area—and checked where he was. He didn't expect to get further than that. When his mother wasn't obsessively using the Light Box, he would ask his avatar to come up with interesting plans. And if his mother asked, Ben had given it strict instructions to lie about his whereabouts. But lately, she'd stopped asking, which suited him just fine. She said to a friend that a lack of male presence in the house had made her only son 'wilful and difficult to manage'. Ben hadn't understood exactly what she meant by that but he knew there were certain things he had to do without her. She was a girl, and girls didn't always understand.

Having forgotten to bring a compass the week before and with no idea where he was, he remembered to pack it this time. It was the last item he'd placed in his bag and it sat atop everything else as a reminder of his forgetfulness. Peter had lent him the compass for a couple of weeks in exchange for some of his antique comics. It had been a good trade. Ben had already read those stories a hundred times. The compass complemented his adventure stories. Along with the map, it would help him get where he needed to go and, more importantly, back again. Peter had told him to check how the compass pointed to his house so if he got lost, he could find his way back. Ben had been confident of his ability to read and understand maps but checked anyway. The needle had wobbled uneasily over East. He wondered whether Peter might consider a permanent trade on the compass for a few more comic books. Or, he could simply tell him he lost it. He would decide later.

The sight of his strawberry jam sandwiches and a carton of juice in his backpack made him drool a little. A sudden chill ran through his tiny body when he realised the man was watching his every move. He instinctively clutched the bag tighter, worried the spy was after his most precious item—his compass. Cautiously, he risked a glance to see if he was still looking at him. He was.

'Hello,' the man said.

A barrage of questions rushed into Ben's mind. Why had he wasted so much time thinking about his mother?

The man continued. 'What's your name?'

A suspicious thought crossed Ben's mind, and he wondered if the man knew his mum. 'What's yours?' he demanded.

'My name's Stephen. Forgive me for staring but I don't live up here and I have never been this close to your kind. I have only read about you or seen photos. Can you tell me what you are?'

Ben's brow creased. Then it came to him. 'Oh, I'm English. And this is New London.' He tried in vain to calm the millions of butterflies that tickled his tummy. 'Are you from Syria or Nepal? I didn't know they spoke English like us.'

Stephen briefly shook his head. 'Neither place. I live here, just like you. I just don't live in this city.' They both sat perfectly still, an eerie silence building between them. Then Stephen spoke again. 'Forgive me. I should rephrase my original question. What do you call yourself?'

'I suppose you mean my name,' Ben said, a little confused. If he really was a spy, he should have known that. 'Do you know my mum?'

'Who is your mother?'

'Diane Watson.'

'I don't know anyone by that name.'

Ben nodded, satisfied with the answer. Stephen looked trustworthy enough. 'My name's Ben. Pleased to meet you.' He thrust out a small hand towards Stephen who hesitated before accepting it. Stephen's cold hand surprised him and he reflexively pulled his hand away. The stranger did the same but more gently, rubbing the back of his hand where Ben's small fingers had rested.

'Your hand is warm. Warmer than I'd expected, to be honest,' Stephen said.

'I was going to say yours is quite cold!' Ben relaxed a little.

'I guess there are some notable differences between us.'

Ben had so many questions he wanted to ask, but he didn't know where to start. The temperature of Stephen's skin seemed like an easy place to begin.

'Why is your hand so cold?'

'It has always been this temperature. This is quite normal for me. Why is yours so warm?'

'Everybody's hands are warm. You're the one that's different!'

Stephen nodded. 'I wonder what else is

different about us?'

Even though he'd only just met him, Ben could tell he and Stephen would become friends. But he was a little stiff and would need to loosen up before he met the rest of the gang. He wondered who Stephen would like better—Peter or his avatar.

Stephen moved and panic gripped hold of Ben. He threw out another question, worried his new friend was thinking about leaving. 'Why is your skin colour so strange? I mean, your neck is really pale, but your face is brown.' He reached out to touch a visible patch on Stephen's neck. Stephen pushed his hand away.

'I wear a covering because my skin is unable to tolerate the strong rays of the sun,' he answered clinically. 'The covering is patchy in places and produces inconsistent results. My skin is the colour you see on my neck. Can you tell me why yours is so much darker in colour?'

Ben smiled. 'My teacher says it's because I have mel—melon in my skin. It helps turn my skin to brown,' he said, holding up his arm to look at his olive complexion. 'You should know that already, because a grown-up told me. But maybe you don't 'cause it looks like you never tan!' He giggled briefly.

They both sat in silence as an engine-red automated bus pulled up to the kerb. Several people alighted from the back while a queue disappeared into the front. They could hear several beeps as passengers scanned their identity chips on the touchpad to the left of the computer-guided navigation system. Neither of them made a move for it.

Spotting the black-haired boy a week ago, Stephen

had trusted his instincts that told him he was the one to approach. Even though the child seemed harmless enough, Stephen's nerves jangled at his closeness to him. Ben was beginning to trust him and his curiosity could give Central Council the answers they needed. He planned to take advantage of his curiosity, even if it meant pushing through the insane fear that was telling him to go.

There were great risks associated with being out in the open, but he hadn't even begun to explore the differences between their species yet. He could tell the complexity of the questions were troubling Ben but he needed to press on. Intellectually, the Surface Creature's children were less advanced than their Evolvers were, but he didn't know how to communicate in any other way. He hadn't studied the younger ones in detail, only the older Surface Creatures. He realised his mistake in not doing so. He had assumed the approach would be the same.

Those aboard the automated bus stared through the window at Stephen and Ben sitting together on the bench. Instinctively, Stephen wrapped his coat tighter around him and pulled the lip of his fedora downwards. He touched the static eliminator in his pocket that absorbed the static his body naturally emitted. The disguise had been necessary and it was painfully obvious at that very moment just how much. His proximity to so many Surface Creatures terrified him, even though he had the ability to outrun all of them.

He battled the constant urge to flee but he couldn't run; another part of him wanted to know what they were. He was drawn to the child for reasons he couldn't explain. This mission was too important to all the Indigenes—he needed to stay. Out in the open, he was vulnerable without his kind to protect him; this was his mission and he was alone. As the automated bus moved off, the danger temporarily passed.

Stephen no longer recognised the place he sat in. So much had been altered in the last thirty years; the Indigenes' living environs and the raised platforms where the Central Council had once stood to speak to the population were gone. He could no longer pinpoint the exact areas where he used to play or where the dome-shaped environs had once been. It was as if they had never existed and the Surface Creatures had always lived there. Beyond the city borders, in the great outlying expanse and beneath the soil, it was a different story. There lay the real planet, the one that the Indigenes understood.

He checked the time and chastised himself for wasting precious minutes lamenting a past life that no longer existed, that they would never get back. He needed to get the conversation back on track and get Ben talking some more. Not wanting to scare him off, he pondered his next question. Would the boy have been so willing and open if he knew what he was or how dangerous he could be?

But before he could speak, Ben asked another question. 'Why don't you have any hair?'

Stephen thought about his answer. Considering some of the photos he had seen, he hadn't expected that to be an obvious difference. 'I don't need it where I am from.'

The child swung his little legs on the bench then leaned forward to look at Stephen's eyes. He fired out another question. 'Your eyes are funny looking. Can you see like we can?'

While Ben was too young to understand the

complexity of the answers, a certain level of astuteness allowed him to ask precise, pointed questions. Again, Stephen opted for the truth. He needed to take a few calculated risks. 'I am capable of seeing in the dark, so I have no need for eyes like yours. I'm wearing protective lenses so that the sun doesn't damage my eyes. They're unable to tolerate the bright light.'

Ben nodded but didn't show any adverse reaction. Stephen had been right about his earlier assumption: the boy was interested in learning, but his ability to understand or keep information hadn't fully developed yet.

'Are you cold?' Ben continued.

It was an unusual question. 'Why do you ask?'

'Because you have been shivering for the last two minutes. I was just wondering if you were cold.'

'Actually, the opposite. I am too warm.'

'How come?' The child reached over to touch Stephen's hand. His first instinct was to pull his hand away but instead he allowed him to make contact.

'My body does not react well to this environment. I don't know how to regulate my core temperature here. I live within an entirely different atmosphere.'

'Why? Where do you live? New Taiyuan? I hear that's hot. It's not that hot here, you know. It's only going to get to twenty degrees today.'

Stephen understood why Ben thought he lived in a hotter climate. His blood would have been thinner, making it harder for the body to insulate properly in a colder place. But the opposite was happening: his core temperature was heating up while his extremities remained cold.

'That wouldn't explain your pale skin though.'

Ben frowned and puckered his lips.

'No, it would not,' Stephen said. 'And no, I do not live in New Taiyuan. I told you, I live here.'

Ben leaned back into the contours of the bench and swung his legs in unison. Stephen crossed his legs from right to left and rested his hands on his knee—a pre-rehearsed move. He wondered whether it would be better to regroup and organise another meeting with him. When he checked the time again, his priorities changed. 'I have to leave. I need to be somewhere else,' he lied, and made a move to stand up.

'But I don't want you to go.' Ben folded his arms tightly across his chest and stared impudently at Stephen. 'I want you to stay here. You don't have my permission to go.'

'I'm afraid I will be late for another engagement if I stay.'

'B—b—but—I want you to stay here.' Ben's lip quivered and for a moment, it looked like he might cry.

The boy's reaction was a good sign. It meant he would be open to meeting up a second time. Whether Stephen could bring himself to show up again was another matter entirely.

'Could we meet again, but somewhere else?' he asked, keeping a close eye on the Surface Creatures that had gathered at the bus stop. It was far too exposed here.

Ben's eyes lit up and he gave him a gap-toothed grin. 'Where?'

'A place not too far from here. Belgrave Square Gardens—do you know it?'

He nodded eagerly. 'I go there on my own. I like to play on the swings and monkey bars.'

Stephen suggested they meet the following Saturday at the bench near the large tree in the gardens. It should be sheltered enough there. He tipped his hat to the boy—another practised move—and swiftly departed.

Ben watched Stephen leave, noticing how he moved quicker than everyone else. He'd said some funny things about his eyes and skin and other stuff that he didn't really understand. In his head, he started planning his secret trip for the following Saturday. His mum would probably sleep in again so he didn't see a problem with getting out of the house unnoticed. If he needed to, he would lie and say he was going to play with his best friend. Peter would cover for him if he promised to give him some toys in exchange for his silence.

He decided it would be too early to tell Pete about Stephen. He wanted to keep his new friend a secret for a while longer. But his avatar would need to know, since his mum would most likely question it first. Since he'd figured out how to bypass the child protection features on the Light Box and had taught the avatar how to lie, that would not be a problem. His mother was oblivious to his knowledge of the inner workings of the Light Box.

Ben didn't feel like going home yet. It was only seven thirty. He decided to look for the bench in Belgrave Square Gardens that Stephen had mentioned in preparation for next week's meeting. Within minutes, an automated bus arrived and he scanned his identity chip as he boarded. Too excited to check if he still had his compass, he settled on his seat and looked out the window as the bus sped off in a northerly direction towards the gardens.

5

Earth

Laura O'Halloran hurried across the road towards the nearest replication terminal for lunch, one of many located close to the Earth Security Centre, in Sydney. She waited for the first set of doors to open, then stepped into the cavernous core, along with fifty or so others. The doors closed behind them and they huddled together in front of a second set. The air inside the core was decontaminated, an action that triggered the second doors to open. She pushed forwards into the terminal and removed the gel mask from her face—the air wasn't poisonous inside. Peeling apart the Velcro strips that covered the zipped part of her grey ESC uniform caused her blonde hair to fuse briefly with one side of the strip. She tugged the strands loose and tucked her hair behind her ears, then unzipped the top section so that her skin could finally breathe.

The first smell that greeted her was a mix of lavender and stale body odour that lingered heavily like the unpleasant air outside. Not entirely convinced that the air inside was any safer to breathe, she held her breath as she joined the queue of people waiting to use one of the replication machines, knowing she would have to draw in the sickly air at some point. In front of Laura was a small dark-haired woman.

Judging by her hunched-over appearance—a side effect from overuse of the genetic manipulation clinics—Laura placed her age to be somewhere in the hundreds. When a bulky and sweaty man joined the queue directly behind her, she exhaled, defeated. She could hold her breath for a week, but in heavily populated areas such as these, there was no escape from the toxins, crawling over her thin, pale body like a snake looking for warmth. Patrons' eyes were also on her, as they always were when she wore her ESC uniform.

The queue inside the narrow corridor moved forward in an efficient way. She never bothered trying to cut in further up the line, since somebody was always ready to put queue-jumpers back into place, or worse, at the end of the queue. That was the only good thing about living among twenty billion people: efficiency and speed were what people cared about enough to control. As she neared one of the replication machines, the woman in front of her selected a beef stew and a glass of water. Laura ordered a chicken sandwich and a Coke. Noticing her choice, the woman turned around to speak to her.

'Don't order that, dear. There's something wrong with the chicken replica. Looks and tastes like solidified porridge. Quite disgusting.' Her nose wrinkled.

'What's good?' Laura asked.

'Anything except the chicken. Larry, who runs this place, says they're trying to get replacements for some of the particle cards but the companies are adamant there's nothing wrong with them. Going to have to fix the graphic cards too, he says. They're years old now and don't work properly. Have you seen how unappetising some of the choices look?

Should take those foods off the menu, if you ask me.'

'Thanks for the advice.' Laura changed her food order to lamb slices with potato cakes and mint jelly. As she collected her choice from the base of the replication machine, she noticed the old woman nod her approval.

The line progressed in an orderly way towards the pay station.

She had felt eyes on her the moment she walked into the replication terminal, but now it was as though one set was burning a hole in the back of her skull. She turned around and a man in his early forties, with slicked back hair and a beard, was looking straight at her. His jeans were secured tightly with an old belt to prevent them from slipping off his beanpole-shaped body. She had seen many like him before—the city was filled with junkies. His eyes were wild with anger.

It wasn't the first time she'd been challenged in public and it wouldn't be the last. 'Can I help you?' she asked.

'You lot over there think you're so fucking great.'

Laura sighed. 'Is there something you want to say to me?' She braced herself for a verbal attack; she had largely become immune to the abuse her uniform attracted.

'My mother is in debt because of you. Owes your crowd a ton of money. She can't sleep 'cause she's expecting your lot to break down her door and arrest her.' The man wagged his finger in her direction. 'What are you going to do about it?'

'You need to take it up with the World Government. I work at the ESC,' she said.

On Level Four—Document Control and

Storage—where she worked, her job was to file away information about tax matters. In other sections, workers checked, processed and filed traffic violations and countless transactions that the inhabitants of Earth had charged to their accounts. ESC had nothing to do with setting taxes or chasing down tax evaders—that was the World Government's job.

'Same fucking thing if you ask me,' the man said, leaving his place in the queue and walking over to her, his finger pointed at her face and hatred in his eyes.

Laura shrank back but there was nowhere to go. She could smell his putrid breath on her face. She could see the track marks on his right arm as he used it to block her path.

The man's finger was now inches from her. 'You lot are all the same. Sucking the life out of innocent people like me and my family. You make me sick.'

It was the large sweaty man behind Laura who squared up to him. He placed a hand on the junkie's chest and said calmly, 'Looks like you're queue-jumping. Either you go back in line or I throw you out the door. Your choice. If you're lucky, I might not break every bone in your body when I slam you into the pavement.'

The junkie backed off and rejoined the queue, his eyes still seething with hatred.

Laura, who had been holding her breath, let it go. 'Thanks,' she said to the large man who grunted once in response.

At the pay station, she scanned her identity chip. She walked unsteadily into the adjoining eating room, still a little shocked by her confrontation with the city's most hated type of resident.

The square eating area was larger than the corridor with the machines. She found a not so quiet—but much coveted—spot by the window. She stood as she ate her lunch, hoping the junkie wouldn't bother her again. She noticed the large man enter the room and stand between her and the door. He didn't acknowledge her. When the junkie finally entered, his eyes searched the room. He lost interest in Laura as soon as he saw the brick wall of a man who had created a buffer between them. For once, she was grateful for the packed conditions of the terminal.

She picked the fat off her lamb slices and gazed out at the dark, smog-filled day. It had been ten years since the sun last shone, when she was just twenty-six years old. Since then, the sun's access to the Earth's surface had diminished rapidly and there was less warmth getting through every day. Like others, she had noticed the chill and the need for extra layers of clothes. She was used to wrapping up well but it was only getting worse.

In the thirty years since her parents' emigration from Dublin to Sydney, Laura had enjoyed sun and temperatures in Sydney that exceeded twenty-five degrees Celsius, just like every other Sydneysider. But the lack of sun caused her more problems than most. With a barely visible ball of light providing little or no heat, the temperatures struggled to surpass a modest ten degrees in high summer. Her golden hair no longer shone. Her previously sun-kissed complexion was now pale and pasty.

As she took a bite of her lamb, she wondered if she would ever set eyes on the sun again. Exilon 5 had sunlight in abundance—a planet she dreamed of living on—but early selection was not a guarantee.

The World Government's transfer programme had changed more times than she could count, and working at the Earth Security Centre didn't seem to give her any special rights. Currently the selection policy was a lottery, a change from the previous volunteer arrangement. But with only a small percentage of the population having transferred, when she might be able to move was anyone's guess.

The city still carried evidence of the catalyst that had changed Earth's atmospheric conditions. The current generation had blamed the habits of older generations, but had not done enough to stem the changes. Posters on walls announcing the arrival of the Go Green revolution were everywhere. Back then, their unglued edges had flapped in the wind. Now, the wind was gone but the posters remained, tatty and faded. More pressing issues overtook the need to remove them. The Go Green project was the World Government's answer to counteracting global change. But as industries became self-sustainable, green energy had not become the cash cow they had hoped it would.

At the turn of the twenty-second century, efforts to go green had surpassed all targets just as the need to raise more funds for space exploration dominated the government's agenda. The World Government and its twelve controlling members needed a quick way to raise cash and so they heavily taxed green energy because of its popularity. Businesses and industries suffered and only the strongest survived. There were more skyscrapers than houses in the city and most had been converted into apartments to cope with the ballooning population. Laura lived in what was a former shoe factory in the middle of the Haymarket district.

She snapped out of her thoughts, noticing that she had done little more than push the food around her plate. She stuck her fork in a piece of lamb and nibbled at it. Food didn't excite her taste buds anymore; she ate the bland food because she had to. One half of the potato cake remained on the plate. The taste was marginally worse than the food in the ESC cafeteria, but still edible. Deciding she'd had enough, she dropped her leftovers into one of the waste incinerators that were placed around the room.

As she headed for the exit, she turned around. The junkie was still looking at her, but with less confidence than before. She hated how people turned on her because of the work she did. They were always too quick to define her character by the uniform she wore. In many ways, the ESC was a great place to work, filled with admirable, hardworking people. She respected the Centre's tireless efforts, not only to protect the Earth from unknown dangers but from people themselves.

The only chance she would have to move to Exilon 5 was if she worked hard—either that or she would push for a better job; she'd heard that the higher levels had a better chance of becoming part of the current job transfer programme. The purple-uniformed workers on Level Five entered her thoughts. In ESC, their presence in the corridors commanded instant respect. She wondered if she had worn a purple uniform instead of a grey one, would the junkie have been so quick to attack her verbally. She shook her head. Any admiration of the Level Five workers was limited to the people who worked at the ESC.

Before the outer door opened, Laura begrudgingly affixed her gel mask to her face. The frigid air hit her and she pulled her coat tightly around her. She stepped out on the plain street, remembering when trees and plants used to grow in the city. Not anymore. It was sad to see the trees change from having plenty of leaves one year, to so few the next, until they stopped growing altogether. Perennial plants that had once bloomed brightly never broke the surface of the soil again. She'd almost forgotten what flowers looked like—almost. Wild animals were the next to go, although the city had done well to hold on to some domesticated ones. Humans were the only species strong enough to adapt.

She arrived back at the ESC building, her security chip allowing her to gain entry through the invisible medium-level force field that surrounded it. The public area to the front and the newest and brightest section of the Centre was the only part without an active force field. Striding past the atmosphere-controlled pond that was home to a few varieties of fish, she bounded up the crescent-shaped steps and into the former Anzac War Memorial building entrance. Recognisable by its pink granite exterior, it remained largely unchanged since it was designed by C. Bruce Dellit and completed in 1934. The World Government had added the public section to the memorial building about fifty years ago, as part of its attempts to regenerate a declining city.

White granite covered the floor and part of the walls. Various sculptures and figure reliefs hugged the upper part, protected by a symphony of stars that formed a crescendo across the dome-shaped ceiling. The gold stars, one hundred and twenty in total, were a stark reminder of one of the many wars of the past and the volunteers that had fought during a more primitive time. A Rayner Hoff sculpture, named

'Sacrifice', once stood in the centre of the room. The sculpture, with its golden sun and fiery arms that blazed outwards with beauty and grace, had been relocated to the public foyer of the Security Centre. Sitting in its place was the turbo lift, linking to the underground levels.

Laura pressed her right thumb on the flat plate beside the turbo lift doors and waited for the system to read her security chip. Her clearance allowed her access to the first four levels below; the remaining six levels required an updated chip. The lift doors opened and within seconds, she arrived at Level Four—Document Control and Storage.

She stepped out into a glass-covered foyer. Looking up she could see workers on Level Three walking above her. When she looked below her, where Level Five was, she saw nothing as usual; she expected that it had been an intentional move on the ESC's part.

Level Five, officially known as High Level Data Storage Facility, was where the World Government sent its high-security documents. Those who didn't work there had christened it the Abyss because of the joke that sensitive information was often lost never to be seen again. Fanciful ideas had been entertained over many lunches that the facility was actually in an entirely different country and that the purple-uniformed workers who walked the halls were planted as part of some elaborate ruse.

As Laura made her way towards corridor ten, where her office and workstation was, she noticed a Level Five worker walking in the opposite direction. Her heart skipped a beat at the rare sight of a purple uniform on her floor. The dark-haired woman neared and she risked speaking to her.

'Hello.' The word came out croaky, not like her voice at all.

The woman briefly glanced in her direction. She nodded once but offered no reply. As soon as Laura had walked passed her, Daphne Gilchrist, the ESC's CEO, appeared like a ghost from the wall and walked in a diagonal line across the floor.

'Shit,' she said under her breath.

She watched the red-haired woman march towards her with purpose. Gilchrist wore a grey trouser suit, her stocky frame cleverly hidden by the feminine folds of the fabric. Her cobalt-blue eyes contained little emotion. Her faint smile was detectable only by the small crease on one side of her genetically altered face. She was in her late eighties, but looked no older than sixty-five.

She waved a scanner over Laura's hand. 'Laura O'Halloran,' her voice boomed loudly.

Reluctantly, Laura rooted herself to the spot. 'Yes,' she replied, clearing her throat.

'Why were you addressing a Level Five worker?'

'I—I was only saying hello.' It was a weak defence and she knew it.

'You know the rules. You are not cleared to talk to the higher levels.' Gilchrist's eyes were boring into her like the junkie's eyes had done in the replication terminal—only her look was more subtle, and far more dangerous. She tapped her index finger on the top of the scanner in that way she always did when something was bothering her.

'It was a mistake. I apologise,' Laura said.

'Consider this your only warning,' Gilchrist said coldly. 'Get back to work.' With that, she turned back the way she had come and disappeared through the glass wall. Laura wondered if there was a hidden door, but only for a brief moment—the CEO was probably watching her.

She carried on to corridor ten and walked the length of the passageway to the door at the end. She scanned her chip on the security plate, and her full name, photo and title flashed up on the screen, along with the length of time she'd been absent.

Unsteadily, she walked into the room and up the centre aisle. On either side, dozens of white workstations sat in neat rows, one hundred and twenty in total. Each row was divided into sections of six.

Janine, a co-worker, was the first to notice her. 'What's wrong?' she asked.

'Just had a run-in with Gilchrist.'

'Over what?' Her eyes widened.

The rest of the workers had stopped what they were doing and were watching her closely. She reached her chair and grabbed the armrest just as her legs buckled underneath her.

'I was caught talking to a Level Fiver.'

'Shit—and she pulled you up on that?' said Chris, another co-worker.

'Came out of nowhere.'

'Yeah, she does that. There are secret doors everywhere in this place.'

'And some guy was abusive to me in the terminal.'

'You can't seem to catch a break today, can ya?' Janine's tone turned cocky suddenly.

'Do you have a sympathetic bone in your body?' Chris asked Janine.

Her face reddened. 'I'm just saying, I'm glad it wasn't me. Laura can take it. She's impenetrable. I'm a lot softer.'

Chris rolled his eyes.

Laura ignored Janine, the drama queen. She might have been emotionally stronger than her, but she certainly wasn't made of titanium.

She activated her workstation and the screen whirred into life. Thousands of documents awaited her. Before the end of the day, there would be another one hundred thousand added to the list, not unexpectedly since they were looking after all the inhabitants of Earth. Encrypted information sent electronically to the Security Centre contained thousands of layers of code that were stripped out before reaching Level Four. The workers had to sort and re-encrypt the information before sending it for long-term storage in the main computer database on Level Nine. In addition, Laura's job was to redirect any classified material to Level Five.

While the computer system could more than handle the workload, the ESC considered document sorting to be a lesson in character building; it weeded out the workers who weren't cut out for life there. On the outside, thousands of workers waited to take their place, people who had scored high on the aptitude test and were biding their time until a vacancy arose. Loyalty was not a common word when there were more people on Earth than available jobs. The best way for Laura to keep her job or progress further was never to complain.

She wished she'd asked the junkie what his name was, so she could see how much he owed and to whom he owed it. People who screamed publicly about family debts were usually careless with money. Gambling, drug addiction, unnecessary organ purchases and genetic manipulation treatments that were not covered by the World Government longevity programme usually topped the list. There were plenty of genuine debt cases too, but she wondered if his mother's debts were because of her son's habit.

'Are you still mad at me?' Janine said to Laura.

She had already forgotten about her. 'No Janine, I'm not mad at you.' She spoke to her as a parent might speak to a child.

Janine refused to let it go. 'Look, it's not my fault you got into trouble at the terminal. What did you say to them anyway to go off on you?'

'I never need to say anything to them. The sight of me is enough to set them off.'

'I always wear my overcoat. I sweat like hell when I'm inside, but at least they can't see my uniform,' Janine said haughtily.

'I'll keep that in mind,' Laura said through gritted teeth. There were plenty of things she wanted to say to Janine but a pleasant working environment was far more important to her.

'Have you heard they're running a lottery in Darlinghurst?' Chris said.

'Not Haymarket?' Laura's voice was louder than she'd planned it to be.

'Not yet. Don't know what made them pick there. Point Piper and Rose Bay too,' Chris said. The World Government had changed the transfer programme to a lottery-based selection process because of the low numbers of volunteers who had made the initial move. Laura hadn't been old enough to apply for the programme back then. 'My mate says they're going to focus on Perth after this.'

'What? That's it—just three areas?' Laura stood up now, her anger palpable. 'Did they say when they were coming back to Sydney?'

Chris held his hands up. 'Don't shoot the messenger. Look, you know how these things go— how often they change their mind? Right now, Australia is one of the countries they're focusing on. You never know what might happen.'

Laura sat back down, her shoulders slumping in a defeated way. There was no hope for her if she remained a Level Four employee, permanently under the radar. She needed to do something that would get her noticed.

She resumed her review of the documents in front of her. All of a sudden, she was pissed off with the world. Earth was a disaster. People had forgotten how to live. The planet had sucked the life out of everyone and Level Four was sucking the life out of her. Even in the work environments where creativity was encouraged, free thinking was still capped by technology. People could offer suggestions, but ultimately the computer decided which path to follow. Discouraged from thinking for themselves, workers obeyed without question.

When Laura had started working at the Centre three years ago, she had been grateful for the opportunity to work at the second most prestigious organisation on Earth. Three years on and she'd seen many people come and go. Some, overwhelmed by the experience, had ended up choosing less daunting careers. Others who had diligently served their time were rewarded with better opportunities, plus a chance to escape Levels One to Four. Promotion was still a possibility but the wait was killing her; she was sick of being just another forgettable statistic. During her darkest days, she'd wondered on many occasions whether the organisation was the right fit for her. But upon reflection, and when she thought about what a move to Exilon 5 would mean to her and her mother, she remembered why it had always been her goal to work at ESC.

Laura shook off her annoyance, watching now as new documents pooled on the screen in front of her. Scrolling through the countless numbers, she selected a few for spot-checking. One of the documents listed names for non-payment of taxes. The first name was a Mrs Annette Billings of Toronto, Canada. Seventy-six years old, she had failed to pay her outstanding tax following receipt of a new heart. It was her first violation. She complained that she was waiting on eye replacements and had not seen the reminders. Noted beside her name were the words, *Has received goods. First Warning Issued.* She paid her arrears within the extra time allotted.

There were seven hundred other entries on the long list, all with similar stories. The seventeenth name was highlighted in red: Mr Robert Fennell, originally from Wales, but now residing in Tokyo. Fifty-eight years old. *Failure to pay apartment taxes. Issued with second warning. No further failures will be tolerated.* He promptly paid any outstanding balances, including arrears.

As Laura continued to search through the reams of names, she wondered whether life on Exilon 5 would be any different to paying taxes, taking abuse from random strangers, or following orders. Her mind wandered as she wondered what she could do to stand out from the crowd.

6

Early on Saturday morning, Galen Thompson hurried around his tiny apartment in Richmond, Virginia, as he got himself ready for work. He struggled to navigate around the furniture that was jammed tightly into the three hundred-square-foot box he called home, and unavoidably bruised his leg on several pointy edges in the process. Cursing aloud, he continued in his time-restricted search for his shoes. He should have remembered where he left them. The place might be microscopic in size, as were most apartments on Earth, but it still surprised him how many things disappeared on a regular basis or wound up in the last place he looked.

When he moved into the bedroom, his communication device shrilled in his ear. Galen activated the earpiece and spoke into the microphone that protruded like a thin wire from the side of his face.

'Hello?'

'Galen. It's me.' It was his father.

'I'm a little busy now. Can this wait until later?'

'Are you alone?'

'I'm at home and I don't really have time to talk—shit!' Galen bent down to rub the pain out of his big toe.

'What's going on there?' He could hear the

tension rise in his father's voice.

'Nothing, I just kicked the bed, that's all.' He got down on all fours and searched under the bed for his shoes. They weren't there. He got up and checked the living room again. 'Dad, what do you need?' he said urgently after his father had fallen silent.

'Are you on your way to work?'

'Yes, and I'll be late if I don't find my damn shoes. The train's leaving in ten minutes.' The silence seemed longer now between questions. Galen knew what was on his father's mind.

'Dad, if you don't say it now, I'm hanging up.'

'Your mother and I were talking—' his father began to say.

He could guess the rest: conspiracies, double agents, secrets, lies. It was present and accounted for in all of their conversations.

'I know what you're going to ask and no, I haven't found any evidence of suspicious activity.'

'How well do you know your overseer?' His father's tone was more urgent now.

Galen worked as an Air and Space controller out of the Hartsfield-Jackson Atlanta (HJA) docking station. A former airport, it was the largest in the world at the beginning of the twenty-first century. The defunct airports had become the ideal locations to convert into docking stations. Seventy-five in total had been built on Earth.

'Stuart?' Galen laughed. 'Well enough to know he's not messed up with anything like what you're suggesting.'

'Okay, maybe not him, but the others.'

He felt around on the floor under the sofa for his shoes. His hand touched one and then the other. He pulled them out. 'Well, I don't know all of them, only the ones on my shift. I'm still a trainee, you know that.' He graduated from Air and Space Control Academy at thirty-one and, for the last two years, had carried out his training at the HJA docking station.

'Well, who *do* you know on your shift?'

'I dunno—Maria, Paddy, why?' Galen pulled each shoe on, not remembering having taken them off just twenty-four hours ago. Last thing he'd recalled was heading straight for the bedroom to sleep for a solid eighteen hours. He didn't even remember undressing, but he had been naked that morning.

'Your mother says the ESC is showing an interest in your docking station. She seems to think it might be connected to higher-level matter; ESC is storing secret files in another part of the building, away from higher-level workers. She doesn't know which of your colleagues they're looking at.'

Galen stopped. 'Looking at them for what exactly?'

His father sighed. 'I don't know. Tampering with records, she says—something to do with the transfer programme. It's still early days, but we've been waiting too long to expose the ESC and World Government for what they are, to ignore any leads.'

Galen thought of Paddy, his eighty-three-year-old Irish colleague. While his bark was worse than his bite, he couldn't imagine the man being involved in anything illegal. Then there was Maria, his Argentinian co-worker whose positivity and gentle nature were not obvious traits of a double agent. After years of ignorant bliss, his father's paranoia was finally rubbing off on him.

Time was running out for him. 'Dad, I have to go.'

'I'll call you later,' his father said and clicked

off.

Galen glanced in the hall mirror and was immediately grateful he had. He grabbed a comb from the hall table drawer and ran the metal teeth through his unruly black hair, swearing softly under his breath. He should have got up earlier; he always left things until the last minute. He pushed his fringe back from his thin face and out of his closely set green eyes. He touched his slightly hooked nose with his finger and, not for the first time, considered altering it at one of the genetic manipulation clinics. But his mother would never forgive him, since the nose was a genetic trait passed down from her side of the family. His older brother had inherited the perfect Thompson genes—sandy hair, blue eyes and a perfectly oval face. Galen had been a quiet skinny teenager, the polar opposite to his sibling's extroverted and popular persona. By the time Galen reached his twenties, he had grown out of his awkward phase. Although he gained bulk in his body, he still hadn't developed the height or popularity of his handsome older brother.

With a quick stroke of his hand, Galen smoothed the creases out of his taupe uniform as best he could. He ran into the kitchen and grabbed a bagel from the replication machine. He took a bite out of the tasteless dough and looked around his apartment, suddenly reminded of how much was on loan from the World Government: his home, his replicated food machine, the uniform he wore. Very few people owned property unless they were the filthy rich proprietors of subsidiary organisations.

He glanced at the time projection on the wall, grateful for the spare five minutes to eat. He took another bite of his bagel, grateful to be one of the lucky ones in finding a good place to live. A decent sized apartment was difficult to come by, but not when you worked for Air and Space Industries—a World Government subsidary. As well as being larger than most apartments, he did not have to share with anyone else. That was one of the perks of being a trainee controller. Outside, hundreds of buildings similar to his lined the streets, all tall and narrow with dark, minimalistic designs—just like the Japanese designers had built over the centuries. Rows of similar buildings stood unified like soldiers protecting their barracks, while their foundations tunnelled deep into the Earth.

One of the downsides to renting was the list of restrictions imposed on the tenant. While most rules were standard, Galen found some restrictions a little strange.

'Only one visitor at any given time.' The building had been designed for optimal usage of space, not structural integrity. While buildings could hold double the current occupancy of three thousand tenants, tenants could never exceed the maximum threshold—for safety reasons, they were told. Thanks to his paranoid parents, Galen now believed the rule was a smokescreen, giving the government a free hand to keep an eye on its people and possible free thinkers.

'Children are not permitted to live in this block.' Families were mostly restricted to one of the 'child friendly' neighbourhoods.

'You must not personalise the apartment's interior.' This was because of the short-term rental arrangements in place. Galen had no plans to live there long-term.

As he finished off the last piece of his bagel,

his father's phone call still nagged at him. While he had grown up overhearing his parents' theories on the World Government's supposed plans, he'd been mostly kept away from the discussions. When his brother turned fifteen, his parents had included him in conversations that were to become more sinister, like their investigation into his grandfather's death. Just five years ago, they started to involve Galen.

He understood now why his parents had been so over protective of him as a child. He and his brother had grown up in one of the 'child friendly' neighbourhoods in Boston, a place that packed families in so tightly, accidents and murders were common occurrences. It was usually over the little things too, like hanging washing ten centimetres over the boundary line of a neighbour's tiny yard. But later, his parents had swapped the neighbourhood for an apartment after his brother had moved out. Galen had come to know every part of his new home while he waited for his parents to return; sometimes they were gone for a few hours, other times it was days on end. Their determination to find out what happened to his grandfather, his father's father, kept them away.

'Workplace accident,' said his dad, reading the top line of his own father's death certificate. 'Can you believe it? My father was one of the most conscientious employees at that ship building company. Hell, he even designed the damn machine they say killed him. I just can't believe it.'

While they hadn't been around much when he was a child, now his parents had done a one-eighty and were too involved in his life. He reckoned it was because of the guilt they still felt for leaving him alone. The mystery surrounding his grandfather's death still haunted them but matters of a more recent nature had caught their attention—the ESC's interest in his docking station for one.

An alarm sounding in the distance broke Galen out of his thoughts and he checked the time. Still tired, he pulled open his apartment door. It might be another week before he'd see the inside of his apartment again. He popped an Actigen into his mouth, a pill that would allow him to skip sleep for a few days. He shuddered with pleasure, as it coated each fibre of his body in an adrenaline-laced liquid. Employees at the docking station were encouraged to take the drug, even though there were legal limits about how long they could keep workers from adequate rest and recovery. The rules were often bent when Actigen was used.

As he walked the short distance to Richmond's bullet train station, he thought about his colleagues. Did he really know them? Were his parents right to be suspicious? Why was ESC so interested in the HJA docking station? Ahead of him was an eight-hundred-mile journey to work. The magnetically levitated train, capable of speeds up to nearly eight hundred miles per hour, would reach its destination in little over an hour, giving him far too much time to mull it over.

7

Galen sat on board the bullet train, hearing a gentle whine as the carriages magnetically levitated above the tracks. He saw nothing inside the dark tunnel except for the advertisements that ran the length of its walls. At first glance, the ads appeared to be static, but on closer inspection, they moved at the same speed as the train, which gave the illusion that it was the carriage that was motionless.

He thought more about his parents' interest in his co-workers, not convinced that any of them were involved in anything illegal. Having worked there for two years, he was sure he would have noticed if something was amiss. But ESC rarely showed so much interest in something—or someone—if there wasn't more to the story.

Ten minutes before the train arrived at its destination, his earpiece vibrated. He answered it.

'Galen. It's me again.'

'What now, Dad?'

'Are you on the train?'

He sighed heavily. 'Where else would I be?'

'Give me your identity code.'

He held his left thumb over the communication device and waited for the inbuilt scanner to check his ID. He heard a tiny beep.

'Satisfied?'

His father's tone became stern. 'We talked

about this attitude of yours. This is not just for your safety; it's for all our safety. What we're doing is extremely risky, you know that.'

Galen rolled his eyes. This was a regular occurrence now, having to confirm his ID for his dad any time he was out in public. His dad, an engineer and now involved in the spaceship design programme, had deliberately followed his father into the same trade that took his life.

'Tell me your date of birth.'

He smiled half-heartedly. 'You're kidding me, right?'

His dad's tone was serious. 'I'm certainly not.'

He looked around the train, packed with so many people that nobody dared move. He whispered, 'Can't you just trust me that I'm your son? Do you go through this same crap with Paul, or is it just me because of where I work?'

'Watch your language and tell me your date of birth.'

'Twenty-first of June.' Galen kept his voice low.

'Good, now tell me your real one.' His father had procured a fake identity chip for him, which showed a different birth date—only his family knew the real one.

'One eight, oh eight.'

'Now, listen to me. Your mother and I want you to find out what memos the ESC has sent to the docking station. It should tell us who they're looking at. Pay attention to what your colleagues are saying, in particular your overseer—he must know something. Report back as soon as you can. Your mother tells me there's a chance it could be connected to something else—something more high level. Can you do that for us? And please be careful.'

'And what *exactly* am I looking for this time?' The instructions as usual, were vague.

'Sorry son, I can't tell you anything except that your mother is more anxious than usual.' There was a trace of worry in his tone.

Galen noticed the different energy that was driving his father; as usual, he would only tell him the basics. Without key information about ESC's primary motive, what could he really do to help his parents?

'And what's Paul doing to help?'

'Your brother is still in Cambodia. We thought it best not to disturb him.' Paul, a teacher, had been drafted in to educate the ethnic groups that still lived in the jungle about how the permanent changes to the environment would affect them. Their refusal to become part of mainstream society, or to move out of the wooden houses they had built there, made things difficult for everyone involved.

'I'll do my best,' Galen said half-heartedly. It was the same thing he always said each time he was asked to help. He was tired of being a part of his parents' obsession. He wished they would get over their guilt and leave him be.

He arrived at the Air and Space Traffic Control Observation Deck (ASCOD) with five minutes to spare before his shift started. He stepped inside the long oblong room and scanned it for signs of Stuart McWilliams, his overseer. Several domed sections formed the roofline, made of high-density glass. If the sun still shone bright, a three-sixty view of the area above them would have been a pleasant sight. But in current conditions, all they saw was endless images of a broken city, smothered by low-lying black and grey clouds. The wall panels containing computer visualisation screens each displayed different images—space debris, planets in the solar system and the area immediately above Earth. There were several workstations in the centre of the room. He heard almost imperceptible beeps as fingers glided over the monitors there. Reports were whisked away to a central computer housed in a secure area of the HJA docking station. Maria and Paddy, two of his colleagues, stood in front of the visualisation screens, traversing the entire galaxy with a flick of their wrists.

At full capacity there was enough room for twenty people, but that day Maria, Paddy and a communication operative were the only ones on duty. It suddenly occurred to Galen that he had never worked with any other controller and he now wondered if his overseer had organised it that way, to limit his contact with others. It was no secret that his mother worked at the ESC.

His father often reminded him of how lucky he was to have found such prestigious work at the HJA docking station; improved healthcare and genetic treatments led to longer life expectancy, and it wasn't so easy to hold on to the better jobs. There were plenty of dead-end jobs available, but those weren't meant for people like him with a high IQ. His mother's influence at the ESC had fast-tracked his chances of securing a decent job. At the time, he had been unsure about her reasons for doing so, but now her intentions were clearer even if the detail of what they wanted him to do today was not.

Galen shook his head; their suspicions are all nonsense, he told himself. He took another step forward into the room just as his overseer emerged from his tiny office. While Stuart busied himself with

Maria and Paddy, he walked over to the workstation area and ran his fingers along the white desks. Paddy relocated to a workstation to log the final report of his shift, not noticing Galen walking casually around the area to see if any of the monitors were live. It was a long shot, he thought, but maybe Stuart had used one and left a memo open. Then he could finally quit his second job of acting as his parents' eyes and ears.

Galen shook his head again, feeling uncomfortable about spying on his colleagues. He cursed his mother. Why was his mother ruining his life? Why had he allowed her to use her influence at the ESC to get him work? Out of the corner of his eye, he noticed Stuart turn his head. He noticed one of the screens was active and was about to read the document when Stuart yelled at him.

'Galen, you bloody eejit, what are you up to?'

Galen's face reddened and he immediately backed away from the area. 'Nothing Stuart, just waiting for Paddy to finish, that's all.'

'Well, stop hovering around like that. You're making me nervous.' Stuart shoved one hand into the pocket of his uniform. The other twitched as if it was independent from his body.

Paddy looked up for the first time since Galen had entered the room. 'What the hell are you doin' standing all the way over there? I've been waitin' for ya. Come on!'

Galen noticed how Stuart shuddered when Paddy spoke. Paddy had always been open about his preference for a quiet life; it paid less and controllers got fewer perks than overseers, but he said he never suffered with anxiety and regularly slept like a baby. Stuart once described Paddy's personality as rough around the edges and difficult to control.

Stuart interrupted Paddy: 'Are you finished logging your report? Because don't swap over unless you are.'

'Yes, boss,' Paddy said. As soon as Stuart turned his back, Paddy gave him the finger.

What Galen saw were two similar people with equally fiery tempers that emerged in different ways. But he found both Paddy and Stuart easy enough to work with. He admired his overseer's affinity for hard work and his sharp-tongued honesty. His parents talked in so much code these days that he preferred knowing where he stood with people. Except for the temper, Stuart reminded him a lot of his old man, having seen him jump through hoops to seek approval for the safety features on board the newer ship designs. Stuart was never afraid to make the hard calls when others would have crumbled under the pressure. It was a job Galen saw himself doing one day.

'C'mon, boy. Move your backside,' Paddy said.

Galen replied wearily, 'I'm coming, Paddy. Just relax, will you?'

'Don't bloody tell me to relax. I'm not the one who's just had a nice twenty-four-hour rest at home. I'm dead on me feet. Come closer. I need to show ya somethin'.' He continued to log his report as he spoke.

Galen didn't argue. Stuart had disappeared out of sight—to get a coffee, he imagined.

Paddy cocked a suspicious eyebrow. 'You gonna give me trouble today?'

'No trouble,' Galen said, wondering if Paddy's grouchy exterior hid anything more sinister. He thought about the ESC memos again. He couldn't quite see it but maybe the old man was good at hiding his secrets.

Paddy flicked the monitor over to the duty change-over screen. Two thumb placeholders appeared. Galen placed his right thumb on one side and Paddy put his on the other. The system scanned their security chips. Paddy stood up and faced him, his expression more serious. He spoke quietly.

'Okay, there have been a few anomalies around a couple of the planets. Could be just space debris. There are also a few crafts arriving today. If you run into any difficulties, Maria will look after you.' His elbow suddenly connected with Galen; bone hitting bone sent a shockwave of pain coursing through Galen's arm.

Hearing her name, Maria turned away from the viewing screen. 'Don't worry, Galen, nothing we can't handle.' She crossed one finger over the other and flashed a quick grin at him.

Galen vigorously rubbed his arm to dispel the pain.

'You goin' soft on me boy?' Paddy narrowed his eyes. 'Got somethin' to hide?'

'No,' he said defensively dropping his eyes to the floor.

'Well in that case, we're done here.' Paddy picked up his DPad and his private communication device. He stuck the latter into his ear. He pulled on his coat and flipped the hood up. 'See you in twenty-four hours. Don't screw anything up while I'm gone.' He slapped Galen hard on the back, so hard that he staggered forwards.

Stuart had reappeared, this time with a cup of coffee in his hand. He didn't comment on the rough play between the two men. 'Galen I need you over here, now.' He took a sip of the liquid and made a face. 'I bloody hate this stuff.'

Paddy hummed a tune and skipped out the door, giddy with the promise of sleep, Galen imagined.

Sulky faced, he repositioned himself beside Maria in front of one of the high-resolution viewing screens.

'He doesn't mean anything by it. It's just his way of having fun,' Maria explained. She wore her jet-black hair in a long plait, which hung down her back like a frayed rope. Her Argentinian olive-coloured skin offset perfectly the mandatory beige uniform.

'Are you kidding me? That's what you call fun, is it?' Galen grumbled. 'He treats me like a little kid sometimes. I'm sick of being thought of as just another person to make up the numbers.'

'Something you want to talk about?' Maria asked gently, her words heavily accented.

Galen flushed with embarrassment. 'Just forget I said anything. I'm having a bad day, that's all.'

'He's fond of you, you know. Thinks of you as the son he never had. Did you know his wife wasn't able to have children?'

Galen shook his head. No, he didn't. He also didn't know what to say at that moment. Uncomfortable with the silence that followed, he turned his full attention to the screens in front of him.

The satellites orbiting the planets could beam a clear view of the solar system on the visualisation screens. Three top-of-the-range satellites orbited the Earth, which gave them even sharper images of space immediately above its atmosphere. Galen checked the outlying areas of space where the passenger ships could meet debris, while Maria closely monitored his work. He couldn't wait until the training phase of his job was over; fastidious in her attention to detail, Maria rarely missed any mistake he might make. But in contrast to Paddy and Stuart, she was remarkably easy-going.

An attractive woman for a sixty-three-year-old, Maria was not short of admirers. The Glamour treatment offered at the genetic manipulation clinics had sliced twenty years off her appearance, but it was her deep brown eyes that revealed her true age. Galen gazed at her. He could tell she found the attention she received from men a little disconcerting at times, probably because of her sexual preferences. Paddy had told him her attraction to women was not decided at birth, but triggered by an event in her life—what that had been, he wouldn't say. She always tried to dress in a way that didn't accentuate her looks, but there was little she could do about her genetically determined Argentinian curves.

Maria finally turned around and caught his gaze. The look in her eyes caused Galen's face to redden. Wordlessly, he turned his full attention back to the screen. Behind him, he could hear McWilliams's impatience build as his tongue clicked mercilessly.

'Okay, how about we concentrate on a little work now,' Maria said.

Galen nodded sheepishly.

'Earlier, Paddy recorded debris collecting in Section Fifteen. I'm going to need you to carry out a sweep of that area, near the rings of Saturn. We've been getting some strange readings from there all day.'

'First line of defence, right?' Galen smirked.

'Yeah, like hell we are,' Stuart quipped. He

89

placed his head in his hands. 'Jesus, where did this headache come from? I can just tell it's going to be one of those days.' He stormed off to refill his coffee cup.

There was a private joke among docking station workers that the controllers were the first line of defence for Earth if an attack ever happened. But Earth Security Centre's collaboration with the World Government meant that the planet's protection was far from being left in the hands of a trainee and a Level Three Air and Space controller.

Galen moved to a free section of the wall and began his search, using his body to control the images that sprang into life. One panel displayed real-time images of the Earth's atmosphere; another was a zoomed-out image of the remaining solar system, waiting to be navigated. He circled both hands in an anti-clockwise motion that activated the zoom. The screen responded instantly and the visual increased by one thousand per cent. Sweeping his hand from left to right, he traversed the solar system easily, slowing down and zooming in when he reached Saturn. He pulled his palms towards him, drawing the image in closer. He tapped twice into the air and closed in on the area of interest. As he flew through the rings of Saturn, he modified his search trajectory until he reached the correct section. Galen immersed himself in the image and pretended he was in space. Flying was all he'd ever wanted to do, ever since he was a child with a toy plane and a dream in the Boston neighbourhood.

In Section Fifteen, Paddy's logs showed up as a bright beacon of red. Galen furrowed his brow but struggled to see anything out of the ordinary. 'What am I looking at? What did Paddy see exactly? Maybe the debris passed by, or could it be a faulty sensor on the satellite at Saturn?'

Stuart, who was shadowing Galen, nodded once. 'Possibly a fault.' He spoke to the communications operative. 'Get the maintenance robots out there to check on the satellites.'

While they carried out their checks, Galen conducted a full sweep of the system. He zoomed out until it filled just half of the visualisation screen. To the right of the great expanse, high-resolution images of Earth were contained in a single panel. The ESC memos sprang to mind and he made a mental note to check the monitor in Stuart's office on his next break.

Galen concentrated solely on the slipstream paths, the same route the passenger ships would navigate when returning to Earth. With one due to arrive the following day, he could not afford to make a mistake.

'Visual of recorded debris at coordinates 15.67, east of Saturn,' Maria's silky voice confirmed.

'Yes, I see it now. How did I miss that?' He quickly zoomed into the coordinates Maria had given him. 'I can confirm it's a meteor fragment.'

'That's what I'm seeing here.'

'I have visual of more debris at coordinates 105.47, north of Venus,' Galen said.

'Similar meteor confirmation, but doesn't appear to be an immediate threat in its current position.'

'Good work, you two,' Stuart said. He put down his cup.

The next two hours passed in a similar way. While they confirmed a number of meteor sightings, no unauthorised ships had wandered unintentionally into the solar system. With high-tech equipment at their fingertips, they could spot any ships before they approached the hidden side of Jupiter.

At the end of each hour, Galen used one of the workstations to log his hourly reports. As he sat in front of the monitor, he wondered whether he could remotely link into Stuart's office; all he needed was the name of someone they were interested in. He quickly dismissed the idea—red flags would be all over Stuart's monitor the next time he checked it.

Stuart emerged from his office with a DPad in his hand. 'Okay, you two, we've got a cargo craft landing in the next hour. I need you to concentrate because nothing is going to mess up my safety record, do you hear me?'

'Yes, sir,' they replied in unison. Galen moved to the wall panels again and this time, concentrated on unseen problems—not flight paths and weather patterns that the computer could handle, but problems that the modern machines kicked up because of the way they moved. Vertical velocity could be a bitch at times. The HJA docking station had held a clean sheet for nearly twenty years; the last recorded death was the result of a piloting error.

For fifty-four minutes, Galen and Maria checked essential weather and atmospheric patterns until there was little else to do except wait for the pilot to make contact. With one minute to go before descent, she came within range of the station and connected with the communication operative: 'Captain Jenny Waterson. Craft 766-C seeking permission to land.'

The communication operative ran her voice through a recognition programme. 'I have confirmed your identity. Please hold,' he said.

Stuart turned to Galen, who was still running a series of last-minute checks. 'Give me your status, lad,' he said.

'Just a few more seconds,' Galen replied vacantly as he dashed from one sector to the next.

Ten seconds passed and the pilot's voice rang out again. 'Craft 766-C seeking permission to land. Can you confirm status?'

'Galen, hurry up. What's the word?' Stuart's voice crackled. Angry red blotches appeared on his neck, caused by a sudden rise in blood pressure.

'Just one more second. I'm almost there.'

Stuart moved to stand directly behind Galen. 'One more second. Always one more. Come on, lad—hurry up. I need an answer from you now.' He called Maria's name to get her attention.

She shrugged. 'He's got a system.'

'You two have me on death's door. For Christ's sake, Galen, the captain hasn't got all day.'

Galen continued his scan of the one hundred-mile area above the Earth's surface, not heeding his overseer's words of warning. He could feel Stuart's eyes burning a hole in the back of his head. Finally, he gave him the thumbs up to go ahead.

Stuart exhaled. 'About bloody time. My heart isn't able for this shit anymore. Remind me to have a wee chat to you later about improving your response time.'

'Craft 766-C, you are clear to land,' communications advised the pilot. 'Dock twelve is available. Set down on the port side of the hold.'

'Roger that,' the captain replied.

Communications disabled the outer perimeter shield, sitting one hundred and fifty miles above

Earth and enveloping the planet like a security blanket. Once the descent began, it would take only minutes for the craft to reach the landing plate. They would need to shut off the inner perimeter shield that encompassed the docking station and landing plates in a protective bubble.

Galen paced back and forth, staring at the problem he'd been too distracted to find: an idle wind pattern at vertical eighty miles picking up speed ahead of the craft's arrival.

8

Captain Jenny Waterson radioed in from the space above the Earth's outer perimeter force field, seeking permission to land. It felt like too long before she received the okay to go ahead.

'Craft 766-C you are clear to land. Dock twelve is available. Set down on the port side of the hold,' they told her.

'Roger that,' she said, before ordering the on-board computer to establish outgoing radio silence. She kept the incoming audio link with HJA active in case they ordered her to divert. The computer beeped once.

'Damn it, they cut that fine,' she mumbled, once the outgoing link had been severed. She ran a hand through her tightly cut platinum-blonde hair. Her blue eyes shifted relentlessly as she readied for the next step of the descent.

As soon as she could, she engaged the autopilot. Her posture still rigid, she exhaled slowly to steady her nerves and calm her rapid heartbeat. Time was not a luxury she could afford with just a narrow window to get the beginning of the descent right. If she missed her slot, it would screw up her schedule and Calypso Couriers—a subsidiary company of the World Government—wouldn't easily forgive her lateness. She was already on thin ice with

95

them. Any infringement could mean the early termination of her employment contract.

At seventy-five, Jenny was one of the more experienced pilots on their books. Her perfect flight record meant she was costly to keep and her employers had been looking for any excuse to get rid of her. With younger, less expensive pilots itching to spread their wings, it was only a matter of time. But she wasn't about to be erased from anyone's books and was determined to give them no reason to fire her.

Jenny knew the hold-up was down to the conscientious Galen Thompson. She bristled with annoyance that Stuart had put him on the roster during her shift; Galen was still too inexperienced. But she had known Stuart a long time and shouldn't have been all that surprised. He encouraged controllers to develop their instincts naturally but that method of training brought with it a measure of unpredictability. Now was not the time for uncertainty, and the more she thought about it, the angrier she became.

She forced her attention back to the descent, a process that had already begun. A male voice spoke through the communications system. 'Strong winds at vertical eighty miles. Be on alert. Looks like a hurricane is building.'

She reactivated the outgoing link and confirmed receipt before resuming radio silence once more; she would need every ounce of her concentration until she arrived safely at the magnetic landing plate at the docking station. Tweaking the craft's movements during descent was extremely dangerous because of the heat build-up caused by a fast drop into the atmosphere. Already her palms were damp, brought on by the fear of the unknown that accompanied each free fall.

She remained in orbit over the landing coordinates at the docking station, just above the Earth's atmosphere. The thrusters engaged sporadically, realigning the craft as it tried to pull in a different direction. It began its descent, dropping into the non-existent atmosphere and through the deactivated force field. The thrusters blasted again to maintain the correct position. On the screen in front of her, she monitored the increase in atmospheric density as the computer relayed progress through the audio channel.

'Density at ninety per cent, ninety-five, ninety-eight—'

Once it reached one hundred per cent, the thrusters would force the craft into a computer-guided free fall. Even though Jenny was well strapped in, she still braced herself for the imminent drop—there would be no warning. She dried her moist palms on the trouser leg of her military-green uniform and blew out a sharp breath.

'—one hundred per cent density achieved.'

There was a sudden jolt as she felt a push downwards. Thrusters disengaged and acceleration increased as the craft dropped towards the surface. Less than a minute passed; the craft had reached one hundred and eighty miles above the docking station, and was heading straight for the middle of the storm.

The craft reached the edge of the storm and winds twisted violently around it, trying to knock it off course. The computer realigned its position but there was no let up in the conditions. Jenny watched the screen like a hawk as the craft lurched to the left and then right. She poised her slender hands over the controls. She only had to touch them to transfer the power back to her.

She had to work from instinct. The force field surrounding her craft would do little to protect her or the cargo from an impending smash. The craft continued to rock from side to side, creaking and moaning as the computer tried to steady the motion.

Then it hit the inner circle of the storm. A mass of blackened clouds swirled one way, then another, as they turned sharply to take repeated shots at the craft. Jenny's heart beat wildly in her chest. She tried to keep her mind clear and her thoughts steady, but sweat soaked her back as the strain of the psychological challenge took hold of her.

She fought the temptation to grab the controls and pilot the craft manually. The craft's tilt variance remained on the edge of the danger zone for three whole minutes.

'Come on Jenny, keep it together.' She fought against her inner panic. 'You've done this a hundred times.' No matter what she did, she couldn't stop thinking about all the things that could go wrong. Ever since Calypso Couriers had told her a month ago that her job was on the line, she'd spent sleepless nights worrying about it. Now she second-guessed every action she made, actions that under normal circumstances would have been entirely instinctual.

The craft rocked and rolled. Jenny's breathing became laboured as she kept her hands hooked in a claw-like way over the controls. She pinched her arm to distract herself. It worked, for about two seconds, then the panic crept into her bones again. She prayed for the first time in twenty years since she started work as a pilot. She didn't know if anyone was up there or even listening to her.

But something changed—the weather became calmer. She smiled briefly and released a slow breath. She would survive this fall and many more that followed. When the craft finally dropped below the black mass and into the grey, lifeless atmosphere that hung over the cities, she thanked whatever invisible being had intervened. She relaxed her hands easily enough but struggled to loosen up her body. The descent continued and the craft dropped effortlessly to within fifty miles of the docking station, where no wind existed except for that created by her own spacecraft.

As soon as the tension broke in her body, her stomach began to heave. She clutched at it, as her body finally registered the rocking motion and the vertical drop. Overpowered by strong nauseous feelings, her stomach twisted and lurched in protest. As a distraction, she pushed even harder on her stomach, even though the action only made it worse. She hadn't eaten anything for the last six hours; in hindsight, that had probably been a good thing. There was nothing to throw up, although she'd no interest in testing that theory. Other pilots had told her that wind topped the list of the worst things to meet. In the training room, Jenny, along with a dozen others, had been shoved vertically, horizontally and exposed to the greatest G-force in cockpit simulations. Even though she'd been through it several times, she had never got used to it.

When the craft's motion finally settled, so too did her stomach. The descent continued smoothly while the speed intensified. A minute later and the craft was directly over the landing plate at Dock 12.

Once in range, Magnetic Levitation kicked in and the landing plate was magnetised with a positive field. The blocks on the underside of the craft took on a similar charge. A sharpness rippled through the entire craft as the magnets tried to repel one another. It pushed upwards and the force field absorbed some of the effect.

With only twenty feet to go, polarisation switched to the lowest levels and the craft glided gently into place, levitating just metres above the landing plate. Jenny regained control and engaged the thrusters. She switched off the magnetic field and guided 766-C smoothly into the hangar bay, setting it down on the port side. She disengaged the thrusters and force field. Emerging slowly from her chair, she took a moment to peel her sweat-soaked uniform away from her back and legs.

She made her way to the back and stood at the exit door, eager to place her feet on solid ground once more. She scanned her security chip on the touch pad.

'Thank you for flying with Dresden Spacecrafts. We hope your journey was satisfactory,' the automated voice boomed, as the exit door was released.

'Pleasure was all mine,' she said sarcastically as she stumbled over the threshold. The next time she saw Stuart McWilliams, she would give him a piece of her mind.

9

Exilon 5

At 6 a.m. on Saturday, Bill Taggart willed his weary body out of bed after another sleepless night. His first attempt to open his eyes failed and he fought hard against the urge to rest for a few minutes more. Eventually, his hands jerked back the covers in one swift motion and he flung his legs over the side of the bed, both actions in direct conflict with what his brain wanted him to do. He gave his ITF-owned apartment the once over before shuffling to the bathroom.

He splashed icy cold water on his face; the drastic temperature change shocked his sluggish system back into life. He felt instantly more awake, even though he didn't look it. He noticed how drawn and thin his face had become from a couple of years of sleep deprivation and a manic diet. Beneath his eyes, he sported an impressive set of black circles, each about the size of the rings of Saturn—he was beginning to look his age. He could undergo genetic treatments to correct the damage, including some that delayed the ageing process. All were widely available to the public, in particular the Glamour package that sliced twenty years off a person's appearance, but he preferred to see his real face every morning, not a modified version of himself. It was what Isla had preferred too. In his own way, he was honouring her memory by staying true to his original appearance.

'There are far too many people walking around with the same face,' she had said to him when Bill told her he was considering using one of the manipulation clinics. 'Wouldn't you prefer to look unique?' Isla was five years older than him, and a little wiser.

'It wouldn't be much,' he said. 'Just a little skin lift to rejuvenate my face.'

Isla made a face. 'It always starts there and then people find they can't stop fiddling with their genetics. A little skin lift turns into a telomere injection. Before you know it, you've turned back time so much you're a teenager again.' Geneticists had figured out how to isolate the gene that controlled the body's natural ageing process. While the telomeres within the body's chromosomes naturally shortened, geneticists found they could lengthen them by injecting a growth hormone into the telomere. This halted the ageing process and dramatically reversed the outward signs of those advancing years.

'I would never go that far,' Bill had said to her, before teasing, 'Well, maybe if I was fifty, so I could snag a younger woman.' Many times, he'd reminded her of his preference for older women.

Isla's expression turned serious. 'Try to look past the exterior, Bill. So many people still judge others by how they look. People are complex and are never what they seem to be.' Her words brought the image of the World Government's CEO, Charles Deighton, to mind and he had to agree with her analogy.

In the six months before her disappearance, Isla's personality had changed drastically. After one of her trips to Exilon 5, she had become suspicious about everything and lost that carefree attitude of hers. When Bill had tried to talk to her about it, she became defensive.

'You're all the same. Why can't you leave well enough alone? Why are you always trying to mess around in things that don't concern you?' she said.

'Is that aimed at me?' He raised an eyebrow.

'Not specifically. Well, yes—maybe.' Isla hung her head low.

'Love, what are you talking about?'

'Just leave it, Bill. I can't talk about it.' She turned her back on him but suddenly changed her mind. She grabbed hold of the lapels on his jacket and looked him dead in the eye. 'Don't jump to obvious conclusions. Do you understand me? It's an easy out. Always search for the truth.'

The passion in her voice had caught his attention. The pain in her eyes confirmed what she'd been feeling. It had not been one of her common lectures, but a warning that he hadn't seen coming.

He stood at the mirror a little longer than usual as he thought about that conversation and the many others that followed after that night.

'Have you ever heard of Morse code?' Isla asked him one evening over dinner in their private apartment in Nottingham on Earth.

Bill shook his head and grabbed a chicken leg from a bowl in the centre of the table. He took a juicy bite from it. 'Can't say that I have.' Juices ran down his hand. Savagely, he licked his thumb and forefinger.

'Dad uses it. He once told me that he can listen in on any conversation in the world.' Her father had worked for the communications section of the World Government. While he'd insisted he didn't listen to every conversation, he had known of others who were less moralistic about it.

That piqued his interest and his brow furrowed. 'How?'

'Through the equipment that we use every single day. It acts as a relay—bounces the sound around and comes through as an echo on the line. It's clear enough to make out conversations.'

'Shit.' He dropped the chicken leg noisily on the plate in front of him. The thought of another person spying on him suddenly agitated him. 'Is he listening in now?'

Isla placed both hands on his arm. 'No. He gave me a sound interrupter. We can't hear it, but it disrupts the sound enough so that it plays back as gobbledygook.'

Bill relaxed a little and wiped his greasy hands on a napkin.

'Not everyone listens in, but he says that there are some who would. Dad was sure the World Government was taking notes. Before he went on his last mission, he gave me the sound interrupter and told me to leave it on permanently. It's the reason he uses Morse code to communicate.'

'Morse code? How does *that* work?'

'It's a series of beeps or clicks, each linked to a letter, word or phrase. You can talk to another person this way. He has tried to use it in public but he says it draws too much attention.'

In that moment, he envisioned Isla's father in one of the food replication terminals, banging on his food tray while another patron did the same. He grinned at the image.

'I know, I know, it's impractical,' she continued, almost reading his thoughts. 'But there has to be a better way to communicate without—being *seen* to communicate.'

She shared something she had read recently, gesturing more animatedly than normal. 'I've been reading up on it and one story stuck with me. Back when Ireland was ruled by the English, Irish was still the primary language of the country up to the eighteenth century. But the nineteenth century saw Irish decline as a first language in favour of English. Why? Well two things: because of the Great Famine and because the English prohibited its teaching in schools. Many Irish leaders also saw Irish as being too backward and pushed for the more progressive English language. They were right to in the end, but Irish people felt that their heritage was being stripped away by English rule, so they continued to teach the language to their children. When the struggle for independence began in the late nineteenth century, the soldiers communicated back and forth in Irish because the English couldn't understand them. A secret language.'

'I like that, Isla. The idea of others listening in any time they want has rattled my cage. You're suggesting what—that we develop our own language?'

'Why not? Doesn't have to be a spoken language. I haven't really thought about it beyond that, but I will.'

Isla had once told Bill that the chats with her father ignited a deep obsession within her to search for a solution to that problem—of how to converse safely in public. He expected her to bring it up again but when she didn't, he assumed she had given up on the idea altogether. His brow creased at the memories, in particular the conversation about the secret

105

language. What did she mean by it? He had to let it go. Besides, deciphering a riddle without all the parts would be a waste of time.

He ran a hand over his two-day-old stubble. 'Grooming will have to wait, Isla,' he said, recalling how she always hated the way the start of a beard scratched her face. He'd always made a special effort to be clean-shaven for her.

He dressed and went to the kitchen to make a fresh pot of coffee. When it sizzled, he filled his mug to the brim and rooted through the almost bare cupboards for something to eat. He settled on a box of replicated cereal flakes and munched on dry handfuls of the stuff. As he ate and drank, he stifled a yawn. He knew the lack of sleep would only get him so far. When his body and mind finally drifted into a deep coma-like sleep, there wouldn't be a damn thing he could do about it. But this was the life of a man who worked unsociable hours and existed in a permanent state of paranoia while searching for a truth he wasn't even sure he would find answers to.

Bill reviewed the files from the week before, noting the Indigene's plans to meet with the boy that morning between 6.45 and 7 a.m. at Belgrave Square Gardens. He and his team had watched the boy and alien interact for a while as they talked at the bus stop. Bill had relocated to the café directly across from their position while his team maintained a discreet distance.

When he first saw the Indigene, he had expected to feel nothing but hate for it and the race that had taken his wife away from him. It was how he'd felt when he first saw footage of the young alien captured a year earlier, and what had driven him to become part of the current mission. The alien had been wild and animal-like in its behaviour—expected traits from a seemingly uncontrollable and thoughtless race. But this Indigene was different: it moved and talked like a human. It had been a long-held belief that the entire race was wild. Now it seemed as if the opposite was true—that they were more intelligent than humans had considered them to be. The fact that the Indigene could con a boy into believing it was just like him was both fascinating and unsettling to him. Both parties had conversed quite freely, so language had to be one of the Indigene's inherent skills. Using a pair of magnification glasses, Bill had watched the Indigene closely from his seat in the café; its posture was wrong, almost forced. A pained expression flashed across its face. Then the Indigene smiled. Why? Such a human act.

His team on the ground had reported the alien's last sighting to be at one of the underground station entrances. When they lost track of its movements, Bill had followed the boy to Belgrave Square Gardens and watched as he stopped briefly to look at a wooden bench before moving on to the swing area.

He had approached the boy and realised that, although they could still capture the alien, the boy may well be their best shot at getting the information they needed. The sight of his approach unsettled the boy enough for him to jump off the swing. Bill's attempts at a genuine smile did little to relieve the tension and the boy dug his feet into the sandy earth, preparing for a confrontation.

'I'm Bill Taggart,' he had said. 'I work for the World Government on Earth.' The boy's expression changed but not in a good way. He looked around nervously so Bill held out his hands. 'You aren't in any trouble. Please don't be scared.'

The boy had eyed him suspiciously. 'Do you know my mother?'

'No, I don't,' Bill replied honestly. 'What's your name?'

'Ben.'

Bill had noticed his body relax.

'How old are you?'

'Eight.'

'Can you tell me about the man you were speaking to at the bus stop earlier?'

'Why do you want to know?' Ben had tensed up again.

'He's not in any trouble. I only want to ask him a few questions.'

A sudden breeze rushed through the trees above their heads and lifted leaves from their branches. The leaves danced and swirled around Ben's head. Ben dug his feet further into the sand. Bill had wondered for a moment why the boy had so eagerly accepted friendship from a complete stranger—and a potential killer—at a bus stop. He needed a new angle and threats might work.

'Well, we can always go ask your mother about your new friend.'

Ben struggled to free himself from the soft earth. He fell to his knees before clambering to his feet. 'No! Don't tell my mum. She doesn't know I'm out here. Please! Don't say anything to her!'

'It's okay,' Bill had soothed. 'I won't if you just tell me what I need to know.'

The boy moved closer. His voice rose as if he was trying to convince Bill of his innocence. Ben told him the stranger's name, recalling his own observations about Stephen's odd appearance. Even though Bill's skin had prickled at the thought of the Indigene using a human name, he listened as the story spilled effortlessly from the boy's lips. On occasion, Bill had to ask a different question when it appeared as though the boy was heading off on a tangent. The information had been a mixed bag and through the eyes of an eight-year-old boy, the Indigene may not have seemed so out of place. If anything of significance was shared between them, Ben may have been too young to understand it. He'd at least managed to get the time and place of their next meeting.

Bill had reached inside an oversized bag that hung across his body, and felt around for the soft object he'd brought with him. He handed the special teddy bear to Ben. It had been fitted with an audio-visual recording device. Ben eagerly accepted the reward for his betrayal.

'Don't forget to bring it along to show your new friend next week,' he had urged him.

Bill hoped his chat with Ben Watson the previous week would pay off as he anxiously waited for the morning's meeting to begin. He ran a hand through his coarse hair, and gave thought to the Indigene and its attempts to look more human. Was that why Isla disappeared—because one of them had tried to befriend her? The very thought made him sick to his stomach.

He sucked tentatively on the rim of his coffee mug, trying not to notice that the contents had completely cooled; it was the caffeine he was after and it worked whether the liquid was hot or cold. But it tasted vile, which made it more difficult to swallow with each mouthful—and his stomach was in knots. He refilled his cup without emptying the cold contents. The old coffee turned the steaming black liquid into a lukewarm fusion. The taste only marginally improved but at least he could drink it.

He checked the time again—it was now six fifteen. Bill activated his DPad and scrolled through countless news articles and official reports generated by the World Government and Earth Security Centre. Some were about the initial move to Exilon 5.

The reports reminded him of when Isla had changed careers about two and a half years ago. Bored in her teaching role, she'd expressed an interest in helping the newest residents of Exilon 5 to settle in.

'I feel useless stuck in this classroom while the population is going through these changes. I need to do something constructive. I need to satisfy my altruistic side.'

Bill laughed. 'Well, you're not being entirely altruistic if you're satisfying your own needs.'

She punched him playfully and had counteracted with one of her cleverly disarming arguments. What she had said exactly, he now couldn't remember.

Isla had turned her attention to training and became a Task Force soldier, winding up working for their military outfit. At the time, the Indigenes weren't a threat to humans and ground patrol duties had been light.

It was around the same time—three months before her disappearance—that Isla had made another drastic change in her life. Bill couldn't quite believe what he was seeing. 'What have you done to yourself?' he said.

She became defensive. 'What? It's my hair. I'll do what I like with it.'

'But—it's all gone,' he gasped. Isla had been wearing her military uniform and steel-toe boots, and had her hair cut so short that it altered the very angles of her face.

'Well, you never liked it anyway,' she had said coldly. 'It doesn't seem important to hold on to such frivolous things when there are bigger problems in the world.'

'Well, I never wanted you to do this to yourself.'

'Like I said, Bill, it's not important.'

The World Government had not been able to say whether Isla was dead—there was no body—only confirming to Bill that it had happened when she confronted one of the Indigenes near the city border of New Copenhagen. But he had an issue with the World Government version of events. He knew his wife better than they did and he couldn't imagine her confronting an Indigene. More likely, she had tried to reach out to it. Even though her personality had changed during her stint on Exilon 5, her core beliefs remained the same.

He could sit there all day thinking about her, but the memories prevented him from moving forward with the mission at hand. He shook his head, opened one of the official World Government reports about the initial move to Exilon 5 and forced himself to read it.

Grey skies, frigid temperatures and a vanishing sun—the clear signs that Earth was changing. The first layer formed like a skin on boiling milk that strangled the sun's attempts to reach the surface below. The sudden change in air temperature had been a shock to the people, and made it feel as though they had just walked into a giant refrigeration unit.

After passing on four unsuitable exoplanets, Exilon 5 became their last hope. The terraforming process, along with the liquid chemicals that seeped into the soil, made it possible for plants and trees to grow more effectively.

While stationed on Exilon 5, the ITF's role had initially been to help new transferees to adjust to their new home. But the alarm of living on Exilon 5—an alien world— had been too much for some people and their behaviour became increasingly erratic. The World Government ordered them to be separated from the rest of the population because the new planet would exist as a place where humans existed harmoniously and no longer traded life for technology.

The report said: 'We intend to reintroduce technology until it complements the human lives that use virtual systems as a replacement for thinking. Exilon 5 will give the people new opportunities to re-learn the basics of thinking, feeling or just being, as well as accessing several forms of technology in a safe and productive way.'

The land beyond the city boundaries, known as no man's land, was undeveloped. The ITF military patrolled the areas day and night, armed with Buzz Guns and Impulse Tasers. Transport arterial routes swept outwards, connecting one city to the next. Black markets dominated the undeveloped land either side of the roads that connected to the cities. In the black of night criminals operated freely, taking advantage of the shortage of technology on the planet and making a living out of swindling the desperate and vulnerable. No matter how many times the ITF smashed the operating rings, fresh businesses would always emerge unscathed in alternative places. It was on such a night that the animal sound was heard. The noise had originated inside the border limits, where animals were strictly forbidden.

Bill opened a video file, which was an interview with one of the ITF officers. He had been the first to arrive on the scene. Sweating and shaking, the officer visibly struggled to communicate what he had seen. He alone had seen the bright, shining eyes of the animal that had wandered inside the city limits. Calling for backup, he then decided to approach the animal alone. For the interviewer's benefit, the officer held his hand up like a gun as his eyes searched the room. Acting it out seemed to help settle his nerves.

'Eyes fixed on me, then looked away.' His eyes flitted from the interviewer to a spot on the wall. 'I heard the animal. It sounded like it was injured. But when I got closer, I couldn't believe what I was seeing.' The officer slapped his hands down on the table and leaned forward.

Surprised by his move, the interviewer leaned back in his chair. 'What was it?' he finally whispered.

The officer laughed cynically. 'Two boys, crouching over what I think was a wolf. The smell of blood turned my stomach. There was so much of it.'

The interviewer leaned forward. 'So you're saying they killed the animal. You were right to report this illegality. The biodome animals are protected.'

The officer shook his head and leaned back, his eyes wild as he tried to explain. 'No, you've got it all wrong,' he whispered through gritted teeth. 'They were eating it.' He drank heavily from a cup of water that had been placed in front of him and resumed his story.

'I thought the attacker had been an animal of

some sort because of its body contortion, its reflective eyes, its primal interest in the wolf. I was unable to retrieve my Buzz Gun without attracting attention to myself. While I waited for backup to arrive, I took a step in its direction. I was trying to corner it, you know, to make the catch a little easier? But that's when I saw something that chilled me.' He swallowed hard.

The interviewer leaned in closer. 'Saw what exactly?'

'It looked at me and smiled. *Smiled*, for God's sake! I mean what kind of animal was it? What creature of God's making looks and acts like a wild animal, then takes time out of its killing spree to flash its pearly whites at me?'

The interviewer sat back in his chair.

The officer continued with his story. 'I felt a rush of cool air pass right by my face.' He used his hand to show what happened. 'We caught one of the bastards. The second one managed to escape.'

'That's a good thing,' the interviewer said encouragingly.

The officer leaned forward again. 'Have you even seen this thing?' He closed his eyes. 'I can honestly say I have never seen anything like it in my whole life.'

Bill closed the video file and opened another labelled, Initial Examination of Species 31. It was recorded by Dr Frank Jameson, a bio-physician who had carried out the first assessment of the captured young Indigene male. According to his file, Dr Jameson worked for a company on Earth called Bio Technologies. Bio Tech specialised in genetic manipulation therapy and disease control, and was another of the World Government's subsidiaries.

The doctor used a roving camera that recorded events by tracking subject motion. While the laboratory's interior was sparse, the setup was far from basic; the New London-based laboratory was using the most up-to-date equipment. Bill noted the request for high-spec equipment had been approved by the World Government CEO, Charles Deighton.

Dr Jameson stood alone and looked into the camera. Nervously, he touched his sandy-coloured hair and neatly trimmed beard. His height was not easy to gauge until two other doctors entered the room; he towered over them. All three wore white boiler suits over their civilian clothes. He flipped up the hood and pulled the drawstrings closed. It puckered around his face.

There was palpable excitement among the tight-knit group as Dr Jameson introduced Doctors White and Henshall. Two assistants added to the team that already consisted of two men and one woman. The room they were in measured about fifty by forty feet. To the left was a small workstation where one of the assistants sat at a research monitor. A stainless-steel shelf ran almost the full length of the back wall. A large sink sat in the middle and took up almost a quarter of its length. To the right was a tray with various cutting tools, including a laser scalpel. Off to the side was an airtight flexible membrane containment unit with an examination table inside.

Dr Jameson motioned towards it. 'We control the unit's gaseous composition through our workstations. We can pass through safely without breaking the seal or compromising the atmospheric configuration inside. The membrane has tiny memory particles that scan our security chips to allow entry and exit from the unit. Mostly used for infection cases and detainees, today we will be using the containment unit for both.'

A short while later, one of the assistants wheeled the young male Indigene in and gently placed its small body on the examination table. Dr Jameson entered the containment unit first with the two doctors behind him. The roving camera hovered above.

Dr Jameson spoke formally. 'Species 31 will remain sedated until a time when we are ready to wake it. We haven't altered the gaseous composition inside the membrane, as it seems the alien is quite capable of breathing our air without any difficulties. We can only conclude at this early stage that it requires the same gaseous composition as humans to survive. We will be bringing the alien round shortly, but we don't know if it has the capability to understand us, or whether it speaks any language at all. How useful the information will be from Species 31 is anyone's guess.'

Bill examined the 3D body scan of the Indigene that accompanied the video. Physically, it looked like a human and its size was comparable to that of a twelve-year-old boy.

As the roving camera trained in on the young Indigene, a flicker of movement caught Bill's eye. It wasn't until the Indigene's breathing pattern changed, from long even breaths to short sporadic bursts, that the doctors also noticed.

Jameson turned to Dr White. The camera mirrored his movement. 'How much sedative did you give him?' White threw out some numbers. Jameson nodded, his brow creasing with worry. He spoke into the camera, but kept his eyes trained on the alien.

'What we have given to Species 31 is a dose designed for a human, but we can't be sure if we have over or under-medicated the alien.' Jameson turned to Henshall. 'I think we should wake it.'

The female doctor nodded and prepared a syringe filled with liquid. The roving camera focused in on her and she explained. 'This solution will counteract the administered sedative.'

White monitored the young Indigene's heartbeat, which registered at forty over eighty. It continued to breathe in uneven, short breaths.

Dr Henshall tied a piece of rubber around the upper part of the Indigene's arm and pulled it tight. She slapped the arm in several places.

'I can't find a vein,' she said.

'Just use the same one as before,' Jameson suggested.

She examined the arm and pulled in an extra source of light to help. 'There's no evidence of the original entry point.'

'Then you're going to have to guess.' Jameson tapped his finger in the crease of his elbow. 'Insert it here.'

Henshall applied too much force and the titanium needle broke twice. On the third attempt, she broke through the skin and everybody waited nervously, including Bill. It only took a minute for the young Indigene to stir from its drug-induced sleep. It blinked its eyes open, but squeezed them shut just as quickly, straining against the harsh lights within the facilities.

'Dim the lights by two-thirds. Now!' Jameson began pacing back and forth.

The laboratory plunged into near darkness and instantly took on a more sinister look. The young

117

Indigene tried to open its eyes again and this time seemed more comfortable with the level of light. Its glazed eyes looked around, appearing to be confused by what it was seeing.

'The alien's eyes seem to be photosensitive. See the lack of pigment here?' The lead doctor stopped pacing. The roving camera nose-dived for a better look.

The Indigene, trapped beneath leg, body and arm restraints, began to panic, twisting its arm until one broke free from the wrist clamp. White, Jameson and the assistant rushed to restrain the alien while Henshall struggled to strap down the rogue arm.

Jameson yanked the hood off his head and pushed his sandy hair out of his eyes. He blew out a breath. 'We are attempting to place further restraints on Species 31. It seems—to have—broken—shit, this thing is strong. I need help over here!' He trailed off and his arms shot up to protect his face.

The Indigene's free arm flailed around wildly. A low guttural snarl escaped from deep inside its throat. The twisting and thrashing gave way to violent convulsions directly beneath the doctors' grip. They instinctively let go and backed away from the table. Jameson shot a look at Henshall.

She shook her head without engaging the doctor's eyes. 'That wasn't me.' She stood motionless and stared at the Indigene.

'White, help me hold it down.' Jameson tried to restrain it once more. 'Give it the anti-convulsion drug, quickly.'

Henshall picked up another liquid-filled syringe and quickly pushed it into the alien's arm. The needle bent again, but the skin yielded to her urgency. They only let go when the convulsions stopped. All four stood back from the table, watching and waiting.

Jameson was silent. His mouth opened but he couldn't explain what had just happened.

Bill opened a new recording. The same three doctors came into view, more composed than before.

The young Indigene lay motionless on the table. The surrounding area resembled something out of a horror story: bed sheets and bandages littered the floor, cutting instruments that had been placed neatly on the tray before, were now haphazardly tossed back.

Jameson clicked his fingers at the assistants when he noticed the camera was still recording. They quickly removed the debris from the floor. Surprisingly, there was a lack of blood and no telltale incisions on the Indigene.

Jameson cleared his throat and pushed his hair out of his eyes. 'At first we thought the epidermis was translucent in colour, but on closer inspection it was actually opaque and not as delicate as we first expected. In fact, it's several times more durable than human skin. The laser scalpel had trouble penetrating the outer layer. Skin pigmentation is not visible. I'm not even sure there are melanocytes present in the toughened layer. Species 31 is capable of regeneration. We cut it several times but it healed in less than a minute, even in posthumous conditions.' He touched the Indigene's face with his finger. 'The eyes lack pigmentation, which probably explains its photosensitivity. It can see better in the dark than we can.'

Bill had read about a case in the early twenty-first century; children in East Asia and South America were recorded as having the ability to see in the dark.

Their eyes resembled round glowing dots in low light, much like a nocturnal animal's eyes. At the time, doctors had attributed the mystery to the rare condition Leukoderma. Leukoderma stripped pigmentation or melanin production in random areas of the skin, leaving visible white patches. In even rarer cases, the condition could affect the eyes. The medical world turned its attention towards the increase of these nocturnal children cases but the story lost momentum when nothing beyond Leukoderma could explain it.

Bill tuned back in to Dr Jameson's monologue.

'There's no sign of hair papillae anywhere on Species 31's body. We also found low levels of red blood cells in its body, other than trace remnants in the digestive system.' For the benefit of the intended audience, Jameson explained further. 'Human blood accounts for seven per cent of bodily fluids. In Species 31, it accounts for less than one per cent. When we sliced the skin open, a clear fluid secreted out. It's what gives the alien its translucent appearance.'

Dr White picked up three items and showed them to the camera. 'We discovered these, in the alien's nasal cavities and in the back of its throat. We think it's an air filtration device. It would explain the scarring we found on its lungs. Species 31 didn't die because of anything we did. It died because of too much oxygen to the brain.'

Bill turned off the video and leaned hard into the chair. He shook his head, trying to dislodge the disturbing image of the panicky young Indigene from his mind. He checked the time projection on the wall.

It was six forty and edging closer to the meeting time. He closed all files and opened the communications channel on the DPad to try to pick up the wireless signal from the teddy bear. He located the unique signature code although the sound was muffled and images were grainy at best. The only explanation he could give was that the bear was inside the little boy's backpack.

Centring the entire investigation on Ben Watson was a bold step and it concerned Bill that he could place the eight-year-old in danger so easily. He was not thinking clearly; he needed personal answers and with Ben turning out to be their best lead, there were no other options open to him. All that mattered was that the boy made it to his scheduled meeting.

Bill picked up a tiny earpiece and shoved it into his ear canal, continuing to hear only muffled sounds. He thought about the Indigene called Stephen and wondered why it had chosen to give itself a human name. Was it the easiest way to blend in?

Pouring himself another cup of coffee—his sixth that morning—he scooted his chair over to the window and stared at Belgrave Square Gardens. Was it luck that the ITF had chosen to rent this very apartment? But even with the magnification glasses, he couldn't see the bench where the two were due to meet, which was hidden behind a myriad of leafy trees.

He reasoned he was safer where he was—in his apartment. He didn't trust being so close to the Indigene. If there was an opportunity to apprehend it, he would tell his team to make their move. For now, the recording device would act as his eyes and ears. The bear would offer an innocuous way to get in close without actually having to. Surely the Indigene would not suspect an innocent toy?

He checked in with his team that remained on standby in the gardens, near to where the meeting would occur. With moments to go, the images changed from grainy to clear. He hit the record button on his DPad and leaned forward, staring hard at the screen.

10

After Stephen's departure the week before, Ben Watson worked hard to come up with an escape plan for the following Saturday. He hoped his mother would be sleeping late again.

He planned his escape one evening and roped in his avatar to help. At first, his avatar had been concerned that he was going to meet a stranger alone, but Ben told it that he'd known Stephen for ages. The lie hung between them like a dead weight but since Ben had disabled the Light Box's A.I. learning features, there was nothing more to say.

That morning, he rose early and crept towards his mother's room. He held his breath as he cracked the door open just a notch. The sounds that drifted towards him put him at ease; little could rouse her when she slept that hard. But if she did wake, his avatar would tell her the story exactly as they had agreed it. With his backpack fully stocked, he carefully placed the stuffed bear the investigator had given him on top of everything else.

He arrived at Belgrave Square Gardens with minutes to spare, far too giddy to care if anyone was following him this time. He skipped lightly towards the empty bench and sat down. Then he carefully pulled the bear free from its temporary prison and placed it beside him.

Watching Ben from behind a cluster of large replicated trees, a bout of empathy washed over Stephen for the boy who was always alone, a feeling that seemed to replace the fear and disdain from the week before. He shook his head, trying to dislodge the feeling, and evoked images of his dead parents to serve as a reminder of what the Surface Creatures were capable of. He thought of Pierre and Elise, the elders of District Three, and struggled to agree with their more open-minded opinion of them. Pierre had told him not to be so quick to judge—advice he said a friend of the Indigenes had given him. Who that was, he wouldn't say.

Stephen moved his body rapidly and repetitively until the movement resembled nothing more than a shadowy blur; in the early morning light, there were many shadows to focus on. He was aware of the military figures that hovered close by, as they had done the week earlier. They weren't difficult to spot, and he had identified each one by their different scents. He idly wondered why they had allowed the meeting to happen between him and the young child again, and if they were being driven by something other than a wish to capture or kill him. Like before, he needed to be careful about the amount of time he spent on the surface. He could already feel the sun's heat beginning to build. His protective eye lenses and the correct balance of air would only last so long.

Sudden thoughts about how the Surface Creatures had attacked their planet thirty years ago entered his mind while he waited for the park to empty a little. The tunnels, colder than the surface had been, had protected his race from the blasts' severity, a move that was only supposed to be temporary until the worst of the airborne chemicals had dissipated.

He remembered as a child how big the heavy door, which stood between the air-controlled environment and the tunnels leading to the surface, had looked to him. His childlike strength had not been able to deal with the weight of the door made from the impervious omega rock. He had tried to open it many times but he could not leave District Three without his parents' permission.

The explosions had tainted the surface air but there were new whisperings in the district that the air was once again breathable. In the corridor leading to the omega door, Stephen had watched the first of the exploratory groups, covered in outfits the females had made, take their first step up top since the air had been chemically damaged. One by one, they had returned, their faces sullen. In the midst of the Indigenes' efforts to reclaim the surface as their own, Stephen had pieced together details about the conditions outside through their many conversations with each other.

'Nothing remains,' said one.

'Everything is covered in a thick, lingering dust,' said another.

Their cities, their homes, the places where they once socially gathered, discussed, meditated, no longer existed. The atmosphere, heavily polluted with harsh chemicals, still aggressively burned their throats. When they had returned to the district, their coughs had lasted days. A few struggled with life underground while most adapted, creating large cavernous rooms off the tunnels that already existed. Those who possessed a heightened spatial awareness had sped up the excavation by being able to analyse the rock's composition and find its weak spots.

The years passed and Stephen had kept his own notes about the conditions of the surface as seen through others' eyes. If the scientists' and his own calculations were correct, then the last of the chemicals should have been absorbed by the land. Excitement and expectation coursed through the residents of District Three, but an unexpected change in Exilon 5's atmosphere had quickly halted that excitement. News about the new atmosphere containing high levels of oxygen and some nitrogen, was not good. The high oxygen levels made the air too corrosive for them to breathe. The elders had ordered the districts' entrance points to be hermetically sealed and the areas beyond were redesigned to give them everything they needed. With their main food source gone, they had to create a synthetic protein compound that eliminated the need to hunt above ground. While the compound didn't satisfy their hunger in the same way, it had been vital in helping to keep them alive.

Thoughts about resurfacing had stayed with the Indigenes. Good memories remained about the grey and obtrusive skies and the tiny glints of sunlight; with little or no wind, the cloud line had rarely shifted. The sun's strength, greatly diminished by the clouds' mass, had kept the air temperature at a constant five degrees centigrade; the Indigenes were more suited to living in cooler conditions. Advanced visionary capabilities allowed them to see in the dark and into light, to break it apart into its seven strands of colour. Living on the surface was similar to being inside a giant prism.

Stephen hadn't quite understood the obsession

of some to return to the surface, even after the news about the new atmosphere was released. It frightened him to learn that his parents had joined an independent group that would surface to discover the changes for themselves.

In the oxygen-rich atmosphere on the surface, the independents soon struggled for breath. Elise, an elder, had stayed with Stephen while he watched his parents on a monitor inside one of the district's rooms. Tightness had spread across his chest and he balled his fists. Without giving it a second thought, he bolted for the omega door, figuring he was strong enough to open it now.

Elise sped after him, grabbed his arm before he could leave and wrapped him up tightly in her embrace. She pulled him back inside the room.

'Pierre, do something,' she had pleaded with her husband. 'They're in pain. I can feel all of them.'

'He shouldn't be watching this,' he had said.

'He wants to see.' Several times, Elise had tried turning Stephen's head away when his parents' distressed faces came into view, but each time he fought her.

'They shouldn't have done this.' Pierre shook his head.

Even then, Stephen had known he was not referring to the independent group but to the Surface Creatures who had carried out the explosions.

'Tell the others to get out there, now!'

Hearing the elder raise his voice like that had scared Stephen enough to move closer to Elise's side. It was the first and the last time he ever saw Pierre angry.

Strange patterns had soon begun to appear in the weather; yellow and orange hues suddenly streamed through shafts that were connected to the surface. They were forced to seal them when the tunnels began to heat up. Soon after, the Surface Creatures arrived.

As Stephen's mind threatened to wander into a more recent past, he caught himself when he noticed that Ben had arrived. He watched and waited while the boy skipped towards the bench and sat down. He then removed something from his bag and placed it beside him.

Stephen ran over to the bench and sat to Ben's right. The area was secluded and there were very few Surface Creatures about. Those who passed by didn't pay them much attention.

The black-haired, wiry-framed boy leapt when he noticed Stephen suddenly sitting beside him. He clutched his chest and threw a hand over his stomach, bending over at the middle. 'Holy cow! You scared me! Where did you come from?'

'Just over there.' Stephen pointed to their right.

The boy followed his finger until his eyes rested on the cluster of trees. 'Well, don't scare me like that again. I'm not supposed to be here. If my mum finds out—'

'I forgot you don't move at the same speed,' Stephen said. 'That was a natural pace for me.'

Ben eyed him more curiously now. 'How fast can you move?'

'Five, six times your speed, I imagine.'

'Cool.'

Stephen casually pointed to the fluffy object sitting between them. 'What's that?'

Ben's face broke into a toothy grin. 'It's a teddy bear, silly! You can't get them anymore, but this one was a present. His name is Snuffles, because his nose looks funny. Kinda upturned. Do you like him?' He held the bear up as high as possible, so Stephen could get a better view.

'Present from whom?'

'My Dad.'

Stephen looked into the reflective black eyes of the toy, but made no move to take it from Ben. Instead he brushed his hand lightly across the furry exterior. It felt so soft.

Ben pulled the bear down and sat it on his lap, angling it in a way that gave Stephen a perfect view. 'How long have you been here for? Were you waiting for me by the trees?'

'No, I arrived moments before you did,' Stephen lied.

'This is really early,' Ben began to chatter. 'Why are we meeting in these gardens instead of at the bus stop? Why did you want to meet at seven in the morning? I know why I'm out this early—it's so my mum doesn't check on me. I like to go on my adventures, you see and she doesn't know anything about them. She wouldn't understand them, not like you do.'

Stephen did not attempt to improve his rigid and uncomfortable posture on the bench. He allowed his eyes to focus blankly in front of him while he used his peripheral vision to scan his surroundings. He listened quietly as Ben rambled on and on about nothing in particular. When it seemed like he wasn't going to take a breath anytime soon, he moved into a more comfortable position.

Ben paused in his relentless chatter and looked up at Stephen, eagerly waiting for him to speak.

'I have chosen this time because there are less of you about. As you can see, I'm quite different to you,' Stephen said. Ben nodded. 'Besides, this seems to be an hour that you are most comfortable with. We met at the same time last week, if you remember.'

Ben laughed once. 'Oh, yeah. I forgot.'

Ben stopped talking, suddenly worried that his constant babbling might end up driving Stephen away. He glanced at Stephen's outfit and wondered if he owned any other clothes besides the long brown trench coat and matching hat. Not for the first time, he wondered if he was dangerous.

He tried hard to think of some grown-up questions to ask and staring into the strange eyes of his new friend brought one to mind. 'Why is the skin on your face a different colour to your arm?' It was a question he had asked the week before.

'I'm wearing a special covering to protect my skin from the sun, and to avoid unnecessary questions about my appearance.'

'Why? What's wrong with it?'

'Nothing, as far as I'm concerned. My skin is perfectly normal to me.'

'But it's not even ten degrees yet! It's not very warm. Why do you need to protect your skin?'

'It reacts differently to yours if exposed to the elements. I prefer a cooler climate and little or no sun.'

Ben's eyes flickered from Stephen's covered face and neck to his patchy arm where the artificial skin had lost its pigmentation. 'Your skin is funny looking. It looks see-through but it's normal on your face.'

Stephen nodded, crossing his legs and folding one hand on top of the other. 'It only appears that way. It's actually opaque.'

'If you ate something, would I be able to see it go into your stomach?'

Stephen shook his head.

'Well, what's the point then? That would be much cooler if you could.'

'It's normal to have this type of skin where I am from,' Stephen answered clinically. 'Yours, however, is strange.' He tilted his head slightly. 'You explained to me last week the reason for its earthy colour. I'm curious today about its solidity. I wonder if it's also waterproof like mine.'

Ben shrugged. 'I don't know what that means.' He squeezed the bear's soft stomach repeatedly with his tiny fingers, feeling something hard move inside the bear as he did. He tried picking up key words like 'earthy', 'solidity', 'waterproof' and putting them together in a sentence that made sense, but it was beyond him.

Stephen reached into a waste receptacle that was at one end of the bench. He fished out a half-empty bottle of water. Unscrewing the cap with one hand he extended his other to Ben.

'May I?'

Ben shrugged again and held out his arm.

Against every natural instinct, Stephen grabbed hold of the child's wrist and straightened out his arm. It felt warm to the touch and caused the ends of his fingers to tingle. He poured the cool liquid from the bottle over the child's arm. It rolled off effortlessly and beaded in areas where the surface flattened out.

'That's interesting,' he said, releasing Ben's wrist. He had never physically touched one of them before. He tried to calm his breathing while his fingers continued to tingle. He grabbed hold of them to stem the feeling.

'What is?'

'Well, it's nothing really,' he replied, rubbing the sensation away. 'It's just that we may look different on the surface, but there are similarities in the way our bodies work, at least in terms of the epidermis layer.'

The expression on Ben's face caused Stephen to backtrack and simplify his last sentence. 'What I mean is the outer layer of our skin essentially does the same thing.'

'So?' Ben shrugged.

'Because we think we know so much about you,' Stephen tried to explain. 'I realise now we don't know as much as we first thought.'

Ben stifled a yawn. 'Do you live in a house?'

'No, I don't.'

'Well where do you live then?'

'Near the train station.'

'Really?' He screwed up his little face. 'I wouldn't like to live there. It's all dark and cold. Why don't you just live up here with everyone else?'

'Because we can't survive above ground for long. It's also doubtful we would be accepted here.'

'Which station do you live at? Is it Charing Cross or Waterloo? Because I've been to both and I guess I could visit you there sometimes.'

'I don't live in the station itself, but I can see how you might think that.' He decided it was better to keep back certain details.

An all-female group entered the park and performed a quick succession of warm-up exercises against a nearby tree. Starting with a comfortable walking pace, the oldest female scrutinised the pair as they passed. Stephen consciously tugged on his hat, pulling it further over his eyes. The female let out a sudden gasp when his partly covered arm fell into her view. She looked ahead and increased her pace, attempting to catch up with the group. He watched them and readied himself to leave if they doubled back. He waited until the last of them was out of sight.

A movement under his left elbow broke his concentration and his eyes quickly darted to the source of the motion. Ben continued to shuffle his bum on the bench. He opened his backpack and seconds later pulled out a sandwich wrapped in plastic. He placed it on his lap and ripped open the parcel. While Stephen had been curious about their food choices, the boy's sandwich emitted a smell that he didn't like.

Ben picked up one half and took a bite. He chewed hungrily.

Stephen couldn't stop staring at his food.

'Want some?' Ben held out the part he had slobbered over.

'What's in it?'

'Bread, butter and strawberry jam. I replicated it myself.' He held it just under Stephen's nose.

'Please take it away,' Stephen said, holding a hand over his mouth as his throat reflexively gagged.

Ben shrugged. 'You don't like jam?' He took another bite. The offer was short-lived.

'I can't eat that.' He suppressed another gag.

'My mum says I can't drink milk because I'm allergic. Is it the same as that?'

'My diet is different. My stomach cannot process a lot of the foods that you easily consume.' A sudden breeze caught the food smell and swept it away. His stomach settled.

'What do you eat then?' Ben licked off a blob of jam that had dropped on his thumb.

Stephen decided it was better to avert his eyes. He sat rigidly and stared at a nearby sculpture of a female holding a child. 'We survive mostly on the blood, and sometimes meat, of animals. We need large amounts of iron in our diets.'

Ben's mouth opened and his eyes became unusually wide. He loosened his grip on the sandwich. 'Are you a vampire?' he whispered. 'They drink human blood though, not animals. I don't want you to eat me, please. My mum would kill me if I got myself killed!'

From the Surface Creatures' literature, Stephen was vaguely familiar with the stories. 'No, I am not a vampire.' He struggled to suppress a laugh; the images of sharp fangs amused him. 'We eat animals the same way your species did during early civilisation periods. We just don't require heat to alter their composition, as your stomachs prefer. We don't hunt with tools—we use our physical strength to overpower the animal.'

'Oh,' Ben said. He took another quick bite of his sandwich. 'My mum buys meat pies sometimes and they are very nice. There's animal in those. I could bring you one if you'd like. Then you wouldn't have to kill any.'

'That won't be necessary.' Stephen smiled a little, then it faded as he remembered why he was there: he was looking for answers. He shifted his thoughts away from the tolerance that was slowly building for the child.

Ben finished his sandwich and sucked loudly

on the straw of his juice box. He squashed his back into the contours of the bench and pulled his legs up so that his feet were perched on the edge. He wrapped his free arm around both legs to keep them in place.

'Why do you eat iron? Is it like the stuff you get in a scrap yard? I wouldn't think that tastes nice.'

'My body does not produce many red blood cells because I don't live in an oxygen-rich atmosphere,' he explained. 'We require less oxygen to breathe and because of our bodies' low levels of haemoglobin, we are naturally deficient in iron. Our stomachs absorb the iron directly from the blood. It gives us strength.' Stephen was pleased that the boy was comfortable in his presence. Soon it would be his turn to talk. 'We survive on a different composition of gases than your species. That's why it's difficult for us to stay up here. We live somewhere where we can control the air we breathe.' He paused to allow Ben time to digest the information.

'If you can't survive here, then how are you breathing the air?'

Stephen thought privately about the boy's intelligence. Even though he wasn't capable of understanding everything, he had intelligently linked many of his questions. 'We have created a small device that helps us to breathe on the surface—to all appearances naturally. However, I can't stay here too long.'

Stephen realised, and not for the first time, that he'd broken many rules, including his plan to keep an emotional distance from the boy. He had already shared a dangerous amount of information and could only guess the military had heard everything. But he had to take risks; it would be impossible to arrange a third meeting. From this moment on, the Surface

Creatures would begin to set traps for the Indigenes, possibly tagging the food source to uncover the location of their districts. That day's meeting with Ben had to count.

He turned the tables and asked Ben a host of questions, checking the time before questioning him about the Surface Creatures' physiology, the types of foods and drinks they enjoyed. He moved to forms of entertainment—what they liked to do, where they liked to go. A clear pattern started to emerge that caused Stephen to ball his fists; he would never accept that the Indigenes and Surface Creatures had anything in common.

But he still had one question left, the reason he'd risked his life to come to the surface—who were they? The response might not give him or the Central Council the answers they wanted, but it was still something he needed to ask. He turned to face Ben fully. 'I would like to return to our discussion last week when I asked what you call yourselves. Do you remember what you said?'

'I told you, I'm English. Did you forget?'

Stephen shook his head. 'No. Perhaps I need to be clearer with my question. What does your species refer to itself as? We only know you as Surface Creatures.'

While Ben scratched his head, Stephen was acutely conscious of his fast-approaching deadline. Suddenly, the child smiled. 'Oh, you mean human?'

'Ah, human,' Stephen said, nodding once. 'Thank you.' On the outside, he appeared to be in control; beneath his icy exterior, his heart raced at over seventy beats per minute. Every part of his body strained against the temptation to flee. His sudden need to bolt without explanation overpowered any rational thoughts he had.

Similar to the week before, he could feel the military's murderous eyes on him as they bravely stepped out of hiding and into his peripheral vision. They were a problem that he didn't need—they would be tracking him again and he needed to outrun them. They'd already seen what he was capable of. This time, he was sure the military would be ready.

Humans. Stephen struggled to think about the word without feeling panic. He leapt from his seat and sped past the military's location. As his feet pummelled the earth, there was only one thing he was sure of: the Indigenes needed a plan and they needed it now.

11

Exilon 5

Fifteen minutes before its exit from Belgrave Square Gardens, Bill Taggart could tell that the Indigene wanted to leave. Their undercover operation was not as covert as he would have liked, since two of his reporting officers had moved out of cover moments before. While he'd been unable to see who they were, their voices told him it was Officers Caldwell and Page. There had been no orders given, and certainly not one for them to move in.

Isla had complained to him regularly about the ITF military's bullish behaviour out on the field. She had used negotiation skills of a cool head and a clear mind when approaching potentially dangerous situations. While Bill had respected her approach, he had equally worried about the 'types' that would try to take advantage of her.

'It's my teaching background,' she said when Bill had asked her how she put up with their behaviour.

'They're loose cannons. I don't want you getting caught up in their mess and ending up dead,' Bill argued.

Isla touched his face gently—he remembered her hand had been warm. 'That's never going to happen, Bill. I'm smarter than they are. I see where the problems are long before they've decided to go it alone.'

He shook his head. 'Like raging bulls, that lot. Glaikit bastards.'

'I know, but beneath the bravado, they wouldn't dare risk anyone else's life. Punishment for that is death.'

'And that's supposed to make me feel better about everything? What about the time that detainee attacked you because one of the officers got cocky and shoved him in your direction?'

'The officer didn't know I was there. It was an accident.'

'It always is.'

'Look Bill, I'm no fool, so stop treating me like one. I know what I'm doing.'

His wife had always been strong-willed, but was physically at a disadvantage in comparison to her beefed-up colleagues. It wasn't that he didn't trust her, it was more that he hadn't trusted the others. It pained him to think that the very thing he'd warned her about may have come true. He tried not to think about the reasons why Isla might have met her end; it hurt too much and he felt a lump rise in the back of his throat. He swallowed hard to dislodge it and worked even harder to bring his attention back to the task at hand.

Pacing back and forth in his ITF apartment in New Westminster, he cursed like a drunken fool as he helplessly watched his team ruin their best chance at getting what he needed. He'd been perfectly clear with them: keep a reasonable distance; don't move in unless he gave them the signal. He hated certain military types and their petulant attitudes; they were impossible to work with. But if he didn't accept the help on offer, the commanding role would go to someone else—orders from Deighton. Now the Indigene was gone; part of the plan had been to capture it and they had lost the advantage of surprise by moving in early. Bill's chance to find out more about Isla's true fate was slipping away.

If the Indigene disappeared, it was unlikely to reappear for some time. Bill wondered why it had risked making contact during daylight hours when they could see and track it easier. Although the alien had blended in, its choice of clothing made it stand out, but not enough for New London residents to question its presence.

Bill fiddled with his earpiece and tried to connect with someone on his team. 'Caldwell! Page!' he shouted into the tiny wire-like microphone. 'What the hell just happened out there? I gave no orders to move in. State your position now.'

The silence that ensued only aggravated him more. He exhaled sharply and massaged his aching temples. Didn't they know what was at stake here?— crucial answers to many important things. As far as his team knew, the mission was about gathering information on the alien race for the World Government. They weren't aware of Bill's true motives for being on the case, nor would he ever discuss it with them. How was he supposed to find out the truth with a group that didn't recognise their inferior rank? Who was really in command here?

At the first mission briefing, the ESC had provided Bill with details of the military he would be assigned. They suggested using people already stationed on Exilon 5. He had agreed, thinking it would be helpful if the team knew the terrain. He expected the officers to become his eyes and ears, freeing up his time to think about more important matters, such as how to get closer to the Indigenes. But their lack of experience in surveillance had bothered him. Now he struggled to find common ground with the guerrilla warfare enthusiasts at his disposal.

Bill twitched involuntarily—the gallon of coffee he'd consumed had him teetering on a knife-edge and he was about ready to jump off it. His previous lethargy had been replaced with nervous energy and palpitations. He perched on the edge of his chair and impatiently drummed the DPad with his fingers as he waited for a response from someone—anyone—in the field.

Knowing what he did about the Indigenes, he really should have discouraged Ben Watson from going to the meeting, but he had needed the boy and the teddy bear in place so he could watch the alien. While the skin covering had altered its appearance, its likeness to humans, both physically and in its mannerisms, shocked him. When the alien had looked into the bear's eyes, a chill ran through his entire body. Instinctively, he'd looked away from the screen, unable to meet the eyes of one of Isla's potential killers. After taking a moment to calm himself, he forced his eyes back to the screen, long enough to notice the brown contact lenses.

Then there were the other differences: their ability to create technology and adapt to the human environment made them imaginative and highly intelligent. Yet their senseless killing of human beings didn't match this description. The Indigene had also mentioned that their race had lived on the surface before the humans arrived. Since reports of them hadn't come to light until a year ago, Bill had to assume the terraforming explosions had destroyed their habitats and forced them underground. Had the alien simply been curious when it went to meet the boy, or was there a different, more sinister reason?

Unlike others who wanted to study the Indigene, Bill was sure of one thing: if he ever came face-to-face with the one calling itself Stephen, he would kill it after it told him everything about what happened to Isla. But if Bill's team couldn't catch up to it, if he couldn't keep the hope alive that he would uncover the truth, then what would happen? Once he released the new recordings to the ESC, he would no longer have control over the mission.

But the answers were still within his reach and the Indigene had not yet escaped. There were two possible outcomes to that day's information: the World Government would consider co-existence with the alien species, or destroy them. When it came to threats against humanity, their reaction was to destroy the thing they didn't understand. That made his search for answers all the more important. He needed to find out the truth before it died with the Indigene race.

Clutching the DPad tightly in one hand, Bill stared at it for a long time. His brow creased as he waited impatiently for his team to resume contact. He could see the device inside the bear was still recording images but its fate—or the boy's for that matter—were no longer his concern.

He switched the pad to his other hand and dried his sweaty palm on his trouser leg. Stuck inside his apartment and of no help to his team, he thought about joining the pursuit. But he was too far away from the chase to be of any use. He had to rely on the eyes and ears of his team, even though it killed him to know they were the ones in control. Just thinking about their stupidity made his blood boil.

Bill spoke harshly into the microphone once more. 'Caldwell? I know you're out there and I know you can hear me. You're going to have to talk to me sometime. Answer me now, dammit!'

Silence hung heavily in the air as he thought again about leaving the apartment. He stood up, sat down and stood up a few extra times, before eventually deciding to sit on the chair. 'Who's down there? Is somebody going to answer me? Because if I have to come down myself, I'll find you and—' His heart hammered so loudly in his chest that it was difficult for him to concentrate.

An eerie quiet emanated from his earpiece. He took a moment to calm himself before he addressed his team again, more aggressively this time. 'This is Taggart! SOMEBODY had better pick up NOW! I'm not fucking about here.'

Christ, he muttered to himself.

He could feel his heart racing as if it was trying to reach some imaginary finish line in his chest. His hands quivered from a mixture of agitation and stimulants. He swore that after today he was going to give up coffee for good. 'Shit, come on.' Bill tried pleading with his team. He considered telling them everything, but he knew it wouldn't magically fix whatever problems they had with his authority. He ordered himself to calm down; he wasn't thinking straight.

A voice broke through the still air. He leapt out of his skin and swore again.

'Jones here. Sorry for the silence earlier. It was necessary. Over.'

'Jones, what the hell is happening down there?

143

I have lost both visual and audio. Where the hell is Caldwell?'

'Caldwell and Page took off after the alien. It absconded from the gardens moments ago. They are maintaining radio silence for the time being. Over,' Jones replied in a rehearsed, nonchalant military voice.

'Well, where is it headed?' Bill said.

'Towards the underground station. The nearest one is in the Victoria district. Over.'

'How about you stop wasting my time and give me everything you have in one go. I don't need it in pieces.'

He could hear the officer sigh heavily, enough to cause Bill to slam his fist on the table.

Jones let out a small squeak and continued, with more pace this time. 'The alien is only a few minutes away from the main entrance now. It already had an extensive head start on us, so following it has been difficult. The crowds have managed to slow it up for now. Caldwell and Page are on its trail, but if it gets inside the station, we're going to lose it for sure. Over.'

'Jones, I want you to keep this line open. I need regular updates and not when it suits all of you. If we don't capture it today—well, let's just say somebody will need to explain to me and the ESC why they messed up.'

'Roger that, Taggart. Over,' Jones replied.

Suddenly realising who he was dealing with, Bill added quickly, 'Oh, and you'd better make sure it's alive. No one is to harm the alien. Understood?'

Their silence told him what their preference would have been, but it wasn't up to them. He would forgive their poor execution if he could speak to the

Indigene before it was carted off to the ESC or World Government.

Bill got up and paced across the room. The mission should have been a done deal. Everything had been so convenient: the second meeting, the chance to talk to the boy, the recording equipment. If this didn't work, if they didn't get something extra from this meeting, then Daphne Gilchrist would be all over him.

Another voice broke through. 'Officer Page here.' Bill's hands trembled. He sat down and listened as Page explained. 'We are pursuing the alien but it's too quick for us. It seems to know the streets pretty well. Over.' Her breathless words indicated that she was on the move.

'Don't you dare lose it, Page. If it gets into the tunnel system, then we won't have a hope in hell of tracking it.'

'I understand that, Taggart, but you need to know it's not looking good.'

'I don't want to hear it, Page.'

'The alien knows we're following and has altered its pattern through the crowds to try to shake us. As I've already said, we can't match its speed.' Page took a few deep breaths before continuing. 'It's at the corner of Buckingham Palace Road and Victoria Street, and now has a clear view of the underground's entrance. I've got to go. Over.'

'Shit.'

Radio silence ensued and a few tense minutes followed without an update. Bill tried to practise patience but failed. Abruptly he stood up and imprinted a healthy set of tread marks in the already worn carpet. They had to capture the Indigene before it reached safety; he needed it alive and unharmed.

When the World Government scientists and geneticists got their hands on it, there would be no opportunity to question it about its real purpose for talking to the boy. When they finished their extensive tests, he doubted they would keep the alien alive. His team's best chance of capture was to reach the Indigene before it entered the station. But it knew the underground tunnels for the Maglev train better than the humans who had built them.

He continued to pace back and forth, his uneasiness increasing as he thought about the similarities between the two races; he tried to ignore the small trace of fascination that accompanied those thoughts. The first sightings on record had reported a crude and animal-like race, something that seemed well founded. It also stated that the creatures possessed subhuman intelligence; a gross misinterpretation.

Aliens possessing superior intelligence? Bill shuddered at the possibility. If they were superior in intellect, were their two races so incapable of living together harmoniously? What if they'd managed to survive so long because they killed others that opposed them? Had they perceived Isla to be a threat to them? They must have, he thought. But going on the Indigene's behaviour that day, something didn't seem right. Something else didn't fit the reports.

A new voice shrilled through Bill's earpiece. He jumped again, but this time not as high; the adrenaline was depleting and he was beginning to feel sluggish. He needed a break.

'Caldwell here. We are in Victoria station. Over.'

He could hear his heart beating loudly in his ears. 'Well, did you capture it?'

'It's gone.'

12

Stephen ran for the eastern exit to Belgrave Square Gardens as fast as he could, his movements so rapid they created an invisible distortion in the air. He worked hard to distance himself from the military, skipping and stumbling over the uneven terrain in equal measure. With the exit in sight, he launched himself towards the gate just as a group of men entered. He immediately twisted and stretched his body around them, creating a sudden gust of wind that knocked one of the men's hats off his head. The man retrieved it and stared after an already empty trail. Getting to the safety of District Three was Stephen's primary concern, where he could breathe unhindered and find protection.

Stephen sprinted to Upper Belgrave Street in the New Westminster area but was forced to slow his pace right down to blend in with the dense crowd there. Instead, he weaved in and out between the humans. He could hear the train in the distance. He was close to the Victoria bullet train station where he could reach the tunnels leading to District Three. The elders would be waiting for him to report something positive back. He had nothing good to tell them; he was sure Pierre and Elise would be as shocked as he was when they found out what the Surface Creatures were. 'Human'; he repeated the word until a new chill coursed through his already cold body. In all of the literature he'd read, not once had there been any reference to humans. Other words had described their race: people, dreamers, philosophers, engineers.

The crowd slowed him down so much it forced him to deal with the volume of humans in another way, so he mimicked the actions of those around him. Yet to master the art of moving slowly, he became uncoordinated and started bumping into others. Some looked up from the impact while others kept walking. He threw an occasional apology their way to calm the more agitated among them. Attract as little attention as possible, he thought. Being so close to the humans made his skin crawl, and he wondered how they would react if they knew what he really was.

Coming to the end of the road, he took a sharp left on Hobart Place. The military were hot on his trail; he could smell them. That he could pick up their scent at all meant they were already too close. Stephen quickened his pace as he reached the road where the station was located. Hidden from view, a line of humans waited for a replication terminal to open. Distracted by his pursuers, he almost collided with the first person in the line. He skidded to an almost stop, leaned away from the crowd and accelerated along the length of the line. His heart pounded in his chest as he narrowly escaped harm.

The area around Grosvenor Gardens was heavily crowded, forcing him to slow down once again. There were so many humans—how would he keep it together long enough to get to safety? The military were also getting closer. Their scents were coming through much stronger now. He turned his head just as they arrived at the corner of Hobart Place where he had just been. *How are they keeping up?*

Then he realised what his mistake had been. He

shook the distractions from his mind that slowed his movements, and tried to pick up a new pace that was faster than theirs. The crowd hindered him and with the military pair bridging the gap, he gasped as the underground station fell into view. Stephen quickened his pace until he was just a short distance away from the entrance but a sudden mass exit of humans from the station building blocked his path to safety. His body strained with the effort of not getting close, but there were too many of them. He took a deep breath and going against every natural instinct, burrowed in deeper, right into the core of the swell. His body became rigid as they knocked and jostled him about. Right then, he was alone and completely vulnerable. Tears began to form and he felt the lenses in his eyes move with every blink.

Without his natural defences of speed and strength to protect him, he was just like them—weak and useless. Stephen realised that the crowd could overpower him at any moment, but he reminded himself that he was strong and he would fight as many of them as was necessary. The train tunnelled through the dark pits below, and the familiar low rumbling rose to his ears as it rode the Maglev rail.

Stephen struggled to keep his walk slow and deliberate, lowering his head to try to make himself seem more invisible to the people around him. Once inside, he could navigate the halls with speed and dexterity, but not out here where he struggled to use his speed effectively. But if *he* was struggling to get through, his pursuers would be too. In the areas where the crowd thinned out, he risked speed; the gap between him and the military was too narrow.

With one final push, he ran inside the station and headed for the tunnels. A queue had already formed at the gate. Ignoring it, he leapt over the stile. Alarms shrilled and people yelled loudly, but he tried not to think about it—survival was his only concern.

Stephen took long elegant strides towards the tunnels that veered off in a westerly direction and arrived on an almost empty platform; a train had just passed. Tilting his head slightly, he could hear the military voices approaching from the level above him. This time, he was sure they would follow him into the murky depths of the train tunnels. He wasted no time and leapt off the end of the platform onto the tracks, hitting the ground running. He followed the tunnel for about a mile in a westerly direction until he reached a section that split off in two directions. He took the left tunnel and carried on for another two miles. To the right he felt around for the opening he could not see with the brown lenses still in his eyes. He found it and squeezed through a narrow gap, one of many they had created across the railway network. He pulled both lenses out and placed them in his pocket. He would return them to Anton later.

The narrow gap linked to a series of passageways that led to the core of his district, each one protected by a false wall. In the low oxygen and pitch-black environment only small insects survived; the military would at least need safety equipment to follow him. Without the lenses, Stephen could once again see the subtle markers that had been carved into the false walls. There were hundreds of dead ends across the Victoria passageways and only twenty or so that led to District Three. He suddenly noticed the strain in his lungs begin; his filtration device was almost out of power, and with trace amounts of breathable air in this part of the maze, he too would suffocate. He shortened his breath and kept moving towards District Three. With his coordination affected, he stumbled through the miles of tunnels, taking left and right turns when the markers appeared. Along the way, he activated false doors to close behind him.

A mile on and the power had drained completely. An intense burning sensation seared Stephen's lungs as he tried to suck in anything that would keep him alive. He recognised the omega door that led into the sealed environment. Recognition software scanned his genetic code and authorised his entry. The impenetrable door slid back into the rock face and he jumped inside, his breathing now ragged. He continued to take short uncomfortable breaths.

The outer door sealed shut, while a smaller one leading into the inner sanctum remained closed. He could hear the first of the air pumps as it whirred into action. His lungs burned more aggressively with the effort of keeping him alive. With his breathing aggravated and painful now, he mentally willed the pumps to work faster. The larger of the two sucked the contaminated air out of the chamber, while the smaller one released air from inside the controlled environment. He fell to his knees as he struggled to stay on his feet and remain conscious. When the inner door finally released, he crawled inside and yanked the pieces of the air filtration device out of his throat and nose. Gasping wildly at first, his breathing calmed as soon as he drew in several breaths of familiar air into his weakened lungs. His body relaxed as he lay on the floor, exhausted from his efforts to stay alive.

Stephen stood up slowly, ignoring the dizziness that accompanied the action. He wanted to rest for longer, to think about the events that had just happened, but he didn't have time. He stumbled forward, fighting against his body's warning to stop and rest as he went looking for Pierre and Elise. He needed to tell them his news so he could understand what their next steps would be for the Indigenes. However, he had a plan of his own that he wanted to suggest to them.

13

Earth

Jenny Waterson was left to sit on a chair in the hold for half an hour before a thin, pale man emerged from his office, DPad in hand, and walked towards her.

'About time!' she muttered to herself. The anger she felt for Stuart McWilliams hadn't abated much and she still wanted to speak to him about using a trainee—a bloody trainee!—to guide her descent. But as the man approached, she groaned as she instantly recognised him as the same docking attendant who had failed to find her name on the incoming flight charter. She rolled her eyes and stood up.

'Hello there! Sorry to keep you waiting. I had important business to attend to.' He proffered his hand. 'Welcome to the HJA docking station. Is this your first time?'

She resisted the urge to slap the thirty-year-old's pasty-white face. Instead of taking his hand, she signalled for him to stop where he was. Slightly bemused, he waited for her to offer up further instructions. She closed her eyes and drew in another deep, steady breath. Her eyes snapped open and she deliberately released her breath into his face. 'Sorry about that. Bumpy trip. It always takes a while for me to come back down to earth, so to speak,' she lied. What she really needed was a stiff drink and a different attendant.

The attendant flipped his eyes upwards and muttered something under his breath about pilots not having the stomach for it. He said it quietly enough, but Jenny just about made it out. He motioned her closer with his hand, then ran his fingers through his auburn hair like a comb. She shuddered, wondering whether the World Government would care if useless people like him disappeared from the world.

'Now, let's see who you are,' he said.

Her skin crawled at the sound of his nasal whine. She shook her head at the fact he continued to pretend not to recognise her.

'Place your thumb here,' he ordered as he flipped the DPad around to face her. The computer scanned her chip and the words 'Captain Jennifer Waterson, Grade 4 Pilot' flashed up on the screen. Her photo appeared beside her name.

The attendant's eyes lingered on it for a moment before looking at Jenny. 'The photo doesn't match,' he said.

She'd already been through this with him the day before. 'As I said to you yesterday, I recently cut my hair and changed the colour.' She ran a hand over her cropped, platinum-blonde hair. The photo on file showed her with a brown, shoulder-length style. Her face was younger than her age. Training kept her body lean and she was physically strong.

'I see,' he said, puffing his chest out. 'Ms Waterson, can you verify your cargo on board, please?'

'That's *Captain*, if you don't mind,' she quipped before adding, 'I'm returning from Saturn with xenon compound.'

Earth's atmosphere contained minute amounts of stable noble gases helium, neon, argon, krypton and xenon, as well as traces of the radioactive noble gas radon. In 2087 they discovered that xenon existed abundantly in compound form within Saturn's recently uncovered supply of water. Xenon compound was primarily used as a propellant for spacecrafts but was also used in laser technology.

'Ah, yes, I have you here now,' he confirmed, wirelessly scanning the on-board content through his DPad. 'Well, I guess that's the paperwork sorted.' He hit the screen firmly with his finger.

The ground staff looked on restlessly as they waited for the instruction to unload. Jenny could tell from the way the staff whispered and elbowed each other that they did not like the attendant. But the attendant appeared to enjoy his superior role, even though his only job was to record the arrival and departure of pilot and cargo. He finally indicated to the ground staff to remove the cargo and when his back was turned, a few proceeded to give him the finger. Jenny struggled to suppress a smile.

'Something funny?' he frowned.

She straightened her expression. 'Eh, no. Still a little giddy after the flight, I guess.'

He clucked his tongue like an intolerant old man. 'How soon will you be flying again?'

'In an hour. I'm delivering cargo to the ESC in Sydney.'

'Right you are, ma'am,' he said. 'I guess you'll be back with us again in no time at all.' Before he finished the last sentence, he'd already turned his back and was walking away.

Jenny hated being talked down to and she

especially hated the use of the word 'ma'am'. It was outdated and represented women of a certain age— she was only seventy-five. 'Moron,' she muttered loudly once the attendant was out of earshot.

She stomped out of the hangar and headed straight for the docking station's canteen where she planned to eat her own body weight in food. It had been eight hours since she'd set off, and six since she'd last eaten anything. While there had been a range of foods available on board the craft, what it made up for in nutrients, it lacked in taste. She wasn't particularly fond of eating cardboard, and that's exactly what it had tasted like when she tried one of their reconstituted apple and winterberry pies.

She arrived at one of HJA's four self-service canteens, nestled in the eastern part of the station, and looked around the long room that had enough space for eight hundred seated workers. The place was divided up into several rows of black tables and white chairs. Pressed up against the longest walls were dozens of silver and black replication machines. Several workers queued for their food.

She grabbed a tray and joined the queue on the left, hoping it was the shorter of the two. It wasn't busy so she moved quickly enough to a vacant machine. She ordered beans on toast, with a side order of sausage, a chicken pot pie, two black coffees and three pieces of chocolate cake. Finding a free seat, she sat down hard on the bench and wolfed down her main meal and one of her pieces of cake. She could feel the exhaustion kick in while she sipped on her coffees and started on the second piece of cake, but she consoled herself with the knowledge that her current shift was ending after her run to

Sydney.

Jenny lived in Brisbane, Australia, in one of the downtown apartment blocks that once overlooked the city's river, a prime spot until the government filled it in over fifty years ago to build more apartments. The view out her window was nothing special; nor was any of the rest of the city nowadays. On the positive side, from Sydney it would only take her forty minutes to reach home on one of the high-speed trains. Then she planned to get some real shut-eye during her eight-hour break.

While nursing her cooling cup, she spotted Stuart walking into the canteen. Her previous annoyance at him returned but with food in her stomach, it didn't feel as venomous.

She'd always considered Stuart to be handsome, but like many men he'd vehemently refused to have work done on his face, claiming it was for 'metrosexual' men only. He had chestnut-brown hair and strong blue eyes. His face was dotted with expression lines that he said gave it character. His slightly expanded middle stretched the uniform he wore. The one thing he could never accept was going grey or losing his hair, and he had privately availed of the 'Bald be Gone' genetic treatment.

Following her divorce and after raising her child, Jenny had discovered a love of flying and enlisted at the Air and Space Control Academy. It was where she had first met Stuart. They spent a number of years as controllers working side by side in the docking station at Auckland, New Zealand. At fifty-five, she began her training as a pilot in earnest, having completed just four years as a controller. Stuart remained where he was, eventually taking up the role of Operations Overseer in Auckland when the job was offered to him.

Stuart waved at Jenny and mock-staggered over to her table. Some of the patrons muttered under their breath as he passed, saying something about McWilliams being 'a disgrace, showing up in that state and still drunk on the job, no less'. But he was a teetotaller and had been for as long as she could remember. Under other circumstances, she would have laughed raucously at her friend's dark humour, but she was not in the mood.

'I see you found me then,' she said flatly, keeping her eyes fixed on her cup.

'Not hard in this place,' he said holding up both thumbs. 'Our very own tracking devices.' He sat down opposite her. 'What happened to your hair?'

Jenny ran a hand across the nape of her neck. 'I fancied a change.' With back-to-back shifts, she found she had little time or patience for personal grooming.

'I think it looks good on you.'

She sighed wearily. 'Stuart, if you haven't guessed already, I'm pissed off with you.'

He raised a single brow. 'I can't imagine why.' He looked at the empty dishes on the table in front of her, most of them licked clean. There remained a piece of chocolate cake. He kept a close eye on it.

'Galen almost cost me my job, you asshole!'

'Jesus, Jenny, calm down.' Stuart looked around nervously. 'Watch your volume, will you?'

She knew what he was looking for—a single roving camera that was hovering over a group of trainees in one corner of the room. When her voice rose, it turned around to look in their direction.

Jenny lowered her voice, but the anger was still there. She leaned forward. 'Do you know what

Calypso Couriers said to me a month ago? That my job is on the line. I always knew it would be a risk when I reached Grade Four but I didn't think they would actually warn me. I can't take any chances, Stu—not anymore.'

'I'm sorry, Jen, I didn't know.'

The anger subsided a little when she heard the word 'sorry'.

The roving camera gave up on them and turned around to focus on the trainees again. Several of the trainees looked nervous, shifting uncomfortably in their seats; others tried to act brazenly, as if the camera's presence wasn't an issue.

'Why couldn't you have given me Maria?'

'I did, she was supervising him. Look, Calypso are a bunch of shits if you ask me. Why don't you consider going out on your own again? You still have that rust bucket in storage, don't you?'

Jenny thought about that. Yes, she did still have her old spacecraft and it was a long time since she had done freelance piloting work—it was how she had started out in the industry after getting her pilot's licence—but she didn't relish the idea of being her own boss again. She had got used to receiving a steady wage at the end of each month.

'I don't know, Stu. Seems like a lot of hassle after a steady job of—what has it been now—twenty years?'

He leaned forward and grabbed her hands. 'Look, if they're causing you such grief, then quit before they try to fire you. You deserve better than this.' He let go.

Jenny exhaled and unenthusiastically picked up her fork. She scooped up some of the chocolate cake and shoved it into her mouth. It had the texture of sponge but it tasted like dirt that had been sprinkled with cocoa powder. She had tried real chocolate cake once before, in Cantaloupe restaurant—it had been heaven on a fork. The excessive cost associated with dining there meant she couldn't afford to visit too often. The memory of what food should taste like, in comparison with what the replicators produced, was difficult to live with.

'I know you don't want to hear this but Galen still needs to learn. If I don't let him practise, I might as well just tell him to stay at home and put his feet up because he's no good to me.'

'You're taking unnecessary risks, Stuart. You know that.'

A strange expression crossed his face. 'It wouldn't be the first time.'

'What do you mean?' She eyed him curiously.

'Nothing.'

She lowered her fork. 'Shit—Stu. What have you done?'

'Nothing!' He pushed the plate closer to her. 'Eat your food.'

She shoved another lump of cake into her mouth. She felt a little sick, but she needed the calories. 'Promise me you won't use him on my schedule again.'

'I wouldn't have allowed anything to happen, you know that.'

She did.

'Why don't you take some proper time off? I mean more than the six or eight-hour layovers they give you.'

Jenny eyed him curiously.

'I'm just saying, you look stressed,' Stuart said. 'I know it's not ideal, given the circumstances, but you need to start thinking about your health.'

'If I take time off now, I might as well hand in my resignation.' She threw her hands up and her voice rose again. 'My stress is keeping me sharp.' The camera turned around again, seeking them out.

Stuart quickly changed the subject. 'How's your daughter?'

'Eleanor's doing well.' Jenny's volume normalised. She finally put down her fork and pushed her plate away. She couldn't eat another bite. If she did, she was certain there would be an explosion. 'She's thinking of starting another course in college—decided to change career paths from law to politics. She can't sit still for five minutes, that one. So like her father was in many ways. How about you? Any decent women decided to make an honest man of you yet?'

'Never going to happen. I've had my fill of wives, ex-wives—the lot. I'm planning on living out the rest of my life as a single bachelor.' Stuart remained stubbornly single after his last wife had almost bankrupted him. He'd been married three times before that and was still paying for his mistakes. Luckily, he hadn't fathered any children with them.

'You look stressed, Stuart. Getting enough sleep?' Jenny pushed all the plates to one side and placed her elbows on the table. She rested her chin on her hands.

'Name one person you can think of that gets decent sleep on this hellhole?' he said, gesturing wildly.

Jenny struggled to at first and then smiled: 'Calypso Couriers.'

'I'll toast to them burning in hell.' They both

raised an imaginary glass and mock-toasted to the image.

She smiled, but couldn't shake the feeling that Stuart was hiding something. 'Is everything alright with you?'

'Yeah, why?'

'You're looking a little peaky, that's all,' she said. 'You should give the skin rejuvenation place a go over at the walk-in clinic in Jacksonville. It's non-invasive and gets rid of the bags and dark circles.'

'I'm a real man—everything *au naturel*, including my face. Besides, if I didn't have the baggage, where would I keep my keys?'

'You're a riot—but you already knew that.' A tiny crease formed on the side of her face. 'I'm just saying, you should think about it. What time does your shift end?'

'Three this afternoon. You?'

'One last run to Sydney and I'm done for another eight hours. I haven't had any time off for a full week now. I'm exhausted.' Jenny yawned.

'Don't they know seventy-five is the new forty in this genetic age of ours?' Stuart pulled the plate with the untouched piece of cake on it towards him. 'Commie bastards. Don't appreciate what they have, that's their problem,' he mumbled as he stuffed his mouth with the chocolate dessert.

Jenny agreed, but she couldn't imagine Calypso Couriers recognising her efforts any time soon. She used what was left of her energy to worry about Stuart. Had she known what the immediate future held for her, she would have saved some energy for herself.

14

Galen turned away from the entrance to the eastern canteen. He had stayed there while Stuart and the captain of the spacecraft argued over something. He couldn't hear what it was about but it looked serious. He mentally noted the disturbance as something his parents might be interested to hear about, and he also planned to delve a little deeper into Captain Jenny Waterson's background. Perhaps it wasn't someone at the HJA docking station the ESC were interested in after all, but an associate of one of the staff working there.

He started to walk away when his communication device rang. He answered it.

'Galen? It's your father.'

'Dad, I was just going to call you. I wanted to let you know I may have found something—'

'I want you to come meet me and your mother in Sydney. We can talk then.'

Galen's stomach lurched; he didn't relish a face-to-face with his parents and could just about handle his father's probing calls. 'Is that necessary? I can just tell you what I know now. I didn't—'

'Your mother wants to see you.' His father sounded flustered. 'Come to Sydney. We'll expect you as soon as possible.'

Galen disconnected the call and headed back to the observation deck to wait for Stuart to return.

Stuart walked into the office with a grim look on his face as if he had a secret to hide; maybe he did, or maybe he was keeping a secret for someone else. Galen met him half way and Stuart's eyes suddenly became more alert.

'Stuart, I need to ask a favour,' Galen said.

'What is it, lad? Don't you have some reports to file?'

'I do but my father just called and he sounded worried about my mother. He wants me to fly over to Sydney immediately.'

Stuart's face reddened. 'What—now? You're in the middle of a shift!'

'I—I'm sorry Stuart. I wouldn't normally ask but—it sounded serious.'

Stuart stroked his chin and stared at the visualisation screen in front of him. 'Well, it's probably best if you're not here for the next hour or so. The captain of the spacecraft that just landed is on the warpath about something.'

Galen's brow creased. 'What?'

Stuart shook his head. 'Nothing. Be back in two hours. No longer.'

Half an hour later, Galen tripped and stumbled out of the Sydney docking station. He looked around for his parents; they were standing by the water's edge.

'Mom, Dad,' Galen said, as he reached them. His father shook his hand while his mother looked out anxiously over the water. He carried his overcoat over one arm, holding it away from his body.

'What was the hold-up?' his mother asked. 'You're fifteen minutes late.'

'Damn wind again, Mom,' Galen replied. 'A

couple of the passengers were sick on the way down, so we had to wait for the cleaning bots to sort out the mess before we could disembark. Of course, one person had to puke on my coat before I could snatch it away. This is going to stink for days, I just know it.' He wrinkled up his nose.

'Never mind all that. We need to talk,' his mother said, her tone urgent.

'Well can I at least take a breath before you start?' Very tentatively, he put his soiled coat on, delaying for time.

The temperature was beginning to drop as the daylight slowly retreated to make way for the evening time. The night-time air had a different—and not so pleasant—edge to it.

His parents headed towards the area just beyond downtown Sydney known as the Rocks. Galen followed a short distance behind, watching as his father stumbled a few times on the uneven path. His mother linked her arm in his to steady him, and as a precaution. Galen suddenly realised why he was always covered in bruises and walking into every inanimate object he could find in his apartment.

'Did you know they used to swim in the seas around here?' his father began, 'Well, not here exactly, but close by, where the beaches are. Can you imagine what it would have been like to do that?'

His mother pulled away from his father's arm, but kept walking. 'We have very little time. I would rather talk to Galen,' she said. Galen braced himself for the interrogation he was sure he was about to get. When there were fewer people about, she spoke quietly. 'What have you found out at the ESC? Have you managed to catch sight of the ESC memos I was talking about?'

'I haven't been able to look at too much. My overseer keeps a close eye on me—doesn't like me using the workstations when I'm not on duty.'

'Sounds like he has something to hide,' his father suggested.

Galen took a deep breath and was about to explain to him what he had seen between Stuart and the captain, but decided against it. He would look into Jenny Waterson's background first. He didn't want to accuse her of anything without having some proof. 'I'll keep an eye on him.'

His mother took a deep breath and released it. 'That may not be important anymore, Galen. I found a micro file hidden at the ESC. I've looked at it and your father now knows what's in it because I told him, but I haven't been able to copy anything yet.'

'What file?' Galen asked, stopping suddenly.

'Keep walking, Galen,' his father urged. 'Remember, we're just a normal family out for a stroll.'

Galen started walking again, beside them now. He shoved his hands deep into his pockets searching for warmth. 'Well, if what you're looking for is at ESC, what do you need me for?'

'Because I suspect that they've been sending more than just memos to your station,' his mother said. 'The docking stations and ESC are too closely linked for them not to be. If they wanted to hide something, they might try to send it to your main computer.'

'But I told you, I can't access the ESC memos. What makes you think I have access to the main computer?'

His mother fidgeted with the buttons on her overcoat. 'Look, all I want to know is if they've been sending information there, or if it's still all at ESC. You might as well keep looking for those memos—there may be other things going on that are not contained in the micro file.'

'Mom, I want to find out what happened to Grandad as much as you do, but the sneaking around is becoming harder.'

His mother glanced briefly at him, then turned to face her husband. 'I found these; they were with the micro file.' She kept an easy pace as she removed a bundle of letters from her pocket and cradled them protectively.

His father frowned. 'Are you looking for trouble now?'

'You don't know what's in them. They're addressed to that investigator.'

'What investigator?' Galen asked.

His father's brow creased. 'Who—Bill Taggart? Who on earth is writing to him?'

'His wife, I think.'

'Who's Bill Taggart?' Galen asked, but his parents ignored him.

His father shook his head. 'Sounds like they're private letters—you should give them back to him.' But something else caught his attention. 'Wait—why does the ESC have them in storage?'

'Would someone like to fill me in?' Galen asked.

His mother ignored him. 'His wife works—I mean—worked for the World Government. I can tell there's serious stuff in these that she wanted him to know, but I just can't make sense of them because they're coded. Why go to the effort of writing them in the first place?' She waved the bundle around in the air.

Galen watched as his father pushed her hand down. 'Put those away, will you?' He looked around nervously. 'First thing you're going to do is put those back where you found them. It's bad enough you stole the micro file. We don't need the government on our asses over these going missing. Where's Bill Taggart now?'

'On Exilon 5, investigating the Indigenes.'

'Seriously,' Galen interrupted. 'Could someone explain to me what's going on?'

Spotting a bench nearby, his father dragged Galen's mother over to sit on it. 'I'll be back in a minute,' he said to her.

He turned and walked with Galen for a short while, telling him what he could about his own father's disappearance. The detail about Bill Taggart and the World Government's investigation into a race called the Indigenes was new.

'So you see, your mother and I have gone too far with this and we don't know how to get out of it. We must keep going, if only to get answers for a man I highly respected.'

Galen frowned. 'And Paul knows about this?'

'Your brother knows as much about it as you do now.'

Galen and his father walked back to where they'd left his mother only to find her helping some old woman with her mask.

'Are you having problems?' they heard her ask the woman.

'Damn mask. Can't seem to get it to fit today,' the old woman wheezed. The poisonous air was seeping into her lungs, making it difficult for her to breathe.

'Here let me,' she offered. She removed the old

169

woman's mask, then held it over her face again and waited for the gel to activate. 'You need to hold the mask in place for a few minutes to give the gel time to form to the shape of your face. Only then will you get that tight seal you're after.' She waited until the structure softened, adhered, and then became rigid before removing her hand from the old woman's face. 'There.'

The woman breathed in deeply, gratefully. 'Thank you so much,' she said before shuffling on.

His mother proceeded to walk along the water's edge, more distracted than before. They followed her. 'Thanks for coming, Galen,' she said, strangely calm now. She kneeled dangerously close to the edge and dangled her hand over the water.

'Careful dear,' his father warned.

Galen wondered what would happen if she plunged her hand into its cool depths—nothing good, he imagined. The water's monochromatic appearance hid a highly toxic secret—only deadly bacteria lived there now. As if his mother had heard him, she withdrew her hand, picked up a stone instead and threw it at the water. It skipped once and then sank.

'So what now?' Galen asked as they all stood together.

'If the information on the micro file is true, we have to tell people,' his mother said. 'We have to get the truth out there somehow.'

His father grabbed hold of her hand. 'I hope you're not thinking of doing something on your own. I agreed to this as long as all of us were careful.'

Her expression hardened. 'And I promise you I will be, but people have a right to know what's going on.'

His father's expression turned grim. 'I never

asked you to go this far and neither would my dad. This is turning into an obsession—a dangerous one.'

She laughed and shook her head. 'This has turned into something huge—much bigger than your father's death. I'm sorry to be so blunt, but it has. If I had known—if either of us had known—what the World Government was up to back then, we would have tried to do something about it. Don't tell me you wouldn't have tried to help. When I think about what they've done to those poor Indigenes, it only encourages me to do more.'

As Galen listened, he realised his dad hadn't quite told him everything about the race on Exilon 5.

'Please don't do anything stupid,' his father said.

'I won't, but I can't sit around waiting for those fools in the government to make amends—to right their wrongs. I have to do something to move things along.' His mother's tone changed. 'There's this girl at the ESC, Laura O'Halloran—they're going to use her. But maybe I can get to her first.'

His father spoke sternly. 'Sweetheart, listen to me, don't do anything without speaking to me first. Do you hear me?'

Galen's mother nodded, but her expression revealed something different.

His father drew in a deep breath and released it. 'Look, how about we all go and grab a bite to eat? What do you say, Galen?'

Galen shook his head. 'I think I've lost my appetite.'

That afternoon, Laura O'Halloran paced herself. With so much documentation to sort through, she was eager to avoid a potential burnout. She had another thirteen hours left of her shift and the rate of document delivery to her monitor didn't look like it was slowing down. *Spread the work out evenly, take regular breaks from the screen.* She obeyed the mantra religiously; when the light-starved office brought on a bout of depression that a shot of vitamin D couldn't fix, things were usually bad. Following the mantra had helped her through darker moments.

While her father had suffered from regular depression, Laura's own was triggered by seasonal changes. Since the season never changed, she was caught up in a perpetual loop. Most times the vitamin D shot worked—a vitamin normally provided by the sun—to keep the darker thoughts at bay, although, not always. While she had never seriously considered terminating her life, she was familiar with the termination rooms the World Government had provided to deal with a population that lived longer. The oldest living human on record was one hundred and sixty—a vast increase since scientists had cracked the 'age' code.

Having amended the law to legalise what was once a criminal practice, termination rooms could now be found everywhere. In the beginning, news reporters had seized the opportunity to create mass hysteria and quickly mounted a campaign against the rooms' existence. But when the government announced to the public that the rooms were free to use, the people got behind them.

She remembered when her great-grandfather had used one. He had once been a sweet elderly man who turned bitter due to lifelong regrets about the things he had not done. On his one hundred and fiftieth birthday he'd told his family he was ready to die and his increasing frailty had cemented his decision. Her great-grandfather's identity chip had contained a dormant chemical and when he placed his thumb in a specially designed receptacle in Sydney's termination room, he was injected with a second chemical that mixed with it to form a lethal toxin. He placed his right hand on a flat plate, which punctured his palm with a thousand tiny needles coated in a mood-enhancing drug and hallucinogen. It felt no worse than pins and needles, he told them.

Laura and her mother Fionnuala had accompanied him that day. Her father, who suffered from depression, hadn't been mentally strong enough to attend. While it wasn't a bad way to end things, surrounded by loved ones, Laura wasn't quite ready to check out of life just yet. Those had been happier times for her and Fionnuala, back when they used to talk. Her father's unexpected death a few years later had turned her mother into a recluse.

The loneliness Laura felt overwhelmed her at times and became another negative thought for her to battle against. While she had friends at the Security Centre, she certainly wasn't close to any of them. She couldn't talk to them about her deeply strained relationship with her mother—or she wouldn't. She tried to imagine what response she might get from Janine if she told her about her sad life and her Seasonal Affective Disorder: horror, disgust—pity maybe? Or how about all of them, but not necessarily in that order.

Laura shook the thoughts from her mind and stood up from her workstation. She stretched out her back, which was rigid from sitting the same way for too long. She took a quick stroll along the centre aisle to help release pent-up energy and relieve stiffness.

She would have killed for an hour in the Energy Creation room on the second floor, a perfect opportunity to take a brain break from mundane information about people who wouldn't think twice about verbally abusing her in public.

Laura routinely stopped to touch her toes and stretch out her lower back until the blood flowed to her cheeks. When she stood up, her pasty-white face looked momentarily healthy as if it had been pinched by the biting winds that used to dominate the shorelines of Dublin. She continued on, wildly swinging her arms to get the circulation going between her shoulders. She tossed her arms one way and swung one leg the other. Having completed a few rounds, she promptly stopped at Janine's workstation.

'Having fun are we?' Janine had a strange expression on her face—something split between humour and jealousy.

'My back is killing me and I am close to collapse. I'm dead on my feet.'

'Just sit down then, will you? Stop torturing us with your boring exercise routine and take another Actigen.'

'Would love to, really, but I'm at my limit of four this week. They aren't working anymore.'

'Look, I've got work to do and you're disturbing me,' Janine said.

'And there it is,' Chris said, keeping one eye on Laura as she bent over to touch her toes.

'What?' Janine said, the irritation clear in her voice.

'The inner bitch.'

'Rack off, Chris.'

'I've made my point and you've just proven it. So what if she's exercising? I for one am enjoying the distraction.'

'You just want to get into her pants.' Janine spat out the words.

'So? What man wouldn't?'

Laura tried to ignore them but she felt her cheeks heat up anyway. 'Stop talking about me like I'm not here. And Chris, watch your mouth.'

'Well then, do what Janine suggested and sit down.' Chris sounded slightly offended.

'I need to get over the hump first. I'll feel better in a moment.'

'Why bother?'

'Because exercise helps me in more ways than one. I know it doesn't look like it now but—'

'There's only one type of exercise I like to do,' Chris said suggestively.

Janine pulled a face. 'Oh, keep your thoughts to yourself, for once—please.'

'I don't know how you lot can sit there for hours without moving a muscle.' Laura jogged lightly on the spot, ignoring the male eyes that watched her chest rise and fall. 'Chris, any word from your friend on the lottery yet?'

'You're not going to like it. Perth now, Melbourne next, then Europe.'

'Shit.' Laura stopped moving.

'Why do you want to go so badly?' Janine asked, eyeing her closely.

'I don't,' she replied a little too quickly. 'I'm just interested, that's all.'

Janine's eyes narrowed. 'Seems to me like it's more than that. What does your family think about it?'

Laura's heart picked up a beat as she worried about them delving too far into areas that were off-limits. 'My mother will probably end up coming with me.'

'And leave all this behind?' Janine swept her hand around the room. 'You'll never get another job as good as this on Exilon 5. You'll probably have to work as a cleaner. Bet you wouldn't like that so much. I hear the pay is shit.'

'Janine, what the hell crawled up your butt today?' Chris said.

'Nothing. I'm just enquiring about Laura's eagerness to leave Earth, that's all. She gets so excited every time the lottery sniffs near Haymarket.'

Laura had just about had her fill of Janine and her petty sniping. Janine was jealous of all women, even though she pretended not to be. Beneath all the bravado, she was insecure and wildly lacking in any personal ambition. Laura rubbed her tired eyes with her fingers and began the short walk back to her desk.

'Is that it?' Chris said. 'No more exercise for today?'

'Bite me.'

'Give me a reason.'

Keen to move the focus on to her, Janine said, 'Would you two stop with the sick flirting already and let me tell you what I've heard.' Heads shot up as everybody stopped to pay attention. Janine was a sure thing for the gossip and she flirted with every male in the building to get it. For the workers on Level Four, her powers of persuasion had proven to be quite useful in the past. She was usually able to pass on information before other levels heard it. Janine enjoyed an audience and innocently twirled a few strands of her long brown hair between her fingers while pausing for effect. She took a deep breath. 'There's a massive meeting being held in Gilchrist's office today. All the security heads are going to be at it. Tom from Level One heard it from Julie, who knows someone who works near Suzanne Brett's office.' Brett was the overseer for Level Five and directly under Gilchrist's command.

A low whisper carried around the room. 'Yeah, I saw Daphne Gilchrist in the lobby this morning, flanked by her minions.'

'That woman puts the frighteners up me,' Chris said.

'All women scare you,' Laura retorted. 'Any of those who have a bit of power that is.'

'Not all women, just the ball breakers. I guarantee every man in the ESC is protecting his manhood as we speak. She has the power to castrate men with her eyes if they look at her for too long.'

'Exaggerate much?' Janine said.

'I speak the truth,' Chris replied innocently. 'Did you know that her voice is so loud during meetings it can shatter unbreakable glass?'

'You are so full of shit.'

The room exploded into peals of laughter. Another person spoke. 'Does anyone know why they're meeting? I can't remember the last time all security heads were in one room.'

'Since when are we ever told about anything in this place?' someone said. 'I barely know what the replicated specials are in the cafeteria let alone important business that might *actually* concern us.'

While everyone guessed what the meeting was about, Laura stayed silent. She didn't remember the last security meeting, guessing it must have been before she started with the ESC. She couldn't shake the feeling that came over her, that something wasn't right.

15

Exilon 5

Bill Taggart gathered his surveillance team in the heart of no man's land, an area of rocky terrain that stretched between New London and the next city on Exilon 5. The sky was a deep blue, speckled with tinges of purple and green. The occasional cloud floated across it, providing little protection for the road maintenance workers spread out across acres of the red and gold-tinted stony landscape. A single road that provided the only access in and out of New London, lent a sense of normality to a seemingly chaotic city. Soon, when funding came through from the government, a dozen similar roads would cut across the surface close to the city to offer a vital transport network between cities.

Bill could hear the animals were close by, probably on the hunt for that easy kill. Resurrected from preserved animal DNA, the animals were housed in special biodomes on the borders of the six cities. Each dome contained a variety of predators, vegetarians and birds alike, living together as natural companions as well as enemies. It was common for the predators to move beyond the biodomes—lions, wolves, coyotes—as they instinctively hunted for a life without boundaries. But their ventures were usually short-lived. The animals would retreat to the safety of the domes where a meal was always guaranteed.

Bill purposefully brought his team to a spot ten miles from New London's city limits. He knew the predators only ventured out a mile, maybe two at most, where food was most likely, and by staying downwind of the biodomes, there was less risk that the animals could pick up their scent. He didn't want to risk bringing the team back to his ITF apartment; with the ITF listening, it would never have been a private affair. What Bill had to say to them was off the record.

There were seven people on the surveillance team, including Bill, and among those were the male and female officers who had disobeyed him— Caldwell and Page. He positioned himself in front of the team, his arms folded tensely across his body. He directed his first question at the duo. 'Tell me what happened after you deliberately disobeyed my direct order not to move in.'

Page, spoke first. 'We did exactly what we needed to do.'

'What the hell does that mean?'

Caldwell interrupted. 'She means there was no danger to the overall mission. We needed to get close to the alien, so we made the call and moved in. It didn't see us, so I'm not really sure what the problem is.'

Bill pinched the bridge of his nose a little too tightly, leaving behind a red mark. 'Are you absolutely positive it didn't see you? How could you tell? It's an alien, which we know very little about. Do you know something about its abilities that we don't?' His eyes scanned the length of the group. Everybody stood at military ease, staring uneasily at a blank point in front of them. Except for Page and Caldwell, no one else dared to make eye contact.

'No, we're not saying that,' Page said. 'What we're saying is that we took a calculated risk before the alien disappeared. Whether it panned out your way or ours, the outcome would have been the same.'

'Would you like to hear what I think?' Bill didn't wait for an answer. 'It seemed pretty obvious to me that the Indigene knew exactly where you were. That was made all the more obvious when you moved in, the same movement that spooked it and sent it hurtling out of the park at breakneck speed. You then decided to chase it and wound up losing track of it. If any of this seems unfamiliar, please feel free to interrupt.'

'We didn't lose it,' Caldwell said. 'We know exactly where it went—into the Victoria underground station. We tracked it all the way.'

It was at times like these that Bill remembered why he preferred to work alone. He looked the stocky military man in the eye. 'But did you catch it?' he asked, slowly emphasising each word.

'No, but—'

'Then ipso facto, you lost it.' He clapped his hands together so loudly it made Officer Page jump.

The rest of the group stayed silent.

'No offence, Bill, but Special Ops was never a right fit for this mission,' Caldwell continued. 'This is pursuit and catch—plain and simple. That's what we're all trained for. We did everything humanly possible to catch our subject. I don't see how you being there could have changed the outcome.'

Bill's eyes widened and his face deepened in colour.

Page tried to defuse the situation. 'Officers

Wilson and Garrett followed the alien as far as the westbound platform, but it had vanished by the time they got there. A follow-up search of the tunnels turned up nothing. We think one possibility is that it may have exited from another station, further down the line.'

Bill's anger temporarily subsided and he rubbed his aching eyes with the heel of his hand. 'So, here we are back at square one—again.' He suddenly craved a hot cup of coffee and a nice piece of pig meat lasagne from his favourite restaurant. But first, there was this small matter to deal with.

'We do have something new,' Page suggested. 'We have the recording device. Audio *and* visual.'

Bill frowned. 'Yes, but apart from a handful of trivial new facts, we still don't know what they are or, more importantly, what they're going to do next.'

'Next?' Page asked.

'Yes! Next, Page,' Bill said, struggling to keep it together. 'Why they are here at all. Why they are killing people.' The chance to question one of the Indigenes had slipped through his fingers.

I've failed you, Isla. In Bill's head, Isla replied, 'It's not your fault, not this time.'

Bill groaned as he thought about the person he'd have to explain the failure of the mission to: Daphne Gilchrist, the CEO of the Earth Security Centre. It had taken years for him to build a decent reputation, but now that reputation looked at risk of coming unstuck. He'd almost guaranteed the World Government and the ESC a result from that day's operation but now he had nothing new to give them— no alien for him or ESC to question. He had assured them the Indigene wouldn't be expecting them at the meeting and, at first, he hadn't thought it was aware

181

of their presence. Upon reflection, he now realised that he was the one who had been played all along.

Around noon, Bill disbanded the meeting and headed to Cantaloupe alone. The smell of home cooked meat always drew him back there, evoking childhood memories of his parents and their monthly Friday family meals. His mother had scrimped and saved each month so she could afford to buy the raw ingredients on the black market. It was the only place people could get them and invariably the most expensive.

He took his usual seat by the window and ordered lunch. Sitting quietly, he rested his head in his hands and thought about the day's events. Today had been the best opportunity for him to find out more about what happened to Isla. Could he have done anything to change the outcome? He no longer doubted that the Indigene had an agenda when it agreed to meet the boy for a second time. Ben Watson had been targeted for a reason, but what was it? Something was pushing the alien's desire to know more. Had its priorities changed?

Bill wondered if the Indigene race's existence had been peaceful before humans had arrived. What if humans had been the catalyst for their change—fuel for their hatred? Historically, many species had suffered at the hands of humans in the pursuit of greater and more powerful outcomes. But that did not give the Indigenes the right to kill humans in retaliation for whatever mistakes the government had made years earlier.

The anger inside him subsided and he felt drained—both emotionally and physically. He was sure that the Indigene would now disappear; it had already taken a massive risk by surfacing during daylight hours. But something else about the alien bothered him. The intel reports were highly inaccurate about them being a sub-intelligent race: the filtration device, the artificial skin and the ability to communicate were all signs of intelligence. Possessing advanced technology like that would surely make the race even harder to track.

Bill tried to imagine what Isla would have done. She had never been one to listen to idle gossip. He reluctantly admitted that she'd have been fascinated by the Indigenes and would have worked hard to understand them. For the first time, Bill thought about Stephen in a different way and wondered what his story was.

Moments later, the waitress arrived with a plate of lasagne, a side order of bread and a strong cup of coffee. His stomach gurgled as he scooped mouthfuls of the lasagne into his waiting mouth. Two minutes later, he was mopping up the remaining tomato juice with his last slice of bread. He sat back in his chair and rubbed his distended belly. When he'd worked directly for the World Government, he was fit and toned, but ITF didn't enforce the fitness rule and since Isla's death, there hadn't been any reason to keep it up. His diet of coffee and fatty meat products didn't help his slowly expanding waistline either. He could feel the heartburn beginning to set in. He sipped on his black coffee and tried to relax.

Sitting into the curve of his chair, Bill silently observed the people of New London on the streets outside. Although the numbers had eased off, the transfer programme to Exilon 5 had progressed as expected. The World Government had done well to ease the residents into their new life. Walking the streets of Exilon 5 without a care, they would never truly appreciate how lucky they were and what they had left on Earth: the poor air, the gel breathing masks, the overcrowding.

Bill caught a glimpse of one of the flashy digital library signs, beckoning people inside with its tacky neon colours. People weren't interested in history, how far space exploration had come or who had discovered Exilon 5. All they cared about was when the rest of the technology would transfer to the planet. Bill understood that the delay in transfer had been as much about keeping it out of the wrong hands as the cost of relocating it.

Many exoplanets had been discovered over the last century and a half, including one called COROT-7b in 2009, which had the same density as Earth, but none of the planets could support human life. When he was a child, his father had told him about the ship designs, how they were improving each year and that soon they would discover a suitable planet. The first of the people-carrying ships had been in operation since 2115, before he was born. They'd designed a hyper drive, invented by a lecturer in Astrophysics in Trinity College Dublin. Professor Tessa Gogarty had also been a propulsion engineer and her contributions had helped to revolutionise space travel. Years later, and just as his father had predicted, Exilon 5 was discovered at the same time the Gogarty Hyper Drive 8.0 was used in the newer ships. The new hyper drive shortened the travel time between Earth and Exilon 5. Currently, the journey only took two weeks.

Bill jumped when his communication device shrilled loudly in his ear. Its unique tone identified it as a call from the Earth Security Centre. With the earpiece firmly lodged, he activated it.

'Bill, is that you?' Daphne Gilchrist rarely dispensed friendly greetings.

'Yes,' he replied. His heart pounded so loud in his chest that he was sure she could hear it.

'Charles Deighton asked that I contact you directly. I'm reading through your preliminary report at the moment. Not looking good, is it?'

There were a small number of patrons in the restaurant. He tried to keep his voice low. 'I know. There were problems with the personnel I was assigned.' He emphasised the word *personnel*. 'They disobeyed a direct order.'

'Not my problem, Bill. This was your operation. You were in charge and you promised results. This is not a result that either Charles or I are interested in,' she said coldly.

Bill couldn't have agreed more. He tried to sound positive. 'The mission wasn't a total write off. We got some extra data on the Indigene that could be worth analysing. I've already sent you a subsection of it. The rest will follow later today.'

'Ah yes, the data. It's being analysed by our team at the Centre as we speak,' Gilchrist said. 'Have the rest of it here in the next hour.'

There was a brief silence. Bill tried to think of something worthwhile to add.

Gilchrist saved him the trouble. 'There does seem to be *some* new information there that may prove useful.' A brief silence followed. 'Still, it's not what we were expecting. I assume the Indigene's whereabouts is still a mystery?'

'My team followed it as far as the track before it disappeared into Victoria's tunnels. We think it exited from another station.'

185

'In your opinion, what are the chances of the alien reappearing any time soon?'

'Slim, I would think. It knows we were watching.' Bill cringed as he thought about the basic things he should have been aware of.

'There's a passenger ship leaving for Earth tomorrow. Be on it. I'll see you at the ESC for a debriefing in two weeks. Out.' Gilchrist severed the connection quickly. Bill was relieved; the less time talking to her, the better.

He blew out a sharp breath and leaned forward, knowing an order to return home meant that he was off the case. The waitress caught his eye and held up a beer bottle. He waved her away and turned to look out the window. The opportunity to track down Isla's killers was slipping through his fingers. He would need to somehow convince Gilchrist to keep him on the investigation so he could continue his search. But with the Indigene gone from sight and unlikely to reappear for some time, returning to Earth was the only option left.

He headed back to his New Westminster apartment and did two things: he prepared the video and audio files to be sent to the Earth Security Centre, and he tossed his meagre possessions into his suitcase. He briefly closed his eyes—even though he'd filled up the tank with food, his mental capacity was now operating on fumes. Today's result had been a massive setback, not only professionally, but personally. He cursed the military officers for the hundredth time that day. It would be a long time before he would trust anyone again.

His head pounded and his eyes drooped, but he was so pissed off that rest wouldn't come. Instead, he placed his suitcase by the door, sat down and reviewed the files carefully over the next hour, in the hope that there might be a clue that he'd overlooked. He found nothing. He fired off the remaining results to the ESC via their encrypted channel.

Deeply agitated by the order to return to Earth, he paced back and forth in his apartment. Going back to Earth and living in the apartment he shared with Isla scared him. He wasn't ready—the memories were too raw. He couldn't relive them, not while she was still out there, unaccounted for.

16

Earth

Daphne Gilchrist paced back and forth at the top of the large meeting room, which adjoined her office on Level Seven. The underground room was built to be impenetrable, as were all the levels in the ESC, except for those numbered one to four where the security was lighter. An oval-shaped walnut table dominated the room. Twelve hand-carved chairs hugged its edge. A circular cream and black rug sat on the oak floor. A solitary painting hung on one wall—a concentric pattern of rings in black and charcoal grey. The image represented the force fields that surrounded the lower offices and was intended to suggest that they were in safe hands.

Sitting around the table were Suzanne Brett, overseer for Level Five, and nine representatives for the various ITF security branches ranging from San Francisco to London to Bangladesh.

'Gentlemen and Lady,' Daphne said looking briefly in Brett's direction. 'What are we going to do?'

They sat in silence around the glossy walnut table as they pondered the question. In their respective ITF branches, each of them was powerful; in Daphne's office, they were just subordinates, something she was quite fond of reminding them. Her father had been a strong, domineering character, ruling his home with an iron fist. She despised her mother for showing weakness in his presence. She'd understood her father's reasons for setting such strict rules: people were unpredictable and needed to be reined in. Daphne always felt his influence had helped her to become the successful businesswoman she was today, while her mother only convinced her that she would never become a doormat.

Wearing a grey trouser suit, Daphne looked younger than her eighty-eight years. Her red hair hung to the nape of her neck and was curled neatly under. She took her seat at the head of the table and tapped a single, clear-polished nail on the table's lacquered surface. Except for the sound of breathing, it was the only noise in the room. To her right sat her male personal assistant. Daphne liked to hire men, enjoying the power she had over the opposite sex. Men were also easier to read. Whenever she glanced in his direction, he tried to look busy. Her assistant was using a DPad to record the meeting details. She didn't like to use the roving cameras because they tended to record too much. With the DPad, she could cut out anything that might show her in a bad light.

'It appears from Bill Taggart's preliminary report that we face a problem. In fact, we're miles away from where we expected to be at this stage in the investigation. What I need are solutions and I need them now.'

Daphne's cold, hard eyes scanned the faces in the room and dared someone to speak first. She insisted on the formality of raising a hand before speaking—it was the Japanese equivalent of bowing and another way for her to assert her position of power. She had worked as CEO of the Earth Security

Centre for the last twenty years. In business life, it was still a man's world, but she had learned to play the game the way the men did. She constantly battled with those who tried to undermine her appointment. If they were waiting for her to slip up, they would be waiting a long time.

Simon Shaw, head of the London ITF office, tentatively raised his hand. She locked her dark blue eyes on his thin face as he cleared his throat.

'I can vouch for Bill Taggart. He's the best investigator to come out of my office. His performance on other missions has been exemplary and I am personally quite confide—'

'I know exactly where he came from,' Daphne interrupted. 'I placed him there myself. Sounds like you're reading out his résumé to me. I don't need you to recite his credentials—it's offensive. So, if that's all you have to say Shaw—'

He continued, slightly rattled. 'No. What I'm trying to say is that we should wait until Taggart gets here for the debriefing. I'm suggesting we hear him out. I'm confident he will find another way forward.'

'I'm sorry Shaw, but we can't live on the faint hope that Mr Taggart will know what to do,' she said. 'That's our job. What happened this morning was no mistake. His team executed his plan as instructed and it failed. Are you so arrogant as to try to convince me otherwise? Where was that ingenious backup plan of his this morning?'

Shaw raised his hand but she ignored it. She had no time for touchy-feely emotions. 'Someone else that is not part of the London office, please.'

He withdrew his hand, clearly angry and mortified.

The representative from the Bangladesh office

raised his next. 'Was there an issue with the military personnel Taggart had been assigned?' he asked. 'I heard there was insubordination among the ranks.'

'Nothing more than usual with those flat heads,' Daphne said. 'I'm looking for suggestions, people.'

The rep from the Tokyo office stood up and bowed respectfully to his host. 'Please, Ms Gilchrist-san. How much does Taggart know about our current situation?'

Apart from Junsuke Sato, Daphne didn't respect any of them. She'd spent a large chunk of her working life in Osaka and had learned how to do business the Japanese way. While she didn't gain the respect as a woman in power there, she still admired their no-nonsense approach to work and traditional views of home life.

'Konnichiwa, Sato-san,' she responded with a brief, but respectful bow. 'Other than the basics, nothing. Shaw, care to elaborate?'

'He still thinks he's on a fact-finding mission. He knows very little about the Indigenes or where they came from. As you instructed, I fed him the false background files.'

'Good. Taggart will be back on Earth in two weeks. We will speak to him then. He's scheduled on the next passenger ship which departs Exilon 5 tomorrow.'

Sato looked concerned as he asked, 'What about his wife? Is that affecting his judgement? What does he know about her?'

'He still thinks the Indigenes killed her and I don't plan on correcting that. Right now, he's more useful to me fighting against them than with them.' She continued to tap her nail on the table, this time, more quickly.

'Is he a risk?' Sato continued.

Daphne shook her head. 'He is manageable. Shaw will see to that.'

'But what if he finds out about her?' Sato pressed her on the issue.

She laughed a little. 'I really don't see how that's possible Sato-san. He doesn't have access to that information and I'm certainly not about to tell him, are you?'

Sato shook his head and sat down.

The Bangladesh rep spoke again. 'What exactly do the Indigenes know about us?'

'Very little, if Taggart's files are anything to go by—although the revelation about what we are must have come as a shock,' she sneered.

'Have the files been processed yet?' the San Francisco rep asked.

'Brett?'

'Not yet,' Suzanne said. 'We're sending them down to our high-level storage facility on Level Five. They will be processed later on this afternoon.'

'Brief me straight away when that's done,' Daphne said.

'I am worried now because we do not know what information the Indigenes have on us,' Sato said. 'Do we at least know what their plans are?'

'No, we don't. I can assure you of this much, we are putting in place proper measures to make sure no harm comes to us. From what I understand, the meeting was innocuous enough—an innocent exchange of words between a man and a child. I don't think they will act on their new findings—at least not straight away. I'm still looking for suggestions from the table.' None were put forward. 'If nobody has anything more to say, we'll have to break up until we've given this situation some more thought. I'm disappointed that we haven't come up with at least one idea.' Daphne moved to stand up.

'On a related matter,' Suzanne said without raising her hand. Daphne sat back down and locked her hard eyes on Suzanne's ice-blue pair. 'We are short of people in Level Five. We've lost two because of illness in the past week and we haven't been able to replace them yet. With the extra work coming our way, we'll need an extra body to pick up the slack.'

'Investigate the pair and if they are lying— well, you know what you have to do; I will not tolerate any security breaches from Level Five,' Daphne said, exhaling sharply and snapping her fingers. 'Who do you have as replacement?'

'I have some options available to me in Document Control and Storage but the specific person I am recommending is Laura O'Halloran,' Suzanne said.

'What can you tell me about her?'

'Three years on the job. No social life outside work. Lives alone. Only child. Has a mother that she doesn't visit. Father is dead. Volunteers for extra shifts when they arise—'

'Sounds like the perfect candidate to manipulate. Inform her of the promotion effective immediately and make her swear to all-out confidentiality. The last thing we need is for the human population to get wind of an alien race occupying their saviour planet. The transfer to Exilon 5 needs to go ahead as planned.'

Suzanne nodded.

'Oh, and for God's sake, make sure her clearance is restricted. I don't want her getting access to Level Eight information unless I give the order. Taggart's files should be clean enough. Need-to-know only. Got it?'

'Understood.'

Daphne exchanged a brief look with Suzanne that the others didn't see.

An hour later, Suzanne burst into Document Control and Storage followed closely by the overseer for Level Four. Work ground to an immediate halt as everyone stopped to look up at the unexpected visitors.

'Carry on with your work,' Suzanne barked.

'Yes, carry on everyone.' The overseer mimicked her order, visibly rattled by her presence.

Laura stared at her screen, trying very hard to look busy and not be distracted by their presence. Instead, her ears honed in on the noises around her as she tried to work out their distance from her workstation. She could hear Suzanne's uniform swishing noisily between her legs. She looked up long enough to see them moving down the centre aisle, destination unknown.

She had only met Suzanne Brett once before, when she started. She hadn't warmed to the woman's chilly desk-side manner, but Laura was smart enough to know who she needed to keep on side if opportunities were to arise. Suzanne's black hair and tight mouth only added to her icy demeanour. The women who occupied the top positions were generally hard asses. Possessing knowledge that others would do anything to get their hands on was a lot for a person to handle. She was aware of how little interaction there was between various ranked ESC staff; the workers in purple uniforms on Level Five pretty much kept to themselves. Laura promised that if she was ever promoted, she would keep in contact with her former colleagues, no matter how much they annoyed her.

She continued to study the screen while her mind wandered. *Why are they here today? Is there something wrong?* She was nervous now as she ran through the possibilities in her mind. When the swishing sounds abated, she tensed up. She cautiously looked up and was surprised to see that her overseer and Suzanne Brett had disappeared from the centre aisle. A finger covertly tapped her on the shoulder and she jumped first, then turned around slowly, flushing with embarrassment at the realisation they were there for her. The room fell silent and Laura couldn't help but notice the relief on her co-workers' faces that it wasn't them they had come for. Suzanne's eyes bored into her while her overseer hovered uneasily in the background.

'Laura O'Halloran?' she asked.

'Yes?' she replied cautiously. Suzanne may not have known her name but her overseer certainly did.

'You are being relocated as a matter of priority. Get your things.'

'What—where?' Laura tried to glean some information from Suzanne's sour expression. Nothing. She glanced at her overseer who simply indicated it was time to go. She stood up and gathered together her meagre possessions. 'Where am I going?'

Silently, Suzanne took the lead and the overseer walked behind Laura as they guided her towards the exit. Panic grew inside her. *Was this good or bad?* She realised she was powerless to do anything other than what they asked.

The curious looks on her colleagues' faces followed her and she caught a word from Janine's lips as she mimicked a call sign. *Later.* No doubt Janine would be talking about her as soon as she left.

When would later even be? She didn't know.

Suzanne led her to the turbo lift and called it. While she and her Level Four overseer waited in silence, Laura struggled to hold her tongue. 'Where are you taking me? Have I done something wrong?'

The lift arrived and Suzanne entered first. Her overseer shoved Laura inside.

'Thanks for your help, Phil,' Suzanne said. 'I'll take it from here.' She placed a hand on the overseer's chest and prevented him from following. As the doors closed, she quickly retracted her arm and left him on the other side. The doors remained open long enough for Laura to see him mouth the word 'bitch'.

'One floor down,' Suzanne said.

At first, Laura thought it was a command for the lift. Then it finally registered with her where she was going—Level Five. Her heart kicked into a higher gear.

'Hold out your right thumb.' Suzanne ordered.

Laura complied wordlessly and Suzanne jabbed her with a sharp instrument. Laura winced, but didn't pull away her thumb. She felt energised, giddy and childlike at the same time; this wasn't a reprimand, it was a promotion. Suzanne Brett was upgrading her security chip.

The lift doors opened. 'That will give you access to Level Five,' Suzanne said coldly. 'But before I can take you there, I need you to do one thing.'

They stepped out into an unremarkable corridor. If it hadn't been for the number five flashing like a beacon in the turbo lift, Laura wouldn't have known what floor she was on; the grey walls and carpet gave no clues. Suzanne ushered her into a small room two doors down from the lift where a seated man waited for her. The unfriendly man wore the familiar purple uniform of the Level Five workers. It was adorned with many accolades but not as many as Suzanne's uniform. Laura could tell he was somebody important in the ESC.

'Please, take a seat.' He pointed to the chair. A musky scent wafted in her direction.

She sat down and looked around her. The door sucked shut. Suzanne remained inside the room, standing in one corner.

The purple-clad man thrust a DPad at her. 'Read this out loud.'

Laura jumped and shakily read the full text of the document.

CONFIDENTIALITY AGREEMENT

You are entering into an area which contains highly sensitive documentation.

You are not permitted to discuss the information you see with anyone.

You must only divulge information to an employee that is of a higher rank than you.

If you do anything that is in direct violation of this agreement, you will be severely reprimanded.

> Place your security chip at the
> bottom of the screen if you comply
> with this agreement.

Briefly, Laura wondered what reprimand they were referring to, but she put aside the negatives and focused on the positives. She decided to ask later about the induction programme, the one designed to ease her into her new role.

In the back of her mind, something nagged at her. This was all happening too fast and it was a little too good to be true; she wasn't scheduled for promotion for another two years and hadn't heard of anyone being fast-tracked.

Then she asked herself if she really cared. She'd heard rumours that the higher levels had a better chance of getting picked from the lottery list for transfer to Exilon 5. Without hesitation, Laura placed her right thumb on the marker and accepted her new role on Level Five.

17

Exilon 5

A low murmur ran around the Gathering Room where the Central Council and representatives for the Indigenes met. The room was located in the southwest section of District Three. Constructed out of omicron rock, its natural sound-insulating properties kept the discussion private.

Pierre and Elise, the Central Council elders, stood on a raised platform alongside Stephen. The room was filled to capacity with fifty representatives. From his elevated position, Stephen noted the concern on the Indigenes' faces as he relayed the information from the child, Ben Watson. The elders held hands to show their solidarity.

Each district had elders that presided over them. Pierre and Elise, both one hundred and twenty years old, were the eldest serving council members among them and in charge of District Three. For the benefit of the representatives in the room, they altered their appearances until they seemed tranquil and in control. But Stephen could tell there was nothing tranquil about their current moods; it was a trick. If the Central Council members fell apart in a crisis, how could they expect others to follow their direction?

Stephen struggled to keep his emotions in

check as his heart raced, aggravated by terror and confusion. As accurately as he could, he relayed the information Ben Watson had told him. When he revealed to the room that the Surface Creatures were human, the atmosphere shifted seismically. Hairline fractures appeared in Pierre and Elise's armour, their worry slipping through on their near-translucent faces.

He looked down at the sea of faces before him, and instantly regretted honing in on his friend, Anton. Anton's eyes had bugged, his mouth agape, Stephen snatched his eyes away and focused on the group as a whole, trying not to single out anyone in particular.

'Please. Everybody needs to calm down,' Pierre urged as the agitation in the room increased tenfold.

Instinctively, Elise leaned in closer to her husband and whispered something to him. Stephen reasoned Elise was probably reading the emotions in the room; she was an empath and it was what she did. Questions soon hit the raised platform.

'What does this mean for us?'

'What are we going to do now?'

'What will happen to us if they discover our districts?'

Pierre fanned his hands. 'Please, we aren't going to help matters by panicking. We will arrive at a solution together, I promise you. Right now, we aren't in any immediate danger and I urge you all to calm down.'

Elise added. 'We have an advantage. They don't know what we are so they won't be looking for us straight away. That gives us time to discuss a strategy.'

'Stephen,' Pierre whispered quietly, 'Elise and I need to speak with you and Anton privately. I will ask Leon to join us.'

Stephen knew what Pierre was going to suggest: for the first time, Central Council would decide without the consensus of the representative group. Vigilantism could be a real threat across the districts if all Indigenes found out about the humans at the same time. Pierre needed to protect them with an undemocratic decision.

Pierre addressed the room again. 'I urge you not to act alone or divulge the information to the others until we've come up with a collective strategy. We need to protect ourselves. Currently, we have the upper hand.' The group agreed. 'I assure you that we will consult all representatives throughout this challenging process.'

A deliberate lie.

Fifteen minutes later, Pierre and Elise gathered in Council Chambers along with Anton, Stephen and Leon. The rectangular room was large and contained a bookcase filled with Indigene and human literature that divided the room in half. Behind the bookcase was a bed that Pierre sometimes used when he was working late. Stephen stood motionless beside Elise, while Anton paced anxiously across the room. Leon, a long-time friend of the elders and Anton's father, projected an image of calm similar to his peers and stood with his hands interlocked behind his back.

They discussed the other information that Stephen had purposefully held back from the representatives.

'What do they call it?' Leon asked him.

'Earth.'

'And this is the human's home planet, where

they originate from?'

'As I understand it,' Stephen said.

'And why have they come here to destroy us?'

'I'm sorry, Leon, I don't know that much. The child was helpful but equally naïve about the way of the world.'

'We shouldn't make any hasty decisions today,' Pierre said. 'We need to understand their motives. It may be our only defence to learn as much as we can about them before they discover what we are.'

'Well, where better to learn about them than their home planet? I say we go now,' Anton said eagerly.

'Easy, Anton,' Elise soothed and placed a gentle hand on his arm. She looked into his eyes. 'We'll probably need to discuss this a little more.' When Anton met her gaze, he instantly relaxed.

'Anton might have a point though,' Pierre said. 'Other than what we know already, we have no clue about what the humans are up to. We know that they were watching Stephen and the child. They're already familiar with our physiology and how it differs from theirs. This latest meeting will only feed their curiosity.'

'I'm curious to know why they are watching at all,' Leon said. 'Apart from Anton, we can all remember the day when the explosions happened. We know that their species can't be trusted.'

Yes, Stephen remembered watching the explosions with his parents from the safety of the tunnels, as they destroyed two-thirds of the Indigenes that were on the surface that day. 'I have the strongest reason to hate them,' Stephen said. 'I wish I could say for certain that they are all the same—it would be easier to believe that—but something nags at me to think otherwise.'

Pierre's eyes brightened. 'What do you mean?'

'I couldn't sense any malice from the child, only curiosity. But then there's the other thing—that they kill innocents so easily.'

'Stephen, your senses rarely let you down. Why not trust them?' Pierre suggested.

Stephen picked up a particular tone in the elder's words, almost as if he was willing him to go with his gut instinct. 'Why are you so eager to push me towards accepting them?'

'I'm not asking or telling you to do that, only that there may be other reasons behind their actions that we haven't yet considered.'

Curious now, he held his elder's gaze. 'Like what?'

Pierre gave nothing away in his appearance but rushed his explanation. 'Nothing specific—let's consider all options. How would you feel about going to Earth to find out more about them?'

Stephen let the matter drop for now. 'It can only help. We need the upper hand if we are to decide how we will move forward.'

At hearing the news, Anton smiled and paced the room again.

Elise looked uneasy. 'I don't have a good feeling about this. It's too dangerous.'

'I'm sorry, wife, but I tend to agree with Stephen. We have to be proactive,' Pierre said. 'It feels as if we're being backed into a corner. The Indigenes that the humans call Shadow People are dangerous and uncontrollable. If we do nothing, who knows what they'll do next? We are no longer safe. Stephen and Anton must go.'

'You want to risk the lives of our best two?' Elise argued.

'It's because they are the best that I'm considering this. It *will* work.'

'I agree with Pierre. We don't have a choice.' Leon gripped Anton's shoulder tightly. 'Stephen, Anton, are you up to the task?'

Stephen glanced at his grinning friend and nodded. 'Yes, I think so.'

'A passenger ship is scheduled to leave orbit tomorrow. Presumably, it's destined for their home planet,' Pierre said.

Elise persisted. 'At least send a backup group with them, Pierre.' She turned to Leon. 'This is madness allowing them to go alone. They won't be able to protect each other if anything happens.'

Pierre shook his head. 'I understand your concerns but if we send too many, they'll be noticed.'

Leon spoke to Anton telepathically. Anton responded with a nod. 'They'll be fine, Elise. They know how to look after themselves.'

'How can you let your only son go so easily?' Elise said.

'It's what Amelia would have wanted. We raised our son to think for himself.'

Pierre turned to Stephen and Anton. 'What do you two think?'

Stephen agreed. 'It will be safer if we do this alone. There will be less chance of them noticing us. If they do detect us, they might think it's a solo mission rather than an organised attack on humans.'

'Anton?'

'I say we give these humans something to think about.'

'This shouldn't be seen as an aggressive

mission,' Pierre said. 'You are going there to add to the information we already know about their species. Most importantly, you will be depending on each other for survival, so rational thinking is called for. Is that clear?'

Anton reluctantly nodded.

Stephen observed Anton closely—there were many intelligent Indigenes but none with his friend's ability to create and adapt technology. He was by far the youngest of their technological protégés and many of their kind publicly acknowledged his talents. He had invented the air filtration device, which changed the way their race hunted. Anton buzzed with enthusiasm; the difficulty lay in curbing it. But in a life or death situation such as this, there was no other Indigene that he wanted watching his back.

Pierre flipped his attention to the finer details of the trip. 'Anton, give us an update on how you're progressing.'

Anton's demeanour brightened; one thing he enjoyed talking about was his inventions. When he launched into full explanation mode, he was difficult to interrupt. 'Well, thanks to Stephen's first expedition last week, I was able to improve the artificial skin's pigmentation. We should be able to blend in better now. I've updated and improved the existing air filtration device. It will now work for two full days without the need for power. I've devised mobile recharging units that we can carry. It should give us an indefinite clean air supply.'

'What about getting on the ship? Won't the fact that you don't carry identity chips be enough to trigger a warning?' Leon asked.

Anton smiled cheekily at his father. 'That's where I've devised the perfect solution. On a recent trip to the surface, I asked one of the mission groups to bring back several identity chips if they could do so without getting caught. They also brought back a security chip from a worker whose thumb had been accidentally cut off.'

Pierre and Elise's mouths hung open in horror. 'They didn't?'

'Don't worry, he was dead at the time—died in an unrelated accident. Anyway, they won't be able to pin it on us. There's a black market for this kind of technology. The humans will blame the scavengers long before we're ever suspected of the crime.'

Pierre shook his head. 'Continue, Anton.'

'I have designed a security chip that should be a decent enough replacement. I've temporarily re-routed the tracking device that was embedded in the one we borrowed. They are sophisticated designs and it won't be long before the chip figures out what I've done and will try to repair itself. If it manages that, it's wired to communicate with a central unit before it destroys itself. Presumably, they will try to find the chip so they can arrest the human responsible for tampering with it. Just so you know, I disconnected it half an hour ago, so I've just an hour to update you. Then we need to get the real chip as far away from here as possible.'

'No pressure then,' Leon said.

'None at all.' Anton smiled. 'We have the fastest runner among us.'

'Well, you'd better hurry then,' Stephen said. 'It seems as if I've something urgent to attend to directly after this.'

'Anton, why do you also need the identity chips?' Elise asked. 'Won't the security one be enough?'

'Both chips are present in human bodies. Depending on their age or skill level, they may have one or both activated. We know they definitely scan both when humans leave the planet. The computer checks that they're still compatible and that they haven't been tampered with. I designed a generic identity chip that the mission group used to replace the ones they took. In theory, the workers they removed them from shouldn't notice anything is wrong, unless they try to leave the planet.'

'Is that a likely occurrence?' Leon asked.

'Unfortunately anything is possible, Father. I hope to have gone and returned home before they discover any of that. It's a risk we have to take.'

'I agree,' Stephen said.

'I plan to insert the identity chips in our left thumbs. The security chips that I've designed should fool the system as long as the other chip is an original. Stephen will be known as Colin Stipple, an underground station operations manager, and I will be Bob Harris, road maintenance worker. That's the information that came back when I scanned the originals into our systems—that's what the logs will refer to us as when we attempt to board.'

'I'm proud of you, Anton,' Leon said, smiling.

'Well, it wasn't all me. I had a little help.' Anton was referring to his team of scientists.

'Please try not to get killed out there,' Elise said. She looked sombre.

'That isn't part of the plan,' Stephen reassured her.

Pierre placed a gentle hand on his wife's shoulder. 'When does the ship leave for Earth?'

'Tomorrow at noon,' Stephen said. 'That will also be the hottest time of the day. It's going to get uncomfortable and dangerous. We'll need to keep our bodies fully covered and that's bound to attract unwanted attention.'

'Don't worry about the temperature,' Anton said. 'I have cooling packs that we can wear inside the coat. We should be fine until we get on board. Oh, I forgot to mention, we are going to have to inject our food directly into our stomachs. We won't be able to eat normally with our filtration devices permanently in place. I've modified the synthesised protein packs, so there should be minimal side effects.'

Stephen grimaced. 'Sounds—challenging.'

'Well, for all our sakes, you two had better be safe,' Leon said, before adding, 'There's just one small problem. What are we going to tell the representatives?'

'Nothing, for now,' Pierre said. 'The less they know about what we're up to the better.'

'In the meantime'—Anton removed the security chip from his pocket and dropped it into Stephen's hand—'Get rid of this, will you?'

18

Tired, thirsty and anxious about the trip home, Bill Taggart ran a hand over the stubble on his face, which would soon be classified as a beard. He would have plenty of time to clean up on the two-week trip home to Earth, just in time for his debriefing with Gilchrist. Today wasn't about personal grooming. He left his ITF apartment in New Westminster for what he expected would be the last time. At street level, an automated military vehicle waited to take him to the nearest docking station, located fifteen miles outside New London's border.

The vehicle travelled quickly through the city and he tried to commit to memory the feel of the place—not just the city and Cantaloupe restaurant, but the entire planet. He watched people stumbling out of bars and on the street—feeling happier after a drink, he imagined. The strong sun cast the shadows of Sunday strollers as they sauntered along with rolled up sleeves and smiles on their faces. City parks were full to the brim with squealing children while chatty parents carried picnic baskets. He rolled down the window and dangled his left arm out, feeling the glorious build up of heat on his skin. Just then he realised how much the city calmed him, even though it was where the Indigenes also lived. Isla's death was also easier to cope with when he felt calm. He dreaded returning to Earth—a year was a long time to be away.

The vehicle pulled up close to the docking station a few miles outside of the city. Bill stayed inside the cabin as he checked out his surroundings. Set in the flatlands, the station was sparsely designed in comparison to the cutting-edge style of the ones on Earth. A large prefabricated cabin served as the main building where passengers walked through to get to the spacecrafts docked on the other side. White tarpaulin hung precariously outside the main doors, shielding the sun from sensitive eyes. The passenger ship waited in orbit for the travellers to arrive.

Exilon 5's docking stations had such a temporary feel to them that Bill wondered how much priority the World Government was giving the current transfer programme; they were well behind on their quotas. The new lottery arrangement had increased the transfer numbers, but planning and developments on Exilon 5 were slow. Twenty billion people remained a wildly ambitious target.

He stepped out of the vehicle and was faced with three queue options; the layout had changed since he'd last been there. One was marked 'Detainees', which didn't describe him—he was leaving a free man, even though he didn't always feel like one. Officers armed with deadly Buzz Guns hovered close by. The second line was for 'Workers', many of whom appeared to be engineers and labourers returning to Earth for work reassignment. The last line, labelled 'Other', provided no clue about who fitted this category.

His previous feelings of calm faded into the background. Fuelled now by little sleep and a short fuse, he tried the worker's line. Unapologetically, he elbowed his way to the front, ahead of the hundreds that waited. Tempers flared and comments flew in all directions around him. His failures the day before were playing on his mind and he was distracted enough for their annoyance not to bother him.

A young officer stood on guard at the head of the queue. He moved to block Bill's path.

'Hang on a minute! Where do you think you're going?' the officer said, holding his arm out. 'Can't you see there's a queue behind you?'

Bill skidded to a halt and reached inside his shirt pocket. He pulled out his credentials and held them within inches of the young man's face. 'I am a high-level employee of the World Government.' Nodding towards the waiting craft he said, 'I'm scheduled to travel today on the passenger ship.'

'Well, there's still a queue, you know,' the officer said uneasily. 'I have to process all these people first. They've been here for at least a couple of hours.' His confidence shrank with every word.

'Tell me your name,' Bill said, struggling to control the frustration and anger that seethed inside.

'Um, Officer Ridge.'

'Well, ummm Officer Ridge, I *know* there's a queue,' he said hotly. 'But I'm on official business, you see. I have to get on board that craft, and you're going to let me pass by now. Unless, of course, you would prefer to speak to Deighton about this?'

An eerie silence descended behind him as people craned their necks and stood on tip toes to catch a glimpse of the action. Expecting the young officer to reprimand him for his behaviour, Bill took a discreet step backwards. Although he didn't look like he had it in him, he could still report him.

But the officer struggled to find his earlier composure. 'That won't be necessary,' he said, fumbling with his DPad.

Bill wasn't surprised. The crowd behind him was audibly disappointed.

The officer tugged nervously on the collar of his uniform as he ran his finger down the passenger manifest. A few moments later, he turned the clipboard around to face Bill. 'Place both thumbs here,' he said. A bead of sweat trickled down his neck. Bill heard sniggering behind him.

His name and clearance flashed up on the screen. 'Investigator William Taggart, International Task Force,' the officer read out loud. 'Ah yes. I'm afraid it seems you're in the wrong queue.' He looked relieved, a little smug even. 'You need to be in the 'Other' queue, over there.' He pointed to a large white tent, where just ten people waited, and promptly turned his back on Bill.

Stephen and Anton stood in the queue, quietly observing the people around them. Stephen stood rigidly, eager to avoid coming into contact with any of the humans.

A stout man in front talked loudly to the tall man beside him.

'Definitely could have stayed for a lot longer. Going home again is shit,' the stout man said.

'Yeah, I know what you mean,' the tall man replied. 'Guaranteed sunshine during daylight hours—the ability to breathe without wearing those stupid masks? Remind me why we're going back there?'

'If we don't, the gov'ment will track us down anyway and we'll never be able to return here. Let's not give them any reason to leave us behind—'

Stephen watched curiously as a man charged up

the outside of the queue, knocking the stout man's arm as he passed. The officer ahead stopped him. Anton became agitated.

The stout man grumbled. 'What the hell? Did you see that? He just pushed right past me shoulder. Someone thinks he's more important than the rest of us. Never in my life have I got such a rough shove in a queue.'

An argument unfolded between the officer and the queue-cutting man. Stephen and Anton listened closely.

His annoyance slipping away, the stout man let go of his arm. 'Oh, forget what I just said. Looks like there's a fight about to happen.' He tried to make himself taller. 'What's he saying now, man? I can't hear 'em all the way up there. Crap, I wish we was closer so we could throw a proper ear on them.'

Even his taller friend struggled to catch anything meaningful. He stood on his toes to get a better view, relying on the mumblings ahead of him to piece the conversation together. Anton helped him out. 'The man is telling the officer that he's not going to queue and he wants to pass now.' Stephen shot Anton an angry look.

'Sorry, they were annoying me,' Anton replied.

The stout man turned around. 'Er, thanks.' He gawked at Anton's appearance.

His tall friend craned his neck towards the front. 'Looks like the kid's about to crap himself.'

The stout man forgot about Anton and shot his head around.

'Ah, it's all over. The kid backed down already.'

'Without a fight? What a baby.' The stout man clucked his tongue and looked curiously at Anton again.

Stephen elbowed him.

'I couldn't stop myself,' Anton said. His agitation increased.

Stephen noticed it. 'What?'

'I think I recognise him,' Anton said in a low whisper. He was pointing at Bill Taggart. 'From the restaurant. He was the one sitting at the table by the window when I was recording those scenes for you. He looked directly at me a couple of times.'

'Do you think he might recognise you now?' Stephen asked.

'No, he didn't pay me much attention—seemed distracted by something. I don't think he would remember me from just one sighting. Do you think he could be involved in the surveillance on us?'

'I'm sure of it. He was sitting in a café last week, the one located across from the bus stop.'

Remaining perfectly still, Stephen and Anton committed to memory the name Investigator William Taggart, as the wind carried the words to their ears.

Bill boarded the craft that held just twenty other World Government employees. The fact that he didn't recognise any of them did not surprise him; his job didn't allow him much freedom to get to know others. He moved towards an available seat and pulled the restraints tight across his body, remembering how rough the last journey had been. The trip took less than ten minutes to reach the outer perimeter shield.

Orbiting fifty miles above the planet's shield was the passenger ship. Bill recalled a story he'd read about how the ship's designer had struggled to get engineers to take his design seriously. But when a prototype was built, its practicality outweighed any previous modern ships in operation. The ship was a mile high from base to tip and two miles long; a tubular core ran through its entire length. The front section was rounded like the early rocket ships. Circumnavigating the core was a trio of wheel-like structures, attached via interconnecting tubes or 'spokes'. The 'wheels' housed sleeping pods, while the tubular core allowed the ship's crew to run the ship without coming into contact with the passengers. It carried an electrical charge and did not need propellants to navigate it. But a standard amount of fuel was carried on board all the ships for when it was ever needed. Powered by a Faster Than Light drive, the ship used the slipstream between planets and harnessed the planets' natural magnetic fields to navigate a path home. The fields exerted a force against the ship's electrically charged exterior to keep it on course. Solar wind power enhanced its top surfing speed. Paying homage to the much-loved bicycle, it was listed as a functional yet quirky looking ship, developed by an even quirkier designer with a passion for all things round. The World Government continually challenged their engineers to improve on the journey time of two weeks. Bill read somewhere that they'd already developed a prototype FTL drive that could do just that.

The craft docked successfully inside the main hold of the ship. Bill disembarked and waited in line for further instructions. The longer he stood there, the harder it was to stay awake; his energy levels were at an all-time low, as though he'd just run a virtual marathon. He wanted two things: an easy registration process, and a place where he could lie for as long as he needed.

There were two sleeping options on board: Dormant or Active. Actives were housed in sleeping quarters in the rim of one of the wheel-like structures. Dormants were placed in suspended stasis in sleeping pods for the entire trip. Located in a separate wheel, their vitals were continually monitored throughout the entire journey, and an hour before arrival, they were revived with an anti-stasis serum containing a large dose of multivitamins and a barely legal dose of Actigen.

A female officer waited up ahead as the high-level officials formed an orderly queue. She hummed a tune as she ran a finger down a list. 'Not too many on board, I see. We are already off to a good start.' She smiled at the waiting group. Her gentle face and warm eyes won over the all-male group. 'Looks like I got the easy list. I'm assuming everybody has been on board this type of ship before?'

They nodded.

'Good. But I'm going to need to run through everything once more. Protocol.' Glancing up briefly from her DPad, she launched into the rules and regulations from memory.

'The journey takes two weeks. There are two accommodation options available to you. Option one: you can stay in normal mode, during which you will be provided with sleeping quarters and have access to a fully stocked kitchen. You will be charged for your stay and board. Option two: you can avail of one of our sleeping pods. You will be fully sedated and sleep suspended until you arrive at your destination. You will not need sustenance during your animated suspension, but you will be administered with a nutrient pack upon revival. The cost of option two is cheaper than option one, of course. All expenses will be recorded on your identity chip and the information stored at the World Government headquarters until payment has been recouped. Is everyone clear?' The group nodded again. 'Now, I need you to line up on the left-hand side, and when you reach me, please state your accommodation requirements.'

Bill kept his eyes on her as he moved forward, inching closer one body at a time. 'Option one— sleeping quarters,' he said when it was his turn. He placed his thumb on the DPad.

The way the registration officer smiled at him sent an unexpected burst of warmth rippling through him. He clutched at his chest, feeling guilty. In that moment, Isla spoke to him. 'I might have to keep my eye on her. Looks like I'm not the only one vying for your attention.' Bill grimaced at her words—nobody would ever replace his wife, but he had no more energy to think about it.

The officer's brow creased suddenly. 'Are you all right?' She placed a hand on his arm.

Bill didn't move it away. 'Yes, I'm fine. Just a little heartburn, that's all.' His eyes shifted nervously as the lies spilled from his lips. He noticed she was very attractive.

The officer narrowed her eyes at first, then her face softened with understanding and she smiled again. She removed her hand and gestured for him to pass.

A small crease formed on his lips. He kept his eyes focused on the ground in front of him as he walked past her, embarrassed for feeling like a schoolboy with a crush.

Bill arrived at the sleeping quarters he'd been assigned and noted the dozen individually sized units that ran along the wall. He punched in a code for one of them, climbed in, closed over the side flap and locked it, happy he'd chosen to stay awake for the journey to Earth. While he hated travelling any distance, he didn't relish the idea of being under for two solid weeks. Besides, he needed to consider what he would say at the ESC debriefing. Without the files, he'd have to prepare his argument from memory; all his files were with the Security Centre. The only things he had in his possession were his clothes, some personal items and his recollection of yesterday's events.

He tried not to think about where his career might go next but he couldn't. Would he be fired? That was a strong possibility. Would he be reassigned? An even stronger likelihood. What he needed to do was get back on track and continue in his search for the truth.

These and other thoughts turned around in his mind as his head edged closer to the pillow. As soon as it hit the soft cushion, his eyes drooped as if weights hung from each lid.

19

Earth

The previous morning at home, Laura had made an overdue call to her mother. It was four years since her father had taken his life and she knew Fionnuala would be in an even worse mood than usual. While depression ran in the O'Halloran side of the family, her mother had no such excuse and should have emerged from her grief by now.

After years of hating him, Laura had only recently forgiven her father for killing himself. It was so different to the way her paternal great-grandfather had died, even though he had battled with the same problems. When her father's death received coverage from the local news, Fionnuala had been mortified by the sudden interest in her family. While her mother liked to get attention, it was the wrong kind. Laura still endured her emotional outbursts about the press intrusion that day.

She remembered how she'd found Fionnuala at home, huddled in a corner of the living room, while her father's body hung in a noose. Laura had tried everything to revive him. Fionnuala was no help; she'd always been useless in a crisis. While she'd always known her efforts were in vain, she struggled to forgive her mother's inaction that day. A deep rift had quickly set in between them. If she was to learn anything from her father's death, it was that she wouldn't become another statistic on the World Government's books. She would stay until the end, just like her great-grandfather had.

During the video call the day before, Laura found it hard to maintain eye contact with Fionnuala and barely listened to her latest ramblings. Fionnuala didn't need to work—she lived comfortably off the proceeds of her husband's termination-friendly insurance policy. More recently, she had begun to notice an increase in her mother's addiction to the Light Box. Yesterday, she'd detected a slight incoherence in her voice that suggested she was tipsy. Her mother's self-pity was nauseating and childish. Laura reckoned she had always known about her mother's dependency issues. If she was being honest, Fionnuala didn't really need her help—she just wanted someone to complain to.

Her mother's remarks had the ability to cut deep. After one of her dark periods, where she would blame the O'Halloran bloodline for her husband's depression, she would remember to apologise a few days later for the things she had said. It had been a year since Laura last visited her in person. She briefly considered telling her mother about the lottery update and her new promotion to Level Five, but felt it wasn't the right time. Fionnuala wouldn't have been happy about a 'bothersome' move to another planet. In the end, Laura would probably have to force her to go to Exilon 5.

Following her meeting with the unfriendly man the day before, Suzanne had escorted her to the door of Level Five. 'You can't speak to anyone about the work you do here. Do you understand?' She had gripped her arm just a little too tightly. 'You'll be given access to extremely sensitive information and your work will be monitored twenty-four/seven while you're at the Centre. Understand?'

Laura nodded but had been more interested in what lay beyond the door. When they'd finally entered Level Five—a place she'd previously believed did not exist—she was disappointed. The only real difference between Level Four and Five was the size of the room, with just twenty-four isolation booths facing towards the centre aisle. Twenty-two of them were occupied. Suzanne had marched her down the aisle and deposited her at a vacant booth. Nobody moved or spoke to her. She was instantly reminded of the robots that supervised the cleaners at the bullet train stations.

'You can take this one. Someone will contact you shortly. For now, just sit here quietly.' Those had been Suzanne's last words before she marched out the door like her backside was on fire. Unsure of her role, Laura sat still like her co-workers. A few hours later, she received orders to go home and rest, which she dutifully accepted; she had worked without a proper break for two weeks.

The following day, she arrived into work partially refreshed and very excited. She'd been told that it would be all hands on deck. Important information was on its way to the High Level Document Storage Facility. She sat in her booth and stared at her monitor, expecting it to spring into life. Two hours later, it still remained blank and she felt cabin fever begin to set in.

Pushing aside her boredom, Laura tried to muster up excitement about her new promotion—there was nothing better than the congratulatory high-fives from others to confirm she was doing the right thing. Chris and Janine, her old colleagues, popped into her head. Janine would be hungry to hear some gossip about Level Five, but she'd have to be selective about what she told her; she didn't need half the organisation finding out and it being traced back to her big mouth. Suzanne Brett's chilling warning the day before reminded her to proceed carefully. She wondered how happy her former colleagues would be for her.

Sitting in her booth, Laura scanned the lacklustre surroundings of Level Five. Beyond the twenty-four booths, there was a water station, a bulletin board that displayed a different motivational quote each day, and a vacuum tube with a direct link to Gilchrist's office. Today, the bulletin board read: 'We are the sum of our counterparts.' Cryptic and utterly irrelevant, she thought. How about: 'Laura, your work station will spring into life in t-minus eight minutes.' The place lacked personality. Maybe she'd been naïve to expect that the lower levels would be given the same aesthetic attention as Gilchrist's office had.

She wondered again whether it was a good idea to talk to Chris and Janine. She understood the rules the unfriendly man had given her but she wasn't sure if that included scheduled breaks, when she was technically off the clock. Now that she wore the purple uniform, she knew others would view her differently.

Her co-workers' disinterest in her since her arrival was the same. On some level, she could understand that; she was a stranger among them. She rose to her feet, feeling the insular vibe in the room—and not for the first time. On Level Four, there had always been time for a quick chat. On Level Five, it was as if the isolation booths were designed to keep people in as well as out.

Laura decided it would be up to her to make the first move. She walked along the centre aisle and stopped at booth one.

'Hi, I'm Laura,' she said breezily and thrust her hand out to the woman. The woman ignored it. Laura shrugged and moved on. She went to the next booth and rattled out the same line. The response didn't change. She worked through six more people with none showing any interest in chatting with her. She decided to quit and walked back to her booth.

A voice boomed from behind as she moved away. 'Hey you, new girl.'

Laura spun on her heels just as the man from booth ten stood up. He motioned for her to return. She complied, wary of his serious expression. 'Since you are *clearly* unfamiliar with the way this place operates, I'm going to enlighten you a little. Pay attention.'

A little rude, she thought. She glanced around to see if anyone else was listening, but the other workers showed no interest in their conversation. She made eye contact with the beady-eyed, black-haired man, even though it made her uncomfortable to do so.

'Don't bother speaking to or getting to know anyone here.' He pointed a finger at her. 'Nobody is interested in you or your story. Have you been briefed yet?'

Laura nodded.

He stopped pointing at her. 'Well then, you should know that they are as serious as shit when it comes to this place. You *will* be monitored like they said, and if you have to take breaks, for God's sake make sure they're sanctioned ones. This isn't like the holiday you've been having on Level Four,' he sneered.

Laura really wanted to walk away but she was afraid to move.

He continued. 'The information we receive within these four walls is extremely confidential and highly sensitive. What we retain up here'—he tapped the side of his head—'can get you killed in an instant. Remember that and learn who your enemies are, because you're already in a room with twenty-two of them.'

An uncontrollable gasp escaped from her lips. The fact that nobody else was laughing convinced her she should take the threat seriously.

'Right now, you're wondering who the hell I am. Well, I'm just like you. I came from another floor some time ago, but I've learned to survive here and you will have to do the same. When you stepped through that door, you became one of us, so learn the rules fast.'

Laura opened and closed her mouth like a floundering fish, trying to think of something to say. All she could think of was: 'What rules? Are there more I should know about?'

'You are not my problem. Figure that out for yourself. But know this—they're always watching. Now, I suggest you go back to your booth and wait until they send your work programme to your monitor.' The man broke off his intense stare and sat down. In an instant, his face softened and he resumed his duties, as if the conversation had never happened.

She walked quickly but unsteadily back to her booth and sat in her chair, her heart thumping wildly; the man's words had left her shaken to the core. She hadn't taken Suzanne too seriously the day before because she was always aggressive towards others. Now she decided the advice from her new 'frenemy' in booth ten wasn't to be ignored. According to him, they were always watching. So, who was watching her now?

'What on earth is she doing? Is she trying to get to know them?' Daphne said. 'Does she still think she's in Document Control? I thought you warned her off. I can't afford any insubordination at this level, Brett.'

'Don't worry,' Suzanne assured her. 'I briefed Chuck beforehand. He is going to drive the message home for us. Watch this.'

Both women watched, quietly amused as the man from booth ten delivered his fine-tuned and well-rehearsed speech. Daphne smirked as a visibly shaken Laura O'Halloran walked unsteadily back to her desk.

'That ought to keep her in line,' Suzanne grinned. 'Chuck is a seasoned pro. Pulled that same line with the others. They haven't stepped out of line since.'

'Can we trust her?' Daphne asked flatly, ignoring her subordinate's attempt at humour.

'After that, she'll be afraid to use the facilities without asking permission from you first.'

'Good. As soon as you have them ready, give her Taggart's files for processing.'

'Are you sure?' Suzanne said warily. 'She has no experience at this level. We have twenty-two other operators at your command, all with ample experience.'

'It's exactly for that reason that she's getting them. If anything should go wrong, she'll be easier to control.'

After another painful hour of nothing to do, Laura felt the uneasiness creep into her mindset. Her stomach growled, which only added to her woes. Any more time spent thinking about the creepy little man and she might have to take an unsanctioned break. She was beginning to understand why no one talked to the workers from Level Five. She suddenly craved companionship outside the immediate vicinity. Not a moment too soon her monitor sprung into life. She exhaled deeply. *Finally.*

Her excitement rose again and she duly put aside her reservations about the workers in the Abyss. She watched as the first page of instructions fed through to her monitor. She read silently as each sentence appeared:

> Worker. Welcome to the High Level Data Storage Facility.
>
> The information that is stored here is extremely confidential. When the high-level files are decrypted upon arrival at the Security Centre, the outward tagging system, that is the tag that indicates the level of security on the file, is stripped.
>
> This is done to prevent the computer from automatically storing the file in the central database, which requires twenty-four hours notice for retrieval. It is an automatic security measure for all files with clearance levels of Five and above.

The Level Five and higher files sent to this location need to be investigated by the Data Analysis Unit on Level Six, before they are sent for storage to the central database. Therefore, all files of this nature must be accessible at any time, day or night.

All workers in this facility are required to process each file when it is received. Files are then manually stored in a maximum security, but fully accessible, database within the Analysis Unit on Level Six.

You are required to process each file as it comes into the waiting area. The security level is printed in the file. You must re-tag each one before a new encryption code is embedded. If you receive Level Eight files by mistake, they should be redirected to booth sixteen immediately. Alternatively, please create a blind copy of the information using one of the spare discs and deposit it into the vacuum tube on the wall.

Due to the sensitive nature of these files, you are not permitted to discuss the contents with anyone. Please place your right thumb at the bottom of the screen before continuing.

Laura blinked furiously. *Is this a joke?* A separate message flashed up asking for confirmation before she could continue. She shook her head and complied wordlessly. The screen flipped over to a pooled list of waiting files.

She couldn't quite believe it; the only difference between this job and her previous role was the security level tagging and re-encryption of the files. Otherwise it was the same old filing job. She tried to remember the bigger picture: the move to Exilon 5. She wondered how long she'd have to do the same crappy work before that would happen. The thought depressed her enough that she considered taking another vitamin D shot.

She stared at the list and watched as some of the files disappeared from view. Booth numbers flashed up beside random files, as they were processed: sixteen, nine, eighteen. It was at that point when she realised that the mysteriousness of the Abyss didn't exist. The unfriendly workers probably had good reason for being that way.

A thought suddenly depressed her: she could wind up doing the same job for the next five to ten years. She hadn't given much thought to how long the others had been here, but now it was all she could think about. For a fleeting moment she felt sorry for them until she realised she was one of them.

Rational thinking took over. Don't they have computers for this stuff? Can't they just write a programme that would do this job? Or is it that they don't trust technology and human intervention is the only way to make sure the files are stored correctly? If anything went wrong, they could blame the human operator. Far easier to prosecute a human than a tin can, she thought cynically.

Suddenly Level Four didn't seem so bad. Briefly, Laura considered a transfer back to Document Control and Storage, but she guessed that was no longer an option since they had her locked in through contractual agreements. Brushing her negative thoughts aside, she willed herself to open the first file that hadn't already been claimed by another booth. She felt the tears coming. *Give it a chance, Laura. You haven't even started and already you're quitting.*

She discreetly wiped a tear from the corner of her eye and looked at the document. It was a memo from the World Government to Head of Operations, Suzanne Brett, about a staff member at the Centre. It read:

> Dear Ms Brett,
>
> It has come to our attention that a member of your staff has leaked confidential information to a person or persons outside the Centre about the status of various bank accounts and their details. I can only assume it is so they can get access to the funds. This matter was brought to our attention by our insider, who had been offered the information in return for stolen goods. We are happy to let you deal with this staff member.
> However, if we find that storage-bound information is leaked in the future, we will have no choice but to intervene.
>
> Sincerely,
> Tom Billings

Overseer for Security Matters
World Government

She noted the clearance level at the top of the document was Five and closed the file. She then tagged it and ran it through the re-encryption programme that had been placed as a shortcut on her monitor. All the files that came into Level Five seemed to have the clearance embedded somewhere in the document, which meant she was forced to search for it. Speed reading was a skill she had honed over the years. At least she could put one of her skills to good use.

She picked another random document simply marked as confidential. In fact, most of the documents had no title—for security reasons, she imagined. It would take hours for her to go through everything, the same tired routine each time. She opened the unclaimed document. It was another memo from the World Government to Suzanne Brett, this time about security chip clearance.

> Dear Ms Brett,
> It has come to our attention that a number of workers have attempted to access certain security areas within the Centre without correct authorisation. Our monitoring team at the World Government flagged up their security chips. You have twenty-four hours to fix the problem or suspend the workers involved.
> If you do not comply, we will have no option but to intervene.

Sincerely,
Tom Billings

Overseer for Security Matters
World Government

She noted it was marked with that day's date and had been sent within the last ten minutes. She wondered who the workers were. Okay, don't piss off the World Government, she thought. She tagged it as Level Five and ran it through the re-encryption file, same as the last one. She checked the clock for the hundredth time that day and wished she could be somewhere else.

20

Bill Taggart wandered the passenger ship's empty corridor, calling out in the vain hope that someone might hear him. Nobody answered his calls. An eerie silence filled the ship, just as a bout of uneasiness caused the hairs on his arms to stand up. Where the hell was everyone? He forced one foot in front of the other, moving silently along the dark tube-shaped passageway.

Overhead lights illuminated each of his steps as if the ship knew where he was going. He wasn't even sure himself. A strong urge to connect with someone drove him on. Could he really be the only one on board? He didn't trust anyone else; he couldn't afford to. Yet an overwhelming need to see another human was a stronger pull than his immediate safety. He needed to know he wasn't alone. As he moved forward, the darkness behind him deepened like a black hole. His body tensed. He kept moving quietly and tentatively.

The place felt strangely unfamiliar to him. It shouldn't have—the ship was his second home. He had memorised every corner so others couldn't hide from him.

But something was wrong here. He wasn't sure what that was but he could feel it.

The air suddenly turned against him, tightening around his body, making it difficult for him to

232

breathe. He instinctively grabbed his throat, trying to force it open and suck more air into his weakening lungs. He dropped to his knees and stared helplessly ahead of him.

A male figure appeared out of nowhere. 'Don't be afraid,' he said. 'Let me help you.'

Bill stared hard at the man, feeling his body relax. As quickly as the suffocation had started, it began to lift. He clambered to his feet no longer feeling the strain on his lungs. His heart drummed unevenly as the dark shape glided gently towards him.

The man wore clothes that didn't fit his frame. A sudden calm took hold of Bill and he didn't feel afraid—he was relieved. He watched quietly as the figure stopped within a foot of him. He tried to explain away the feeling of familiarity for the figure; other than the outfit, the shape bore no other distinctive features.

'Who are you?' he asked of the blackened mass.

'Don't ask questions you don't want answered,' the man said. He did not recognise the voice.

The dark figure removed his hat. Bill stared at the man's face, but saw nothing; he had no expression, no features.

He reached out to touch the shape in front of him but his hand sliced easily through the wispy cloud that instantly reformed into a solid mass. Mesmerised by the effect, he let his inhibitions go. He tried to work out if this was real or a dream. It felt real enough.

The man moved in closer and Bill tensed up. More uneasiness spread through his body but it was too late. Catching sight of a shiny object in the man's

233

hand, he raised his arm a second too late as the knife sliced effortlessly across his throat.

Passenger Ship

Bill awoke with a start, sweating heavily and feeling claustrophobic. His throat was constricted and he struggled to breathe normally.

Gasping for air, he twisted and turned in the cocoon-like sleeping unit on the passenger ship. The air hung oppressively around him. There was resistance on his arms and legs, as if something was holding them in place. Remembering the restrictive size of the unit, he stopped struggling.

He fumbled in the dark, trying to find the unit's lock. His face flushed with the exertion. He moved his head around, searching for new air. There was none. He twisted awkwardly and tried to bang the lock with his fist to force it to release, but he quickly lost strength. His efforts were no more effective than a child's would have been. Light-headedness caused his head to swim.

'What the f—' he mumbled as he slipped in and out of consciousness. Shaking his head to clear the daze, he fought to think straight. He turned his back to the lock and repeatedly slammed his elbow against it.

'Holy mother of—' Bill cried in pain when the metal catch caught his funny bone. Rubbing the pain out of his elbow between each attempt, he flinched each time it connected with a hard surface. The impact lessened as the physical exertion drained him of energy.

He continued to pound on the lock, determined

to unlock the flap before every last breath in his body was used up. 'Open up. For Christ's sake, please open,' he whispered. In the air-starved environment, the panic built up inside him.

He shifted to his side and closed his eyes, feeling as helpless as he'd been in his dream. He wanted to fight but he didn't have it in him. He was weak. Isla was shouting at him to keep trying. What could he do? He felt a hot tear fall from his eye and stream down his face. He didn't have the strength to wipe it away.

Suddenly, cool air rushed over him and he hungrily sucked it into his lungs. The oxygen instantly invigorated his weak muscles as if he had injected life straight into them. Feeling his strength return, he moved, but didn't try to get out—there was no hurry.

Bill wasn't sure how long he lay there—seconds, maybe minutes. Time had lost all meaning. He felt cold arms reach in and lock around his form. The sleeping quarters were still dark and he couldn't see anything. He didn't fight. He allowed whomever it was to pull him free.

His head hit the floor with a thud. He ignored the pain as he swallowed another lungful of sweet oxygen-rich air. Blinking furiously, he managed to focus on the figure of a man hovering over him. Cool fingers momentarily rested on his neck. The man spoke clinically to someone else in the room. 'His pulse is strong. They all seem fine now.'

Bill blinked, trying to dispel the tears and focus on the men's faces. He squeezed his eyes shut and opened them again, but they had suddenly vanished from view. Gingerly, he felt the bump that was beginning to form at the back of his head. As quickly as he could manage, he sat up to assess the danger. His eyes darted around the room but there was no sign of the men that had helped him moments ago, correction—that saved him. *What were they doing outside of the units anyway? Weren't they also trapped?*

He kept his back flat against the wall, his head spinning wildly out of control, as he tried to make sense of it all. He braced himself for a possible attack. As he looked around him, things started to make more sense. Scattered across the hard floor were nine other people, all moving around in a similarly sluggish way. Bill crawled forward, fighting off his dizziness as best he could while he felt each body for a pulse. They were all alive.

'What happened?' he asked one man, who was lying on his back and staring at the ceiling.

'I—I couldn't breathe. The lock was stuck. If it hadn't been for those two men—' He didn't finish. Instead he closed his eyes and released a long, satisfying breath.

When the dizziness subsided long enough for Bill to stand without falling over, he walked the halls in search of someone in charge. He found a senior officer and realised how valuable his World Government credentials were as the officer rushed to explain the situation, with obvious embarrassment.

'I'm sorry, sir. There was a power failure in Section Seven, where your unit and fifty others are located. The situation is now under control.'

'How the hell does a ship this size have power failures?' Bill asked. He gently touched the golf ball-sized lump that had formed at the back of his head. He winced.

'Normally the backup power supply takes over,

sir, but because it didn't engage immediately, the computer shut off the oxygen levels to that area.'

'Surely the computer is smart enough to detect when the sleeping quarters are being occupied,' Bill said.

The officer's face reddened. 'Um, normally, sir, but the computers on board this ship are designed to save power, um, not to detect life on board.'

He worked out the rest. 'So, when the computer knocked out the oxygen to that section, the sensors locked the units so we couldn't escape?' His words were dripping with sarcasm.

'Er, not quite, sir. The sensors assumed they were unoccupied and lockdown was initiated to prevent tampering with unused units, sir.'

'Good to know we're in such safe hands,' Bill said cynically.

'Yes, sir,' the officer agreed, seemingly missing the point.

'Well, if it wasn't for your officers, we would have all suffocated in there. Please thank them for me. I didn't manage to get a good look at their faces, so I don't know who they were.'

'Sir?'

'Your officers,' Bill repeated.

The senior officer stared blankly at him, before answering in his best military tone. 'Of course, sir. Immediately.'

Bill squeezed his eyes shut as a stab of pain shot through his tenderised elbow.

'Do you need medical help?'

'No, I'll be fine,' he said and began the walk back to his sleeping quarters. Out of earshot of the officer he added, 'You'd probably only try to harvest my organs for donation.'

Stephen and Anton watched the exchange between the official and Bill Taggart. Tucked into a darkened doorway, they spoke quietly to one another.

'Would they really try to harvest that human's organs?' Anton asked.

'We know they are killers, so anything's possible,' Stephen said as he watched the investigator walk away.

'I'm glad you decided to help those people in the end.'

'I was this close to ignoring their screams.' Stephen held his thumb and forefinger a small distance apart.

'I don't believe that. You're nothing like the other Indigenes.'

'But I have every reason to be.'

Anton's brow creased. 'Are the humans as bad as you say they are? Pierre's opinion seems to differ.'

'Pierre is practical. He prefers the option with the least carnage.'

'Seems like we should wait to see what we find out before judging them.'

Stephen smirked. 'You sound like Pierre.'

'Well, he isn't an elder for nothing.'

'The very fact that they are human bothers me.'

'I know, but no matter what they are, we can't treat them as immediate enemies. It would make us no different to them.'

'But we *are* like them.' Stephen pointed out.

'Look, he's alone now,' Anton gestured after Bill. 'Why don't we just approach him—demand answers from him about why they are investigating us?'

'No, I'm not ready for that yet. Besides, we can't be sure if we can trust him. I think we should wait until we get to Earth.'

'But what if we lose him? We don't know where he's going.'

'We will soon enough. It won't be long before we arrive on their planet and then we can track him.'

A memory of the district's Evolvers entered Stephen's mind—they had also been tracked by the humans. In hindsight, it had been an error on some Indigenes' part to allow their young to hunt without supervision. Stupidly, their choices had revealed their race's existence to the humans. Central Council's perfect democratic society was showing signs of wear.

Stephen had also been hunting that night and had not been aware of the pair's dangerous proximity to the city border. They all heard the wolf baying in the distance, but soon recognised the change in pitch that told them the animal was on the back foot; an easy kill was too tempting. Unaware of how close the humans were, Stephen was stopped dead in his tracks by the light from a single torch. His hunting party of six gathered around him and looked on helplessly as the Evolvers were moments away from being discovered.

The young pair had continued to play games with the wolf, teasing it until it was unsure which one of them posed the bigger threat. One Evolver danced for the wolf, moving his feet quickly and effortlessly, distracting and diverting its attention away. The other curled his spine into a crouched stance, lowering his arms and legs until he was inches from the ground. Resting his full bodyweight on his toes and the tips of his fingers, he kept his bloodthirsty eyes on the prey.

The wolf stood perfectly still. A blood-curdling screech emanated from the dancing Evolver. The other, still low to the ground, drew back his lips to show a set of teeth strong enough to rip the wolf in half.

Stephen had recognised the prelude to an attack: the low guttural snarl coming from the wolf, the flash of its razor-sharp teeth. The wolf only moved backwards when the Evolvers inched closer. The animal leaned back on its haunches, its muscles visibly shaking with tension.

Stephen had seen the human creep in from the left but stopped as soon as his light exposed the truth. The smell of iron filled his nose. The Evolvers shook with excitement as a crimson waterfall of blood spilled from the wolf's neck.

As soon as the first Evolver had been surrounded, Stephen grabbed the second Evolver and ran.

Stephen's ragged breathing broke him out of his thoughts about the Evolver. He tilted his head back and carefully pulled out the three sections of the filtration device. He pulled the spare set off his belt and adjusted the larger part at the back of his throat with his finger. He wiped down the depleted sections and placed each one carefully in the recharger unit that also hung from his belt.

Anton waited for him to finish before speaking again. 'So, how are we supposed to get off this ship without being noticed?'

'The same way we got on. Will the chips work at the exit point?'

'In theory they should. Disembarkation should be straight forward enough,' Anton said. 'Getting around the planet—well, I haven't figured out how we're going to manage that just yet.'

21

Earth

One document after another appeared on Laura's monitor, churned out in the form of an endless, mind-numbing list. In a short space of time, she viewed various memos between the World Government and its subsidiaries about security matters. While some issues were minor, others might become serious if they weren't dealt with swiftly. Even though the detail contained in the documents was more interesting than it had been on Level Four, she was just about ready to call it quits.

Out of the corner of her eye, she spotted a blinking folder on her monitor, staring at it for a moment and positive it hadn't been there a second ago. There had been no folders for her to choose from; the files were listed chronologically one after another. Booth numbers and names flashed up beside files and then disappeared; booth one; her frenemy in booth ten; booth sixteen. She deliberated what her next move would be: should she ignore it and carry on, leaving someone else to process its contents? What if she was *expected* to open it? With no clear guidance coming from anyone, she decided to play it safe and leave it.

Twenty minutes later, the folder icon was still winking at her and Laura wondered if the other workers could see it on their screens. She was about to ask someone when she remembered the cardinal rule: don't speak to anyone. She glanced around her, not seeing a single head move but hearing intermittent beeping as dozens of fingers glided over touch-activated monitors. Laura realised that several of the booths that had been occupied before were now empty. Had she become so absorbed in her own duties that she hadn't noticed anyone leave? Suddenly eager for a change of scenery, she logged downtime for a bathroom break through her monitor. A clock flashed up on-screen and a two-minute countdown commenced.

In the bathroom down the hall, she splashed cold water on her face, allowing it to drip down her neck where it soaked into her collar. She leaned against the steel-top counter and stared at herself in the mirror; the face that looked back seemed older than the day before. Her blonde hair, which had started out as a neat ponytail, was now a mess. She took it down and tidied it up. Her green eyes were missing their usual sparkle. Her skin was more pale than usual. Her clothes hung loosely on her frame. She'd lost weight recently and it didn't suit her.

As Laura leaned towards the mirror, she struggled to remember the reasons why she worked at the ESC in the first place. She was tired—not just physically, but emotionally. The toil of working towards something that was never a guarantee hit her all at once, but she did the same thing she always did when she felt this low: she gave herself another vitamin D shot, pulled on a smile and went about her business as if none of it bothered her. She patted her face dry with a paper towel and went back to work. At her workstation, the folder was still blinking on her monitor. Laura ignored it. Instead, she randomly selected a file from the list that was increasing exponentially the longer she sat there.

Hours passed in this way as Laura processed files as efficiently as she could and still the ominous folder flashed on her screen. Odd. Why hadn't anyone else picked it up and processed it? she wondered. Then she considered the possibility that she was the only one who could see it. Tentatively, she selected it. A folder labelled 'Private' opened to show nine documents, all with the security tag 732-554-ITF-TGT. A number of them had the prefix 'to be re-filed' attached.

She opened the first document and scanned the contents. The name Bill Taggart appeared repeatedly throughout the document. She wondered who he was, guessing that the TGT on the security tag stood for his name. ITF, it explained in the document, stood for International Task Force. She read on. Words that caught her attention as she scoured the document for the clearance level included 'Exilon 5', 'investigation' and 'meeting', which featured quite heavily. The document appeared to be a preliminary report sent a week ago. About two-thirds in, she found the clearance level embedded deeply within the document, almost not seeing it. She closed the file immediately, tagged it and yawned as she ran it through re-encryption.

Laura opened the files sequentially. The documents labelled 'for re-filing' contained both video recordings and notes. She was unsure how to file a document that contained more than one element. Should she process the components separately or together?

'Video and text together in the same file,' she

said to nobody in particular. 'Do I tag together or separately?' While she waited, her heart thumped erratically. She hadn't planned on breaking the cardinal rule.

All noises stopped and the silence that followed was deafening. She pushed up from the desk and cast her eyes slowly around the room. There was only one person looking at her: the woman from booth sixteen who handled Level Eight information. While asking questions had been standard practice on Level Four, she felt awkward about asking one here.

'Together,' Sixteen replied flatly.

'Thanks.' Laura dropped back down into her seat. *There, that wasn't too difficult.* She tagged the two files without reading the text. She had found the clearance attached to the video file, simply titled 'Examination'.

It wasn't until she had opened the sixth document in the list of nine that alarm bells started ringing. A document labelled 'to be re-filed -732-554-ITF-TGT', upon opening, had a different name 'Autopsy of Species 31'. Her eyes widened and her interest in her work did a sudden one-eighty. Luckily, nobody could see her sitting there with her mouth agape.

She started putting everything together now. The words 'Exilon 5', 'investigator' and 'meeting' suddenly developed some meaningful context, but she was still unsure how 'meeting' connected with anything. *A meeting with whom? Species 31 perhaps?* Did the alien autopsy pre-empt a meeting? What if the meeting didn't go according to plan?

As she speed-read the document, she was tempted to labour over the contents, but she didn't need the hassle from Brett, her new overseer. Key phrases rose to the surface: translucent skin, photosensitive eyes, discovery of object lodged in back of throat and nasal cavity. What am I looking at? she wondered.

Laura re-read the information until the words didn't make any sense. She closed her mouth, straightened up and readjusted her body. She stood up and pretended to stretch. As she did, she looked around to see if anyone else had seen what she had. Sixteen was watching her, so she dropped the charade and sat down.

Her brief glimpse into a darker side to work on Level Five came as a surprise. There was no way this information was being conveyed publicly. She would have heard something already if it had been. The warnings from the beady-eyed man rang true. *What we retain can get you killed in an instant. So learn the rules fast.* She still had no idea what the other rules were.

Laura didn't know how dangerous it was for her to view the Taggart files. But how could it be if it was her job to process them? They had sent her the information freely; surely the files were innocent enough? In the back of her mind, something nagged at her to be careful. She ignored it. Driven on by an insatiable curiosity, she opened the remaining files.

22

Daphne Gilchrist sat alone in her glass-walled office on Level Seven. She had increased the tint on the windows so that the people outside couldn't see into the room. She had a perfect view of what they were doing. It was how she liked to operate—always one step ahead of others.

Leaning forward in her plush leather chair and propping her elbows up on the gleaming mahogany table, she listened as a female doctor spoke. Stationed on Exilon 5, the doctor had just discovered a replicated identity chip and was showing her close-ups of the microscopic device, which was three times the size of a flat pinhead. Stellar wave technology ensured that the communication link between them was crisp and clear. Daphne was pleased about the World Government's investment into new technologies, delivered through its countless subsidiary organisations and companies.

She looked into the monitor that sat on her desk. As a precaution, she had placed a piece of cloth underneath its base to protect the expensive table and its rich sheen. The pretty doctor's face filled the screen.

'As you can see, Daphne, it is a very advanced design,' she said.

With her cold and experienced eyes, Daphne shot her a warning look. The doctor was young and unfamiliar with the right way to address the CEO of a major organisation on Earth. Only Charles Deighton was on a first name basis with her because she'd been afraid to correct him. Ms Gilchrist—or Chief—would suffice; it was the Japanese way.

The doctor took the warning in her stride and Daphne seethed beneath her icy exterior. She survived on inflicting fear wherever she went. In an instant, this woman had unhinged her and only one other person could do that. She disliked women, preferring to give them a wide berth. Men were much easier to read and were far more understanding of her iron-fisted approach.

'If you looked at an original chip and security chip side by side, you would see they both have an inbuilt communication thread so they can talk to each other.' Daphne watched as the doctor tapped the active thread on the replica identity chip with a minuscule pointer. The thread squirmed under the microscope as if it were alive. 'This replica is mirrored after an identity chip. The thread here is composed of nerve receptor molecules, which normally receive signals from a cell. The security chip's thread has the same molecular structure, except it has extra molecules called ligands that act as agonists. The agonists stimulate the receptor to send signal information, using the cells as a go-between.'

Daphne ran one hand through her red hair and tapped a polished nail from her other hand on the surface of the table. She watched the doctor as she spoke, feeling her dislike for the woman beginning to show on her face. The woman's dark hair was gently pulled back from her face and tied into a loose bun. Green eyes that placed her high up the genetic transfer list complemented her soft-looking face. In that instant, the doctor reminded her of Isla Taggart.

'Shall I continue?' the doctor asked, slightly bemused.

Daphne realised that she'd been caught staring off into the distance. She waved dismissively for her to carry on.

'The original and security chips will also work independently of each other. The identity chip is the first to be implanted at birth; the thread remains dormant until the recipient receives a security chip. Once that happens their connection is live. Equally, if you remove one, they both revert to their original state and can work as single units. But without two original chips present, they can't be activated together, as the unique connection no longer exists. Unfortunately, you need to activate a pair simultaneously to see if the connection has been severed.'

'Did the host try to leave the planet? Is that how the replicated chip was discovered?'

'No. Bob Harris presented with an infection yesterday.'

Naming her patient made the doctor far too emotional as far as Daphne was concerned. She wished it had been a male doctor who'd discovered the anomaly. Men wanted to be told what to do and when to do it. Women got too emotionally involved and she was sure that was where Isla Taggart had tripped up. If only she had left well enough alone... Daphne shook her head; she would never be tripped up in the same way. With no living family outside the ESC's glass confine, there was very little for her to get emotional about. Men knew that her mind was quick and to the point. Plus, she could pull out the female card when necessary—it always seemed to be needed at some point or another.

'Did he try to remove it?' Daphne asked the doctor.

'He said he didn't. The chip is developed out of his DNA and has been designed to become part of his body—completely and utterly compatible in every way. For the most part, it remains inert. He said he hadn't tried tampering with it either. Apart from yearly upgrades due to changes in his work status and living arrangements, he'd forgotten he even had it—that was until a month ago.' The doctor paused before continuing. 'He was in a lot of discomfort, poor guy. Didn't see it coming.'

There it was again: the emotional response. 'And?' Daphne said, feeling her patience run thin. She tried to pick up the pace of the conversation.

'Well, the microchip is an integrated circuit device encased in a polymer compound. The compound is created by taking a DNA sample from a baby, then mixing it with the liquid solution. As you know, the identity chip is then inserted under the skin of the left thumb. As the human body grows, the chip adapts to the host. The silicone breaks down over time, releasing a compound that partially solidifies the saline, holding the chip in place. Over time, the DNA polymer and saline fuse, providing the final housing over the circuitry. It's entirely natural and, in practice, identity chips never need replacing, just updating, which can be done with a simple tweak.'

Daphne's time to talk was limited but the doctor didn't hurry with her explanation.

'The security chip is developed from a section of the identity chip,' the doctor continued. 'It's the DNA marker that makes them so unique. If one or both chips were removed from a host, they wouldn't work in another human. It is, therefore, pointless to sell them on the black market, as is currently happening. The public's general lack of knowledge is the reason the market remains so lucrative.'

'So, it was stolen?' Daphne said.

'Yes, but it doesn't make sense to replace it with something else; the chip is tamper-proof and will eventually destroy itself if physically removed. Replacements shouldn't work. That's why this replication model is so amazing.' The doctor produced side-by-side images of an original and replicated chip. Daphne saw no difference.

'It even has a similar thread like the original one,' the doctor said. 'And it works—can you believe it? Whoever designed this knows a lot about genetronics.'

'What about the replication? How was it discovered?'

'The replication is superb,' the doctor said. 'Aside from being able to attach itself to the host's DNA, it works as if it's the real chip. As I've already explained, the originals must be activated simultaneously to see the problem. Fortunately for us, Bob Harris has a rare condition.'

'How is that fortunate?'

'Bob has a super-charged immune system that rejects the presence of foreign matter. He will never get sick. Only a handful of humans have this affliction.'

'Knowing your area of expertise, Doctor, can I go so far as to assume you are under-qualified at this point to brief me on genetic anomalies?' Daphne said. The doctor's credentials registered her as a nurse. It was her field training in scientific studies that had accredited her with the title of doctor. It was why she was on Exilon 5.

'Actually, I'm more than qualified to advise you on the subject. I studied anatomy extensively before turning my attention purely to the sciences.'

Daphne was unimpressed. She allowed the doctor to carry on, only because she needed her; she would find a satisfying way to punish her some other time.

'His unique immune system means he's protected from the most aggressive medical conditions that still exist, rare as they are. The original chip bonded to his internal network because there was DNA present in the chip. Take away the DNA and his system will try to reject the foreign object. That's what happened here—his body fought the invasion and turned it into an infectious mass because the chip had nowhere to go.'

'Is that how you found it?' Daphne asked.

'His thumb had blown up to twice its normal size. I didn't notice the incision until I examined the area more closely.'

Daphne had heard enough. 'Your analogy has been helpful, Doctor. I will be sure to pass on details of your cooperation to your superior.' She allowed the lie to surface. If anything, a damning report would follow. 'Out.'

With a flick of her index finger, the screen changed and a new face popped up.

'Did you hear everything, Charles?' She smiled; it was not something she did often but he was the only person she felt the need to adjust her personality for. It was instinctual, as if that simple action might save her life one day.

Staring back was the one hundred and nineteen-year-old face of Charles Deighton, CEO of the World

Government. 'Yes. Exciting times ahead, don't you think? It appears our friends are more advanced than we've given them credit for.' His voice crackled with age.

Daphne noticed how old Deighton was looking lately. Even with all the treatments to stay young, old age was catching up on him; his hair was full, but beginning to lose thickness; his skin had lost its elasticity and was starting to sag south. It was a degenerating larynx that gave the raspy sound to his speech. Although he'd been scheduled to have his larynx replaced, Deighton admitted he'd become familiar with the way his voice sounded and liked it. He said it gave him a mysterious edge and he enjoyed being an enigma. Daphne thought the rasping made him sound like there was a permanent frog lodged in there somewhere. Every time he spoke, she fought the urge to clear her own throat.

'They've moved on technologically, there's no doubt about that, and they're learning faster than we originally thought they would,' Daphne replied before adding, 'It appears we may have a stowaway on board the passenger ship. The manifest flagged Bob Harris's name twenty minutes ago. How would you like us to proceed?'

'Nobody is to interfere!' Deighton's words were venomous.

Daphne instinctively recoiled from her monitor. In a hurry, she forced a smile. 'Of course, Charles. I hadn't intended on sending out an order without clearing it with you first.'

Deighton quickly regained composure. Smiling now, he added, 'The ship won't be here for another twelve days. We'll send a special team to meet and greet our new friend upon arrival.'

23

On her second day in the new job, Laura O'Halloran desperately searched for a new distraction. Her former colleagues came into her head and now seemed as good a time as any to catch up with them. She arrived at the cafeteria located on the second floor of the Earth Security Centre and grabbed a tray. She ordered beef stew and a glass of lemonade from one of the replicator machines, then placed the items on the tray and picked it up. Scanning the room for signs of Chris and Janine, she saw they were sitting in their regular spot in one corner of the room.

As she approached them, Chris gave her a look that sent a chill up her spine. He dropped his eyes to the table and pretended not to see her. Instead, he whispered something to Janine who sat with her back to Laura. With each step Laura took, their location seemed to move further away, and she now wondered if the purple uniform was a turn off. Determined to cast off her doubts about how others viewed Level Five workers, she kept going. She trained one eye on legs jutting out from underneath tables that threatened to trip her up before she arrived safely.

But as she neared them, her uneasiness increased tenfold and a second chill washed over her just as she reached their table. The intense conversation they continued to share didn't help matters. Janine's eyes met hers briefly; there was less warmth than normal in them, if that was even possible.

Laura struggled to think what to do. While she didn't care for Janine's insatiable need to poke around in others' business or Chris's sexist attitude towards women, she needed them. She needed them to tell her the move to Level Five was the right thing to do. She needed Chris to tell her that the lottery had made a mistake all along and that Haymarket was back on their radar. So she swallowed hard and, just like she had done before, she plastered on a fake smile and pretended that none of this bothered her.

'Hi guys. My day has been crazy!' she said as breezily as she could manage. 'Mind if I join you?'

'Actually, we do,' Janine replied flatly.

Chris kept an eye on the roving camera that was hovering around the room; now it wasn't looking in their direction. He kept his voice low. 'You're going to get us into trouble. You know we can't be seen talking to you. You need to stick to your lot. Bugger off.' He shooed her away with his hand.

Laura had expected their reaction but she wasn't willing to give up without a fight. She needed people, interaction; she was going stir-crazy on Level Five without it. Was there any way to change their mind—allay their fears about her new position?

She placed the tray on the table and hunkered down to their level. She gripped its edge to steady herself. 'Look, I know what the rumours are but they're just rumours, right? I mean how much trouble are we really going to get into by talking to one another? We used to work together, for Christ's sake.'

Janine refused to make eye contact with her. Laura wasn't sure if it was fear of the unknown or plain jealousy that was driving her former colleague's current attitude towards her.

'Oh shit,' Chris said. The trio watched in horror as the roving camera hovered over to their table. 'See what you've gone and done now? Talk your way out of it.'

'Yeah, you're good at getting what you want, aren't you?' Janine said, the words sticking in her throat.

'If you care about us at all, you'd better fix this.' Chris said. Spittle landed on her face.

The camera moved in close to them. An electronic voice boomed through the device. 'What's going on here?' It scanned Laura's face.

She stood up, the blood rushing back into the lower part of her legs where she had temporarily cut off the supply. She could see her reflection in the golden ball. It was the first time she had seen one of the cameras up close. It was shimmering and bright—it was also very close to her face.

She cleared her throat while thinking about what she might say. It would be easy to drop the pair in it, to save her skin; she felt no loyalty towards them since they were too busy saving their own. Janine's currently cold attitude had put her right off her former colleague. She wondered how she'd put up with her snarly personality for so long, since it was in direct opposition to hers.

Laura looked at them both, then at the camera.

'I was just asking—'

'Just asking what?' the camera voice said. Laura pictured a fat bald man sitting at a control panel somewhere in ESC getting great pleasure out of making her squirm. It was the easiest way for her to talk to one of these things since she struggled to think of it as a living entity. It wasn't a person—nor was it person-operated—but it did contain artificial intelligence. She was tempted to stick her tongue out, to see if it understood the meaning of her gesture.

She took a gamble. 'I was just asking them if they knew where the swipe cards for the machines were.' The cards were used to reset the replication machines that were designed to run on cycles. At the end of a cycle, the food quality was at its worst and the machines needed a simple reboot to begin it again. 'My stew has a metallic taste to it and I wanted to reset it.'

The camera scanned Chris's face, then Janine's. 'Don't you three know each other?'

'Yes,' Laura replied honestly. 'We used to work together on Level Four.'

'You're not supposed to be talking to each other. I will have to report this.'

Laura noticed the look of fear on Chris's face. She couldn't see Janine's but she could sense her coolness.

'I only asked them *because* I know them. I don't really know anyone on Level Five yet but I promise, this will be the last time.'

She meant it. She was done with the pair of them.

The camera made a humming noise as it continued to hover effortlessly in the air. 'The cards are to the side of the machines, where they always are.'

'Sorry about that. I'll check again.'

It lingered on her face a little longer—or the fat bald man did—before moving away.

Without another word, she blew out a breath and walked over to the machine without giving a backwards glance to either Chris or Janine. She reset the nearest one and ordered another stew. To keep up the charade, she dropped the original dish in one of the waste receptacle units.

As she sat down, she could feel dozens of eyes on her. She was angry at Chris and the imaginary camera operator, but mostly at Janine and her knack for making people feel unwelcome. The people around her all regarded her warily. Laura began to wonder if the warnings she had received weren't just for her. She wondered if her former colleagues had also been threatened.

Appetite well and truly gone, she tried to act as if everything was still normal. She forced down a gulp or two of lemonade that tasted more bitter than usual and took a rabbit-sized bite of her average-tasting stew. After an uncomfortable few minutes, she abandoned her lunch and went back to work. She immersed herself fully in her work. No further files appeared about Bill Taggart.

24

Passenger Ship

Stephen and Anton sat in the recreation room aboard the passenger ship. A brief orientation at the start of their journey, plus their own explorations, had given them a good idea of the massive layout. The room was sparsely decorated; tables and chairs were huddled in a space spanning the size of a football pitch. According to an information robot, the room was mainly used to accommodate diners when the cafeteria was full. Stephen imagined that at busier times, the place would be jammed to the rafters. He was grateful it wasn't like that now.

Sitting down was part of the pretence to fit in with everybody else. They were not alone in the room. At another table, two humans sat together and a third sat alone in a different section. While they had company, they needed to keep up the charade and act as human-like as possible. Despite all their preparations, they still didn't blend in as well as they would have liked. Others were noticeably stand-offish with them.

'Our outfits are drawing too much attention,' Anton said quietly. He provided cover for Stephen while he discreetly injected a synthesised protein pack directly into his stomach cavity.

Stephen drew in a long breath and grabbed the

edge of the table; the untested side effects of injecting protein in this way gave him crippling stomach cramps. Anton waited for him to regain his composure. He moaned and doubled over in his seat, clutching his stomach as lightly as he could—any sort of pressure seemed to make things worse. He tried to control his pain cognitively, but having company in the room made it difficult for him to concentrate. His moans began to draw attention. He tried to straighten up and relax. The spasms doubled him back over. He waited for the pain to plateau, but not before it delivered a crunching blow to his midsection.

Anton had warned him about prolonged use of the protein packs; they hadn't been designed to be used in this way. He tried his best to deal with it, while Anton kept an eye on the trio across the room.

'I'm sorry,' Anton said. 'The first thing I'm going to do is correct the protein imbalance. I was under a little pressure before we left.'

Stephen groaned again in response to a sharp pain that felt like it was ripping his body in half. He tried to placate his friend in the lulls between spasms. 'Don't worry about it, please. It will pass soon en—' The pain cut him off.

Anton shook his head. 'I should have done more tests. It wasn't ready.'

Stephen drew in a long breath. 'The alternative is starvation. I'll take this fleeting pain over the other option any day.'

Anton's eyes darted around as soon as he noticed movement in the room.

Stephen jerked his head up and his eyes found the source of the commotion. Coming towards them were two of the humans, looking dangerously interested in them.

'Don't let them get too close,' he whispered. 'We can't allow them time to study our appearance.' He felt his stomach muscles jerk and spasm again. He tried to limit the movement, but he was caught firmly in its vice-like grip.

'Hey you!' the stout man from the queue earlier said to Anton, while nodding in Stephen's direction. 'What's wrong with your friend? You need a doc or somethin'?'

The men edged closer with slow, unsure steps until there was just a couple of table lengths between them. Anton stood up and spoke quickly. He tried to smile. 'He is feeling sick—he doesn't like to travel.'

A series of unusual noises emanated from Stephen.

Both men stopped dead in their tracks. The stout man spoke again. 'Gerry here,' he elbowed his taller friend, 'knows CPR and worked as a nurse for a stint. Didn't you Gerry?'

'Eh, sure but—' the tall man replied.

'Well go and help him will ya? Don't just stand there.'

'I'm not sure about this—looks serious enough. I think he might need a real doctor or something.'

The stout man turned to his friend and quietly mumbled. 'Well, you can still take a look, can't ya? You're embarrassin' me.'

'Er, sure, I guess,' he replied unconvincingly. He took a step towards them.

Stephen watched as Anton readied to block his path. Then the stout man spoke again. 'Hey!' He looked from Stephen to Anton and back again. A stubby finger jabbed in their direction and a glimmer of recognition passed across his face. It was enough to stop the tall man's advances—for the moment.

'Weren't you two standing behind us in the queue for this rust bucket?'

The tall man nodded and smiled. 'Oh, yeah, I think you're right—in the queue.'

'The worst is coming, Anton, get rid of them,' Stephen whispered.

Anton cleared his throat. 'I'm sorry, but my friend here needs his space because he feels like throwing up. Unless you'd like to be covered in his stomach contents, I suggest you move back as far as you can.'

The stout man was the first to concede defeat, and his shadow wasn't far behind him. 'Don't want to see no sick,' he said, holding up his hands defensively. 'Can't stand the sight of anythin' oozing out of bodies and such. I'm already feeling chunks moving around me own stomach as I think about it.' He clutched his midsection.

'Me neither,' his friend added.

The stout man shot him an odd look. 'Whatcha talking about? You're trained for this kind of thing.'

'Only lasted a month at nursing school. Once we started the practical shit, I was out of there, as quick as you like.'

The stout man shook his head. 'Useless.'

Both retreated wordlessly and headed straight for the exit. Talk of vomit was enough to move the remaining passenger.

Soon after, Stephen felt the worst of it pass. 'That's better,' he said, breathing out slowly. 'I don't want to go through that again for another day at least. By the way, what's "throwing up"?'

'Apparently, if the Surface Creatures—I mean humans—eat too much, it shoots back up their oesophagus without warning. As I understand, not too many of them are fond of witnessing it.'

Stephen straightened up. 'Well, whatever it looks like, good thinking. We might need to use that excuse in the future. That was too close for my liking. I don't like the idea of *them* getting that close. We need to make a better effort to keep under the radar from now on. Maybe we should ditch these hats back at our sleeping pods—we'll look more natural without hair than permanently wearing a hat indoors. We should also try to stick to darkened areas as much as possible.'

Now that they were alone, both of them stood—a more natural position for them. 'Referring to them as humans is going to take some getting used to,' Anton said. 'What are we looking for when we get to Earth?'

'Answers, plain and simple,' Stephen said, pacing quietly. 'Something that'll explain how it is they exist at all, and why they're intent on destroying us.'

As they made their way back to their sleeping quarters, Anton asked, 'Why him?'

Puzzled, Stephen looked at him. 'Who?'

'You can't stand being near any of them but you went out of your way to choose the child called Ben—why?'

Stephen shrugged. 'Because I saw something in him that the others didn't possess—innocence, perhaps. It was easier to be around him.' He stopped and leaned against the wall, exhaling sharply. 'I don't know, Anton. I can't explain it better than that.'

25

Earth

Galen Thompson stood beside Paddy, Maria and the communications operative inside Stuart's cramped office, where they shoved and jostled for a better position. Stuart rarely used his office, preferring to stand on the HJA observation deck. He'd told Galen that overseeing was a lot like parenthood; if he didn't keep an eye on his kids, sooner or later, they would get into trouble.

The fact that Stuart had summoned all on-duty controllers to his office had Galen worried. He nervously chewed the skin on his left thumb, shifting his weight from one leg to the other. He wondered if his parents' activities had anything to do with them being there, or if his mother had given the micro file to that girl in the ESC—Laura O'Halloran? They shot quizzical looks at each other as they tried to guess what the news might be. Only Galen remained tight-lipped.

The door opened suddenly and Stuart burst into the room, almost knocking Paddy off his feet; the door hit his boot with a heavy thud. His quick reflexes prompted him to throw an arm across his face.

'Shit, Paddy,' Stuart snapped, 'what are you doing behind there?'

Paddy straightened up and pushed his back further into the corner. 'Sorry, boss. No room in here. And what the feck is this all about anyway?'

'Just settle for a mo, I'll tell you in a minute.' Stuart squeezed past Maria, who had been allocated the postage stamp space behind the desk. Normally Stuart would have made some sarcastic comment about how they should stop meeting like this, but he was clearly distracted. Finally, he took his seat, if only to help free up some floor space.

'Alright,' he said, exhaling sharply once he'd settled into the chair. 'We are meeting in here because what I have to say is for your ears only. It's not to be discussed with that lot out there.' He jerked a thumb towards the observation deck, where five trainee rookies were on duty. 'They are far too green to hear what I have to say.'

Galen fidgeted with his hands, sensing that his place was also out there with the trainees—technically he still was one. He couldn't get the ESC memos or the business with the letters and micro file out of his head. He wondered if they were all linked.

Stuart finally noticed his anxiety. 'Got something to say, Galen?'

'Eh, should I even be in here? I mean, I'm not even a senior controller yet.'

'You are one of our top trainees. Stay where you are.' Stuart snapped, throwing a furtive glance at Galen. 'Now what the hell was I saying before I was rudely interrupted?'

Galen flushed with embarrassment.

'Oh yeah, I have some bad news from the ESC.' He leaned back in his chair, managing a thirty-degree tilt before the edge hit the wall.

They all inhaled sharply. Galen looked at

Paddy, who was staring at the floor; Paddy had already told him what the Earth Security Centre was capable of doing.

News from the ESC wasn't usually positive. They only ever contacted the docking stations if there was a security breach, or if cuts were on the way. Because of ESC's relationship with the World Government, they could initiate any changes they wanted. Security matters were most feared, and from what Galen understood, the consequences were pretty dire.

Paddy had told him the grim story one lunchtime about a former colleague of his who'd been caught abusing his security-level clearance. Nothing too serious, Paddy recalled. His colleague had been obsessed with bettering his career and had broken into the personnel office to gain insider knowledge on his competition. While they hadn't physically caught him, the ESC had recorded an unusual amount of activity in Section Three. Within hours, security had arrived to escort him off the premises. Paddy never laid eyes on him again. He had often wondered what happened to the man but knew the chances were slim that the World Government would waste good resources keeping him in some high-security facility on the outskirts of town. No, Paddy told him, it was far more likely that they'd done away with him.

Stuart continued talking as Galen's concern flipped over to his parents. He swallowed loudly.

'As you know, we're expecting a passenger ship from Exilon 5. It's scheduled to arrive Sunday week. I've been informed by ESC that there has been a breach of security and there's a possible stowaway on board.'

Paddy looked relieved but his expression soon

changed. 'I don't understand, Stuart. Why's this time any different from the two other incidents that occurred last year? It happens.'

'While I would normally agree with you, the ESC is taking this very seriously. They're sending over military personnel to monitor activity before and after the ship arrives.'

'Who is this mystery stowaway?' Maria said.

'Some worker called Bob Harris,' Stuart said. The group shrugged. They weren't familiar with the name. 'I know, I don't recognise it either, but apparently it means something to them.'

'Falsification of departure records again?' Paddy asked.

'No, not this time. An identity chip was stolen and used to gain access to the ship. Whoever is using it is of great importance to them.' Stuart glanced at the door and lowered his voice. 'You didn't hear this from me, but the order is coming directly from Charles Deighton.'

Paddy let out a low whistle.

'So, the military are taking over next week,' the communications operative said. 'For how long?'

'As long as it takes for them to get what they want, and ruin a perfectly good working week in the process. It's going to get a little crowded in here. I need you all to keep clear heads. I don't want to give the ESC any reason to shut this place down. Are we clear?'

'Understood,' they chimed together.

Laura immersed herself in work and had little or no time off during what the ESC had described as a hectic period in the calendar. They weren't sure when the double shifts on Level Five would end, they told her, only that it would be soon. Not really in a position to negotiate an early release from duty, she accepted that her presence was necessary. Her own shift was finishing in twenty-four hours and it couldn't come quick enough for her; she was barely able to keep her eyes open. She decided against taking a fifth Actigen pill that week, even though her employers had advised it.

When the effects of the last Actigen finally wore off, which would be in about three hours, Laura would attempt to grab an hour's sleep on Level Two. Alongside the gym, the ESC had installed sleeping quarters so they could keep their staff on round-the-clock shifts. It was more time-efficient than sending workers home, although by law they had to, eventually. Strangely enough, the government had maintained the law that prevented a worker from being confined indoors for more than a week at a time.

Laura felt what she could only describe as insurmountable tiredness. She'd never felt this way before, even during her worst shifts on Level Four. No, this was something completely different. On the one hand, she didn't mind keeping busy. It was a distraction for the most part; it wasn't like there was anyone waiting for her at home, including her mother. On the other hand, she'd had her fill of looking at the same walls and was eager to avoid her former colleagues in the corridors above. Just one more day, she reminded herself, then she planned to go straight to bed and sleep for twenty-four hours.

As she stared at the grey partitions encasing her isolation booth, she began to see spots. The lacklustre interior of Level Five was beginning to sap whatever mental strength she still had. She had started to reorganise items on her desk as a way to distract herself—her monitor, a communication earpiece and an inactive DPad—lining them up neatly against the edge of the table or the length of the partition. Her personal effects were in the drawer as instructed by her overseer, for fear they might be a distraction. She'd always felt distractions were healthy and she needed them more than most.

The Actigen wasn't working as effectively as it should. The adrenaline kick was nowhere in sight, probably because it was the fourth pill she'd taken in a week. The sleep breaks on Level Two weren't restorative enough. Running on a dangerously low tank of energy, light-headedness was beginning to cloud her judgement.

Laura walked to the back of the room and requested water from the H2O replication terminal. As she did, the woman from booth sixteen arrived with a disc in hand and deposited it in the vacuum tube to the right of her. Sixteen waited until she heard the familiar sucking noise that told her the disc was on its way to Gilchrist's office before returning to her seat. She didn't look at Laura.

Laura was too tired to care about her colleagues' indifference anymore. Lifting the tiny cone-shaped cup to her lips, she drank thirstily and requested a refill twice before she was mildly satisfied. But the hydration effects did little to lift the edge off her mood, or ease her thumping headache. She returned to her workstation, keeping her eyes firmly locked on the floor—a habit she'd developed over the last week as a way to avoid eye contact. She sat down, closed her eyes and rubbed her temples. It wasn't entirely the Actigen's fault—there was something else playing on her mind. She was having trouble forgetting the Bill Taggart files and the information contained within them. She had been overwhelmed by their content but her own plans to transfer to Exilon 5 carried more weight—it was her chance for a fresh start. Knowing that a world existed where sunshine was guaranteed was driving her through the worst days.

Nothing was safe on Earth, including the fragile mindset of the people who lived there. Laura understood the reason for the move; something had to be done to secure their future survival. But the sudden appearance of an indigenous species was changing the World Government's focus and that worried her. Time was running out for the lottery and there appeared to be no resolution to the problems of transferring the entire population. She wasn't sure what the government had planned for the Indigene race but the documents led her to believe they were still in an exploratory phase that could last indefinitely. It made sense because they had sent an investigation team to the planet, led by Bill Taggart.

'Indefinitely' also described the status transfer plans that were on hold and she wondered how long she would have to wait. With problems like overcrowding and a diminishing air quality on Earth, she had no intention of facing such a future.

On the one hand, she was desperate for a new life and new hope. On the other hand, she couldn't help but feel sorry for the Indigenes whose very existence was threatened by the arrival of humans. Apparently the explosions on Exilon 5, which had terraformed the planet, almost wiped out their entire race. Evidence in the earlier files, which recounted an officer's close-up experience and detailed the autopsy of Species 31, categorised the Indigenes as an aggressive and primitive species. But Laura had been surprised to read about the new information on the Indigene called Stephen and his meeting with the boy. The previous evidence about their aggression had been wrong.

Two keywords stood out from the latter files: 'Intelligence' and 'Adaptability'. She didn't know if that was a good or bad thing, but she reasoned that if any race was going to survive it would be the most adaptable one. Stephen's image was now etched in her memory. She'd also memorised Bill Taggart's unique and naturally aged face, right down to the grey flecks in his hair and the number of lines on his forehead. But now, every time she closed her eyes their faces would appear, making sleep impossible. She wondered if she would recognise either of them if she met them in person.

So what would happen next? It appeared the investigations were continuing so the government could gauge the Indigene's level of threat to the human population. Considering the level of investment to date, that was understandable, she thought. But there was a danger the affair could become one big PR disaster; with hundreds of millions having already transferred to Exilon 5, it would be difficult to keep the other race's existence a secret forever. In addition, the planet was too big an asset to relinquish control of easily.

Laura guessed the government would stay and fight. With time running out for humans on Earth, it would be impossible to find another planet with such exacting requirements in a short time frame. Why not try living side by side? Laura mused. Was the planet not big enough to accommodate everyone? Couldn't

271

the Indigenes just live somewhere without humans interfering? Was that the reason for the ongoing investigation—the World Government was working out if everyone could live side by side? She badly wanted to believe the Indigenes were peaceful, but humans had already threatened their existence. From the reports, it wasn't clear how they felt about the humans' presence.

With only twenty-four more hours of her shift remaining, Laura realised she needed to stop thinking about it to conserve what little energy she had left. She reckoned she could drag her body around the office for another day, as long as she managed to get some decent shut-eye at the end of it.

Lunchtime came around and Laura gratefully clocked off from the system. Even after her humiliating experience with Chris and Janine a week ago, she'd decided to persist with the idea of taking regular lunch breaks. Apart from it being good practice, she wasn't going to let her former colleagues' petty behaviour drive her away. She just made sure to go at times when they wouldn't be there. The replication terminal across the road and the abuse she seemed to attract there was not an option.

Laura ate her lunch in silence and operated on autopilot for most of it. Her glazed eyes stared blankly at her plate, not really seeing the food in front of her. She didn't register the slight jolt at first as someone sat down beside her, just one seat away. Half expecting to see Chris or Janine there to offer her an apology, she gasped when she set eyes on the dark-haired woman from booth sixteen. Sixteen ignored her. Instead, she scooped food on her fork and shoved it into her waiting mouth. Laura couldn't think of anything else to do except stare at her.

'Eyes down,' Sixteen commanded as she chewed her food slowly. Her eyes remained focused on an area in front of her.

Laura did as she was told. Her previous observations of the woman had been brief. She appeared to be in her mid sixties, her black hair was styled into a neat bob. She had an angular jaw and closely set eyes. Judging from the way she slouched her back, she looked as if she was carrying a heavy burden on her shoulders.

Adrenaline burst through Laura's body, and with it she lost her appetite; she wasn't sure if the adrenaline was real or a delayed effect of the Actigen. Suddenly feeling uneasy, she picked up her coffee mug and took tentative sips of its contents. She gripped the handle so tightly, her knuckles turned white.

Sixteen continued to look elsewhere, but Laura could tell from the woman's body language that there was more to come. She waited until the woman decided to speak to her again. Through small and even mouthfuls of food, the words spilled forth like a cascade. Sixteen spoke quietly so as not to alert the roving cameras, forcing Laura to fine-tune her hearing to catch what was being said.

'This place is not what it seems. On the outside, the ESC seems to be working for the good of the people. You don't know what's really going on here. They are using you. So far they've only shown you things they want you to see.'

Laura was confused. Her eyes widened. What on earth was she talking about? What things was she referring to?

273

'You think you know why you're here,' Sixteen continued in a low murmur, 'but I bet you've questioned your presence on Level Five on more than one occasion. Why do they need *me*? What makes *me* so special? Why did they give *me* the files? It's because you're new. You're less likely to question their motives.'

Laura gasped quietly. *The Taggart files.* It had to be what she was referring to. Her eyes immediately sought out the camera's current location. Luckily, it was busy interrogating someone else.

'This place is a front for something bigger and you and I are pawns in their game. Think about it. The work we do can easily be handled by a computer. So why do they need us? We can't be necessary for the survival of this place, can we?'

Laura wanted to ask why they needed her but decided against it.

Galen Thompson's mother forced more food into her mouth. Shortly after, she spoke again. 'They think you're special, and you may well be. It's for that reason I'm giving you these.' She discreetly reached into her trouser pocket and pulled out three folded envelopes with a tiny micro file taped to the front. 'I think you need your eyes opened a little wider, before they manipulate your good nature and you wind up a pathetic wreck.' Her words were muffled and low. 'To understand what's going on here, you need to know what this place has become involved in. And prepare yourself; you are *not* going to like it.'

Laura desperately wanted to make eye contact with Sixteen but something told her it was a bad idea. Instead, she felt around blindly under the table until she retrieved the letters from her hand. With a shaky grip, she slipped them quickly into the waistband of her trousers. Surprised at how quickly she'd become devious, she tried to settle her racing heart. The adrenaline was agitating her, but her head was telling her to slow down and play it cautiously.

Trembling, she brought her mug up to her lips. 'What are they?' she asked, suddenly more awake and alert than she'd been all week. She took a sip and carefully put the mug down.

Sixteen didn't answer her at first. Instead she finished her meal quickly, keeping her eyes as vacant as they had been at the very start. 'Try not to get caught with them,' she said eventually.

'But I still don't understand. Why me?' Laura said.

Sixteen placed her hands on the edge of her tray. 'Because you have no connection to any of it. You're the last person they'll suspect.' She stood up and headed for the exit, depositing her tray along the way.

Laura feigned disinterest when the woman from booth sixteen got up to leave; the last thing she needed was for the cameras to seek her out. She could feel the adrenaline slowly leaving her system as the blood returned to her extremities. But she still felt jacked up. Her heart fluttered unnaturally, as it tried to return to a normal rhythm. If her experiences over the last week were anything to go by, getting caught talking to anyone—including the Level Five employees with whom she worked—was not a good idea. She hoped the authorities would view Sixteen's proximity as an oversight rather than a deliberate attempt to make contact.

Laura battled against the urge to take out the letters and read them; she had to assume eyes were on her at all times, as she'd been told they were by the man from booth ten. She forced herself to stay seated for a further five agonising minutes before leaving the cafeteria as casually as she could.

On her way back to Level Five, she stopped in the bathroom, went into one of the cubicles and quickly locked the door behind her. She removed the letters from her waistband and carefully peeled the micro file off the front, holding it in the palm of her hand. It was the size of an old Australian two-dollar coin with a tiny wire feed extruding from one end. It was designed to be viewed through a monitor, but there was no way she could risk hooking it up in work. Any deviation from regular work would be guaranteed to raise the alarm.

With her curiosity now piqued, Laura needed to see what was on the file and what secrets were hidden in the letters. She thought for a moment and came up with a solution: the hardware control unit for the Light Box could accept files of this type. She had no idea whether they were monitoring her activity at home, but hoped they weren't.

Laura removed her jacket, exposing her bra. She ripped a small hole in the fabric and slipped the file neatly between the padding, then tucked the letters into the back of her underwear until they were secure and she was sure they wouldn't slip down her trouser leg. She washed her hands and tidied her appearance before resuming her duties for the afternoon.

26

Passenger Ship

In the black night sky, the stars melded into one blur of white light. At their current speed, Bill Taggart would be unable to see the constellations like Andromeda, Aquarius and Orion when the passenger ship neared Earth. Since he was young, he'd had more than a passing interest in astronomy. To him the stars signified new beginnings. He liked the simplicity of the sky, of space, of the untroubled planets that existed independently from Earth's mess—anything that suggested life could truly exist without complications.

As it rode the magnetic slipstream between the planets, the ship passed by what looked like two moons. Fleetingly, the light changed from white to grey, then back to white again. A moon: that's what Earth now looks like from space, he thought. It looked nothing like the old photos that showed it as a luminous blue and white sphere.

Bill waited until most people were asleep before he wandered the ship alone. With only one hundred and seventy Actives out of the thousand plus passenger list, the place was quiet at night. It had been a week since he'd left Exilon 5, and while fleeting moments of rest came to him, it was far from restorative. Just when he thought he might give in to sleep, he'd almost suffocated in his sleeping unit. If it hadn't been for those two men—well, he may not have survived.

Since that day, he'd given plenty of thought to the two men. Every time he closed his eyes, he could see them—their faceless silhouettes with eyes that burned bright. But he hadn't set eyes on either of them since, nor was he looking for them. He was maintaining a low profile.

The idea of falling into a deep sleep again scared him and he was trying to stay lucid with Actigen. He knew that clinging on to a chemically maintained consciousness was no substitute for proper sleep; he felt inhuman as his body fought him for outright control. Bill's sleep-deprived mind had fooled him into thinking that his brush with death— the oxygen loss and the unit lockdown—had little to do with a computer glitch, and he'd recently become suspicious of the ship's crew. He was sure that if he spoke to them, he'd be able to tell if they were lying to him. But only part of him wanted to face them. Another part of him said it was bullshit; his suspicions were just speculation—and he was heavily medicated. Then there was the World Government and the things that lurked beneath their shiny, helpful exterior—things that he knew were not above board. But he'd decided a long time ago not to delve too deeply into the secrets of his employers.

Bill moved away from the window and padded quietly along one of the tubular passageways that connected the wheel rim to the hub of the ship. He remained on guard as he navigated his way along the spokes, each step he took illuminating a new section and plunging the earlier part into darkness. He zigzagged along the horizontal tubes that connected to the vertical spokes, trying to make it difficult for anyone who might be following to track his movements.

Several minutes later, he arrived at the recreation room in the centre of the hub. Remembering his earlier idea of confronting the ship's crew but not the reason he'd ruled it out, he strode over to the door that he knew connected the hub to the operational area; he'd seen officers pass through the door several times. He held his security chip up to the access control panel. Expectedly, it flashed red. He told himself to forget about it.

Turning on his heel, a wave of dizziness hit him and he wobbled unsteadily on his feet. He knew it was the Actigen. 'Prolonged usage' and 'side effects' were emblazoned on the side of the packet, words that he'd read and forgotten in a matter of seconds. Now his motor functions were switching off. He'd managed before with little or no rest but he'd never tried to go without sleep for days on end. This time he had taken it too far and his body was screaming at him to stop.

Bill struggled to stay upright and groped around for something to hold on to. He found the edge of a nearby table. As soon as he thought he had a grip, he angled his body towards the seat. An unsteady grip sent him crashing straight to the floor. He lay there, winded, his head groggy and his body limp. He attempted to sit up, but he could only manage a back and forth rocking motion. So he tried rolling onto his side and used his hands to help him onto his knees. Another bout of dizziness almost knocked him back down. He pushed up off the floor and gripped the table again, managing to find the chair this time. The dizziness came at him and he clamped the sides of his head to stop the motion, but his head slipped out of his grip too easily and slammed into the table. He briefly lost consciousness as the hard knock brought him back to reality. He tried to lift his suddenly heavy head off the flat surface. But it was easier to stop fighting and give in.

Bill awoke with a start and was disorientated at first. In the almost-black environment, he concentrated on key features—things that he might recognise the longer he stared at them. He tried to piece together his last movements. The last thing he remembered was sitting in the recreation room before his head hit the table. It had all happened so fast. Now here he was in his sleeping unit with absolutely no memory of how he got there. He wasn't even sure of the time. He felt panic swell inside him. *What the hell happened to me? How did I get here?*

He vowed it would be the last time he would let his guard down. He also vowed to go easy on the pills.

27

Earth

Laura didn't get any sleep that morning in her apartment in Haymarket, knowing that what she had in her possession could get her into a lot of trouble. The projection on the wall read midday and she was still deliberating if she should even look at the contents of the micro file. She'd been dead on her feet the day before, but now, she was unusually alert.

She had spent the better part of the morning contemplating various ideas about what might be on the file, whether they were remotely monitoring her Light Box or if there was a chance that they'd followed her home. She eventually discounted the last idea, having been home almost three hours and with no sign of ESC security at her door. As for the monitoring of the Light Box, it was impossible for her to know since she wasn't a technical expert.

Laura ran her fingers across the unopened letters on her side table, the ones that were addressed to 'Bill Taggart'. She brought the paper up to her nose and thought she could smell perfume. While she'd wanted to tear the letters open minutes after getting them, now she couldn't do anything more than look at them; they weren't meant for her and she sensed they were personal.

Viewing the contents of the micro file was

something within her control but Sixteen's words screamed loudly inside her head, *'to understand what's going on here, you need to know what this place has become involved in. And prepare yourself; you are not going to like it.'* Those very words had stopped her from opening it the second she arrived home. While Chris and Janine could easily entertain the idea that the ESC was involved in foul play, Laura was less influenced by gossip. Now that she might have proof in her hand, it scared her to death. By taking the smallest of peeks at the file's content, there would be no turning back. She realised she could be jeopardising her lottery chances but her curiosity to learn more about who she worked for was stronger than her need to move.

Laura tossed and turned in the bed, wrapping the covers tightly around her, willing herself to sleep. She had been so tired all week, but rest wouldn't come. Eventually she gave up and got up—an action that instantly filled her with fear. What she was about to do terrified her. She walked over to the window and increased the tint just a little.

Her apartment in Haymarket, Sydney, was ten floors up and gave her a clear view of the street below. She reached for a pair of magnification glasses—something she'd found among her dad's personal effects. She'd never had a good excuse to use them before now. She put them on and focused on exposed areas to the front of the building. She looked into the block across the street; the rooms were dark, even where the glass tint was at its lowest and there was nothing to see. She removed the glasses and decreased the tint on her window again.

Slipping into her robe, she tied the straps securely around her waist, as if the action would somehow protect her more. She retrieved the micro file from its hiding place and studied it more closely, turning it over with her index finger. How could something so small be so dangerous? she wondered as she walked uneasily towards the living room.

The Light Box's virtual display hummed into life when Laura stepped into the room. It waited for a first command. She prised opened the cover to the hardware control unit beneath the virtual display and inserted the file's tendril into one of six openings. The opening swallowed it and the two temporarily merged into one. The display changed and a new screen filled the wall, illuminating her apartment in the process. On the left-hand side, a yellow icon flashed.

'Open icon,' Laura said and the screen immediately listed the contents of the micro file. There were ten documents, each one identifiable by a security code, followed by another number. The second number was the date and the files were arranged in chronological order. The information spanned several years. Other than that, the numbers did not indicate what was actually in each document.

'Open first document,' she said. She could feel her heart beating in her throat as she spoke the words. She figured the best place to start was at the beginning and work her way through to the last.

The display changed and a report filled the screen. Laura checked over her shoulder out of a new habit, but except for her furniture, the room remained empty. She sat down on the edge of the nearest chair, unable to relax. The chair's lacquered edge bit into her skin to remind her that she shouldn't get too comfortable. Her palms were clammy with anticipation and she was shaking. This was just the beginning.

The on-screen report had been issued from Daphne Gilchrist to Charles Deighton. At the time of correspondence, Gilchrist was Head of Operations at the ESC, a position that Suzanne Brett now filled, as well as being in charge of Level Five. The document centred around the indigenous race on Exilon 5, something she'd already read about in one of Bill Taggart's reports. It had been written twenty-five years ago, five years after the explosions that had transformed Exilon 5 into its current state. The Taggart reports contained information about the same events of thirty years ago, which gave her a basic understanding of what was being discussed. But as she ventured further into the report, the first mention came of the experiments on the indigenous race. It wasn't clear when humans had carried out the experiments on them, but she assumed it had been at the time of their discovery. The graphic details forced her to stop reading.

'What is this?' She took a long deep breath and sat quietly for a few moments, trying to forget what she had just read. She realised it was impossible to separate the ordinary detail from the experimentations. They were interlinked. There was no other option but to read on. Something deep inside compelled her to continue. As she did, specific details about how humans had interfered in the lives of the Indigenes were laid bare for her to see; there appeared to be no limit to the amount of terror, destruction— and change—the World Government was willing to inflict upon them.

Closing the first document, Laura stood up and paced back and forth across her living room floor. She couldn't quite believe what she was seeing—was any of it even real? It had to be; why would the woman from booth sixteen risk her job, and her life, to give her false data? Reluctantly, she sat down again and willed her voice to issue the next command. The second and third documents opened and she read the content in just minutes. The experiments on the Indigenes weren't mentioned again until the fourth document—a recent one, just three months old. It tied in neatly with the ongoing investigations on Exilon 5, mentioning the investigator, Bill Taggart who had headed up the mission. She was starting to piece together the story morsel by morsel.

But she had no idea at that point what else she might learn. About three-quarters of the way into the fourth report, it was all there; the reason behind the World Government's obsession with the Indigenes had only been given in outline form, but it was enough to explain their motives and expose their lies and secrets. Then there was ESC's involvement. Neither organisation had conducted experiments so they could find out more about the aliens—they already knew everything about them.

When Laura read the fifth document, she gasped loudly. In disbelief, she covered her mouth muffling the only words to pass her lips. 'Oh my God.' Her eyes immediately shot over to her bedside table where she had left the unopened letters addressed to the investigator.

28

May 2163, Earth

'Eleanor, love, it's so great to see you.' Jenny Waterson hugged her daughter tightly as they sat down to dinner in a local Brisbane restaurant. 'How long has it been since we last caught up in person? I can't remember.'

'Hi, Mum. You're looking tired. About two months now.'

She shook her head in disbelief. 'You're kidding? I can't believe how quickly time is passing these days.'

'That job of yours has you working all sorts of hours. When was the last time you took a proper break?'

Jenny mulled the question over as she browsed the digital menu that was set into the table. 'I don't know. When was Christmas?' she replied glibly.

'Be serious!' her daughter demanded.

'Okay, okay, about two months I guess. The last time we caught up probably.' She sighed deeply.

'How long are they giving you this time?' Eleanor asked.

Jenny hesitated before replying. 'Um, a couple of days.' She knew what was coming and she wasn't in the mood for it.

'See? That's what I'm talking about. Last time

you were given a whole week off.'

'Look, love, I'm here to spend time with you, not talk about my work.' Jenny selected chicken teriyaki with Singapore noodles and a glass of red wine from the menu.

'I can't help it, Mum. The way they treat you— well, it's appalling. Maybe you should think about changing careers—working for people who actually show you more respect.'

Jenny looked at her, a little puzzled. 'And do what? I know I'm only seventy-five, but I make good money there. I'm not sure I want to start at the bottom all over again.'

'It's not so bad,' her daughter said, her eyes downcast as she mulled over her dinner choice.

'But you're only a third of the way through your life cycle. Just a baby. Plenty of years ahead of you yet.'

'And you're not down and out!' Eleanor said. 'Look, I can't sit idly by and say nothing about the way they treat you. You're nothing more than a commodity to them. It annoys me to even think about it, especially since you're the best pilot on their books.'

'You know how it works, love. I don't have to spell it out for you. It's my choice to stay and take their abuse.'

'Mum, you frustrate me at times!' she gasped. 'That's why I moved away from law to study politics. I hate the way this world is being governed.' She calmed down before speaking again. 'I'm also a qualified lawyer, so if you need someone to go in and bat for you, you only have to ask.'

'Sure will, love.' Jenny forced a smile and ran a hand across the nape of her neck; she hated arguing with her daughter. 'I couldn't ask for a better lawyer. Just leave everything to me, love. I know what I'm doing. I'll be fine.'

'I wish there was something I could do for you.'

Jenny sighed again and placed her arms on the table. 'There is. Keep me company while I enjoy my first break in months.'

Eleanor conceded the argument with her own sigh. 'I guess I can do that.'

With little warning, Jenny's communication device shrilled loudly and with persistence. Her employers, Calypso Couriers, demanded that she be contactable and to always keep the device on her person.

Jenny saw Eleanor's eyes widen as she reached for the device. 'Don't you dare answer that,' she said.

'I have to. It might be important.' Jenny connected her earpiece without looking at her. 'Yes,' she said flatly, ignoring the face her daughter was pulling. She could hear her mumble something rude.

'All personnel are required to report for duty tomorrow morning. Deighton's orders,' the voice ordered her.

'But you don't understand. I'm not due back until Monday,' Jenny said hotly. The argument was of little use. The line clicked dead. If she didn't show up the next day, she would be fired.

'I told you not to answer it,' Eleanor huffed.

'Let's just enjoy tonight and forget about everything that's wrong with this world.' Jenny smiled, but it didn't reach her eyes.

That week in work, Laura O'Halloran struggled to

order her thoughts in any meaningful way, given the despicable things she knew about her employers. She'd tried to talk to the woman from booth sixteen, but she'd blanked her every time she did. As Chris and Janine continued to keep their distance from her, she wondered who she could talk to. What was the purpose of giving her the information if she couldn't do anything with it? What was she expected to do now—just pretend that everything was normal?

When had her ordinary life changed so much that she was now Sixteen's target? Maybe it was her eagerness to rise above the others that had attracted the woman's attention. But her move to Level Five had only been about increasing her chances at lottery selection. This was never part of the plan. Sixteen was using her to channel her private issues with the World Government. Now she possessed information that was so dangerous, the experience had changed her.

Laura had lost control of something she valued strongly: her right to choose. Sixteen had pushed her on to a train—and a path—not of her own choosing. Knowing what she did about the ESC and World Government, and the decisions they were prepared to take, getting off that train wouldn't be easy. She had tried everything to erase the words and images she had seen emblazoned across the Light Box the week before, but nothing worked. Their activities replayed in her head, and then there was Isla Taggart and the picture of her talking to the Indigenes. In one picture she was laughing at something that had been said, the same picture that had words stamped across it: 'Destroy the evidence'.

Laura reasoned that there was only one thing left to do: she must get rid of the evidence. She would pass the letters on to Bill Taggart and destroy the micro file, in that order. But could she destroy the file now that she knew what was on it? Sure, it would be risky holding on to the coin-shaped file and she wasn't quite sure why she still had it. Maybe she hoped there was a different explanation for what she'd seen, or that the entire thing had been one big joke on her—a rite of passage for the new girl.

No, this was something else, she felt. Sitting in her booth, she pulled on her usual happy face and pretended she wanted to be there, when anywhere else would have been preferable.

29

Galen Thompson watched Stuart, his overseer, pace back and forth along the length of the observation deck; the military muscle had arrived; the operation was in full swing. Their primary role was to apprehend the stowaway on board the ship as quickly and as safely as possible. But until that happened there would be little for anyone to do, which was giving the military ample time to inspect Stuart's operational hub. Galen's own search for the ESC memos would have to wait, the ones his parents said implicated one of the workers at HJA. He wasn't going to take any chances, not with Charles Deighton's men breathing down his neck.

Stuart shadowed the military as they moved from one spot to another. His right hand twitched involuntarily at his side. Galen thought his reaction to the military's presence was over the top. Stuart fixed his communication device in his ear and stormed out of the room. Galen followed him, his interest suddenly piqued. His overseer moved into the corridor. Galen hung back, and tucked himself into a corner.

'Jenny, pick up. It's Stuart,' he whispered. 'Shit. You were right. I've done something terrible. Remember that clean sheet I have? Well, it only happens when I change a few dates and numbers.' Stuart began to pace back and forth. 'Shit, Jenny. If you're there, please pick up. I know you're in the skies now but I really need to speak to you. I don't know what to do. The military are here and they're like a pack of dogs fighting over a bone. What should I do?' Stuart waited a few seconds for a reply and finally disconnected the call. 'Shit.'

Before Galen could move, Stuart had turned the corner and seen him. 'Galen! What the hell are you doing out here?'

Galen flushed a crimson red. 'I was coming to get you. The passenger ship is almost in range. You need to get in there.'

Stuart eyed him closely. 'What did you hear?'

'I just arrived.' Galen held eye contact for as long as he could.

Stuart's tone changed. 'We've been working together for a while now. I hope you won't do anything to ruin that.'

Galen said nothing.

'Come on, the sooner these goons are gone, the better.' He pushed Galen ahead of him.

As the ship edged closer to the docking station, the need for obvious distractions lessened and Stuart appeared to be less tense. Once the ship had passed the outlying planets in the solar system, the military personnel adopted hive-like characteristics and started to move and act as one. With the ship's arrival just an hour away, the communications operative ordered the spacecrafts to rendezvous with the ship at predetermined coordinates. The pilot came into range and connected with the docking station through the satellites that orbited the planets.

The military suddenly hovered over controllers who were checking for debris in the ship's path. The controllers ignored their distracting questions while they completed their checks. The two heads of the military group stood over the communications operative in a threatening manner while he tried to speak to the pilot. Stuart shot over to where they stood and shadowed their every move.

'Ask him if there were any disturbances on board,' the sergeant ordered the operative.

The operative complied and the pilot answered in his earpiece. 'No, there hasn't been anything reported, sir,' he replied flatly.

'Doesn't mean anything,' the corporal said to the sergeant. 'We should still consider the stowaway to be a serious threat.'

'I agree,' the sergeant said and turned around. He jumped when he noticed Stuart standing directly behind him and backed away from him slightly. 'We're going to need everybody's full cooperation until the person we're after has been safely apprehended.'

'Of course,' Stuart replied agreeably and took a step forward. 'If there's anything at all we can do, please don't hesitate—'

'I want to speak to the pilot,' the sergeant interrupted. He grabbed the communication operative's shoulder and thrust out his other hand. The operative handed the earpiece to the sergeant with the cropped military hairstyle and the stiff posture. He shoved it into his ear and spoke gruffly into the micro-thin wire that protruded from it. 'Pilot of the passenger ship. You have a dangerous stowaway on board. Do not approach, under any circumstances. Proceed as normal. The military will be handling this situation on the ground.' The sergeant nodded briefly when the pilot responded, then pulled the earpiece out and tossed it casually on the table, out of the operative's reach. The operative angrily reached across the table to retrieve it.

'Who have you got in the skies at the moment?' he barked at Stuart.

Stuart's temper flared as he replied through gritted teeth. 'Cream of the crop, sir. All experienced pilots have been recalled from leave or other duties and are at your disposal. Will you be sending your own people up with the pilots?'

'Negative. We don't want military presence to scare off this individual. We will apprehend the subject when it arrives. Who will be collecting the fake Bob Harris from the passenger ship?'

'The best pilot we have, Captain Jennifer Waterson,' Stuart replied.

'Does she know why we're here?' the sergeant asked.

'Yes, but only that the person you are looking for will be boarding *her* craft—nothing beyond that.'

'Keep it that way. We don't want the pilot to panic unnecessarily. When we have our man, we'll be out of here.'

Galen noted the strange tone that the sergeant used to describe 'our man'.

The ship arrived five minutes ahead of schedule and hovered in the outer perimeter surrounding Earth. Jenny Waterson waited alongside seven other crafts at the designated coordinates while the ship was steered into position. The crafts hovered silently in the black expanse as the doors of Cargo Hold 1 in the ship's underside winched open like the jaws of a beast. One by one, they entered through the dock and landed on the port and aft sides. Jenny was scheduled to be the second last to enter and the first to leave with her passenger quota. According to the manifest, her passengers would include maintenance workers, architects and road designers—her destination, the HJA docking station. The rest, including several government employees, were scheduled to arrive at Sydney.

Inside the hold, Jenny gently tweaked the controls until she felt the landing skids touch the floor. The craft bounced slightly off course until she corrected it with a flick of her hand. She tried to hit the landing spot again, but the lack of gravity made it more difficult. She tweaked the controls gently until it finally settled on the floor and disengaged the thrusters so it wouldn't move again. While she waited for the confine to decompress, she kept the force field in place. Once the hold was made safe, the eight craft doors slid open to reveal their dark cavernous interiors.

The passengers waited in orderly queues, unaware of the attention being given to the HJA docking station below them. Jenny easily identified the ones that hadn't emerged fully from stasis. Even with the anti-stasis serum injections, it could be another two hours before the passengers—still disconnected from reality—would feel completely human again.

The journey had taken a different kind of toll on others and Jenny noticed one man in particular who was heading for one of the other crafts. An attractive man in his mid forties, he looked physically drained as he shuffled along with the others. His appearance was neat and tidy, his hair combed and his skin smooth, but his eyes said he hadn't slept a wink over the last fourteen days.

From the on-board computer, she downloaded the manifest from the ship officer's DPad using a unique identification code. As everyone filed on board, she requested they all strap in tightly, and reminded them of what to expect on the short and intense journey ahead of them: some might feel sick and should use the bags provided under their seats, she explained.

Jenny manoeuvred her craft out of the hold and headed for the predetermined landing coordinates at Dock 10. One by one, the other crafts followed suit, branching off towards their own destinations. She made brief contact with the communications operator in HJA and received instructions that she was clear for landing. She began her descent, firing all thrusters until she had dropped below the outer perimeter shield, where the remaining leg of the journey towards the landing plate would be dictated by gravitational pull alone.

Stephen and Anton separated when they boarded the craft and sat in differently located seats. Gone were the long brown trench coats and brown fedoras; they were replaced by modern navy blue suits and small black Stetsons, in line with what some of the others had been wearing. Anton had bypassed security in one of the sleeping areas where the Dormants were being housed. While the clothes were not an exact fit, they were at least in keeping with the style. After listening to the pilot's instructions, they strapped in tightly.

Stephen relaxed a little, confident their arrival on Earth would be without problems.

Galen watched through one of the observation deck's viewing screens as Dock 10 became infested with dozens of military personnel. Hidden behind crates, the roving cameras tracked their movements precisely. He expected they would make their move when the passengers disembarked; the military didn't know who exactly was using Bob Harris's identity.

Galen hadn't witnessed a military presence quite like this before. In the back of his mind, he thought about his parents and their obsessive need to court danger. He chewed on his thumb, wondering if the military would go to the same efforts if his mother and father were the ones being sought out. On the one hand, it would be easier if they were—Galen could go back to a simpler life without always having to search for something incriminating. On the other, the World Government would probably deal with his parents' crimes in a cleaner way—in a private place with no witnesses. So why were they hunting a person out in the open, where everybody could see?

The lines on his forehead deepened and he looked around to see how everybody else felt about the intrusion. His eyes settled on Stuart's worried face long enough for his own tension to increase.

'What do you think will happen to the stowaway?' he asked cautiously, reminded of Paddy's story about his ex-colleague. A chill coursed through his body.

'I have no bloody idea,' Stuart snapped. 'One thing I know is if I were Bob Harris, I wouldn't be returning to this crap hole called Earth.'

Galen understood. The stories about Exilon 5 were wildly infectious. Having watched one of the government's videos on the bullet train, it was easy to believe their vision of a lush green, sunny alternative to this destitute planet. He thought about the fate of Bob Harris, but only briefly.

Galen wondered if he should call his parents to tell them what was happening or to fill them in on Stuart's falsification of records; his search for the person of interest and the ESC memos was finally over. But something told him not to. Stuart was not their enemy; he was just a man who made a wrong call. Who knew what brand new danger his parents would seek out if they found out about this?

His attention was drawn back to the screen. The craft had just landed.

While he and Anton waited to disembark with the other passengers, Stephen became distracted by the pilot's low whisperings to someone within the docking station. The female had turned her back to the group and was trying to be discreet. But he'd been able to pick up her conversation.

'Yes, he is,' she confirmed. 'I'm looking at the manifest now. How do you want me to proceed?' Stephen could make out the voice, a male, on the other end of the line. 'Do nothing. This is our operation now, ma'am.'

The pilot shuddered, muttering quietly. 'I fucking hate it when they call me that.' She replied officially to the caller. 'Understood.'

Anton shot an anxious look at Stephen: the humans knew they were on board.

Galen and six others were transfixed by the main screen action. The sergeant had ordered non-essential personnel to stay out of Dock 10 and all other crafts were diverted to alternative docking stations as the entire HJA docking station was placed on lockdown.

A dull ache spread through Galen's legs. He looked around and thought about pulling over a chair to sit on but caught Stuart glaring at him from across the room. Instead, Galen took a deep breath and willed the ache in his legs away. Stuart continued to shadow the sergeant, who had stayed behind on the observation deck. The corporal was in Dock 10 where he waited for further orders from his sergeant. The sergeant continued to hassle the communication operative, who ignored his intrusion as best as he could.

Galen watched the sergeant for a moment. He had two theories about him: either the sergeant felt he could direct the operation better from the observation deck, or he didn't want to be in Dock 10 when the stowaway arrived. Far safer to be up here if the struggle turned nasty, Galen mused.

The sergeant's agitation increased suddenly. He spoke to the corporal. 'Order the docking attendants to scan every identity chip. We need to know which one is ours. I don't care. If you have to. Just make sure it's still alive. Gilchrist's orders.'

While in the company of so many humans on board the craft, Stephen spoke telepathically to Anton. They anxiously waited for the craft doors to open and be ushered to the scanning station.

'They can't catch both of us. Why don't we just make a run for it?' Anton suggested.

'Because I think they've erected a force field around the building. We won't get very far,' Stephen replied.

'So what's left? We can't just give up now. We've come this far.'

'I've no intention of giving up,' Stephen stayed silent for a moment as he ran through the limited options available to them in his mind. When his eyes finally widened, Anton noticed the change.

'What is it?' he asked.

'I think I have a plan, but it's going to be dangerous,' Stephen said. 'How fast can you run these days?'

'Almost as fast as you. You need me to go somewhere?'

'Yes, but try not to get caught. I don't want to be left alone too long with these humans.' He flinched when the woman behind him inched forward and invaded his personal space. 'I don't know what I might do.'

'I can handle it.' Anton straightened up.

Stephen smiled half-heartedly. 'For once, I'm glad to hear you say that. But we need to stick to the rear of the group. If they're going to find us, let's make sure nobody else gets in our way.'

He watched as Anton waited in line with the other passengers. He desperately wanted to lend support to his friend, but in the event the humans were only searching for one of them, there was no way they could be linked. When most of the passengers had filed off the craft, Stephen wasn't surprised when military humans suddenly emerged from behind tall crates that were stacked three high in places; he'd already picked up their sickly sweet scent. Some of the military humans went to stand directly behind attendants just as they scanned identity chips. Passengers gasped when they saw the extra force and tried to figure out the reason for their presence.

The line progressed quickly as cleared passengers were ushered out through a set of doors to the rear of the dock. With most of the passengers having already disembarked, Stephen deliberately remained at the back of the group.

A nervous Anton hoped he could create enough of a diversion for Stephen to get to safety. But that was only part of it. The next part was much trickier: getting Stephen through the docking station's force field. He hadn't told Stephen but he wasn't planning to go with him.

A dozen military eyes scanned the length of the queue, then a second time, paying close attention to the faces. Three sets of eyes lingered on him. He held his breath and stood perfectly still, his adrenaline charged and readied for flight. Their eyes scrutinised his appearance, searching for something—anything—that seemed out of place. They looked from one passenger to the next, eager to find something wrong in the comparison. Anton tried to relax his facial expression and look disinterested. Their eyes eventually moved on to the next person.

Anton steadied his racing heart and released the breath he'd been holding. While the new version of the artificial skin had worked, the identity chips would soon reveal who he was. He drew in a new breath and held it. He reached the top of the line and the attendant motioned him forward. Anton placed his left thumb on the DPad and prepared himself. The name that flashed up sent the military into frenzied overdrive.

Strong arms grabbed at him and tried to force him to the ground. He stumbled, but regained control long enough to twist out of their grip. The military tightened their hold, still believing they had him but it took a second for them to notice that Anton was moving towards the doors to the rear of the dock. While the strength of ten officers was a worthy match for Anton, his speed had surprised them all.

An officer reached for a black object in his holster. The air crackled with uncontrollable energy. Static in the room built up to the point where it nipped at Anton's skin. The static eliminator he carried in his pocket felt hot. He rubbed away the sensation on his arm and bolted for the doors. Hot on his heels were ten military humans.

Jenny watched the action unfold from the safety of the cockpit while just one passenger remained on board. She eventually made her way to where he stood by the open door.

'Must be serious,' she said. 'They don't usually bring out the big guns unless the person they're after is a serious criminal.' She placed a reassuring hand on his shoulder. The coldness that seeped through his jacket caught her by surprise. 'You should stand back from the door. It's too dangerous to go out there when the military are armed. They're always itching to use their damn weapons. I've seen innocents get caught up in the middle of their crossfire. It's almost like they have to shoot at something or they'll die of boredom. Hang back here for just an instant.'

She turned around but spun on her heels when she heard the familiar sound of the craft door sucking closed. Her jaw dropped as her remaining passenger stood with his finger poised over the door's control panel.

'What the hell are you doing?' she cried, about to make a move towards him. 'Get away from there. You have no right.'

She had only uttered the words when he was already standing beside her. She saw a flash of metal and tasted bile in the back of her throat. She gasped in horror at the man's speed. *What are you?* She tried to speak but no words would come.

Stephen spoke calmly as he jammed the metal rod into her back. 'I need you to erect the force field around this thing—now. I will hurt you if I have to. It's a matter of life and death.'

'For who?' Jenny dared to ask. The pressure of the weapon on her skin made her shudder.

'For you, for me. For many reasons that are beyond your comprehension.'

The man's actions terrified her but she couldn't give up so easily. She drew on her experience of dealing with her fair share of difficult passengers. 'Who are you? Tell me why you're here.'

Stephen forced her into the cockpit and shoved her easily into the seat. 'I said erect the force field around this craft.' His voice had become more urgent.

'Why should I?' Jenny pushed her luck. A nervous crackle emanated from her dry throat.

'Because I could snap your neck easily if I wanted to. But I need you—I want to find William Taggart.'

The name was not at all familiar to her. 'Who's William Taggart? What's this all about?'

'Force field first.' He jabbed the rod into her spine once more.

Jenny figured she would live longer if she

303

complied. The dock was free from military personnel as they chased after their person of interest; there was no one left that could come quickly to help her. She considered calling the observation deck, but from what she'd already seen she could be dead before anyone made it to her in time. She pressed a button on her console. 'Done.'

'Find William Taggart.'

Jenny noticed the man's voice was cold, devoid of emotion. 'How am I supposed to do that?' she said. 'I haven't heard the name before. Can you at least tell me where I should begin?'

'He was a passenger on the ship I was on. Find him for me.' Stephen jammed the rounded end of the rod into her rib.

Jenny flinched. 'Okay, okay. I'll help you, but could you ease off first? You're really hurting me.'

Stephen reduced the pressure and Jenny heard his emotion slip slightly as he said, 'I am desperate to find him.'

'What is he to you?' The weapon no longer bruised her skin, but he still held it firmly against her ribcage. She was met with silence. She cautiously turned her head to look at her passenger. It was the word 'desperate' that had caught her attention and forced her to meet the eyes of her assailant. The man's eyes were strange—wild but fearful. 'I will help you,' she said calmly. It was what she had been taught to say if she was ever caught in a hostage situation.

Stephen didn't respond.

She still couldn't figure out whether she was safe or if these were the actions of a frantic individual. She scanned the ship's computer and found the name her kidnapper was looking for. 'Here he is—an ITF investigator. Heading to Sydney, probably going to the Security Centre, I imagine. Can I go now?'

'No. I need you to take me there, but not now. Someone is working on getting us out of here. So I just need you to sit here and be quiet.'

Anton took no time in reaching a room that he quickly identified as the observation deck. He had a good lead on the pursuing group, which gave him an opportunity to wedge the door shut from the inside; that would hold them off, if only for a short while. There were a dozen humans already inside the large room, but not so many that he couldn't deal with them.

Anton's eyes honed in on the military human that cowered behind two others like a scared rabbit. The rest were glued to the spot, staring blankly at the stranger in their midst. He took advantage of that and identified the weakest in the group.

With a crude weapon in hand, he picked out the youngest in the room and made a beeline for him. Without hesitation, he looped an arm around Galen's neck and stuck the razor-sharp end of his weapon into his flesh.

'I need someone to drop the force field around this station,' Anton said.

Stuart stepped forward hesitantly. 'I'm not sure who you think you are, sonny, coming in here and threatening my staff? I won't have it, not on my watch. Do you hear me? Do yourself a wee favour and drop your weapon before you get into serious trouble.'

'I'm in charge now,' Anton replied clinically. 'I

305

said drop the force field.' A snarl crossed his lips, which put everybody on edge. He could feel Galen's body turn rigid beneath his grip.

'Listen here. This is my station. And by the way, *pal*, if anybody is in charge here, it's me, not you.' Stuart calmed his temper. 'Now just let the young lad go. No harm done.'

Anton sensed truth behind the threat, coupled with a real sense of fear. He upped the ante. Making a small incision on Galen's neck, he moved with speed to stand behind Maria and threatened her with the same weapon. He could hear them gasp and knew it was not the violence that had shocked them but the way he'd just moved; he needed to show them he was no ordinary threat. He glanced over at his first target just as a small trickle of blood wept from the tiny cut he'd made on his neck.

'What the hell are you?' Stuart said, moving forward more tentatively now.

'Do you see that craft down there?' He nodded towards the viewing screen showing Dock 10. 'It needs to leave. You need to drop the force field.'

'Why on earth would you think I'd do that for you?' Stuart said hotly. 'All you've managed to do so far is threaten my staff.'

'Because I could kill you all within seconds and you wouldn't be able to stop me.'

Stuart hesitated slightly.

Anton had already shown them what he was capable of doing—he was not like them, that much should have been clear.

Stuart spoke to the communications operative. 'Drop the force field.'

'Are you sure about that?' the operative replied.

Stuart flashed him a look that told him not to

argue. The operative moved to the nearest panel and manually shut off the field.

Stuart stared hard at Anton. 'What's on that craft that's so damned important to you anyway?'

He smiled wryly. 'You have no idea.'

'Well, whoever it is had better not hurt the pilot in any way. If they do, I'll be coming after you—you can be sure of that.'

Anton sensed the truth behind the words but chose not to placate him.

The sergeant took a step forward but remained behind the operative and Stuart for protection. 'You won't get away with this you know.' He wagged his finger in Anton's direction. 'You are trapped here, you fool. You won't last two minutes when my men get here.'

Anton ignored the threat and spoke to Stuart. 'Contact them and tell them they can leave.'

Moments later, the hijacked craft, piloted by Jenny Waterston, rose out of Dock 10 to begin its brief journey to Sydney.

Distracted by its departure, Anton hadn't noticed the military humans enter the room. In a flash, he moved towards Galen again; this time he faced him. He couldn't explain his interest in the human other than that he was drawn to him. He'd assumed it was because the male was the weakest of the group, but there was an easy familiarity that drew Anton in dangerously close. His mannerisms, the way he looked at him, reminded him of his father Leon. In some small way, he began to understand Stephen's obsession with Ben, but not his aversion to all other humans. Galen tensed up and reflexively shot a hand over his neck to protect it. Anton chuckled at the instinctive move.

307

'What are you exactly?' Galen asked.

'If I knew that, human, I wouldn't be here.'

A sudden discharge of electricity made Anton's teeth stand on edge. He slumped awkwardly to the ground as the military moved in.

30

Bill walked quickly through the public entrance of the Earth Security Centre and headed straight for the turbo lift at the other end of the foyer. The public area was bathed in a natural light because of the glass panels that covered the ceiling; set into each one was a reflective pigmentation that magnified tiny shafts of light by up to a thousand times their original strength. Panel images transformed the grey world outside into a blue wonder. It was how the ESC marketed itself: as a beacon of light and hope while the world outside languished in despair and eternal darkness. And it worked, as was obvious from the crowd of eager recruits gathered to hear the history of the building from appropriately trained guides.

Bill snaked a path through the busy lobby, distracted by thoughts about what he would say at the debriefing—get the tone wrong and Gilchrist would stick him on traffic duty. His wife's face came to mind and she was telling him to keep a cool head. He agreed and if he could convince Gilchrist that he was not on the mission for any other reason, she might keep him on.

At first, Bill hadn't noticed the young woman looking at him strangely, but the second he did he jacked up his defences; he didn't know her, but she looked at him as if he was somehow familiar to her. His eyes settled uneasily on her pretty face as he tried to decide how threatening she might be to him. But the young woman's face seemed troubled, her kind face unable to counteract the distressed look in her eyes—eyes filled with deep and dark secrets. The blonde-haired woman held his gaze as she passed. Bill noticed something else behind the eyes—a warning.

He nodded to her once. She didn't reciprocate.

Laura's legs turned to jelly as soon as she saw Bill Taggart walking in her direction. She thought about turning around but she couldn't bring herself to do it. She remembered the letters that were hidden in her apartment and the secret words they contained. For a moment, she wondered why he was at the ESC, but remembered it probably had something to do with his investigative work on Exilon 5.

She held his gaze for as long as she could but when he nodded to her, she froze. The place was crowded and she'd no idea if one of the roving cameras was tailing her, recording her every movement. No matter what else happened, she couldn't let them connect her to the information she had seen. She applied enough power to her legs to carry her out the front entrance and take her home.

The walk to her apartment block in Haymarket took longer than usual and Laura's distracted state of mind meant she hadn't noticed the person following her home. It wasn't until she reached the outer door to her block that the sound of movement was clear. The skies were grey and the street was dark, making it all too easy for someone to attack. With every ounce of strength, she resisted the urge to turn around. Instead, she fumbled around in her bag for an object that could double up as a weapon.

She deliberated how much time she'd need to activate the lock on the outer door and close it safely behind her. It would take her thumbprint to open it, but every movement wasted precious time and gave the advantage back to her pursuer. She had no idea how close the person was, but her skin tingled as if they were nearer than they should have been.

Damn, nothing in my bag. She cursed as she desperately tried to think of a plan B. She wished now she had actually prepared a plan B, or even a plan A for that matter. She should have known that her move to Level Five would bring with it added risks. She was reminded of what the creepy worker in booth ten had said to her: *what you retain can get you killed.* As she waited for her pursuer to make their move, she now believed the warning with all her heart.

Just face whoever it is and act all innocent, she ordered silently. Laura was about to turn round when a hand touched her shoulder. She froze, a reaction that was brought on in part by an icy sensation that seeped through the heavy fabric of her uniform. She still couldn't see who the threatening person was.

'Don't try anything. I'm armed and dangerous,' she said, trying to sound convincing. When she finally managed to look behind her she gasped in shock at the figure that stood inches from her face. It was someone she wouldn't forget in a hurry.

'I wouldn't be here if I had another choice,' Stephen said. 'I saw you with Bill Taggart just now. This is the last place I can think of. I need your help.'

Bill arrived at Level Seven for the scheduled debriefing with Daphne Gilchrist. He took a seat as he waited for her personal assistant to announce his arrival. He was ushered quickly into the large boardroom that was connected to her private office. The place was familiar to him because briefings were common enough, but this time it felt different. He walked inside, expecting to see a full turnout for the significant debriefing. Instead, just three people waited for him. Gilchrist stood at the top of the room, while Suzanne Brett and Simon Shaw, his boss from the ITF London office, sat on either side of the table.

Gilchrist read his thoughts. 'There won't be anyone else joining us today. This is a closed debriefing. The others will be informed in due course about the outcome of today's meeting.'

Bill nodded and took the seat that she pointed to, at the far cnd of the oval table. As he did, his mind raced through the possibilities of what this might mean for him.

'Well, let's begin shall we?' Gilchrist began. 'We've received your files from both meetings and have gone through the evidence. But now I would like to hear your version of events.'

Bill took a short breath before launching into the details of the case. He recounted his orders to the military personnel who'd been given specific instructions that day not to approach the target. He recalled how their advances had caused the target to exit early from the gardens. He identified the pursuit team that had followed the alien and the communication silence they maintained, both of which—he made quite clear to the debriefing group—he had not authorised.

The trio sat in silence. Neither Suzanne nor Simon made a move to comment; they simply nodded as they listened with apparent interest. As Bill continued to recount his version of events and only Gilchrist asked questions, he began to wonder if the other two were there simply for show—or as witnesses. Fifteen minutes later, he summarised.

'So, where do you think we should go from here?' Gilchrist asked.

Bill had given that question many hours of consideration on the journey back to Earth and had prepared a textbook answer for the CEO. 'Well, it's likely the Indigene won't risk surfacing again for some time. My suggestion is we wait.'

'Wait?' She arched one brow suspiciously.

'Yes. Wait a few months and then attempt to track them electronically when they finally resurface.'

'Is that it?' she sounded unimpressed.

'No. We have a list of people on Exilon 5 who have made inadvertent contact with the Indigenes before this. I plan to talk to them to try to get a different angle on our investigations. It also appears that the Indigenes favour hunting at night and have already surfaced in locations already known to us. I'm proposing we set up vigils in the wastelands between the cities, to try to catch them there.' He knew the solutions he'd offered were weak at best, but he desperately wanted to stay on Exilon 5 for as long as possible. It was his best shot at turning the mission around and getting answers about his wife. His heart drummed unevenly in his chest.

Gilchrist rested a clear-polished finger on her lips. 'All interesting solutions, but I'm not sure we have the time, or personnel, to waste on mere chances.'

Shaw and Brett nodded. Bill finally understood their role, which was to agree with everything Gilchrist said in the meeting. He felt a sudden need to defend his position. He assumed that at least Simon Shaw would back him up. 'I would like to stay on this investigation,' he said.

Gilchrist smiled crookedly. 'It's not about what you want, Bill—it's about what's best for this mission.'

The calm slipped away. 'With all due respect, I am what's best for this mission. Just let me pick my team this time and—'

Gilchrist cut him off. 'There was nothing wrong with your team. More likely, it was your poor handling of the situation that led to the breakdown of communication.'

Bill said nothing; if he wanted to save himself from a reassignment to traffic duty, now was the time to keep his mouth shut.

'Thank you, Bill,' Gilchrist said. 'We'll take your points under consideration.' Shaw and Brett nodded, like the lap dogs they had become. 'We'll be in touch as soon as we have more detail about how we'll be progressing this issue.' She spoke with a forced sincerity that Bill didn't like. 'Head down to the docking station. A craft is waiting to take you to your accommodation here on Earth.'

'Where am I going?'

'Washington. Mr Deighton has asked that you be close to head office. You may be called in at short notice.'

As Bill stood to leave, he was thankful for one small thing: at least he wasn't being fired straight away. Maybe he could talk his way back onto the investigation when the heat died down.

As soon as Bill Taggart stepped through the turbo lift

doors, Daphne dismissed Shaw and Brett. She relocated to her private office and closed the door behind her. Taking a seat in her leather chair, she looked directly into the monitor on her desk and clasped her hands together tightly.

The screen changed in an instant and the sergeant's genetically treated face came into shot. He spoke confidently as he recounted the most recent events in the HJA docking station.

'Yes, we have him in custody. We have transferred him to a secured facility in Washington.'

'Good work, Sergeant. Your superiors will receive a glowing report about your team's work today.'

'Thank you, Ms Gilchrist. I appreciate your words,' he gushed.

'Out.' Daphne made a face as soon as the connection was severed; she couldn't stand the military. They were good for one thing only: brute force. Other than that, she had no use for them.

She knew Taggart hadn't been to blame for the breakdown of the operation on Exilon 5; it was impossible to control military personnel at the best of times. The decision to keep Special Ops out of it had been at Charles Deighton's request. He was concerned that Bill was getting too close to the truth about the Indigenes and his wife, and the military were an easy way to rein him in. The purpose of the mission had been to drive the Indigenes out of their hiding places and into their waiting arms. That part of it had gone very smoothly.

Daphne stood up from her expensive desk, brushed the creases out of her blue suit as best she could and ordered her assistant to make travel arrangements to Washington.

Bill left the meeting, feeling both relieved and frustrated. He hadn't been allowed to defend the outcome on Exilon 5, or his place on the mission. Suddenly he wished he could cut all ties with the government and work as an independent. He ditched the idea when he remembered how controlling his bosses were.

He stepped outside into the dull Sydney afternoon and fixed his gel mask in place. In an instant, all the bad memories he had managed to repress about Earth came flooding back, applying a thin coating to his skin. He tried to wipe the feeling off, and with it the memories that burned at him. But they lingered, along with the ghosts of those who had left him behind to survive alone in this mess. He took several steps forward through the badly congested crowds of zombie-like people, reminding himself of the world that existed beyond this one—a better world that was meant for all of them. He pulled at his mask, its tight seal suddenly making him feel claustrophobic. He could see the dead eyes of the crowd watching him, willing him to be the first to pull the mask off, to put an end to this pathetic life. He almost did.

Why was he still here? What was his purpose in this world? To search for answers? He could take his own life and ask Isla himself. But the sadness and desperation that persisted in people's eyes stopped him. He wasn't like them; he still had passion and until that passion completely died, he would fight on.

Bill checked the seal on his mask and increased his step, heading towards the docking station at Sydney's harbour front. From the moment he set foot on the road that ran next to the ESC, he could hear the sound of steady footfall behind him. The streets were busy so he tuned out unnecessary noises and distractions. His senses peaked when he heard a step and a half being taken for every one stride of his. He didn't dare to look back.

The only person he could think of that wanted him dead was Larry Hunt—the man who he'd placed behind bars. Since Hunt was still in prison, that just left his henchmen. Bill instinctively touched the area where they had knifed him some time ago. He quickened his pace and refused to give in to a backward glance. He didn't want to let his follower, or followers, know that he was aware of them. He didn't want them changing their tactics; he knew exactly where they were.

Bill crossed on to George Street, Sydney's main thoroughfare, deliberating if he should try to make a run for it or face them head on. In his mind, he had replayed this moment should it ever arise, and calculated what he might do. Now that the situation was upon him, his thoughts didn't possess any of their usual clarity. As he weaved in and out of the crowds, he felt the urge to stop and confront them; with so many people around, he could use them as protection.

He fought his initial urge and kept moving, hastily deciding to confront his pursuer, but not in the open. Heading north towards the harbour, he stayed on the street that would lead him to the area known as the Rocks. His heart thumped wildly as he tried to thrash out a possible way out of this mess.

An opportunity arose when Bill reached a road junction. He swerved round quickly on to the road heading west and waited for his follower. Confident that they had taken the same route, he ducked into a nearby alleyway and hid behind a series of crates that had been stacked outside an unused replication terminal. He watched out for the feet of his potential assailants as they approached his hiding place. When only one set passed by, he made his move. Emerging from his hiding place, he readied for a fight. But his surprise at seeing who followed him caught him off guard. He forced his shock to one side and quickly moved in, grabbing her from behind and spinning her around to face him. He closed a hand over her throat and slammed her body into the adjacent wall with force. He could hear a dull thud as her head smacked against it.

'Who are you?' he demanded as he took in the face of the young woman whom he'd seen earlier in the foyer of the ESC. Her eyes and mouth widened in horror. He loosened his tight grip on her throat. He repeated himself. 'I said who are you? Why are you following me?'

'Please, you're hurting me,' she managed to say, curling her hands around his threatening arm.

'Tell me who you are then. I saw you at the Security Centre earlier. I want to know why you're following me. Do you work for Hunt?'

'I don't know anyone called Hunt,' she struggled to say. 'My name is Laura, Laura O'Halloran. Please, let me go.'

Seeing genuine fear on her face, Bill relaxed his arm and dropped his hand. Laura rubbed the area where he'd exerted the most pressure and coughed to clear her throat.

He stepped away from her, slightly embarrassed by his heavy-handedness; her slender frame meant she was no match for his strength. He quickly regained composure when he realised he still had no idea who this woman really was. 'Who do you work for?'

Laura coughed again before answering. 'I work for the Earth Security Centre—in the High Level Data Storage Facility. I just needed to talk to you for a moment.'

He considered her answer for a moment and relaxed a fraction. 'You should really think twice about sneaking up on people like that. I could have killed you.'

'I'll try to remember that in future,' she wheezed.

'What exactly do you want to talk to me about?'

'Your most recent investigation on Exilon 5.'

Bill remained defensive. Laura's position at the Centre meant she was privy to that level of information, but he wanted some proof that she was who she claimed to be. 'First show me your credentials. If you are who you say you are that shouldn't be a problem for you.'

Laura opened her overcoat. Underneath she wore her purple uniform; she pointed to the security tags. 'There is also my security chip. But you have no way of checking that right now. I'm afraid that's all the proof I can give you, Mr Taggart. I need you to trust me on the rest.'

'Why are you interested in an investigation of mine?' Bill asked, still unsure about the nature of business she claimed to have with him.

'I've recently been given some information that directly relates to your current case. I also promised someone that I would find you and ask for your help.'

'Who—for what exactly?'

'I can't say here. I need you to come with me. I'm taking a risk just by being here. You need to trust me. Please.' Her voice was shaky.

In all his years working for the World Government, not once had anyone asked for his help. He had been asked *to* help—head up missions, profile criminals, track wanted felons. If this turned out to be a trick, Bill would pay heavily for his trust. But he sensed no malice in her tone. He sensed warmth and genuine compassion from her and it had been a long time since he'd cared about another's cause other than his own.

31

Laura led an uneasy-looking Bill back to her apartment, but there was good reason for him to be there. He had no reason to trust her but the fact he'd made it this far was encouraging. She motioned him inside but he kept a small distance behind her. She didn't blame him for his hesitation; for all he knew, she could be leading him into a trap. The man was on edge and she knew that very little would be needed to push him over. Once inside, she quickly closed the door to prevent the investigator from changing his mind.

She noticed Bill relax a little as he looked around her apartment, which was generous for Earth accommodation. 'How big is it?' he asked.

'Big enough to have a separate bedroom,' Laura said, smiling.

Bill let out a low whistle. 'I've only read about apartments this size on Earth. You can get hold of these easy on Exilon 5, you know. You must be doing well to have been given this, considering you live alone.'

'I do okay. Job perk I guess.' She shrugged, watching as Bill removed a magnetised metal cube from his pocket and attach it to the front of the Light Box's hardware unit. 'What's that?' She pointed to the object that was no bigger than a rolling dice.

'A sound interrupter—so we can talk in

private.'

Laura's mood turned darker. 'Please don't feel like this is a trick. It's not. I brought you here because I need you to meet someone. Before I bring him out, though, I need to ask you to keep an open mind.'

Bill's brow creased in confusion.

She called out to the empty space. 'It's okay. You can come out. It is just me, and I've brought Bill Taggart.'

He saw the investigator tense up as the bedroom door creaked open.

A tall figure dressed in a blue suit emerged from the darkened room. He made a move towards them. 'Hello Bill, I believe you already know who I am,' he said slowly, deliberately, his eyes fixed on the investigator's every move. Obvious anger simmered just beneath the surface. 'I would like to formally introduce myself. My name is Stephen.'

Within the hour, Daphne Gilchrist had arrived in Washington D. C. on a specially chartered craft. Marching through the front entrance of the World Government, she veered off to the left towards a hidden corridor that housed a turbo lift, connecting the surface to the secret underground levels. The levels contained a number of underground bunkers, set deep beneath the streets above; it was where the sergeant had been ordered to transfer the Indigene. The lift took just seconds to reach the requested floor. The door opened and she could see three weapon-carrying officers patrolling the bunker security area. The security system could handle unauthorised entries and escape attempts, but the additional firepower had been at Charles Deighton's request. Taking into account the type of business they carried out at these levels, he hadn't wanted to leave anything to chance. Even though many considered Deighton to be nothing more than a figurehead for the World Government, his main role was to protect the investment of the twelve members of which he was secretly one.

It took a short time for Daphne to gain clearance through the scanning station. Both of her chips were scanned and her DNA sampled and cross-referenced against the database copy. The referencing was an extra security measure; facial manipulation was popular among the radicals pretending to be someone important.

One of the officers led Daphne down a corridor to the door at the end. Waiting for her inside were Charles Deighton and the overseer for security matters in the World Government.

'Ah Daphne, I see you made it.' Deighton greeted her as if they were old friends, kissing her on both cheeks. 'So good to see you.' The words dripped off the old man's tongue like honey. There was an easy yet guarded familiarity between the two.

'Charles! I hope you haven't started without me.' Daphne performed for her boss. 'What's with all the extra security measures outside?'

He laughed a throaty cackle. 'I thought you might comment on that. Can't be too careful these days. You never know who's trying to hurt us.' He nodded towards the flexible membrane containment unit where Anton watched the trio in perfect silence.

'Daphne, you remember Tom Billings? He's here as a witness to the proceedings.' Deighton laughed a little.

'Ms Gilchrist.' The security overseer nodded meekly in her direction, offering his hand. She briefly shook it.

'Looks like we've finally recaptured our most ingenious of creations,' Deighton said, looking at Anton. 'Although, judging by his age, he's more likely to be the product of two of our creations—even better, I'd say.' He smiled; it was a cold, calculating smile. 'It's taken us many years to get here, but I think we finally have everything we need to improve our own situation. Is he talking yet?'

'No,' the security overseer replied. 'He's refusing to cooperate.'

'No matter, we aren't in any hurry,' Deighton said, smiling.

Bill recoiled in horror at the sight of Stephen standing there. He moved backwards until his back hit the door with a thud. He stared at the Indigene that was just a few feet away but regained enough composure to stretch out a hand towards Laura. 'I need you to come over here now. You have no idea how dangerous he is.'

She took a tentative step towards him, but he could see it wasn't in fear—it was self-assured and, with her arms outstretched, it appeared as if she was protecting Stephen from him. 'He's not dangerous, Bill,' she soothed.

'Of course he is! He—they killed my—' He couldn't bring himself to say it.

She took another step forward. 'Your wife?'

Bill's eyes widened. His face reddened. 'What the hell do you know about that?'

'I'm sorry,' Laura said. Her voice was calm, but she visibly shook. 'I have information. I know you're looking for answers. You need to know the

Indigenes are not to blame.'

'It has to be them. Who else could it be?' Bill kept his eyes firmly fixed on Stephen, waiting for him to make a move. He swiped at Laura hoping to grab hold of her arm, but she kept enough of a distance between them.

'The government, Bill—has been all along.'

He dropped his arm and straightened up slightly. 'What?'

'The World Government and my bosses, the ESC, are involved in things they shouldn't be. Isla got too close to the truth. In fact, she got close to the Indigenes and was trying to help them.'

'Yes, and they killed her!' He stared at Stephen, angling his body towards him in a threatening way. Stephen dropped his head and drew back while maintaining eye contact with Bill.

'No!' She closed the gap between them and placed a hand on Bill's chest. Her touch relaxed him a little. 'Not the Indigenes—they had nothing to do with her death. It was Deighton and Gilchrist,' she whispered through clenched teeth.

Bill stared at Laura now and shook his head. 'You're lying. Where are you getting this from?'

'Files about the investigation—and letters.'

'Letters?'

As Stephen took a step towards them, Bill snapped his attention back to the Indigene. He pushed Laura's hand away.

She blocked Stephen's path and pleaded with him. 'Please, I know it's difficult being here with us.'

'Tell me why you were investigating us and I won't kill you,' Stephen said to Bill. 'I don't want to be here any longer than necessary.'

'Please, your fight isn't with us.' Laura placed

a hand on Stephen's arm. 'We are all the same. We are fighting for the same thing.'

'Let him go,' Bill said, making a tight fist. 'If he wants a fight, I'll give him one.'

'Not until he understands what he is,' Laura said. Turning to face Stephen, she added, 'If you still want to harm us after what I tell you, then you have every right to.'

'What are you saying?' Bill's eyes widened at her suggestion. 'Don't you know what he's capable of?'

'Yes, I know everything about him—his origin, his creation.'

Both of them stared at Laura now.

'What are you talking about? What do you know?' Bill almost whispered.

'If you're going to help each other, you need to know everything about him, including where he came from. You have to know what he is. Are you ready for that?'

'Tell me. What is he?' Bill said impatiently, struggling to relax his hands.

Stephen said nothing. His posture rigid, he waited for her answer. His eyes were now fixed on Laura.

She looked from one face to the other. Stephen's eyes widened in anticipation of her next words.

'He's human.' Her words hung heavily in the air.

It was only Bill who shook his head in disbelief. 'He's *what*?' He unclenched his fists.

'Human,' Laura repeated.

'Yes, I know I am,' Stephen confirmed. 'But why are you also called "human"?'

Bill grabbed hold of Laura's arm. He laughed cynically, his eyes burrowing deep into hers. 'What the hell are you talking about? Where did you get this information from?' There was a serious note to the questions. 'How do you know all of this?'

The move clearly surprised her but she tried to stay calm. 'I've recently come into some information that could get me killed if anyone found out I had it. Trust me, I know.'

Bill became eerily still and allowed his eyes to fix on a blank spot on the floor. A sudden thought agitated him and he jumped. The move startled Laura, but not Stephen.

'How many visitors are you permitted to have?' he asked her.

'What?'

'How many visitors. Think!'

She shook her head, confused. 'I don't know. I don't usually have any. Why does that matter?'

He clamped the sides of her arms using his hands. 'How many does this block allow?'

She thought about it for a minute, and realised her mistake. 'Oh, crap, only one!'

Bill raced over to the Light Box's hardware control unit and opened a panel at the back. He removed a small rectangular box from his pocket. Quickly disconnecting the remote sensor, he temporarily re-routed the Light Box signal through it.

'Do you know if they're monitoring your apartment?'

'I dunno,' Laura vacantly replied, her agitation beginning to increase.

'Chances are high that they are. This disruption device is designed to confuse the Light Box sensors. By re-routing the signal through it, we can predetermine the number of signatures it will detect. Right now, it should be picking up just two. Chances are they've already detected the three of us. They're going to send a team out to check the anomaly.'

'What do we do?'

'We have to cut our numbers by one. I need to remove both devices before they have a chance to see them. When I do, there can only be two of us here.' Bill suddenly thought of something. Reluctantly, he addressed Stephen. 'Can you do that fast blurry thing you do?'

Laura was confused.

Stephen nodded. 'Yes, that should work.' He explained to Laura. 'I can move at a speed where I become invisible to the human eye.' He corrected himself. 'I should say, ordinary human eye. It should fool the sensors long enough for them not to detect my presence.'

'They're going to be here shortly. Laura, you need to change into something else,' he said, pointing to her easily recognisable uniform. 'Then I want you to follow my lead.'

Five minutes later, there was a sharp rap on the door, as Bill had predicted. Stephen took his cue and disappeared into a blurry haze right before their eyes. He could see Laura gasp, but admirably, she forced her attention back to the door. With Stephen hopefully undetectable by the sensors, Bill removed both the signal disrupter and sound interruption device and prayed that their combined efforts were enough.

He grabbed hold of a now casually dressed Laura and began kissing her on the mouth, his facial hair scratching her pale and sensitive skin easily. He felt her go limp for a second and then straighten up. He held her in a tight grip—a little too tight—as he jerked the handle of the door open. Two officers stood in the hallway—one male and one female. While both carried Impulse Tasers and Buzz Guns in their hip holsters, he noticed that their hands were poised defensively over the deadlier of the weapons. Neither officer introduced themselves.

'We have reason to believe that you have violated the building safety code. You are registering a third person in the apartment,' one said.

Bill put his arm round Laura's shoulders and pulled her even closer—he could feel her warmth as he held her close. An apple scent wafted up from her hair. 'I'm sorry officers. You see, it's our anniversary—the first time we met—and I only have two hours with this gorgeous woman before I have to go back to work.' He stroked Laura's hair gently. She acted her part and laid her head on his chest

'What career line are you in?' the female asked him suspiciously.

'Shipping. I'm a pilot,' he lied easily.

'Where do you work out of?'

'Sydney mainly.'

'And what about you?' She turned her calculating eyes towards Laura.

Laura hesitated. Sensing her discomfort, Bill cut in. He gently pushed her away. 'Is this really necessary? As you can see, it's just us.' He pretended to be irritated.

'Rules are rules,' the male officer said. 'We're going to have to check for ourselves.'

Reluctantly, they both stood back from the door, and allowed the officers to enter. 'As you wish.

You're free to check.'

Bill's eyes nervously scanned the room; he couldn't see Stephen anywhere. *Damn, he was good,* whatever he was pretending to be.

The officers carried out a sweep of the apartment, visibly disappointed that they hadn't found a third person. Not entirely convinced, the female officer followed up with an independent scan, which still registered just two signatures, apart from their own.

'All clear,' she announced to her partner, sounding unconvinced. She turned to Bill and Laura. 'This doesn't quite account for the third person you were registering ten minutes ago. Care to explain?'

'I'm sorry. That was my fault.' Laura smiled apologctically. 'I had arranged a surprise for my boyfriend. The guy came to install a virtual package upgrade for the Light Box—you, know, the one where you can holiday in any part of the world without having to leave your armchair? He's addicted to his virtual world. Well, the guy was just finishing up, when he came home earlier than planned.' She threw a fake scowl at Bill.

Bill shrugged his shoulders at the officers in a what-can-you-do way.

'Oh, I've heard about that one. Is it any good?' the male officer asked.

'I don't know yet. But I'll let you know if you leave us alone? We were planning a quick trip to Bali.' Bill winked at him.

'One last thing,' the female officer interrupted. 'We need to scan your identity chips. For the record, you understand.'

'Come on, officers,' Bill said, 'we've been fully cooperative here. We just want to get back to our evening with just one hour and fifty-five minutes left of our alone time.' He directed his next words towards the male officer, adding another wink. 'You know how it is, with the crazy work schedules we have to stick to. It's tough enough to get time off under the easiest of circumstances. Am I right?'

The male officer nodded and laughed gently. 'I'm just surprised you have the energy.' His tone turned serious. 'Everything seems in order. Have a nice evening.' He pushed his reluctant-to-leave partner out of the apartment.

As soon as Laura closed the door, Bill removed the disruption unit from his pocket and channelled the Light Box signal through it once more. He placed the sound interrupter on the front panel again. 'That was way too close for comfort.' He let out a long breath. 'We should be okay for the next two hours. Then they'll be expecting me to leave.' He spoke to the empty room. 'You can come out now.' To Laura, he said, 'And then you're going to start from the beginning.'

'What a magnificent specimen he is,' Daphne said to Deighton, while observing Anton from a safe distance on the other side of the room. Even though the containment unit was impenetrable, neither of them was sure how easily the Indigene could manipulate technology. Daphne didn't want to leave herself vulnerable to attack; there would be plenty of time to find out all of Anton's strengths and weaknesses.

'The technological advances the Indigenes have made are better than expected,' she said. 'It appears that the second generation has only improved the design.'

Deighton spoke excitedly to the security overseer. 'You see, they were much more primitive in the beginning—closer to our design really. Time has allowed their abilities to develop naturally, and in such a short space of time too. I imagine the next generation will be even more marvellous!' He clasped his degenerating hands together. A strange mood filled the room.

Just as Daphne took a step closer, Anton dropped to all fours and arched his back.

She stopped dead.

'See what he just did there?' Deighton said. 'They didn't do that when we first created them. Primitive animals. Brutes. Couldn't even talk. Over time, they've adapted, changed so much. It's quite marvellous to see that our species is capable of such adaptability, if managed correctly. It will come in handy for our own future.'

'You see, the Indigenes have only been in existence for fifty years,' Laura explained to Bill. 'They were created from existing humans in the beginning.'

'How is that possible?' Stephen said, feeling his control slip away further as more information became known. 'Our race has existed for thousands of years, not half a century. You are simply misinformed.'

Laura placed a hand on Stephen's arm, a move that was difficult for the Indigene to allow. Her touch was fleeting, but kind. 'I wish I was. I couldn't believe my eyes when I saw the data for myself.'

Stephen shook his head; he set out to understand the humans' motives for killing so many of his kind all those years ago, but if he was to believe Laura, then their motives were no longer the issue—his origin was. He was uncertain if he could trust Laura and Bill but he needed to hear more. He wished Anton was with him.

'Where did you get the data from?' Bill asked.

'I received it from an anonymous tip—anonymous because I don't even know her name.' She laughed once without humour. 'There is a woman who works in the same area that I do, on Level Five. You see, I'd just been promoted to that area about two weeks ago. And you can only imagine how stunned I was when she approached me at lunch and handed me a micro file in broad daylight.'

'What, she didn't say anything—what was on it even?' Bill said.

'No need—the data speaks for itself. She said something alright. That the work at the ESC was not all it seemed to be.'

'That doesn't surprise me one bit. What else?' Bill asked.

'She said I needed to have my eyes opened before they tried to manipulate me,' Laura said. 'The reason she was giving me the information was because I had no obvious connection to it.'

'Any idea what her connection might have been?'

'No idea. She wouldn't talk to me after that.'

'Not unexpected behaviour, given the circumstances,' Bill mused.

'Wait,' Stephen interrupted, having heard enough small talk. 'I need you to start from the beginning. I came to Earth because your species is *still* trying to eradicate ours. I want to know why and to find out how we supposedly became another version of you.'

'Yes, I'd like to know that too.' Bill nodded.

Laura took a seat on the sofa. She leaned forward, resting her forearms on her legs and clasping her hands in front of her.

Both Stephen and Bill stood at opposite ends of the sofa, hovering uneasily over her.

'Please, I need someone to sit with me.' She patted the vacant area beside her. 'You're both making me very nervous, lurking over me like that.'

Bill chose to join her—not on the seat, but perched on the edge of the armrest. Stephen stayed in what was a more natural position for him.

'In the latter part of the twenty-first century, the World Government had seemingly been well informed of the inherent risks to our planet. The overpopulation had already begun, the biodiversity was unbalanced and extinction lists were growing at an unmanageable rate. It was what drove the initial investment in space travel.'

Bill nodded, his head hung low as he listened. 'Yes, apart from the government's early indications, this is all well known.'

Laura continued. 'Well, as you know, their relentless search for a new exoplanet began shortly afterwards, and then they came across Exilon 5.'

'In 2076.'

'That's right. The history books report it was the astronomer Harry Buxton who discovered the planet—this is all true. But what the books don't reveal is that the government in power at the time was busy digging up other facts isolated from this event. They discovered that the planet could support life, but not their own because of incompatible gases. So they looked for other ways to make it happen.'

The event sequence started to make sense to

Stephen. 'Alter its composition?'

'Not at the beginning. While they racked their brains to come up with a solution, plan B was being put into effect. As far back as 2032, they'd involved themselves in a number of genetic experiments on human test subjects.'

Bill reflected for a moment. 'There was an early twenty-first century condition known as Leukoderma that stripped the skin of pigmentation. Then, there were other cases involving children, where the condition appeared to have mutated to the eyes. Details recorded made reference to their eyes shining like bright lights in the dark.'

'Yes, I read the case. It was one of the early experiments carried out on children. Tests were performed, often without the subject's permission. Some were as young as four.'

Stephen shuddered. 'Did these children have superior night vision?'

'Yes, as it turned out, their vision was exceptional in darkened conditions, but much more sensitive in daytime light.'

'As our vision is—' Stephen had yet to hear all the details, but could hazard a guess as to where it was leading.

'I'm sorry, Stephen,' Laura said. 'I know this is difficult for you to hear, but you need to know everything.'

32

Two armed officers joined Deighton, Gilchrist and the security overseer in the room where Anton was being held prisoner. They continued to probe deeper into the reasons why Anton had made the long and dangerous journey to Earth.

Gilchrist took a step towards the containment unit. As she did, both officers shadowed her to stand directly behind her. 'Don't be afraid. We're not interested in hurting you. We are your friends,' she said smoothly. 'I would like to know your name. I'd like to call you something other than Indigene. I'll begin. My name is Daphne Gilchrist.'

Anton remained in his protective crouch and kept quiet—he could sense the lies spilling from her mouth; he could see the tension and apprehension in the way she held herself. Then there was the excitement coming from the old man. He wondered how Gilchrist knew he was an Indigene.

'So, not interested in talking much?' Gilchrist's tone became less inviting.

'What if it can't communicate in the same way we can?' the security overseer said quietly.

'Ah, but it can. I've witnessed one of them talk quite freely with another human being. They have the same ability to learn languages, as we do.' A puzzled look crossed her face. 'In fact, I'm surprised they haven't created their own by now.'

'What if they have?' the security overseer suggested. 'What if they can communicate without words?'

Gilchrist raised a single eyebrow in response to the suggestion.

Anton continued his analysis of her: he could sense her desire to dominate the room and the males within it; she thrived on being in charge. But for all her experience she'd missed the point the younger male had been astute enough to make.

'You can drop the charade now. I'm not buying it.' Gilchrist turned her attention back to Anton. 'I can keep calling you Species 31, but I would rather call you by your real name.'

Anton decided he'd taken things far enough; he figured there might be a better chance of getting information from them if he spoke out loud. 'My name is Anton.'

'Anton!' Deighton spoke up from the back of the room and clapped his hands together. 'What an altogether human name. Not terribly surprising, I suppose, considering what stock you came from.'

'What are you talking about?' Anton straightened up instantly.

'Did you see how fast he just moved there?' Deighton squealed. 'Marvellous advancements— better than any design we could have come up with.'

Anton wondered if Stephen had been able to escape or whether they were holding him in a similar place to this. He thought about asking, but they hadn't once mentioned his name, false or real. It was possible they were still unaware that he was on the planet.

'By the way, using the chips like that was a very clever thing to do, Bob Harris. I assume you had an accomplice?' Gilchrist asked.

No, they didn't know Stephen was here; they were fishing for information. He was relieved. 'Just some useful human who was careless with his identity chip, that's all.'

'So, why were you in such a hurry to get out of Dock 10 then? Our records show it was Colin Stipple who illegally commandeered the flight out with one of our best pilots on board. Who is he to you?'

'Just someone who needed my help in return for a favour. A family member was committing termination, or so he said.' Anton told the story as was agreed. 'He'd expected his travel to be curtailed when he returned here and he made a compelling argument. It seemed important, so I helped.' How easily the lies flowed from his lips in the face of danger.

'How noble of you to help out our kind, considering what we tried to do to yours—' Gilchrist watched him for a moment, her cold, hard stare burrowing deep. Her face lacked emotion.

Anton could tell she was trying to read him: his facial expressions, the way he held his hands, how he stood—anything that might reveal a hidden clue. Unlike Stephen, he bore no ill feelings towards humans, but suddenly he understood why certain Indigenes set out to kill humans such as these.

Gilchrist's face broke into a wide smile. She applauded his performance. 'That's a wonderful story. Fortunately for you, when we spoke to the pilot, she backed up your version of events. Still can't figure out why the bitch lied.'

'I'm afraid it's no story. It's the truth.'

Deighton stepped forward. 'You still haven't answered an important question. Why are you here on

Earth?'

Anton stayed silent while he considered his next lie.

'Look, I know this is difficult for all of us to hear, let alone discuss,' Bill said, 'but I'm having trouble understanding exactly where Stephen fits into all of this.'

Laura swallowed loudly. Bill could tell she was struggling to recount the full details of what had been on the micro file. She continued. 'As I said, the genetic experiments were carried out long before the planet had even been discovered. From the files, it appears that around 2110, while engineers and ship designers were busy perfecting space travel, the World Government had almost perfected something of their own.' She looked at Stephen. He stared back at her.

Bill's eyes widened in horror as he stared at Stephen, finally understanding where this story was heading,

'Yes.' Laura confirmed their silent suspicions. 'They created a race that was capable of surviving on the planet in its original uninhabitable state. They'd given up hope of humans ever living there and without having discovered more exoplanets, they fell back on their contingency plan for the human race. In their mind, the Earth was beyond saving.'

Bill gasped, as the last piece slotted into place. His original reasons for hating the Indigenes vanished. 'They were creating a new breed of human?' he almost whispered. His earlier defensive nature towards Stephen had dissipated. Unusually, he felt comfortable there.

'Yes.' Laura glanced at Stephen. 'He is us, but just a better version of us.'

'Shit.' Bill let out a deep breath. He dropped his gaze to the floor and ran his fingers through his greying hair.

In all that time, Stephen didn't move a muscle. If it wasn't for the intensity in his eyes, Bill wouldn't have known what the Indigene was feeling. Then something else caught his attention about the story. His head shot up and he looked at Laura once more. It unnerved him to even ask it. 'And what had they planned to do with the regular humans?'

'That's where it becomes difficult for me to even talk about it. It makes me sick just to think of it.' She stopped for a moment and placed her head in her hands. After a few deep breaths, she continued. 'Our future existence was being placed entirely in the hands of this super human race. What remained of the human race was going to be wiped out.'

'Double shit,' he said. Even for him and what he'd seen as an investigator, this was a lot to take in. He'd known about his employers' shady past and present, but he never contemplated that they would take it this far.

Stephen stepped forward. There was deep pain hidden behind the brown lens-covered eyes—eyes that now sought out the truth. While Laura and Bill had become sidetracked with the plans for the people of Earth, they'd forgotten about the man who stood before them—a man who'd been unwittingly caught up in a war that was not of his making. Stephen's eyes widened. 'How did I come into existence? Where did I come from exactly? Please—I need to know.'

Laura continued. 'In the early days, scientists

had advertised for human test subjects to become part of their gene splicing and manipulation therapy programmes. It was, of course, fully funded by the World Government.'

'Another non-surprise,' Bill said hotly.

'Some volunteered, but many didn't. Without enough subjects to test, they had to resort to taking people from the street. At first, the tests had been successful enough, they said. But neither the splicing nor manipulation techniques worked too well in those who had inherited genetic diseases from their parents. In the end, their bodies successfully rejected the changes.

'It was through trial and error alone that the scientists discovered that. Later on, when they trialled splicing in people of average intellect with clean DNA structures, the results improved slightly, but there was still little noticeable difference between the before and after test subjects. It wasn't until they tested those with a superior IQ that the genetic splicing and manipulation worked perfectly with their genes. The work done also had a boosting effect on their brain's ability to learn. Take doctors, engineers and professors, as an example—professions with a high IQ—the tests seemed to supercharge their skills somehow.'

Bill had always suspected there was something different, or special, about the indigenous race on Exilon 5. He just hadn't been quite sure what that was—until now. 'So, there really is a race of super intelligent beings on Exilon 5?'

'You only have to look at Stephen to know that's the case.'

'What's your IQ Stephen?' Bill was curious now.

'We don't use human measurements to define our intelligence, but if I was to compare it to your scale, it would be close to two hundred and seventy.'

Bill let out a low whistle. He looked at the Indigene he once regarded as his enemy. While Stephen might still pose a threat, at that moment what he saw was a man whose history had been torn to shreds. He was a man who, suddenly, didn't fit anywhere.

'What do you want from me?' Anton said, becoming impatient and nervous as Gilchrist inched closer to him. He waited for her to make a threatening move towards him.

Deighton chuckled, changing positions. The uniformed officers shadowed his move. 'What *don't* we want from you?'

'Here's a better question,' Gilchrist piped up. 'What is it that you want from us? You're the one trespassing on our planet. You're a risk to our national security. It concerns me that you're even here at all. How did you figure out how to leave Exilon 5?'

Anton didn't know what Gilchrist's exact motives were; he could work out the younger male quite easily but not her, or the older male. He sensed that while it was important to keep them talking, he also needed to question their motives for invading Exilon 5. 'You've attempted to destroy our race. I think I should be more concerned about you. Do you hold no responsibility for your actions?'

'Of course we do, but you cannot destroy what you already own,' Deighton said. 'You can only choose to discard. To destroy is to assume it belongs to someone else.'

Anton struggled to decipher their riddles without knowing all the facts. 'Are you going to kill me?' he asked; he'd gone into this mission knowing there was a good chance he might not return from it.

Gilchrist and Deighton laughed, while the security overseer and the two uniformed officers looked on.

'No, my dear boy,' Deighton said. 'What a waste that would be. No, I have much better plans for you.'

'Care to share your plans with me?' Anton asked.

'Of course not! Where would be the fun in that?'

33

'So, Stephen is human?'

'Yes and no. You see, Stephen is less than fifty years old—am I right?' Laura looked at him. He nodded. 'So, essentially he was the product of two super humans. He's a true indigenous species of the planet. According to the files, anyone older than fifty would have lived ordinary lives as humans at some stage, since the experiments were only completed at that point.'

It was Stephen's turn to gasp.

'What is it?' Laura asked.

'Our oldest Central Council members are well over fifty years old. Are you telling me they were once your kind of human?'

'Yes. I'm afraid that's probably the case,' Laura said.

He shook his head. 'But it's not possible—they have specific memories of being born, of growing up on the planet, and of a life before the one we have now. How can that be?'

'When the early super humans were created, their memories were overwritten with new ones. The scientists rewired the neural pathways. That's why they wouldn't remember their old lives. The government scientists painstakingly created a new existence for these people so they would adapt to the new planet. It worked like a dream as far as I can tell.

Because of your age, Stephen, your memories are real. Any memories occurring earlier than fifty years ago are most likely false.'

'So why is the government trying to kill the Indigenes if they are just like us?' Bill asked.

Laura pulled the band out of her hair and her hair tumbled down out of the ponytail. She quickly ruffled it with her hand. It fell into her face and she tucked it neatly behind her ears. 'Their motives seem to have been more innocent at the start. While putting all their hopes for survival into this new race, they accidentally stumbled upon a way to alter the gas composition on Exilon 5. When they realised that the planet could house ordinary humans, they knew one race would be sacrificed for another. When the explosions happened, it wasn't just to terraform the planet, it was to destroy their creation. Somewhere in the files, they mentioned that neither race could find out about the other.'

'Pity for them that we did more than survive—we adapted even further,' Stephen hissed.

'He's right,' Laura said. 'The first batch of super humans that relocated to the planet resembled us, but was more primitive in behaviour. Their skin was as sturdy as it is now, but their outward appearance was more like how you and I look.' She addressed Stephen. 'I imagine it was the years of living underground that altered the Indigene's DNA and made your appearance what it is today.'

'The toughened skin. How?' Stephen asked.

Laura let out a long, weary breath. The events were visibly taking their toll on her. Bill placed a reassuring hand on her shoulder. He could feel her shaking through her clothes. 'I know this is a lot to explain, but please bear with it. It's important,' he said.

She nodded and continued. 'The genetic manipulation involved experimentation with other species' DNA—animals mostly. Think of the toughened exterior of a rhinoceros, for example; or the night vision of a nocturnal animal, or the regenerative properties of a lizard—the list is endless. They tried various permutations, trying to alter the human code so it would mimic the more interesting properties of some of these animals.'

'What do they plan to do with us?' Stephen asked.

'I don't know. They can't carry out any more explosions on the surface—not with a small number of transferees already living on Exilon 5.'

'What then?'

'I don't know. Look, I didn't get an idea of how this was going to play out. All I can tell you about are the facts on the micro file.'

'Sorry for pushing you so hard,' Bill said. 'We both appreciate what you've done here. Do you still have the file?'

'Yes. I thought about getting rid of it, but for some insane reason I just kept it around. It's yours, if you want it,' Laura said.

Stephen spoke suddenly, causing both of them to jump. 'This transfer you speak of. When did it begin?'

'Around twenty-five years ago,' Bill said. 'Why?'

'And when did it slow down? Far less of you have since settled on the planet.'

'I don't know exactly. A few years ago. Why, what are you thinking?'

'Well, it seems to correlate with the time that

some of our young were captured. Could it be possible that their plans have changed?'

'It seems like anything's possible with this bloody lot,' Bill said.

'So what's our next move in all of this?' Laura said.

'Well, for one thing it's not safe for us to stay here,' Bill said. 'Laura, you'll have to come with me—leave your apartment, your current life behind.'

'What? No! I have a job. A career. I can't just leave it!'

'If they find out what you know, you won't be alive long enough to enjoy it.'

'I was hoping to get transferred to Exilon 5. If I disappear now I lose that chance.'

'Chances are all future transfers will be placed on hold anyway. There are more pressing issues at play here. You need to decide which side you're on.'

'I'm on this side, of course! Why can't I stay where I am? Wouldn't I be more useful to you if I was on the inside?' Laura pleaded.

Bill considered it he but couldn't see how it would work—she would be in too much danger.

Stephen spoke urgently. 'I need to get back to Exilon 5. I need to tell the Indigenes what I've learned here. We have much more to fear than I'd first anticipated.'

Bill looked at him, compassion replacing the anger that had consumed him for so long. 'Of course. Getting you safely off this planet is our first priority.'

'I have another favour to ask of you, Bill,' Stephen said quietly.

'What?'

'I didn't come here alone. My friend Anton was captured so that I could escape. I need you to find out if he's still alive.'

'If the World Government has him, he may not be.'

'I'm prepared for that. But I would still like you to check.'

'I'll see what I can find out,' Bill said.

'Thank you.'

Bill ran a hand through his hair and stopped to touch the bump that remained after his fall.

'How's your head?' Stephen asked.

He looked at him blankly. 'How do you know about—' His expression changed as he realised. 'That was you?'

A small crease formed on Stephen's lips. 'Actually, it was Anton who convinced me to help. I'm glad I did now.'

Bill stared at him and at the same time couldn't stop himself from yawning. Exhaustion had set in, and this heavy input of new information was taking its toll. 'Do you mind if I take a quick nap on your bed?' he asked Laura.

She nodded. 'Take all the time you need. But before you go, there's something else I need to give you.' She went into her bedroom and retrieved three envelopes. She showed them to Bill.

He stared down at them, puzzled. 'What are they?'

'Letters—from your wife,' Laura said tenderly.

His eyes widened as he looked at the envelopes that contained the letters, then at Laura. 'What do they say—I mean, did you read them?' he whispered, swallowing back a lump in his throat.

She shook her head. 'I can't decipher them, they're coded I think. Just take them.' She shoved them closer to his hand.

He grabbed them without examining them, his mouth set into a tight line. 'Wake me up in an hour. We can't stay here.'

Bill closed the bedroom door gently behind him, clutching the envelopes tightly in his hand. He felt different, less angry somehow. There were still questions to be answered but he needed more time to think. He didn't know if he could completely trust the pair in the next room but he was now certain of one thing: the Indigenes were not his enemy.

He kicked off his boots and lay on the top of the bed. Tentatively, he brushed his fingers over the envelopes, not sure if he was ready to read his wife's innermost secrets. He brought one of the envelopes up to his nose; her perfume was faint but it was enough to break down the last wall in his defences. Tears formed in his eyes and he curled up on his side, hugging the letters close to his chest. His eyes, puffy and red, drooped from the effort of keeping them open.

He was tired of fighting. He needed to rest. But he knew the fight was only beginning.

34

Anton woke to the uncomfortable sound of electricity buzzing close by. He sat up and wiggled a finger in each ear to try to stop the persistent noise. Climbing slowly to his feet, he felt a lump on the back of his head, then touched the spot on his arm where they had injected him with something just before he'd passed out. He'd probably hit his head when he fell to the floor. A pleasant chill passed over his skin. He was naked except for a pair of taupe-coloured loose-legged pants.

There was an obvious route out of the room, an open gap, but his skin nipped uncomfortably. The closer he got to the doorless gap the more his movements slowed. By the time he reached the opening itself it felt as though he were treading water. His fingers barely grazed the space before the electrical current momentarily rooted him to the spot.

The human called Deighton came into view outside the opening. He was whistling a tune.

'Let me out of here,' Anton said, his words coming thick and slow. He was breathing too hard. His device! He rolled his tongue over the back of his throat.

'I'd like to, dear boy, but you're far too valuable to me to do that,' Deighton said.

Anton shuffled backwards until he was far enough away from the electrically-charged gap to be able to move freely again. His tongue found the piece in the back of his throat. His hands loosened and he touched each nostril. He released a quick breath. It was only panic that was causing him to breathe hard.

'You've seen what I can do,' Anton said. 'Yet you want someone as dangerous as me around? That doesn't make any sense.'

Deighton laughed noisily. 'I'm quite sure I'm safe. I just saw how effective you were when you tried to breach this room.' He swirled one finger in the air. 'That low buzzing noise is a right irritation, even to my ordinary ears.' He brought his hands behind his back and a strange smile settled into place. 'It's clear to me you don't understand why you're here yet. The others don't either. It's because you're very important to me.'

Anton slowed his breathing right down until the fog in his mind lifted and he could think a little clearer. They had drugged him. He could feel his body attacking whatever it was they had given him. It would only be a matter of time before his immune system counteracted its effects. 'My friends, they're coming for me,' he said.

Deighton dropped his overly friendly disposition and his shoulders tensed. 'Who is coming for you? Are there more of you on the way?'

Anton thought about telling Deighton that Stephen was there too, for no other reason than to buy himself time, but that would be suicide for both of them.

'Yes, that's what I thought,' Deighton said, seeming to visibly relax. 'You've come alone. Or maybe you haven't. It doesn't really matter. I only need one of you anyway.'

Anton slid to the floor and wrapped his arms loosely around his knees. His bare skin was pressed against the cool rock. Ironically, it felt familiar and comfortable, like District Three. He stared at Deighton and tried to read his thoughts, but the old human seemed to carry a technology with him that blocked Anton's abilities. Either that or it was the electricity—or the drugs. He shook his head to clear it. Would Stephen send for help? Would he live out his days as a prisoner? Not if he could help it. But how could he fight against both the drugs and the electricity?

He sighed deeply, a part of him resigned to his capture. 'So what do you need me for anyway?'

Deighton's watery eyes brightened for a moment, but he turned and walked away. Anton heard a door open.

'To help keep me alive,' Deighton called out, his voice echoing eerily in the open space some distance away.

Then Anton heard the door shut softly.

Keep me alive? The three words tripped and tumbled about in Anton's mind. The faint thread of a thought danced before him and he pulled on it.

Deighton needed Anton for something. That meant he had a chance.

* * *

The door to Laura's bedroom creaked more than she had expected it to. She sucked in a breath, only releasing it when the door had finally opened wide enough for her to step inside. Bill and Stephen had been in her apartment for an hour and Stephen was getting jittery about being there; he needed to leave for Exilon 5 to warn his people. But Laura was feeling jittery too; she wanted Stephen out of the apartment in case the two officers returned and caught her out in her lie.

She found Bill lying on top of her bedclothes, the letters from his wife unopened and cradled in his arms. She bit the skin around her thumb as she contemplated leaving him to sleep longer. But Stephen couldn't get home on his own, and she wouldn't be able to live with herself if he was captured because they had been too slow to help.

Laura perched on the edge of the bed and put a hand on Bill's shoulder.

'Hey,' she said softly. Bill didn't move, so she shook him gently. 'Time to go.'

Bill's eyes opened slowly, then widened. He quickly grabbed her wrist. 'What the hell are you doing?'

Laura jerked her arm away, but he had a firm hold on her. Her chest tightened with fear. 'We ... we have to go. Stephen needs to leave. I'm sorry. I had to wake you.'

Bill stared down at her wrist, then loosened his grip almost instantly giving her the opportunity to pull it from him. He glanced away and hastily stuffed the unopened letters into the inside pocket of his jacket. He sat up and rubbed his eyes. 'You shouldn't have allowed me to sleep so long.'

Laura moved to the door, relieved to be beyond his reach. 'You were dead on your feet and you needed it,' she said coldly. 'I'll be outside.' She pulled the door closed behind her.

When Bill emerged a few minutes later Stephen was already by the front door, his navy blue suit wrinkle-free and fully buttoned, his black Stetson in one hand.

'Are you sure you can get me safe passage off

Earth?' he asked Bill, placing his hat on his head.

Bill rubbed his eyes again. 'I'll make damn sure it happens. I just need to make a quick call first—one of my contacts off the grid.' He narrowed his gaze at Stephen, his eyes suddenly alert. 'Don't take this the wrong way, but I don't want to see you here again. You understand?'

Stephen's smile was fleeting. 'If I'm here it means I'm not safe.'

Bill dug his communication device out of his pocket and stuck the earpiece in his ear. Laura listened as he barked instructions to someone on the other end of the line:

'Are you sure it will work? ... Yeah, yeah, Colin Stipple ... It's a hot name right now. People are probably looking for him.' Bill looked at Stephen, then shot his gaze away. 'Yeah, something like that ... Cheers, I owe you one.'

Laura pulled on her jacket and wrapped a scarf around her neck and head, making it into a hood of sorts.

Taking out his earpiece Bill turned around, his eyes widening when he saw Laura. 'And where the hell do you think you're going?' he said, putting a firm hand on her arm.

She frowned at him. 'I'm coming with you.'

'I won't be responsible for another person going missing,' Bill said. Laura could see he was deadly serious.

'He's right, Laura,' Stephen said quietly. 'I don't want you risking your life for me. It was Bill Taggart I needed to find and now I have.'

'Yeah?' She turned the collar up on her coat and felt around for the gel mask in her pocket. 'Well, the last time I checked neither of you were responsible for me. If I hadn't seen the information on the micro file you two wouldn't have learned as much as you did. And since you're both standing in my apartment, I'd say I'm very much involved.'

She didn't wait for a reply. She opened the door and walked out into the communal hall.

'Well, are you two coming or not?' she said, turning back to them when they didn't follow.

Bill shook his head and flashed a smile at her. 'You're one stubborn lady,' he said, walking past her.

'You have no idea just how stubborn, Bill Taggart,' she said.

She pulled the door closed behind Stephen and put on her gel mask. 'Now, let's get Stephen home.'

Acknowledgements

This self-published book is dedicated to all those hard working self-published authors who write brilliantly and spend money on editors and book cover designers so they can produce the best quality book for their readers. Our goal is to compete in a noisy book market by producing our best work possible.

Thank you to my editor, Averill Buchanan, for editing this book in its entirety. Thank you to Andrew and Rebecca from Design for Writers for the really cool cover. I still get great comments about the design.

To my sci-fi-loving best friend who cuts through the crappy first draft ideas so my second draft reads a little more like it should.

Character/Location/Organisation List

I've designed this list to help you to keep track of the characters and locations, if required. I've also listed some minor characters to give you context while reading.

Organisations
- World Government – Comprised of twelve board members, including a CEO. Decision makers for matters on Earth and Exilon 5
- Earth Security Centre – Is responsible for Earth's safety. CEO also operates as a second pair of eyes for the World Government
- International Task Force – Handles the groundwork for the World Government on Earth and Exilon 5. Responsible for policing, deploying military units, heading up investigations etc …

Exilon 5, New London
- Bill Taggart – World Government Investigator. When on Earth, he works out of London ITF office
- Isla Taggart – Bill's wife
- Officer Page/Garrett/Wilson – Part of Bill's investigation team
- Ben Watson – Young boy

Exilon 5, District Three – below the streets of New London
- Stephen – Indigene
- Anton – Indigene and friend of Stephen
- Leon – Anton's father
- Elise and Pierre – Indigenes and Central

Council elders

Earth, Washington D.C. – Location of World Government offices

- Charles Deighton – CEO of World Government

Earth, Sydney – Location of Earth Security Centre (ESC)

- Laura O'Halloran – ESC worker, Level Four
- Daphne Gilchrist – CEO for ESC
- Chris/Janine – Colleagues from Level Four
- Suzanne Brett – Overseer for Level Five
- Penny Thompson – ESC worker, Level Five
- Fionnuala O'Halloran – Laura's mother

Earth, London

- Simon Shaw – Bill Taggart's supervisor at the ITF office in London

Earth, Hartsfield Jackson-Atlanta

- Galen Thompson – Trainee Air and Space Controller at HJA docking station and Penny Thompson's son
- Stuart McWilliams – Overseer for HJA docking station
- Paddy/Maria – Galen's colleagues at HJA docking station
- Jenny Waterson – Spacecraft pilot working for World Government subsidiary, Calypso Couriers and friend of Stuart McWilliams

Purchase other books in the series

Paperback and Digital from all major online stores

Altered Reality (Book 2 in the Exilon 5 series)
Crimson Dawn (Book 3 in the Exilon 5 series)

Prequels to the Exilon 5 Series, digital only

Discover what happened before *Becoming Human* with these prequels:

Echoes of Earth (Bill and Isla Taggart)
New Origin (Stephen and Anton)

Both prequels also available in a digital box set.

Stand alone series, digital only

Derailed Conscience (a dark psychological story)

For a limited time, you can get *Derailed Conscience* for free in digital format. Check out www.elizagreenbooks.com to get started.

Coming soon November 2016: *Feeder,* brand new young adult sci-fi. Check out www.elizagreenbooks.com/books for more details.

Word of mouth is crucial for authors. If you enjoyed this book, please consider leaving a review where you purchased it; make it as long or as short as you like. I know review writing can be a hassle, but it's the most effective way to let others know what you thought. Plus, it helps me reach new readers instantly.

You can also find me on:

www.twitter.com/elizagreenbooks
www.facebook.com/elizagreenbooks
Goodreads – search for Eliza Green

Printed in Great Britain
by Amazon